EX LIBRIS

# THE
# POETIC EDDA

# THE POETIC EDDA
# A BOOK THAT INSPIRED TOLKIEN
## - With Original Illustrations -

### Book #2 of "The Professor's Bookshelf"

Cover images by W.G. Collingwood and W.B. MacDougall

Uniform Title: Edda Saemundar. English. Selections.
Title: The poetic Edda:
illustrated - original text with english translation - including a glossary of terms
edited and translated by Olive Bray;
illustrated by W. G. Collingwood;
introduced by Cecilia Dart-Thornton.
Edition: Revised edition.

ISBN: 9781925110043 (paperback)

Series: The professor's bookshelf ; 2

Subjects: Old Norse poetry--Translations into English.
Eddas--Translations into English.
Vikings--Poetry.

Dewey Number: 839.61

Copyright (C) 2018 Leaves of Gold Press
ABN 67 099 575 078
PO Box 3092, Brighton, 3186, Victoria, Australia

# THE POETIC EDDA
## - A Book That Inspired Tolkien -

### ORIGINAL OLD NORSE TEXT WITH ENGLISH TRANSLATION
*Revised and including a glossary of terms*

First published in 1908 as
'The Elder or Poetic Edda: Commonly known as Saemund's Edda'

Author unknown
Edited and translated by Olive Bray
Illustrated by W. G. Collingwood
Introduced by Cecilia Dart-Thornton

www.professorsbookshelf.com

# THE PROFESSOR'S BOOKSHELF

Welcome to The Professor's Bookshelf, a collection of books that inspired the imagination of Professor JRR Tolkien, author of The Hobbit and The Lord of the Rings.

All our titles have informed the professor's writings in one way or another. In most cases the man himself has revealed their influence in his essays or interviews; in others, his biographers and researchers have uncovered the evidence. Some were widely obtainable and popular in his literary circles, so that he certainly knew of them and there is little doubt he read them.

Tolkien's own drawings adorn the pages of The Hobbit and it is easy to imagine him as a boy, long before the invention of television, poring for hours over the images in his favourite volumes - images that helped shape his creation of Middle Earth.

Where possible we have selected illustrated editions available in his lifetime. Both texts and pictures have been reproduced, and our books are mostly copies of the editions the professor held in his own hands.

Like the celebrated nineteenth century English textile designer, artist and writer William Morris, we at The Professor's Bookshelf reject the notion that illustrated materials are unsuitable for adults. To Morris, who was one of Tolkien's favourite authors, illustrated books for adults presented an opportunity to integrate literature with design and art. In essence, a book is itself an artistic creation. The Professor's Bookshelf celebrates this by embellishing our 'Illustrated' series with the original plates (whole page illustrations printed separately from the text), cuts (illustrations printed within the text), borders, fonts, miniatures, and ornamental capital letters, in addition to our own 'endpapers' and bookplates.

Each Professor's Bookshelf classic opens with an introduction by fantasy author Cecilia Dart-Thornton, about whose acclaimed Bitterbynde Trilogy Grand Master of Science Fiction Andre Norton wrote: 'Not since Tolkien's The Lord of the Rings fell into my hands have I been so impressed by a beautifully spun fantasy.'

Literary scholars have studied the texts in the The Professor's Bookshelf collection, finding threads and motifs linking them to the professor's famous works. On reading them you will be awakened to that vast library of myth, magic, legend and fantasy whose legacy inspired the great English writer, poet and philologist, J.R.R. Tolkien.

# ~ SOME TITLES IN THE SERIES ~

**1. The Song of the Nibelungs (illustrated)**
Translated by Margaret Armour, illust. W. B. MacDougall, previously published as 'The Fall of the Nibelungs', pub. 1897

**2. The Poetic Edda (illustrated)**
Translated by Olive Bray, previously published as 'The Elder or Poetic Edda', illust. W. G. Collingwood, pub. 1908

**3. The Story of the Glittering Plain (illustrated)**
By William Morris, illust. Walter Crane, pub.1894

**4. The Red Fairy Book (illustrated)**
By Andrew Lang, illust. H. J. Ford and Lancelot Speed, pub. 1907

**5. The Princess and the Goblin (illustrated)**
By George MacDonald, illust. Jessie Willcox Smith, pub. 1920

**6. The Saga of Eric Brighteyes (illustrated)**
By H. Rider Haggard, illust. Lancelot Speed, pub. 1891.

**7. The Dragon Ouroboros (illustrated)**
By Eric Rücker Eddison, illust. Keith Henderson, previously published as 'The Worm Ouroboros', pub. 1922

**8. The Book of Wonder & The Last Book of Wonder (illustrated)**
By Lord Dunsany, illust. S. H. Syme, pub. 1912

**9. The Story of King Arthur and his Knights (illustrated)**
Written and illustrated by Howard Pyle, pub. 1903

**10. Grimm's Fairy Tales (illustrated)**
Translated by Lucy Crane, illust. Walter Crane, pub. 1922

For more about the The Professor's Bookshelf series, visit
www.professorsbookshelf.com

Title page of the 1908 edition

## WHAT IS AN EDDA?

The word 'Edda' was attached to a group of mythological stories collected by the great Icelandic historian, Snorri Sturluson (1181- 1241).

Many scholars incline to the theory that the name originally meant 'the book of Oddi', and that 'Edda' is merely a feminine form (agreeing with 'bok') of 'Oddi', the home village of Snorri, where his love for history and literature was first kindled.

# INTRODUCTION
by Cecilia Dart-Thornton

The Poetic Edda, also known as The Elder Edda or Saemund's Edda, is a magnificent and magical collection of thirty-four Icelandic poems, interwoven with prose, dating from the 9th century to the 12th. The original Old Norse verses are printed here, side by side with English translations.

The collection includes the archetypal stories about wise Odin, hammer-wielding Thor, mischievous Loki and the other gods and goddesses of Asgard.

J. R. R. Tolkien readily acknowledged his debt to this source. He was sixteen years old when the Viking Club of London published this beautifully illustrated translation by Olive Bray. Readers of Tolkien's work will easily spot his inspirations—the names of the dwarves in The Hobbit; riddle games; Mirkwood; the Paths of the Dead; an underworld creature being tricked into remaining above-ground until dawn, when sunlight turns him to stone; different races calling a single thing by various names, and more.

In the Poetic Edda the realm where man dwells is called "Midgarth", which translates as "Middle-earth". Elves are mentioned, and there are dwarves called Thorin, Nori, Dori, Ori, Gloin, Fili, Kili Bifur, Bafur, Bombur, and Oaken-shield. The names Thrainn and Thror are mentioned, as is the name Gandalf, which Bray translates as "Wand-elf". Tolkien's Gandalf, of course, carries a staff, or wand.

The poems features a dragon called Fierce-stinger:
"Fares from beneath a dim dragon flying,
a glistening snake from the Moonless Fells.
Fierce-stinger bears the dead on his pinions
away o'er the plains. I sink now and cease."

The language is archaic, so for 21st century readers a glossary is provided at the back of this book, as well as an index of names to help identify all the characters. Bray's lengthy introduction has also been revised for modern readers, and some footnote citations omitted; all else remains exactly as it was in Tolkien's time.

Remarkably in Bray's edition, the original Icelandic text was included. This would have appealed to Tolkien, as a philologist. He must have relished comparing the English words with the Icelandic, page by page.

Illustrator W. G. Collingwood was an English author, artist, antiquary and professor. In 1897 he travelled to Iceland where he spent three months exploring the actual sites that are the settings for the medieval Icelandic sagas. He produced a large number of sketches and watercolours during this time and published an illustrated account of his expedition in 1899. His study of Norse and Anglican archaeology made him widely recognized as a leading authority, and his gorgeous Art Nouveau-style illustrations for the Bray edition are rich with symbolism.

The Poetic Edda, the most important existing source on Norse mythology and Germanic heroic legends, is part of the literature that influenced Tolkien's inner world, informing the creation of The Hobbit and The Lord of the Rings.

Cecilia Dart-Thornton
Author of The Bitterbynde Trilogy
www.dartthornton.com

for
THE PROFESSOR'S BOOKSHELF

(PS: For a better understanding of the Poetic Edda, I recommend reading the last poem, 'Völuspá', first.)

# CONTENTS

# LIST OF ILLUSTRATIONS

*Odin enthroned and holding his spear Gungnir,
flanked by his ravens Huginn and Muninn
and wolves Geri and Freki
by Carl Emil Doepler (1882)*

# BACKGROUND

In Norse mythology there are two races of gods; the warlike Æsir and the gentler Vanir (also known as 'Wanes'). Odin is the first-born of the Æsir, and one of the deities who created mankind. He is also the Allfather of the Æsir and their chief, the High One. Though old, he remains hale and strong, and he is both wise and learned. His thirst for knowledge is unquenchable, and in his quest to learn more he often wanders through the world wearing a hooded cloak made of the sky, or a wide brimmed hat which conceals his face. He prefers to travel incognito.

In his earlier years Odin journeyed to the well of wisdom, guarded by the Jötun (giant) Mimir, where the dew of wisdom seeps in at the roots of the world. There, the High One of the Æsir sacrificed his eye to the well so that he might drink its waters, thereby receiving knowledge possessed by no others. His one remaining eye shines like the sun, and his missing eye, which is dim, is often linked to the moon.

In Odin's eager pursuit of yet more wisdom he managed to obtain mead; an alcoholic beverage made by brewing a mixture of honey and water. According to legend mead is the fermented blood of Kvasir, the greatest mortal poet and *skald* of his time. Drinking mead made Odin fluent in poetry and prose.

The High One of the Æsir is the god of war, battle, victory, hunting and death, but he is also associated with wisdom, magic, poetry, eloquence and prophecy. He has many sons, the most famous of whom is Thor, wielder of the great thunder-hammer Mjölnir. In our daily lives we often speak the names of Odin and his family. Wednesday is named after him (Woden's Day); Thursday is named for Thor and Friday is named for Odin's wife Frigg, who is also a power of the sky. Two other sons of Odin are Vidar, 'the silent god,' who lives in wild Wood-home; and Baldr, whose dwelling-place is fair and shining as his face. Pure is the heart of he who is the best and the most loved of all the gods.

With Frigg, Odin rules Asgard, one of the Nine Worlds and home to the Æsir. His home is Valhöll (Valhalla), the Hall of the Slain, standing high in Asgarth (Asgard). In front of this majestic hall stands the golden-leafed tree Glasir. The hall's roof is thatched with golden shields, and it surrounded by the air river Thund, which roars and thunders when the Valkyries - beautiful winged maidens, the Choosers of the Slain - come riding in with the dead. Half the warriors who die in combat travel to Valhalla, while the other half go to Fólkvangr (Folk-field) in the underworld of Hel, which is ruled by the gentle Vanir goddess Freyja'.

In Valhöll a great host is assembled, and more shall gather; yet they will seem too few when Fenrir, the Wolf, is let loose at Ragnarök, the Doom of the gods. The Chosen have for food the flesh of a sooty-black boar called Saehrimnir, which will never be consumed, however great the throng in Valhöll. Each day the boar is boiled in Eldhrimnir (the fire-smoked cauldron) by Andhrimnir (the sooty-faced cook), and every evening it becomes whole again.

But Odin partakes not of the same food as his Chosen Warriors. He gives the portion from his table to two wolves, Greed and Ravener (Geri and Freki), for he himself needs no food, but mead is his meat and drink.

Two ravens sit perched on his shoulder, and whisper to him tidings of what they have seen and heard. Thought and Memory (Huginn and Muninn) are their names. He sends them flying each day over all the world, and at breakfast-time they return. Thus he is made aware of the things which come to pass, and is called by mortals the Raven God.

The Chosen Warriors have a drink which, like their food, is never failing; but they drink not water, for how should the All-father bid kings and earls and other mighty men to his halls and give them nought but water? A great price would it seem to those who had suffered wounds and death to get such a draught for their pains. But there stands a she-goat called Heidrun over the roof of Valhöll, biting leaves from the overhanging tree. Mead flows from her teats into a vessel so huge that all the Chosen Warriors can drink their fill.

When they are not drinking they engage in sport. Each morning they put on their war-gear, take up their weapons and go forth into the court-yard. There they fight and lay one another low, and play thus till breakfast-time, when they go back and sit them down to drink. These daily conflicts, it would seem, are but a preparation for the last great conflict at Ragnarök.

Another great hall Odin owns in Asgard is named Valaskjálf. This hall is thatched it with sheer silver, and within stands the Hliðskjálf, called the high seat. Whenever the Allfather sits in that seat, he can survey all lands.

# GRIMNISMÁL
## THE SAYINGS OF GRIMNIR

### SYNOPSIS

Grimnismál commences with Odin and his wife, Frigg, sitting in Hlidskjalf, the high seat from which they can look out across every realm. They bend their gaze towards King Geirröth, who is reigning in the stead of his late father, King Hrauthung.

Geirröth and his older brother Agnarr have been raised by Odin and Frigg, respectively. The god and goddess, disguised as a peasant and his wife, had taught the children wisdom. Geirröth had returned to his father's kingdom where he became king upon his father's death, while Agnarr dwelt in company with a giantess in a cave.

In Hliðskjálf, Odin remarks to Frigg that his foster-child Geirröth seemed to be prospering more so than her Agnarr. Frigg retorts that Geirröth is so parsimonious and inhospitable that he would torture his guests if he thought there were too many of them. Odin disputes this, and the couple enters into a wager upon the matter.

Frigg then sends her maid Fulla to Geirröth, advising him that a magician will soon enter his court to bewitch him, and saying that he might be recognised by the fact that no dog was fierce enough to leap up at him.

Odin appears upon earth as a stranger at Geirröth's doors. He arrives in the form best known to men, grey-bearded and clad in a dark blue cloak and broad-brimmed hat, but Geirröth fails to recognise him.

The dogs refuse the attack the stranger. Heeding Fulla's false warning, Geirröth orders his men to capture him. Odin allows this to happen. He states that his name is Grímnir, but he will say nothing further about himself.

Geirröth has him tortured to force him to speak, putting him between two fires for eight nights.

After describing his own home and the joyous life there, Grimnir, tortured by fiery heat, calls to mind the cool, rushing waters which flow from Roaring Kettle, the central fountain of the world, which brings him to the holiest of all places, the Doomstead of the gods, where they assemble daily to hold council and judgment. Here also are two other fountains the well of Mimir, whence Odin draws his wisdom, and the well of Weird, with the Norns who dwell beside it shaping the lives of men. Overhead rises the World-tree Yggdrasil, which Grimnir has just called by the name which in his torment most appealed to him the Shelterer. He remembers now its sufferings the fair, green boughs which stretch over the heavens, and whence fall the dews of life, are being gnawed by spiteful harts the roots, springing;no man knows how deep, are torn by the fierce dragon of the under- world and the mighty stem which rises like the central column of the;universe, rots and suffers from decay.

From time to time Grímnir's narrative is broken by a cry from the god to his faithful Valkyries. Only one person, Geirröth's son, Agnarr (named after his uncle) comes to Odin/Grímnir and gives him a full horn from which to drink, saying that his father, the king, was wrong to torture him.

Odin/Grímnir eventually speaks, saying that he has suffered eight days and nights, without succour from any save Agnarr. He reveals himself to Geirröth as Odin the highest, the god with many aspects and names, who has veiled his god-head and suffered torment in order to instruct and enlighten mankind. Odin promises Agnarr a reward for bringing him the drink, prophesying that he will become Lord of the Goths.

Then Odin/Grímnir turns to Geirröth and predicts his doom. Geirröth realizes the magnitude of his mistake; he has offended the greatest of all the gods. Panicking, he tries to escape his fate. . .

*Sources: Olive Bray and Wikipedia*

*Odin in Torment*

## GRIMNISMÁL

Óþinn ok Frigg sátu í Hliþskjálfu ok sá um heima alla.

Óþinn mælti : 'Sér þu Agnar fóstra þinn, hvar hann elr börn viþ gýgi í hellinum ? En Geirröþr fóstri minn er konungr ok sitr nú at landi.'

Frigg segir : 'Hann er matníþingr sá, at hann kvelr gesti sína, ef honum þykkja ofmargn koma.'

Óþinn segir, at þat er in mesta lygi ; þau veþja um þetta mál. Frigg sendi eskimey sína Fullu til Geirröþar. Hon baþ konung varaz, at eigi fyrgörþi hánum fjölkunnigr maþr sá er þar var kominn í land, ok sagþi þat mark á, at engi hundr var svá ólmr at á hann mundi hlaupa.

En þat var enn mesti hégómi, at Geirröþr konungr væri eigi matgópr ; ok þó lætr hann handtaka þann mann er eigi vildu hundar á ráþa. Sá var í feldi blám ok nefndiz Grimnir ok sagþi ekki fleira frá sér, þótt hann væri at spurþr. Konungr lét hann pína til sagna ok setja milli elda tveggja, ok sat hann þar átta nætr.

*The Chariot of the Sun*

## GRIMNISMÁL

Odin and Frigg were sitting once on Window-shelf, gazing out over all the world.

Said Odin: 'Seest thou Agnar, thy fosterling, how he begets children with a giantess in a cave? But Geirröth, my fosterling, is a king, and rules over the realm.'

'He is such a meat-grudger,' answered Frigg, 'that he starves his guests when he deems that too many are come into his halls.'

Odin swore that this was the greatest lie, and they wagered on the matter. Frigg sent her hand-maiden Fulla to Geirröth to bid the king beware lest an enchanter, who had come into the land, should bewitch him, and she gave them this sign whereby he might be known: no dog, however fierce, would assail him.

Men had lied greatly in saying that Geirröth was not hospitable, but for all that he caused a certain guest to be seized, whom the dogs would not attack. He came clad in a blue mantle, calling himself Grimnir, the Masked One, and would tell nought beside, however much they asked him.

Geirröþr konungr átti þá son tíu vetra gamlan ok hét Agnarr eptir bróþur hans.

Agnarr gekk at Grimni ok gaf hánum horn fullt at drekka ok sagþi, at konungr görþi illa, er hann lét pína hann saklausan. Grimnir drakk af ; þá var cldrinn svá kominn, at feldrinn brann af Grimni. Hann kvaþ :

1.    Heitr est, hripuþr !     ok heldr til mikill ;
        göngumk firr, funi !
    loþi sviþnar,     þót á lopt berak,
        brinnumk feldr fyrir.

2.    Átta nætr      satk milli elda hér,
        svát mér manngi mat né bauþ,
    nema einn Agnarr,     es einn skal ráþa
        Geirröþar sunr Gotna landi.

3.    Heill skaltu Agnarr !     alls þik heilan biþr
        Veratýr vesa ;
    eins drykkjar     þú skalt aldregi
        betri gjöld geta.

4.    Land es heilagt     es ek liggja sé
        ásum ok ölfum nær :
    enn í þrúþheimi     skal þórr vesa,
        unz of rjúfask regin.

5.    Ýdalir heita     þars Ullr hefr
        sér of görva sali ;
    Alfheim Frey     gáfu í árdaga
        tívar at tannfé.

Then the king ordered him to be tortured till he should speak, and they set him in the midst between two fires, and eight nights he sat there.

Geirröth's son, who was ten years old, and named Agnar after the king's brother, went up to Grimnir and gave him to drink out of a brimming horn, saying that the king had done ill thus to torture him without cause; and Grimnir drank. At length, when the fire had waxed so nigh that his mantle burned upon him, he spake:

1. Fierce art thou, fire! and far too great;
flame, get thee further away !
my cloak is scorched though I hold it high;
my mantle burns before me.

2. Eight nights have I sat betwixt the fires,
while no man offered me food,
save only Agnar, the son of Geirröth,
who alone shall rule the realm.

3. Blest be thou Agnar, the God of all beings
shall call a blessing upon thee:
for one such draught thou shalt never more
so fair a guerdon win.

## THE TWELVE HOMES OF THE GODS.

4. Holy is the land which yonder lies
near the world of gods and elves:
in the Home of Strength shall the Thunderer dwell,
even till the Powers perish.

5. Yew-dale is called the realm where Ull
hath set him a hall on high;
and Elf-home that which the gods gave Frey
as tooth-fee in days of yore.

---

5 *Tooth fee, gift to a child at teething.*

6. Bǿr's enn þriþi,     es blíþ regin
     silfri þökpu sali :
   Válaskjalf heitir     es vélti sér
     áss í árdaga.

7. Sökkvabekkr heitir enn fjórþi,     enn þar svalar knegu
     unnir glymja yfir :
   þar þau Óþinn ok Sága     drekka of alla daga
     glöþ ór gollnum kerum.

8. Glaþsheimr heitir enn fimti     þars en gollbjarta
     Valhöll víp of þrumir ;
   en þar Hróptr     kýss hverjan dag
     vápndauþa vera.

9. Mjök es auþkent     þeims til Óþins koma
     salkynni at sea :
   sköptum's rann rept,     skjöldum's salr þakiþr,
     brynjum of bekki straït.

10. Mjök es auþkent     þeims til Óþins koma
     salkynni at sea :
   vargr hangir     fyr vestan dyrr
     ok drúpir örn yfir.

11. Þrymheimr heitir enn sétti,     es Þjazi bjó,
     sa enn ámátki jötunn ;
   en nú Skaþi byggvir,     skír brúþr goþa,
     fornar toptir föþur.

12. Breipablik 'rú en sjaundu,     en þar Baldr hefr
     sér of görva sali :
   á því landi     es ek liggja veit
     fǽsta feiknstafi.

6. A third home is there whose hall is thatched
with silver by blessed Powers;
Vala-shelf that seat is named,
which was founded in former days.

7. The fourth is Falling-brook; there, for ever,
the chill waves are rushing over;
while day by day drink Odin and Saga,
glad-hearted, from golden cups.

8. The fifth is called Glad-home, and gold-bright Valhöll,
spacious, lies in its midst:
there Odin shall choose his own each day
of the warriors fallen in war.

9. 'Tis easily known by all who come
to visit Odin's folk;
with shafts 'tis raftered, with shields 'tis roofed,
with byrnies the benches are strewn.

10. 'Tis easily known by all who come
to visit Odin's folk;
there hangs a wolf 'fore the western door,
and an eagle hovers over.

11. The sixth is Sound-home, where Thiazi bode,
that fearful Jötun of yore;
now Skaði dwells, fair bride of gods,
in her father's former home.

12. The seventh is Broad-gleam; there hath Baldr
set him a hall on high,
away in the land where I ween are found
the fewest tokens of ill.

---

6. *The Icelandic 'Völva' is here anglicised to 'Vala'.*
11. *Jötun - a giant*

13. Himinbjörg 'ru en áttu,   en þar Heimdall kveþa

    . . . valda veum :

    þar vörþr goþa          drekkr í væru ranni

    glaþr enn góþa mjöþ.

14. Folkvangr 's enn niundi,   en þar Freyja ræþr

    sessa kostum í sal :

    hálfan val          hón kýss hverjan dag

    en hálfan Óþinn á.

15. Glitnir 's enn tiundi,   hann es golli studdr

    ok silfri þakþr et sama :

    en þar Forseti          byggvir flestan dag

    ok svæfir allar sakar.

16. Noatún 'ru en elliftu,      en þar Njörþr hefr

    sér of görva sali :

    manna þengill          enn meinsvani

    hátimbruþum hörgi ræþr.

17. Hrísi vex          ok hávu grasi

    Víþars land Viþi :

    en þar mögr          of læzk af mars baki

    frœkn at hefna föþur.

13. The eighth is Heaven-hill; world-bright Heimdal
rules o'er its holy fanes:
in that peaceful hall the watchman of gods
glad-hearted the good mead quaffs.

14. The ninth is Folk-field; Freyja rules there
choice of seats in the hall:
one half the dead she chooses each day
but half the War-father owns.

15. The tenth is Glistener pillared with gold,
and eke with silver roofed;
there Forseti dwells nigh the long day through,
the Judge, and soothes all strife.

16. The eleventh is Noatun; Njörð in that haven
hath built him a hall by the sea;
a prince of men, ever faultless found,
he holds the high built fanes.

17. With brushwood grows, and with grasses high,
Wood-home, Vidar's land;
from his steed that son of Odin shall show him
strong to avenge his sire.

---

14. *Freyja seems here to stand for Frigg, wife of Odin, who
shared the slain with him.*
16. *Njörð in that haven; the suggested meaning for Noatun is
'Ship-haven.'*

18. (21.) Þýtr Þund,     unir Þjóþvitnis
        flskr flóþi í :
    árstraumr     þykkir ofmikill
        valglaumi at vaþa

19. (23) Fimm hundruþ golfa  ok of fjórum tögum
        hykk Bilskirni meþ bugum ;
    ranna þeira     es ek rept vita
        míns veitk mest magar.

20. (22) Valgrind heitir     es stendr velli á
        heilög fyr helgum durum ;
    forn's sú grind,     en þat fair vitu,
        hvé's í lás of lokin.

21. (24) Fimm hundruþ dura  ok of fjórum tögum
        hykk á Valhöllu vesa ;
    átta hundruþ einherja  ganga ór einum durum,
        þás þeir fara viþ Vitni at vega.

22. (18) Andhrimnir     lætr í Eldhrimni
        Sæhrimni soþinn,
    fleska bazt :     en þat faïr vitu,
        viþ hvat einherjar alask.

23. (19) Gera ok Freka     seþr gunntamiþr
        hróþugr Herjaföþr :
    en viþ vín eitt     vápngöfugr
        Óþinn æ liflr.

## THE SKY-ROAD TO Valhöll

18. The Thunder-flood roars, while sports the fish
of the mighty Wolf therein;
o'erwhelming seems the flow of that stream
for the host of slain to wade.

19. Halls five hundred and forty more
hath the Lightning-abode in its bendings,
of all the high roofed houses I know,
highest is that of the Thunderer.

## VALHÖLL

20. Death-barrier stands, the sacred gate,
on the plain 'fore the sacred doors;
old is the lattice and few have learned
how it is closed on the latch.

21. Doors five hundred, and forty more
I ween may be found in Valhöll;
and eight hundred Chosen pass through each one
when they fare to fight with the Wolf.

22. There Sooty-face boils in Sooty-flame
the boar called Sooty-black;
'tis the best of fare, which few have heard
is the chosen warriors' food.

23. Glorying, the battle-wont Father of Hosts
feeds Ravener and Greed, his wolves;
but on wine alone ever Odin lives,
the Weapon-famed god of war.

---

18. *The fish of the mighty Wolf is the sun, or prey of the wolf of
darkness. She shines in the heavens till swallowed by Fenrir.*

24. (20) Huginn ok Muninn    fljúga hverjan dag
jörmungrund yfir :
oumk of Hugin    at hann aptr né komi,
þó seumk meirr of Munin.

25. Heiþrún heitir geit  es stendr höllu á [Herjaföþrs]
ok bítr at Læráþs limum ;
skapker fylla  hón skal ens skíra mjaþar,
knáat sú veig vanask.

26. Hjörtr heitir Eikþyrnir es stendr höllu á [Herjaföþrs]
ok bítr af Læráþs limum ;
en af hans hornum    drýpr í Hvergelmi,
þaþan eigu vötn öll vega.

27. Síþ ok Víþ,    Sækin ok Ækin,
Svöl ok Gunnþró,    Fjörm ok Fimbulþul,
Rín ok Rinnandi,
Gipul ok Göpul,    Gömul ok Geirvimul,
þær hverfa of hodd goþa ;
Þyn ok Vín,    Þöll ok Höll,
Gráþ ok Gunnþorin

28. Vín á heitir,    önnur Vegsvinn,
þriþja Þjóþnuma ;
Nyt ok Nöt,    Nönn ok Hrönn,
Slíþ ok Hriþ,    Sylgr ok Ylgr,
Víþ ok Ván,    Vönd ok Strönd,
Gjöll ok Leiptr,    þær falla gumnum nær,
en falla til Heljar heþan

29. Körmt ok Örmt    ok Kerlaugar tvær,
þær skal Þórr vaþa
dag hverjan,    es hann dœma ferr
at aski Yggdrasils ;
þvít ásbrú    brinnr öll loga,
heilög vötn hloa.

30. Glaþr ok Gyllir,    Gler ok Skeiþbrimir,
Silfrintoppr ok Sinir,
Gísl ok Falhófnir,    Golltoppr ok Léttfeti,
þeim ríþa aésir joum
dag hverjan,    es dœma fara
at aski Yggdrasils.

24. Ravens, Hugin and Munin, of Thought and Memory
wing the wide world each day:
I tremble for Thought, lest he come not again,
yet for Memory more I fear.

## THE WATERS OF THE WORLD

25. Sky-bright o'er Valhöll stands, the goat,
who gnaws the Shelterer's boughs;
she fills a bowl with the shining mead:
'Tis a draught which runs not dry.

26. Oak-thorn o'er Valhöll stands, the hart,
who gnaws the Shelterer's boughs;
run drops from his horns into Roaring-kettle
whence flow all floods in the world.

[27, 28. The names contained in these strophes do not all bear
interpretation and seem to belong to existing, not mythical, rivers,
some of which were to be found in Britain.]

29. Kormt and Ormt and the Bath-tubs twain,
these must the Thunderer wade,
when he fares each day to his throne of doom
under Yggdrasil's ash;
thence Bifrost burns, the bridge of the gods,
and the mighty waters well.

30. Glad One, Goldy, Gleamer, Race-giant,
Silvery-lock and Sinewy,
Shiner, Pale-hoof, Gold-lock, Lightfoot,
these are the steeds which the gods ride,
when they fare each day to their thrones of doom
under Yggdrasil's ash.

---

*30. Yggdrasil's ash, the World Tree.*

31.  Þriar rœtr        standa á þria vega
     und aski Yggdrasils :
     Hel býr und einni,        annarri hrímþursar,
     þriþju menskir menn.

31A.  *Örn sitr        á asks limum*
      *es vel kveþa mart vita ;*
      *öglir einn        hönum augna í milli*
      *Veþrfölnir vakir.*

32.  Ratatoskr heitir íkorni        es rinna skal
     at aski Yggdrasils ;
     arnar orþ        hann skal ofan bera
     ok segja Níþhöggvi niþr.

33.  Hirtir 'u auk fjórir        þeirs af hæfingar á
     gaghalsir gnaga :
     Daïnn ok Dvalinn,    .  .  .  .  .
        Duneyrr ok Dyraþrór.

34.  Ormar fleiri liggja        und aski Yggdrasils,
     an of hyggi hverr ósviþra apa :
     Goinn ok Moinn.        þeir'u Grafvitnis synir,
        Grábakr ok Grafvölluþr,
     Ofnir ok Svafnir        hykk at æ skyli
        meiþs kvistu má.

## THE WORLD TREE'S TORMENTS

31. There are three roots stretching three divers ways
from under Yggdrasil's ash:
'neath the first dwells Hel, 'neath the second Frost giants,
and human kind 'neath the third.

31a. An eagle sits in the boughs of the ash,
knowing much of many things;
and a hawk is perched, Storm-pale, aloft
betwixt that eagle's eyes.

32. Ratatosk is the squirrel with gnawing tooth
which runs in Yggdrasil's ash :
he bears the eagle's words from above
and to Fierce-stinger tells below.

33. There are four harts too, who with heads thrown back
gnaw the topmost boughs of the tree:
Dainn the Dead One. Dvalin the Dallier,
Duneyr and Dyrathror.

34. More serpents lie under Yggdrasil's ash
than a witless fool would ween.
Coin and Moin, the offspring of Grave-monster,
Grey-back and Grave-haunting worm,
Weaver and Soother, I ween they must ever
rend the twigs of the tree.

---

*31. Human kind. These are the dead folk whose dwelling is in the underworld, not the living. We are repeatedly told that Yggdrasil springs from under the earth.*

*32. Ratatosk is the squirrel with gnawing tooth which runs in Yggdrasil's ash: he bears the eagle's words from above and to Fierce-stinger tells below.*

35.   Askr Yggdrasils        drýgir erfiþi
      meira an menn viti :
hjörtr bítr ofan,        en á hliþu fúnar,
skerþir Níþhöggr neþan.


36.   Hrist ok Mist        vilk at mér horn beri,
      Skeggjöld ok Skögul ;
Hildr ok þrúþr,        Hlökk ok Herfjötur,
      Göll ok Geirönul,
Randgríþ ok Ráþgriþ        ok Reginleif,
      þǽr bera einherjum öl.


37.   Árvakr ok Alsviþr        þeir skulu upp heþan
      svangir sól draga ;
en und þeira bógum        fálu bliþ regin,
      æsir, ísarn kól.

38.   Svalinn heitir,        hann stendr sólu fyrir,
      Skjöldr skínanda goþi :
björg ok brim        veitk at brinna skulu,
      ef hann fellr í frá.

39.   Sköll heitir ulfr        es fylgir enu skírleita
      goþi til Varnar-viþar,
en annarr Hati,        Hróþvitnis sunr,
      skal fyr heiþa brúþi himins.

35. Yggdrasil's ash suffers anguish more
than mortal has ever known,
on high gnaw harts, it rots at the side,
and Fierce-stinger rends it beneath.

(Then cries he from the fire-torment:)

36. Would that Hrist and Mist would bear me a horn!
my Valkyries, Axe and Spear-point,
Bond and War-fetter, Battle and Might,
Shrieker and Spear-fierce in strife;
Shield-fierce, Counsel-fierce, Strength-maiden all
who bear ale to the Chosen in War.

## SUN AND EARTH

37. Early-woke, All-fleet, hence must these horses
wearily draw up the sun,
but under their withers the gods, gracious Powers,
 an iron-coolness have hid.

38. There is one called the Cooler who stands 'fore the Sun,
a shield from the shining goddess:
the mountains I ween, and the stormy sea
will flame if he fall from thence.

39. Skoll is the wolf called who hunts the bright sun-goddess
even to the Sheltering grove;
a second fares, Moon-hater, offspring of Fenrir,
in front of that fair bride of heaven.

---

35. *Fierce-stinger, the dragon of the underworld*
36. *Valkyries, or war maidens of Odin*
39. *Skoll, Moon-hater, wolves of darkness. Fenrir, the great Wolf*
*who swallows Odin*

40. Ór Ymis holdi     vas jörþ of sköpuþ,
    en ór sveita sǽr,
björg ór beinum,     baþmr ór hári
    en ór hausi himinn.


41. (40)  En ór hans bröum     görþu blíþ regin
      miþgarþ manna sunum,
    en ór hans heila  vöru þau en harþmóþgu
    ský öll of sköpuþ.


42. (41)  Ullar hylli     hefr ok allra goþa
      hverrs tekr fyrstr á funa ;
    þvít opnir heimar     verþa of ása sunum,
    þás hefja af hvera.


43. (42)  Ívalda synir     gengu í árdaga
      Skiþblaþni at skapa,
    skipa bazt     skírum Frey,
      nýtum Njarþar bur.


44. (43)  Askr Yggdrasils     hann es œztr viþa,
      enn Skiþblaþnir skipa,
    Óþinn ása,     en joa Sleipnir,
    Bifröst brua,     en Bragi skalda,
    Hábrók hauka,     en hunda Garmr.

40. From the flesh of Ymir the world was formed,
from his blood the billows of the sea,
the hills from his bones, the trees from his hair,
the sphere of heaven from his skull.

41. Out of his brows the blithe Powers made
Midgarth for sons of men,
and out of his brains were the angry clouds
all shaped above in the sky.

(The Kettle is taken off the fire in Geirröth's hall.)

42. The favour of Ull and of all the Powers
to him touching first the fire !
For gods can enter the homes of men
when the kettle is raised from the hearth.

## THE TREASURES OF THE WORLD

43. Went the Wielder's sons of old to build
Skidbladnir the wooden bladed,
best of all ships, for the bright god Frey,
ever bountiful son of Niord.

44. Yggdrasil's ash, 'tis the best of trees,
but Skidbladnir of ships,
Odin of gods, Sleipnir of steeds,
Bifrost of bridges, Bragi of skalds,
Habrok of hawks and Garm of hounds.

---

40. *Ymir, a Jötun, the first born of beings.*
41 *Midgarth: In Old English poems also the earth is called Middle-garth.*
42. *When the kettle is taken off the gods can see Odin through the roof opening, come to his rescue, and then hold a triumphal feast.*

45. (44)  Svipum hefk nú ypt        fyr sigtíva sunum,
          vip þat skal vilbjörg vaka :
          öllum ásum          þat skal inn koma
          Ægis bekki á
          Ægis drekku at.


46. (50)  Ölr est, Geirröþr !         hefr þú ofdrukkit,
          . . .            . . . . .
          miklu'st hnugginn,      es þú'st mínu gengi
          öllum einherjum ok Óþins hylli.


47. (51)  Fjölþ þér sagþak,        en þú fátt of mant :
          of þik véla vinir ;
          mæki liggja        ek sé míns vinar
          allan í dreyra drifinn.


48. (52)  Eggmóþan val        nú mun Yggr hafa,
          þitt veitk líf of liþit ;
          úfar'u dísir        nú knátt Óþin sea,
          nálgask þú mik, ef megir !


49. (45)  Hétumk Grímr        hétumk Gangleri,
          Herjan ok Hjalmberi,
          Þekkr ok Þriþi,        Þuþr ok Uþr,
          Helblindi ok Hár,


50. (46)  Saþr ok Svipall        ok Sanngetall,
          Herteitr ok Hnikarr,
          Bíleygr, Báleygr        Bölverkr, Fjölnir,
          Grímr ok Grimnir,       Glapsviþr, Fjölsviþr,
   (47)   Síþhöttr, Síþskeggr,        Sigföþr, Hnikuþr,
          Alföþr, Valföþr,        Atriþr, Farmatýr :
          einu nafni        hétumk aldrigi,
          síz meþ folkum fórk.

## GRIMNIR REVEALS HIMSELF AS ODIN

45. Now my face have I shown to the war-god's sons,
therewith shall help awake,
and the gods shall gather, all glad, to the bench
in Ægir's feasting hall.

46. Dulled with ale art thou, Geirröth, too much hast thou
drunk,
of great treasure art thou deprived,
bereft of my help, and of all chosen warriors,
even the favour of Odin.

47. Much have I told thee, but little thou mindest,
by tricks thou hast been betrayed:
ere long shall I see thy sword, good friend,
lying all bathed in blood.

48. Thy days are run out, the Dread War-father owns
him who is slain by the sword:
the spirits are hostile, behold now! 'tis Odin;
more nigh shalt thou come if thou canst.

(He makes known his names.)

49. They have called me Hood- winker, called me Wanderer,
Helm-bearer, Lord of the Host,
Well-comer, Third Highest, Wave, and Slender,
High One, Dazzler of Hel.

50. They have called me Soothsayer, True and Fickle,
On-driver, Eager in War,
Flashing-eyed, Flaming-eyed, Bale-worker, Shape-shifter,
Veiled One, Masked One, Wile-wise and Much-wise,
Broad-hat, Long-beard, War-father, On-thruster,
All-father, Death-father, On-rider, Freight-wafter
ne'er was I called by one name alone
since I passed through the people of men.

51. (48)    Grimnir hétumk       at Geirröþar,
           en Jalkr at Ásmundar,
         en þá Kjalarr,      es ek kjalka dró,
         Þror þingum at,      Viþurr at vígum,
         Óski ok Ómi,       Jafnhár, Biflindi,
           Göndlir ok Hárbarþr meþ goþum.


52. (49)    Sviþurr ok Sviþrir   es ek hét at Sökkmímis
           ok dulþak enn aldna jötun,
         þas ek Miþvitnis      vask ens mǽra burar
         orþinn einbani.


53. (53)    Óþinn nú heitik,       Yggr áþan hétk,
           hétumk Þundr fyr þat,
         Vakr ok Skilfingr,     Váfuþr ok Hróptatýr,
           Gautr ok Jalkr meþ goþum,
    (54)   Ofnir ok Svafnir,      es hykk at orþnir sé
         allir af einum mér.


Geirröþr konungr sat ok hafþi sverþ um kné sér ok brugþit til miþs. En er hann heyrþi at Óþinn var þar kominn, þá stóþ hann upp ok vildi taka Óþin frá eldinum. Sverþit slapp ór hendi hánum ok vissu hjöltin niþr. Konungr drap fœti ok steyptiz áfram, en sverþit stóþ í gögnum hann, ok fekk hann bana. Óþinn hvarf þá, en Agnarr var þar konungr lengi síþan.

51. They called me Grimnir, the Masked one, at Geirröth's,
Jalk was I named at Osmund's,
Keeler once, when I drew the sledge,
Thror in council, in strife the Stormer,
Wish-giver, Wind-roar, Tree-rocker, Equal-ranked,
Grey-beard and Wizard of gods.

52. They called me Sage and Wise when I duped
the old Jötun who dwells 'neath the earth,
and slew single-handed the glorious son
of that monster who owned the Mead.

53. They call me now Odin, but erewhile the Dread One,
Thund was I called before that,
Watcher and Shaker, Wafter and Counsellor,
Maker and Jalk among gods,
Weaver and Soother, names which I deem
come all from Myself alone.

King Geirröth was sitting by with a half-drawn sword across his knees. When he knew that Odin was there, he rose up desiring to remove the god from the fire. But as he did so the sword slipped out of his hand point upwards, while losing his feet he fell forward upon it, and was pierced through and slain. Then Odin vanished, and Agnar was left to rule long time as king.

---

*51. Tree-rocker, Odin as Wind god. Another meaning suggested for Biflindi is Shield-shaker.*
*52. The old Jötun, Suttung, who owned the Song-mead.*

# ALVÍSSMÁL
## THE WISDOM OF ALL-WISE

SYNOPSIS

Alvíssmál ('Alvíss's Sayings') is a poem collected in the Poetic Edda, probably dating to the 12th century, that relates a conversation between Thor and a dwarf called Alvíss ('All-Wise').

It tells how Thrym, the daughter of Thor, was pledged to a dwarf by the other gods in the absence of her father.

The dwarf, All-wise, is discovered hastening to the home of his betrothed, rejoicing too soon at the good fortune which has won him a bride born of gods. Thus, lost in love-musing, he is met by a rude and way-worn traveller - Thor, returning on foot from some wearying journey.

All-wise does not recognise the father of his bride, and is much injured at the harshness of Thor's address. He has doubtless, if such vanities are permitted to dwarfs, clothed himself in his best as a bridegroom, and now he is taunted with the disfigurements of his race, the pallor of beings who may never see the sun, and his shortness of stature. Nonetheless Alvíss claims Thor's daughter as his bride, saying that she had been promised to him earlier.

The god of Thunder, however, declares himself and refuses the claim, since he had not been at home at the time. If Alviss is to win his daughter, he must answer every question the god poses.

Thor questions the dwarf on the different names which are given to aspects of nature by 'the wights of all worlds' These wights, or beings, include men, gods, Jötuns (giants), dwarves and elves.

Alvíss gives the correct answer to every one of Thor's questions, but eventually, in a surprise twist, he is outwitted. This is the only episode on record where Thor outthinks his adversary; he usually relied on brute force!

*Source: Olive Bray and Wikipedia*

*Allwise Answers Thor*

# ALVÍSSMÁL.

Alvíss kvaþ :

1.  ' Bekki breiþa        nú skal brúþr meþ mér,
        heim í sinni snuask ;
    hratat of mægi        mun hverjum þykkja,
        heima skalat hvilþ nema.'

Þórr kvaþ :

2.  'Hvat's þat fira ?    hví 'stu svá fölr umb nasar ?
        vastu í nótt meþ naï ?
    þursa líki        þykkjumk á þér vesa,
        estat þú til brúþar borinn.'

*The Sun Shines in the Hall*

# ALVÍSSMÁL

All-wise:
1. Ere long shall a bride deck the bench beside me,
we will hasten home together:
swift in my wooing shall I seem to all beings,
but at home none shall hinder my peace.

Thor:
2. What being art thou so pale of hue?
Hast dwelt to-night with the dead?
A likeness to giants I trow hangs o'er thee;
thou wast not born for a bride !

---

*3. The goat-wain, Thor's chariot*

Alvíss kvaþ :

3. ' Alvíss ek heiti,      býk fyr jörþ neþan,
    ák und steini staþ ;
vagna vers      emk á vit kominn :
    bregþi engi föstu heiti firar.'

Þórr kvaþ :

4. ' Ek mun bregþa,      þvít ek brúþar á
    flest of ráþ sem faþir ;
vaskak heima,      þás þér heitit vas,
    sá einn es gjöfir meþ goþum.'

Alvíss kvaþ :

5. ' Hvat's þat rekka      es í ráþum telsk
    fljóþs ens fagrgloa ?
fjarrafleina þik      munu fair kunna :
    hverr hefr baugum þik borit ? '

Þórr kvaþ :

6. ' Vingþórr heitik,      ek hef vita ratat,
    sunr emk Síþgrana ;
at ósátt minni      skaltu þat et unga man hafa
    ok þat gjaforþ geta.'

Alvíss kvaþ :

7. ' Sáttir þinar      es vilk snimma hafa
    ok þat gjaforþ geta ;
eiga viljak      heldr an án vesa
    þat et mjallhvíta man.'

Þórr kvaþ :

8. ' Meyjar ástum      muna þér verþa,
    vísi gestr ! of varit,
ef ór heimi kannt      hverjum at segja
    allt þats viljak vita.

All-wise:
3. I am All-wise who dwell far under the Earth,
I hide in a rock for my home;
I look for the Thunderer, Lord of the goat-wain:
let none break a firm-sworn vow.


Thor:
4. I will break it, who rule o'er the bride as father;
he alone among gods is the giver:
I was far from home when that fair maid of mine
was promised thee ever as bride.

All-wise:
5. What hero is this, who holds in his power
that fair glowing maiden as gift?
Like a far-straying arrow, none knows who thou art,
nor whence all the wealth which thou wearest.

Thor:
6. Winged-thunder am I, wide have I wandered,
son of Sigrani Long-bearded:
ne'er with my will shalt thou win the young maiden
and get thee a wife among gods.

All-wise:
7. Thy good-will then must I speedily gain
and win me a wife among gods:
I would liefer hold in my arms than lack
that snow-white maiden as mine.

Thor:
8. The maiden's love thou shalt not lack,
stranger, who seemest wise!
if thou canst tell out of every world
all that I long to learn.

---

6. *Sigrani, a name for Odin in his form of an old man with a long beard.*

Þórr kvaþ :

9.   ' Seg mer þat, Alvíss !       öll of rök fira

vörumk, dvergr ! at vitir :

hvé sú jörþ heitir      es liggr fyr alda sunum,

heimi hverjum í ? '

Alvíss kvaþ :

10.   ' Jörþ heitir meþ mönnum,      en meþ ásum fold,

kalla vega vanir,

ígrœn jötnar,      alfar groandi,

kalla aur uppregin."

Þórr kvaþ :

11   ' Seg mer þat, Alvíss !       öll of rök fira

vörumk, dvergr ! at vitir :

hvé sá himinn heitir      enn Ymi kendi

heimi hverjum í ? '

Alvíss kvaþ :

12.   'Himinn heitir meþ mönnum,     en hlýrnir meþ goþum,

kalla vindofni vanir,

uppheim jötnar,      alfar fagra ræfr,

dvergar drjúpan sal.'

Þórr kvaþ :

13.   ' Seg mer þat, Alvíss !       öll of rök fira

vörumk, dvergr ! at vitir :

hversu máni heitir,      sás menn sea,

heimi hverjum í ? '

Thor:

9. Tell me this, All-wise, since thou art learned
in the ways of all beings, I ween:
how is Earth, which lies spread before sons of men,
named by the wights of all worlds.

All-wise:

10. Earth 'tis named among men, but Field among gods,
Wanes call it ever the Way;
Jötuns, Fair Green, elves, the Grower,
high Powers call it Clay.

Thor:

11. Tell me this, All-wise, since thou art learned
in the ways of all beings I ween:
how is Heaven, which once was born of Ymir
named by the wights of all worlds?

All-wise:

12. Heaven 'tis named among men, Time-teller among gods,
 Wanes call it Weaver of Wind,
Jötuns, Overworld, elves, the Fair Roof,
dwarfs, the Dripping Hall.

Thor:

13. Tell me this, All-wise, since thou art learned
in the ways of all beings, I ween:
how is the Moon which men behold
named by the wights of all worlds?

Alvíss kvaþ :

14. 'Máni heitir meþ mönnum,    en mýlinn meþ goþum,
     kalla hvél helju í,
   skyndi jötnar,        en skin dvergar,
     kalla alfar ártala.'

Þórr kvaþ :

15. ' Seg mer þat, Alvíss !       öll of rök fira
     vörumk, dvergr ! at vitir :
   hvé sú sól heitir,      es sea alda synir,
     heimi hverjum í ? '

Alvíss kvaþ :

16. ' Sól heitir meþ mönnum,     en sunna meþ goþum,
     kalla dvergar Dvalins ]eika,
   eygló jötnar,       alfar fagra hvél,
     alskír ása synir.'

Þórr kvaþ :

17. ' Seg mer þat, Alvíss !       öll of rök fira
     vörumk, dvergr ! at vitir :
   hvé þau ský heita,     es skúrum blandask,
     heimi hverjum í ? '

Alvíss kvaþ :

18. ' Ský heita meþ mönnum,    en skúrván meþ goþum,
     kalla vindflot vanir,
   úrván jötnar      alfar veþrmegin,
     kalla í helju hjalm huliþs.'

All-wise:

14. Moon 'tis named among men, the Ball among gods,
but the Whirling Wheel in Hel,
of Jötuns, the Hastener, of dwarfs, the Shimmerer,
'tis Year-teller called of elves.

Thor:

15. Tell me this, All-wise, since thou art learned
in the ways of all beings, I ween:
how is Sol which the sons of men behold
named by the wights of all worlds?

All-wise:

16. Sol 'tis named among men, but Sun among gods,
dwarfs call it Dallier's playmate,
Ever-glowing, the Jötuns, Fair wheel, the elves,
All-shine, the children of gods.

Thor:

17. Tell me this, All-wise, since thou art learned
in the ways of all beings, I ween:
how are Clouds of the sky, that with showers are mingled,
named by the wights of all worlds?

All-wise:

18. They are clouds among men, Shower-promise to gods,
Wind-floater called of Wanes,
Rain-omen of Jötuns, Storm-might of elves,
Helm of the Hidden in Hel.

---

*14. Ball, a doubtful word. Some translators suggest Fire.*
*'Hastener', because the sun is pursued by a wolf.*
*16. Dallier's playmate. The sun makes sport of dwarfs who are*
*caught above ground at dawn.*

Þórr kvaþ :

19. ' Seg mer þat, Alvíss !　　　　öll of rök fira
vörumk, dvergr ! at vitir :
hvé sá vindr heitir,　　　es vípast ferr,
heimi hverjum í ? '

Alvíss kvaþ :

20. 'Vindr heitir meþ mönnum,　en váfuþr meþ goþum,
kalla gneggjuþ ginnregin,
œpi jötnar,　　　alfar dynfara,
kalla í helju hviþuþ.'

Þorr kvaþ :

21. ' Seg mer þat, Alvíss !　　　　öll of rök fira
vörumk, dvergr ! at vitir :
hvé þat logn heitir,　　es liggja skal,
heimi hverjum í ? '

Alvíss kvaþ :

22. ' Logn heitir meþ mönnum,　　en lægi meþ goþum,
kalla vindslot vanir,
ofhlý jötnar,　　　alfar dagsefa,
kalla dvergar dags veru.'

Þórr kvaþ :

23. ' Seg mer þat, Alvíss !　　　　öll of rök fira
vörumk, dvergr ! at vitir :
hvé sá marr heitir,　　es menn roa,
heimi hverjum í ? '

Alvíss kvaþ :

24. 'Sær heitir meþ mönnum,　　en sílægja meþ goþum,
kalla vág vanir,
álheim jötnar,　　　alfar lágastaf,
kalla dvergar djúpan mar.'

Thor:
19. Tell me this, All-wise, since thou art learned
in the ways of all beings, I ween:
how is the Wind which wanders wide
named by the wights of all worlds?

All-wise:
20. Wind 'tis named among men, but Waverer of gods,
the wise Powers call it Whinnier,
Jötuns, the Howler, elves, Roaring Rider,
in Hel 'tis called Swooping Storm.

Thor:
21. Tell me this, All-wise, since thou art learned
in the ways of all beings, I ween:
how is the Calm, ever wont to rest,
named by the wights of all worlds?

All-wise:
22. Calm 'tis named among men, Sea-rest among gods,
Wanes ever call it Wind-lull,
Jötuns, the Swelterer, elves, Day-soother,
dwarfs, the Refuge of Day.

Thor:
23. Tell me this, All-wise, since thou art learned
in the ways of all beings, I ween:
how is the Sea which is sailed of men,
named by the wights of all worlds?

All-wise:
24. Sea 'tis named among men, Wide Ocean of gods,
Wanes call it flowing Wave,
Jötuns, Eel-home, elves, the Water-stave,
by dwarfs 'tis called the Deep.

---

20. *Waverer, one of Odin's names as Wind-god.*

Þórr kvaþ :

25.　' Seg mer þat, Alvíss !　　öll of rök fira
　　　vörumk, dvergr ! at vitir :
　　　hvé sá eldr heitir,　　es brinnr fyr alda sunum,
　　　heimi hverjum í ? '

Alvíss kvaþ :

26.　' Eldr heitir meþ mönnum,　　en meþ ásum funi,
　　　kalla vág vanir,
　　　freka jötnar,　　en forbrenni dvergar,
　　　kalla í helju hröþuþ.'

Þórr kvaþ :

27.　' Seg mer þat, Alvíss !　　öll of rök fira
　　　vörumk, dvergr ! at vitir :
　　　hvé sá vipr heitir,　　es vex fyr alda sunum,
　　　heimi hverjum í ? '

Alvíss kvaþ :

28.　'Viþr heitir meþ mönnum,　en vallar fax meþ goþum,
　　　kalla hlíþþang halir,
　　　eldi jötnar,　　alfar fagrlima,
　　　kalla vönd vanir.'

Þórr kvaþ :

29.　' Seg mer þat, Alvíss !　　öll of rök fira
　　　vörumk, dvergr ! at vitir :
　　　hvé sú nótt heitir,　　en Nörvi kenda,
　　　heimi hverjum í ? '

Thor:

25. Tell me this, All-wise, since thou art learned
in the ways of all beings, I ween:
how is Fire, which burns before men's sons,
named by the wights of all worlds?

All-wise:

26. Fire 'tis named among men, but Flame among gods,
Wanes call it leaping Wave,
Jötuns, the Havener, Hel-folk, the Racer,
dwarfs, the Burning Bane.

Thor:

27. Tell me this, All-wise, since thou art learned
in the ways of all beings, I ween:
how is Wood which waxes before men's sons
named by the wights of all worlds?

All-wise:

28. Wood 'tis named among men, Wold-locks among gods,
by heroes Sea-weed of the hills,
Jötuns, Life-feeder, elves, the Fair-limbed,
Wanes ever call it Wand.

Thor:

29. Tell me this, All-wise, since thou art learned
in the ways of all beings, I ween:
how is Night who is born, the daughter of Norr,
named by the wights of all worlds?

---

24. *Wide Ocean, others suggest Silent Water.*
28. *Heroes, the dead warriors in Hel, Icelandic halir, is used else-*
*where for the dead folk (See Vm. st. 43)' and has probably the*
*same meaning here.*

Alvíss kvaþ :

30.  ' Nótt heitir meþ mönnum,     en njól meþ goþum,
kalla grímu ginnregin,
óljós jötnar,        alfar svefngaman,
kalla dvergar draumnjörun.'

Þórr kvaþ :

31.  ' Seg mer þat, Alvíss !       öll of rök fira
vörumk, dvergr ! at vitir :
hvé þat sáþ heitir,        es sá alda synir,
heimi hverjum í ? '

32.  ' Bygg heitir meþ mönnum,     en barr meþ goþum,
kalla vöxt vanir,
æti jötnar,        alfar lágastaf,
kalla í helju hnipinn.'

Þórr kvap :

33.  ' Seg mer þat, Alvíss !       öll of rök fira
vörumk, dvergr ! at vitir :
hvé þat öl heitir,        es drekka alda synir,
heimi hverjum í ? '

Alvíss kvaþ :

34.  ' Öl heitir meþ mönnum,       en meþ ásum bjórr,
kalla veig vanir,
hreina lög jötnar,        en í helju mjöþ,
kalla sumbl Suttungs synir.'

All-wise:

30. She is Night among men, but Mist among gods,
the high Powers call her Hood,
the Jötuns, Unlight, elves, the Sleep-joy,
dwarfs, the Goddess of Dreams.

Thor:

31. Tell me this, All-wise, since thou art learned
in the ways of all beings, I ween:
how is Seed which is sown by the sons of men
named by the wights of all worlds?

All-wise:

32. Tis named Barley among men, but Bear among gods,
Wanes call it Growth of the ground,
Jötuns, Food-stuff, elves, the Sap-staff,
Hel-dwellers, Drooping Head.

Thor:

33. Tell me this, All-wise, since thou art learned
in the ways of all beings, I ween:
how is Ale which sons of men drink oft
named by the wights of all worlds?

All-wise:

34. Ale 'tis named among men, but Beer among gods,
the Stirring Draught of Wanes,
of Jötuns, Clear-flowing, of Hel-folk, Mead,
by the Sons of Suttung, Feast.

Þórr kvaþ :

35.   ' Í einu brjósti      ek sák aldrigi
       fleiri forna stafi ;
    tálum miklum       ek kvep tældan þik :
       uppi est, dvergr ! of dagaþr,
       nú skínn sól í sali.'

Thor:

35. Not e'er have I found in the bosom of one
more learning of olden lore;
but with wiles art thou duped, thus dallying here,
while dawn is upon thee, dwarf!
Behold! Sun shines in the hall.

(As the first ray of sunlight strikes him, All-wise the dwarf is
turned into stone.)

___

33. *'Bear' is an old word for 'barley', and cognate with the
Icelandic 'barn'.*

# VAFÞRÚÞNISMÁL
## ÞE WORDS OF ÞE MIGHÞY WEAVER

SYNOPSIS

Vafþrúðnismál (Vafþrúðnir's sayings) is the third poem in the Poetic Edda. It is a conversation in verse form conducted initially between the Æsir Odin and Frigg, and subsequently between Odin and the giant Vafþrúðnir. The poem goes into detail about the Norse cosmogony.

The Mighty Weaver ia a giant sage, unutterably old and unutterably wise; who sits on his throne throughout the ages, waiting to be questioned by those who dare enter his presence.

In Old Norse tradition knowledge must be sought from bird or beast, from souls of the dead who have gone back to their home in nature, but above all from the giants, that ancient race who were born even before the earth, and were made of a similar substance.

Odin, though a god, is not all-wise by nature, but has to learn, borrow, buy, and even steal his wisdom. He has resolved to contend with the giant whose knowledge is a race heritage

The lay commences with the Allfather asking advice and directions of his wife Frigg as to whether it would be wise to seek out the hall of Vafþrúðnir. Frigg counsels against this course of action, saying that Vafþrúðnir is an extremely powerful Jötun, the most powerful one she knows. Nevertheless Odin continues with his quest.

Odin, a master of dissimulation, disguises himself as Gagnráðr (which translates as 'Wise Counsel'). He enters the giant's hall and stands on the floor before the Weaver with an assumption of humility, begging for the hospitality traditionally afforded to wayfarers. He seeks to obtain Vafþrúðnir's wisdom through the classic mechanism of a wisdom contest.

Vafþrúðnir's response is to accept the wanderer in his hall and only allow him to leave alive if Odin proves to be wiser. If the Weaver had known the nature of his guest he would scarce have asked the Wind god concerning powers of the sky and the steeds of light and darkness, which Odin well knows.

The pair then begin a game of riddling.

During the course of stanza 19, Vafþrúðnir is unwise enough to wager his head in the case of defeat: victory for Odin will result in his death. In stanza 55, at the conclusion of the contest, Vafþrúðnir is obliged to capitulate to Odin's cunning when Odin asks him a question to which only he, and the dead, know the answer. .

*Source: Olive Bray and Wikipedia.*

*Vidar*

# VAFÞRÚÞNISMÁL

Óþinn kvaþ :

1.  ' Ráþ mér nú, Frigg !        alls mik fara tiþir
        at vitja Vafþrúþnis ;
    forvitni mikla        kveþk mér á fornum stöfum
    viþ enn alsvinna jötun.'

Frigg kvap :

2.  ' Heima letja        mundak Herjaföþr
        í görþum goþa ;
    þvít engi jötun        hugþak jafnramman
    sem Vafþrúþni vesa.'

*Odin's Last Words to Baldr*

# VAFÞRÚÞNISMÁL

Odin:
1. Now counsel me, Frigg for I fain would seek
the Mighty Weaver of words.
I yearn to strive with that all-wise giant
in learning of olden lore.

Frigg:
2. Nay, Father of Hosts ! I fain would keep thee
at home in the garth of the gods;
no giant I deem so dread and wise
as that Mighty Weaver of words.

Óþinn kvap :

3. ' Fjölþ ek fór,      fjölþ freistaþak,
     fjölþ of reyndak regin ;
    hitt viljak vita      hvé Vafþrúþnis
     salakynni sé.'

Frigg kvaþ :

4. ' Heill þú farir !      heill aptr komir !
     heill þu á sinnum sér !
    œþi þer dugi,      hvars skalt, Aldaföþr !
     orþum mæla. jötun.'

5. Fór þá Óþinn      at freista orþspeki
     þess ens alsvinna. jötuns :
   at höllu hann kvam      ok átti Hýms faþir,
     inn gekk Yggr þegar.

Óþinn kvaþ :

6. ' Heill þú, Vafþrúþnir !      nú'mk í höll kominn,
     á þik sjalfan at sea ;
    hitt viljak fyrst vita,      ef þú fróþr sér
     eþa alsviþr, jötunn ! '

Vafþrúþnir kvaþ :

7. ' Hvat's þat manna      es í mínum sal
     verpumk orþi á ?
   út né kömr      órum höllum frá
     nema þú enn snotrari sér.'

Óþinn kvaþ :

8. ' Gagnráþr heitik,      nú'mk af göngu kominn
     þyrstr til þinna sala ;
    laþar þurfi—hef ek lengi farit—
     ok andfanga, jötunn ! '

Odin:

3. Far have I fared much have I ventured,
oft have I proved the Powers;
this now must I know how the house-folk fare
in the Mighty Weaver's home.

Frigg:

4. Then safely go, come safely again,
and safely wend thy way:
may thy wit avail thee, Father of beings,
when thou weavest words with the giant !

5. Then Odin went to prove with words
the wisdom of the all-wise giant:
he reached the hall of the Jötun race;
the Dread One entered forthwith.

Odin:

6. Hail, Mighty Weaver ! here in this hall
I have come thyself to see;
and first will try if thou art in truth
all-wise and all-knowing, Giant.

The Weaver:

7. What man is here, who dares in my hall
to throw his words at me thus?
thou shalt ne'er come forth again from our courts
if thou be not the wiser of twain.

Odin:

8. Riddle-reader I am called, I come from my roaming
thirsty here to thy halls,
in need of welcome and kindly greeting,
long way have I wandered, Giant.

Vafþrúþnir kvaþ :

9. ' Hví þu þá, Gagnráþr !     mælisk af golfi fyrir ?
    farþu í sess í sal !
    þá skal freista,     hvaþarr fleira viti,
    gestr eþa enn gamli þulr.'

Óþinn kvaþ :

10. ' Óauþugr maþr,     es til auþugs kömr,
    mæli þarft eþa þegi !
    ofrmælgi mikil     hykk at illa geti
    hveims viþ kaldrifjaþan kömr.'

Vafþrúþnir kvaþ :

11. ' Seg mér, Gagnráþr !     alls þu á golfi vill
    þíns of freista frama :
    hvé sá hestr heitir     es hverjan dregr
    dag of dróttmögu ? '

Óþinn kvaþ :

12. ' Skinfaxi heitir     es enn skíra dregr
    dag of dróttmögu ;
    hesta baztr     þykkir meþ Hreiþgotum,
    ey lýsir mön af mari.'

Vafþrúþnir kvaþ :

13. ' Seg þat, Gagnráþr !     alls þu á golfi vill
    þíns of freista frama :
    hvé sá jór heitir     es austan dregr
    nótt of nýt regin ? '

The Weaver:
9. Why speak, Riddle-reader, standing thus?
take here thy seat in the hall;
and soon shall be seen who knows the more,
stranger or ancient sage.

Odin:
10. Let the penniless wretch in the house of the rich
speak needful words or none:
prating, I ween, works ill for him
who comes to the cold in heart.

I

THE PROVING OF RIDDLE-READER

The Weaver:
11. Say, Riddle-reader! since on the floor
thou fain wouldst show thy skill,
how the Steed is called which draws each Day
over the children of men.

Odin:
12. 'Tis Shining-Mane who draws bright Day
over the children of men;
they hold him best of steeds in the host;
streams light from his mane evermore.

The Weaver:
13. Say, Riddle-reader ! since on the floor
thou fain wouldst show thy skill,
how the Steed is called who forth from the east
draws Night o'er the blessed Powers.

Óþinn kvaþ :

14. ' Hrímfaxi heitir      es hverja dregr
       nótt of nýt regin ;
    méldropa        fellir morgin hvern,
       þaþan kömr dögg of dali.'

Vafþrúþnir kvaþ :

15. ' Seg þat, Gagnráþr !      alls þu á golfi vill
       þins of freista frama :
    hvé sú á heitir      es deilir meþ jötna sunum
       grund auk meþ goþum ? '

Óþinn kvaþ :

16. ' Ifing heitir á      es deilir meþ jötna sunum
       grund auk meþ goþum ;
    opin rinna      hón skal of aldrdaga,
       verþrat íss á á.'

Vafþrúþnir kvaþ :

17. ' Seg þat, Gagnráþr !      alls þu á golfi vill
       þins of freista frama :
    hvé sá völlr heitir      es finnask vígi at
       Surtr ok en svásu goþ ? '

Óþinn kvaþ :

18. ' Vígriþr heitir völlr      es finnask vígi at
       Surtr ok en svásu goþ ;
    hundraþ rasta      hann's á hverjan veg,
       sá's þeim völlr vitaþr.'

Odin:

14. 'Tis Rimy- Mane who draws evermore
each Night o'er the blessed Powers;
he lets fall drops from his bit each dawning;
thence comes dew in the dales.

The Weaver:

15. Say, Riddle-reader ! since on the floor
thou fain wouldst show thy skill,
how the River is called which parts the realm
of the Jötun race from the gods.

Odin:

16. That River is Ifing which parts the realm
of the Jötun race from the gods;
free shall it flow while life days last;
never ice shall come o'er that stream.

The Weaver:

17. Say, Riddle-reader! since on the floor
thou fain wouldst show thy skill,
how the Field is called where in strife shall meet
dark Surt and the gracious gods.

Odin:

18. War-path is the Field where in strife shall meet
dark Surt and the gracious gods:
a hundred miles it measures each way;
'tis the Field marked out by Fate.

---

*17. Surt, a fire giant*

19.' Fróþr est, gestr !      farþu á bekk jötuns,

     ok mælumsk í sessi saman !

höfþi veþja      vit skulum höllu í,

     gestr ! of geþspeki.'

Óþinn kvaþ :

20. ' Seg pat et eina,      ef þitt œpi dugir

     ok þú, Vafþrúþnir vitir :

hvaþan jörþ of kvam      eþa upphiminn

     fyrst, enn fróþi jötunn ? '

Vafþrúþnir kvaþ :

21. ' Ór Ymis holdi      vas jörþ of sköpuþ

     en ór beinum björg,

himinn ór hausi      ens hrímkalda jötuns,

     en ór sveita sær,'

Óþinn kvaþ :

22. ' Seg þat annat,      ef þitt œþi dugir

     ok þú, Vafþrúþnir ! vitir :

hvaþan máni of kvam,      sás ferr menn yfir,

     eþa sól et sama ? '

The Weaver:
19. Wise art thou, stranger, but come now and sit
by my side on the Jötun's seat;
let us talk and wager on wisdom of mind
our two heads here in the hall.

(Odin seats himself by the giant.)

## II
## THE PROVING OF THE MIGHTY WEAVER

Odin:
20. Answer well the first, if thou hast the wit,
and knowest, Mighty Weaver,
from whence the Earth and the heavens on high,
wise Giant, came once to be.

The Weaver:
21. From the flesh of Ymir the world was formed,
from his bones were mountains made,
and Heaven from the skull of that frost-cold giant,
from his blood the billows of the sea.

Odin:
22. Answer well the second, if thou hast the wit,
and knowest, Mighty Weaver,
whence Moon hath come who fares over men,
and whence Sun hath had her source.

---

21. *Ymir, the first-born of the Jötuns.*
22. *Moon, sun, see Grimnismal stanza 31.*

23,   ' Mundilferi heitir        hann es Mána faþir
ok svá Sólar et sama ;
    himin hverfa        þau skulu hverjan dag
öldum at ártali.'

Óþinn kvaþ :

24.   ' Seg þat et þriþja,        alls þik svinnan kveþa,
    ef þú, Vafþrúþnir ! vitir :
hvaþan dagr of kvam,        sás ferr drótt yfir,
    eþa nótt meþ niþum ? '

Vafþrúþnir kvaþ :

25.   ' Dellingr heitir,        hann es Dags faþir,
    en Nótt vas Nörvi borin ;
ný ok niþ        skóþu nýt regin
    öldum at ártali.'

Óþinn kvaþ :

26.   ' Seg þat et fjórþa,        alls þik fróþan kveþa,
    ef þú, Vafþrúþnir ! vitir :
hvaþan vetr of kvam        eþa varmt sumar
    fyrst meþ fróþ regin ? '

The Weaver:
23. The Mover of the Handle is father of Moon,
and the father eke of Sun,
round the heavens they roll each day
for measuring of years to men.

Odin:
24. Answer well the third if thou hast the wit,
and knowest, Mighty Weaver,
whence Day arose to pass o'er the race,
and Night with her waning Moons.

The Weaver:

25. There is one called Dawning, the father of Day,
but Night was born of Norr;
new and waning moons the wise Powers wrought
for measuring of years to men.

Odin:

26. Answer well the fourth, if thou hast the wit,
and knowest, Mighty Weaver,
whence Winter came and warm Summer first
the wise Powers once among.

---

*23. Mover of the handle. This mysterious being Mundilferi is not mentioned elsewhere. Rydberg traces a belief that the heavens were turned by a gigantic world mill. (Teutonic Mythology, p. 397).*

*25. In this passage Ymir is called Aurgelmir. 'Gelmir' in all these names seems to signify the roaring, rushing sound of the elemental powers in chaos.*

27. ' Vindsvalr heitir,        hann es Vetrar faþir,
     en Svósuþr Sumars ; '
   [Vindsvals faþir        var Vásuþr of heitinn,
     öll es su ætt til ötul.]

Óþinn kvaþ :

28. ' Seg þat et fimta,        alls þik fróþan kveþa,
     ef þú, Vafþrúþnir ! vitir :
   hverr ása elztr        eþa Ymis niþja
     yrþi í ardaga ? '

Vafþrúþnir kvaþ :

29. ' Örófi vetra,        áþr væri jörþ sköpuþ,
     þá vas Bergelmir borinn ;
   Þrúþgelmir        vas þess faþir,
     en Aurgelmir afi.'

Óþinn kvaþ :

30. ' Seg þat et sétta,        alls þik svinnan kveþa,
     ef þú, Vafþrúþnir ! vitir :
   hvaþan Aurgelmir        kvam meþ jötna sunum
     fyrst, enn fróþi jötunn ? '

Vafþrúþnir kvaþ :

31. ' Ór Élivágum        stukku eitrdropar,
     svá óx unz ór varþ jötunn ;
   [þar órar ættir        kvámu allar saman,
     því's þat æ allt til atalt.']

Óþinn kvaþ :

32. ' Seg þat et sjaunda,        alls þik svinnan kveþa,
     ef þú, Vafþrúþnir ! vitir :
   hvé sá börn of gat        enn aldni jötunn,
     es hann hafþit gýgjar gaman ? '

The Weaver:

27. There is One called Sweetsouth, father of Summer, but Wind-cool is winter's sire, the son was he of Sorrow-seed; all fierce and dread is that race.

Odin:

28. Answer well the fifth, if thou hast the wit, and knowest, Mighty Weaver: who was born of gods or of Jötun brood, the eldest in days of yore?

The Weaver:

29. Untold winters ere Earth was fashioned roaring Bergelm was born; his father was Thrudgelm of Mighty Voice, loud-sounding Ymir his grandsire.

Odin:

30. Answer well the sixth, if thou hast the wit, and knowest, Mighty Weaver, whence came Ymir, loud-sounding Jötun, the first of thy race, wise Giant.

The Weaver:

31. From Stormy-billow sprang poison-drops, which waxed into Jötun form, and from him are come the whole of our kin; all fierce and dread is that race.

Odin:

32. Answer well the seventh, if thou hast the wit, and knowest, Mighty Weaver, how that ancient Being begot his children who knew not joy of a giantess.

---

31. *Stormy-billow, a mythical river between Asgard and Jötunheim.*

33. ' Und hendi vaxa        kváþu hrímþursi
      mey ok mög saman ;
  fótr viþ fœti        gat ens frópa jötuns
      sexhöfþaþan sun.'

Óþinn kvaþ :

34. ' Seg þat et átta,      alls þik svinnan kveþa,
      ef þú, Vafþrúþnir ! vitir :
  hvat fyrst of mant      eþa fremst of veizt ?
      þú 'st alsviþr, jötunn ! '

Vafþrúþnir kvaþ :

35. ' Örófi vetra        áþr væri jörþ of sköpuþ,
      þá vas Bergelmir borinn ;
  þat ek fyrst of man,      es sa enn frópi jötunn
      á vas lúþr of lagiþr.'

Óþinn kvaþ :

36. ' Seg þat et niunda,      alls þik svinnan kveþa,
      ef þú, Vafþrúþnir ! vitir :
  hvaþan vindr of kömr      sás ferr vág yfir ?
      aé menn hann sjalfan of sea.'

Vafþrúþnir kvaþ :

37. ' Hræsvelgr heitir      en sitr á himins enda,
      jötunn í arnar ham ;
  af hans vængjum      kveþa vind koma
      alla menn yfir.'

The Weaver:

33. 'Tis said that under the Frost-giant's arm grew a boy and girl together; foot with foot begot of that first wise giant, and a six-headed son was born.

Odin:

34. Answer well the eighth, if thou hast the wit, and knowest, Mighty Weaver, what mindst thou of old, and didst earliest know? since I ween thou art all wise, giant !

The Weaver:

35. Untold winters ere Earth was shaped, roaring Bergelm was born; I mind me first when that most wise giant of old in a cradle was laid.

Odin:

36. Answer well the ninth, if thou hast the wit, and knowest, Mighty Weaver, whence comes the Wind which fares o'er the waves, but which never man hath seen.

The Weaver:

37. Corpse-swallower sits at the end of heaven, a Jötun in eagle form; from his wings, they say, comes the wind which fares over all the dwellers of Earth.

---

35. *Cradle (Icelandic luþr) has various meanings including meal-bin box, boat, ark.*

37. *Corpse-swallower is perhaps identical with the raven of Völuspá 47.*

Óþinn kvaþ :

38. ' Seg þat et tiunda,        alls þú tíva rök
        öll, Vafþrúþnir ! vitir :
    hvaþan Njörþr of kvam        meþ ása sunum—
    hofum ok hörgum        hanr ræþr hundmörgum—
        ok vasat hann ásum alinn ? '

Vafþrúþnir kvaþ :

39. ' Í Vanaheimi        skópu hann vís regin
        ok seldu at gíslingu goþum ;
    í aldar rök        hann mun aptr koma
        heim meþ vísum Vönum.'

Óþinn kvaþ :

40. ' Seg þat et ellifta,        alls þik svinnan kveþa,
        ef þú, Vafþrúþnir ! vitir :
    hverir'u ýtar        es Óþins túnum í
        höggvask hverjan dag ? '

Vafþrúþnir kvaþ :

41. ' Allir einherjar        Óþins túnum í
        höggvask hverjan dag ;
    val þeir kjósa        ok ríþa vígi frá,
        sitja meirr of sáttir saman.'

Óþinn kvaþ :

42. ' Seg pat et tolfta,        hví þú tíva rök
        öll, Vafþrúþnir ! vitir :
    frá jötna rúnum        ok allra goþa
        segir þu et sannasta,
        enn alsvinni jötunn ! '

Odin:

38. Answer well the tenth, since all tidings of gods thou knowest, Mighty Weaver, whence Niord first came mid the ^Esir kin- courts and altars he owns in hundreds who was not reared in their race.

The Weaver:

39. In Wane-home once the wise Powers made him and gave him as hostage to gods; in the story of time he shall yet come home to the wise foreseeing Wanes.

Odin:

40. Answer well the eleventh, since they call thee wise, if thou knowest, Mighty Weaver who are the beings who thus do battle in the dwellings of Odin each day?

The Weaver:

41. All the Chosen Warriors are waging war in the dwellings of Odin each day : they choose the slain, ride home from the strife, then at peace sit again together.

Odin:

42. Answer well the twelfth, how all the story of the Powers thou knowest, Weaver. Canst thou truly tell me the secrets of Jötuns and all the gods, wise giant?

---

*38, 39. Æsir, Wanes. These are the two races of the gods; for their war, see Völuspá stanzas 21-24 and the introduction to Völuspá.*
*41. Chosen Warriors, see Grimnismál stanza 21.*

Vafþrúþnir kvaþ :

43. ' Frá jötna rúnum      ok allra goþa
     ek kann segja satt,
   þvít hvern hefk      heim of komit :
   niu kvamk heima      fyr Niflhel neþan,
   hinig deyja [ór helju] halir.'

Óþinn kvaþ :

44. ' Fjölþ ek fór,      fjölþ ek freistaþak,
     fjölþ of reyndak regin :
   hvat lifir manna,      pás enn mæra líþr
   fimbulvetr meþ firum ? '

Vafþrúþnir kvap :

45. ' Líf ok Lífþrasir,      en þau leynask munu
     í holti Hoddmimis ;
   morgindöggvar      þau sér at mat hafa
   en þaþan af aldir alask.'

Óþinn kvaþ :

46. ' Fjölþ ek fór,      fjölþ ek freistaþak,
     fjölþ of reyndak regin :
   hvapan kömr sól      á enn slétta himin
   þás þessi hefr Fenrir farit ? '

Vafþrúþnir kvaþ :

47. ' Eina dóttur      berr Alfröþull,
     áþr henni Fenrir fari ;
   sú skal ríþa,      þás regin deyja
   móþur brautir mær.'

The Weaver:

43. Most truly I can tell thee the secrets of Jötuns and all the gods; since I have been into every world, even nine worlds to Mist-Hel beneath whither die the dead from Hel.

Odin:

44. Far have I fared, much have I ventured, oft have I proved the Powers: what beings shall live when the long Dread Winter comes o'er the people of earth?

The Weaver:

45. Life and Life-craver, who hidden shall lie in the boughs of Yggdrasil's Ash : morning dews they shall have as meat; thence shall come new kindreds of men.

Odin:

46. Far have I fared, much have I ventured, oft have I proved the Powers : whence comes a new Sun in the clear heaven again when the Wolf has swallowed the old.

The Weaver:

47. One daughter alone shall that Elf-beam bear before she is swallowed by the Wolf; and the maid shall ride on the mother's path after the Powers have perished.

---

*43. Nine Worlds. Nine was a mystic number . In Alvíssmál are mentioned worlds of Æsir, Wanes, giants, dwarfs, elves, men, and the dead in Hel, but nine are never enumerated.*

*44. Dread Winter or Fimbul-vetr is the sign of the coming doom of the gods.*

*45. Yggdrasil is suggested by Hodd-mimir's wood, which is clearly the World tree.*

*46. The Wolf, Fenrir.*

Óþinn kvaþ :

48.  ' Fjölþ ek fór,       fjölþ ek freistaþak,
    fjölþ of reyndak regin :
    hverjar 'u meyjar       es líþa mar yfir,
    fróþgeþjaþar fara ? '

Vafþrúþnir kvaþ :

49.  ' þriar þjóþir       falla þorp yfir
    meyja Mögþrasis,
    hamingjur einar       þærs í heimi 'rú,
    þó þær meþ jötnum alask.'

Óþinn kvaþ :

50.  ' Fjölþ ek fór,       fjölþ ek freistaþak,
    fjölþ of reyndak regin :
    hverir ráþa æsir       eignum goþa,
    þás sloknar Surta logi ? '

Vafþrúþnir kvaþ :

51.  ' Víþarr ok Váli       byggva vé goþa,
    þás sloknar Surta logi ;
    Móþi ok Magni       skulu Mjöllni hafa
    Vingnis at vígþroti.'

Óþinn kvaþ :

52.  ' Fjölþ ek fór,       fjölþ ek freistaþak,
    fjölþ of reyndak regin :
    hvat verþr Óþni       at aldrlagi,
    þás of rjúfask regin ? '

Odin:

48. Far have I fared, much have I ventured, oft have I proved the Powers : who are those maidens who pass o'er the sea wandering, wise in mind?

The Weaver:

49. There fly three troops of Mogthrasir's maidens and hover o'er homes of men; the only guardian spirits on earth, and they are of Jötuns born.

Odin:

50. Far have I fared, much have I ventured, oft have I proved the Powers : who shall afterwards hold the wealth of the gods when the fire of dark Surt is slaked?

The Weaver:

51. In the fanes of the gods shall dwell Vidar and Vali when the fire of dark Surt is slaked; to Modi and Magni shall Mjollnir be given when to Thor comes the end of strife.

Odin:

52. Far have I fared, much have I ventured, oft have I proved the Powers : what foe shall bring, at the Doom of gods, to Odin the end of life?

---

49. *Mogthrasir is unknown. The interpretation 'Son-craver ' suggested by G. is doubtful.*
51. *Vidar and Vali, both sons of Odin; Modi and Magni, both sons of Thor. Mjollnir, Thor's hammer. To Thor comes the end: he is slain by the World -serpent. He is here called Vingnir.*

Vafþrúþnir kvaþ :

53.  ' Ulfr gleypa        mun Aldaföþr,
      þess mun Víþarr vreka ;
   kalda kjapta       hann klyfja mun
      vitnis vígi at.'

Óþinn kvaþ :

54.  ' Fjölþ ek fór,       fjölþ ek freistaþak,
      fjölþ of reyndak regin :
   hvat mælti Óþinn,       áþr á bál stigi,
      sjalfr í eyra syni ? '

Vafþrúþnir kvaþ :

55.  ' Ey manni þat veit,       hvat þu í árdaga
      sagþir í eyra syni :
   feigum munni       mæltak mína forna stafi
      auk of ragna rök.
   Nú viþ Óþin       deildak orþsþeki,
      þú'st æ vísastr vera.'

The Weaver:

53. Fenrir shall swallow the Father of men, but this shall Vidar avenge: with his sword he shall cleave the ice-cold jaws of the mighty monster in strife.

Odin:

54. Far have I fared, much have I ventured, oft have I proved the Powers : what spake Odin's self in the ear of his son, when Baldr was laid on the bale fire?

The Weaver:

55. That no man knows, what Thou didst speak of old in the ear of thy son. Thus with fated lips have I uttered old lore and told the great Doom of the Powers; for I have striven in word-skill with Odin's self; thou art ever the wisest of all.

# HÁVAMÁL
## THE WORDS OF ODIN THE HIGH ONE

### SYNOPSIS

Hávamál, presented as a single poem, is in fact a medley of different poems that chiefly offer advice for prudent living and appropriate conduct. For the most part it is composed in the metre Ljóðaháttr, a metre associated with wise verse.

It seems that Hávamál's final author was more teacher than poet; possibly a Christian monk with a taste for antiquarian knowledge. This author had none of the poetic imagination of the writer of Grimnismal.

The first section, Gestaþáttr, the 'guest's section' (stanzas 1 through 79) advises how one should behave when one is traveling. It focusses on etiquette between hosts and guests, and the traditions of reciprocity and hospitality, which were sacred to the Norse pagans.

Stanzas 84 to 110 deal with romantic love and the character of women. They commence with a discourse on the faithlessness of women and advice for the seducing of them. This is followed by two mythological accounts of Odin's relationships with women, known as 'Odin's Examples' or 'Odin's Love Quests'. The first is the story of Odin's thwarted attempt at possessing the daughter of Billing, the second the tale of the mead of poetry, which Odin won by seducing its guardian, the maiden Gunnlöð.

Loddfáfnismál (stanzas 111-138) again expounds upon morals, ethics, proper behaviour and codes of conduct. The section is addressed to Loddfáfnir , 'Stray-singer'.

In Rúnatal or Óðin's Rune Song, (stanzas 138-146), Odin explains how he won the runes of writing. In stanzas 138 and 139, Odin describes his sacrifice of himself to himself. The 'windy tree' from which he hangs is often identified with the world tree, Yggdrasil.

The last section, Ljóðatal, lists eighteen songs, sometimes called 'charms'. We are not given the songs themselves - only a description of their effects. There is no actual mention of runes or runic magic in Ljóðatal excepting in the twelfth song (stanza 158), which takes up the motif of Odin hanging on the tree and its association with runes' 'Svo egríst / og í rúnum fá'g' - 'So do I write / and colour the runes.' Nevertheless, because Rúnatal precedes the list, scholars sometimes reinterpret Ljóðatal as referring to runes, specifically the sixteen letters of the Younger Futhark.

ᚠᛇᚷᛚᛖ ᚹᚠᚤᛇᛏ ᚾᛇᛗᚼ

*Source: Olive Bray and Wikipedia*

## HÁVAMÁL

### I GESTAÞÁTTR

1.  Gáttir allar,
    áþr gangi fram,
    umb skoþask skyli,
    umb skygnask skyli ;
    þvít óvist es,
    hvar óvinir
    sitja á fleti fyrir.

2.Gefendr heilir!   gestr's inn
    kominn hvar skal sitja sjá?
Mjök es bráþr sás á bröndum skal   síns of freista frama.

3.  Elds es þörf   þeims inn es kominn
    auk á kné kalinn ;
    matar ok váþa   es manni þörf
    þeims hefr of fjall farit.

4.  Vatns es þörf   þeims til verþar kömr,
    þerru ok þjóþlaþar,
    góþs of æþis   ef sér geta mætti
    orþ, ok endrþögu.

## HÁVAMÁL

I GESTAÞÁTTR
WISDOM FOR WANDERERS
AND COUNSEL TO GUESTS.

1. At every door-way, ere one enters, one should spy round, one should pry round, for uncertain is the witting that there be no foeman sitting, within, before one on the floor.

2. Hail, ye Givers! a guest is come; say ! where shall he sit within? Much pressed is he who fain on the hearth would seek for warmth and weal.

3. He hath need of fire, who now is come, numbed with cold to the knee; food and clothing the wanderer craves who has fared o'er the rimy fell.

4. He craves for water, who comes for refreshment, drying and friendly bidding, marks of good will, fair fame if 'tis won, and welcome once and again.

5.   Vits es þörf      þeims víþa ratar,
      dælt es heima hvat ;
  at augabragþi      verþr sás etki kann
  auk meþ snotrum sitr.

6.   At hyggjandi sinni     skylit maþr hrœsinn vesa,
      heldr gǽinn at geþi ;
  þás horskr ok þögull     kömr heimisgarþa til,
      sjaldan verþr víti vörum.
  þvít óbrigþra vin     fǽr maþr aldrigi,
  an manvit mikit.

7.   Enn vari gestr,     es til verþar kömr,
      þunnu hljóþi þegir,
  eyrum hlýþir,      en augum skoþar :
      svá nýsisk fróþra hverr fyrir.

8.   Hinn es sǽll     es sér of getr
      lof ok líknstafi ;
  ódǽlla er viþ þat     es maþr eiga skal
      annars brjóstum í.

9.   Sá es sǽll     es sjalfir of á
      lof ok vit meþan lifir,
  þvít ill ráþ     hefr maþr opt þegit
      annars brjóstum ór.

10.   Byrþi betri     berrat maþr brautu at,
      an sé manvit mikit ;
  auþi betra     þykkir þat í ókunnum staþ,
      slíkt es válaþs vera.

11.   Byrþi betri     berrat maþr brautu at,
      an sé manvit mikit ;
  vegnest verra     vegra hann velli at,
      an sé ofdrykkja öls.

12. (11)   Esa svá gott,     sem gott kveþa,
      öl alda sunum,
  þvít fǽra veit,     es fleira drekkr,
      síns til geþs gumi.

13. (12)   Óminnis hegri heitir     sás of ölprum þrumir,
      hann stelr geþi guma ;
  þess fugls fjöþrum     ek fjötraþr vask
      í garþi Gunnlaþar.

14. (13)   Ölr ek varþ,     varþ ofrölvi
      at ens fróþa Fjalars ;
  því's ölþr bazt,     at aptr of heimtir
      hverr sitt geþ gumi.

5. He hath need of his wits who wanders wide, aught simple will serve at home; but a gazing-stock is the fool who sits mid the wise, and nothing knows.

6. Let no man glory in the greatness of his mind, but rather keep watch o'er his wits. Cautious and silent let him enter a dwelling; to the heedful comes seldom harm, for none can find a more faithful friend than his wealth of mother wit.

7. Let the wary stranger who seeks refreshment keep silent with sharpened hearing; with his ears let him listen, and look with his eyes; thus each wise man spies out the way.

8. Happy is he who wins for himself fair fame and kindly words; but uneasy is that which a man doth own while it lies in another's breast.

9. Happy is he who hath in himself praise and wisdom in life; for oft doth a man ill counsel get when 'tis born in another's breast.

10. A better burden can no man bear on the way than his mother wit: 'tis the refuge of the poor, and richer it seems than wealth in a world untried.

11. A better burden can no man bear on the way than his mother wit: and no worse provision can he carry with him than too deep a draught of ale.

12. Less good than they say for the sons of men is the drinking oft of ale: for the more they drink, the less can they think and keep a watch o'er their wits.

13. A bird of Unmindfulness flutters o'er ale feasts, wiling away men's wits: with the feathers of that fowl I was fettered once in the garths of Gunnlod below.

14. Drunk was I then, I was over drunk in that crafty Jötun's court. But best is an ale feast when man is able to call back his wits at once.

---

*13 and 14. 'Gunnlod' and 'That crafty Jötun'. The name Fjalar in the text also belongs to Thor's famous opponent. Possibly it is here used in a general sense for any Jötun.*

15. (14)    Þagalt ok hugalt      skyli þjóþans barn
         ok vígdjarft vesa ;
   glaþr ok reifr      skyli gumna hverr
         unz sinn bíþr bana.

16. (15)    Ósnjallr maþr      hyggsk munu ey lifa,
         ef viþ víg varask,
   en elli gefr      hánum engi friþ,
         þót hánum geirar gefi.

17. (16)    Kópir afglapi,      es til kynnis kömr,
         þylsk hann umb eþa þrumir ;
   alt es senn,      ef hann sylg of getr,
         uppi's þá geþ guma.

18 (17)    Sá einn veit      es víþa ratar
         auk hefr fjölþ of farit,
   hverju geþi      stýrir gumna hverr
         sás vitandi 's vits.

19. (18)    Haldit maþr á keri,      drekki þó at hófi mjöþ,
         mæli þarft eþa þegi ;
   ókynnis þess      vár þik engi maþr,
         at þú gangir snimma at sofa.

20. (19)    Gráþugr halr,      nema geþs viti,
         etr sér aldrtrega ;
   opt fær hlægis,      es meþ horskum kömr,
         manni heimskum magi.

21. (20)    Hjarþir þat vitu,      nær þær heim skulu,
         ok ganga þá af grasi ;
   en ósviþr maþr      kann ævagi
         síns of mál maga.

22. (21)    Vesall maþr      ok illa skapi
         hlær at hvívetna ;
   hitki hann veit,      es hann vita þyrfti,
         at hann esa vamma vanr.

23. (22)    Ósviþr maþr      vakir of allar nætr
         ok hyggr      at hvívetna ;
   þá es móþr      es at morni kömr,
         allt es víl sem vas.

24. (23)    Ósnotr maþr      hyggr sér alla vesa
         viþhlæjendr vini ;
   hitki hann fiþr,      þót of hann fár lesi,
         ef meþ snotrum sitr.

25. (24)    Ósnotr maþr      hyggr sér alla vesa
         viþhlæjendr vini ;
   þá þat fiþr,      es at þingi kömr,
         at á formælendr fá.

15. Silent and thoughtful and bold in strife the prince's bairn should be. Joyous and generous let each man show him until he shall suffer death.

16. A coward believes he will ever live if he keep him safe from strife: but old age leaves him not long in peace though spears may spare his life.

17. A fool will gape when he goes to a friend, and mumble only, or mope; but pass him the ale cup and all in a moment the mind of that man is shown.

18. He knows alone who has wandered wide, and far has fared on the way, what manner of mind a man doth own who is wise of head and heart.

19. Keep not the mead cup but drink thy measure; speak needful words or none: none shall upbraid thee for lack of breeding if soon thou seek'st thy rest.

20. A greedy man, if he be not mindful, eats to his own life's hurt: oft the belly of the fool will bring him to scorn when he seeks the circle of the wise.

21. Herds know the hour of their going home and turn them again from the grass; but never is found a foolish man who knows the measure of his maw.

22. The miserable man and evil minded makes of all things mockery, and knows not that which he best should know, that he is not free from faults.

23. The unwise man is awake all night, and ponders everything over; when morning comes he is weary in mind, and all is a burden as ever.

24. The unwise man weens all who smile and flatter him are his friends, nor notes how oft they speak him ill when he sits in the circle of the wise.

25. The unwise man weens all who smile and flatter him are his friends; but when he shall come into court he shall find there are few to defend his cause.

26. (25) Ósnotr maþr        þykkisk allt vita,
            ef á ser í vá veru ;
        hitki hann veit,        hvat hann skal viþ kveþa,
            ef hans freista firar.

27. (26) Ósnotr maþr,        es meþ aldir kömr,
            þat es bazt at þegi ;
        engi þat veit,        at hann etki kann,
            nema hann mæli til mart.
        Veita maþr        hinns vætki veit,
            þót hann mæli til mart.

28. (27) Fróþr sá þykkisk        es fregna kann
            ok segja et sama ;
        eyvitu leyna        megu ýta synir
            þvís gengr of guma.

29. (28) Œrna mæfir        sás æva þegir
            staþlausu stafi ;
        hraþmælt tunga,        nema haldendr eigi,
            opt sér ógott of gelr.

30. (29) At augabragþi        skala maþr annan hafa,
            þót til kynnis komi ;
        margr fróþr þykkisk        ef freginn esat,
            ok naï þurrfjallr þruma.

31. (30) Fróþr þykkisk        sás fiótta tekr
            gestr at gest hæþinn ;
        veita görla        sás of verþi glissir
            þót meþ grömum glami.

32. (31) Gumnar margir        erusk gagnhollir,
            en at virþi vrekask ;
        aldar róg        þat mun æ vesa,
            órir gestr viþ gest.

33. (32) Árliga verþar        skyli maþr opt fá,
            nema til kynnis komi :
        sitr ok snópir,        lætr sem solginn sé,
            ok kann fregna at föu.

34. (33) Afhvarf mikit        es til ills vinar
            þót á brautu bui,
        en til góþs vinar        liggja gagnvegir,
            þót sé firr farinn.

35. (34) Ganga skal,        skala gestr vesa
            ey í einum staþ ;
        ljúfr verþr leiþr,        ef lengi sitr
            annars fletjum á.

36. (35) Bú es betra,        þót lítit sé,
            halr es heima hverr ;
        þót tvær geitr eigi        ok taugreptan sal,
            þat's þó betra an bœn.

26. The unwise man thinks all to know, while he sits in a sheltered nook; but he knows not one thing, what he shall answer, if men shall put him to proof.

27. For the unwise man 'tis best to be mute when he comes amid the crowd, for none is aware of his lack of wit if he wastes not too many words; for he who lacks wit shall never learn though his words flow ne'er so fast.

28. Wise he is deemed who can question well, and also answer back: the sons of men can no secret make of the tidings told in their midst.

29. Too many unstable words are spoken by him who ne'er holds his peace; the hasty tongue sings its own mishap if it be not bridled in.

30. Let no man be held as a laughing-stock, though he come as guest for a meal: wise enough seem many while they sit dry-skinned and are not put to proof.

31. A guest thinks him witty who mocks at a guest and runs from his wrath away; but none can be sure who jests at a meal that he makes not fun among foes.

32. Oft, though their hearts lean towards one another, friends are divided at table; ever the source of strife 'twill be, that guest will anger guest.

33. A man should take always his meals betimes unless he visit a friend, or he sits and mopes, and half famished seems, and can ask or answer nought.

34. Long is the round to a false friend leading, e'en if he dwell on the way; but though far off fared, to a faithful friend straight are the roads and short.

35. A guest must depart again on his way, nor stay in the same place ever; if he bide too long on another's bench the loved one soon becomes loathed.

36. One's own house is best, though small it may be; each man is master at home; though he have but two goats and a bark-thatched hut 'tis better than craving a boon.

37. (36)    Bú es betra,       þót lítit sé,
          halr es heima hverr ;
       blóþugt's hjarta       þeims biþja skal
          sér í mál hvert matar.

38. (37)    Vápnum sínum       skala maþr velli á
          feti ganga framarr,
       þvít óvist's at vita,       nær verþr á vegum úti
          geirs of þörf guma.

39. (38)    Fannkak mildan mann       eþa svá matargóþan,
          at værit þiggja þegit,
       eþa síns fear       svági *gjöflan,*
          at leiþ sé laun ef þegi.

40. (39)    Fear síns       es fengit hefr
          skylit maþr þörf þola ;
       opt sparir leiþum       þats hefr ljúfum hugat,
          mart gengr verr an varer.

41. (40)    Vápnum ok váþum       skulu vinir gleþjask,
          þat's á sjölfum sýnst ;
       viþrgefendr [ok endrgefendr]       erusk vinir lengst,
          ef þat bíþr at verþa vel.

42. (41)    Vin sínum       skal maþr vinr vesa
          ok gjalda gjöf viþ gjöf,
       hlátr viþ hlátri       skyli hölþar taka,
          en lausung viþ lygi.

43. (42)    Vin sínum       skal maþr vinr vesa,
          þeim ok þess vin,
       en óvinar síns       skyli engi maþr
          vinar vinr vesa.

44. (43)    Veiztu, ef vin átt       þanns þú vel truir,
          ok vill af hánum gott geta,
       geþi skalt viþ þann blanda       ok gjöfum skipta,
          fara at finna opt.

45. (44)    Ef átt annan       þanns þú illa truir,
          vill af hánum þo gott geta,
       fagrt skalt viþ þann mæla,       en flátt hyggja
          ok gjalda lausung viþ lygi.

46. (45)    Þat's enn of þann       es þú illa truir,
          ok þér's grunr at hans geþi :
       hlæja skalt viþ þeim       ok of hug mæla,
          glik skulu gjöld gjöfum.

47. (46)    Ungr vask forþum,       fór ek einn saman,
          þá varþk villr vega ;
       auþugr þóttumk       es ek annan fann :
          maþr es manns gaman.

37. One's own house is best, though small it may be, each man is master at home; with a bleeding heart will he beg, who must, his meat at every meal.

38. Let a man never stir on his road a step without his weapons of war; for unsure is the knowing when need shall arise of a spear on the way without.

39. I found none so noble or free with his food, who was not gladdened with a gift, nor one who gave of his gifts such store but he loved reward, could he win it.

40. Let no man stint him and suffer need of the wealth he has won in life; oft is saved for a foe what was meant for a friend, and much goes worse than one weens.

41. With raiment and arms shall friends gladden each other, so has one proved oneself; for friends last longest, if fate be fair, who give and give again.

42. To his friend a man should bear him as friend, and gift for gift bestow, laughter for laughter let him exchange, but leasing pay for a lie.

43. To his friend a man should bear him as friend, to him and a friend of his; but let him beware that he be not the friend of one who is friend to his foe.

44. Hast thou a friend whom thou trustest well, from whom thou cravest good? Share thy mind with him, gifts exchange with him, fare to find him oft.

45. But hast thou one whom thou trustest ill yet from whom thou cravest good? Thou shalt speak him fair, but falsely think, and leasing pay for a lie.

46. Yet further of him whom thou trusted ill, and whose mind thou dost misdoubt; thou shalt laugh with him but withhold thy thought, for gift with like gift should be paid.

47. Young was I once, I walked alone, and bewildered seemed in the way; then I found me another and rich I thought me, for man is the joy of man.

48. (47)   Mildir, frœknir      menn bazt lifa,
         sjaldan sút ala,
    en ósnjallr maþr      uggir hotvetna,
      sýtir æ glöggr viþ gjöfum.

49. (48)   Vátir mínar      gaf ek velli at
        tveim trémönnum ;
    rekkar þat þóttusk      es þeir ript höfþu :
     neiss es nökkviþr halr.

50. (49)   Hrörnar þöll      sús stendr þorpi á,
        hlýrat börkr né barr ;
    svá es maþr      sás manngi ann,
     hvat skal hann lengi lifa ?

51. (50)   Eldi heitari      brinnr meþ illum vinum
        friþr fimm daga,
    en þá sloknar,      es enn sétti kömr,
     ok versnar vinskapr allr.

52. (51)   Mikit eitt      skala manni gefa,
        opt kaupir í litlu lof ;
    meþ hölfum hleifi      ok meþ höllu keri
     fengumk félaga.

53. (52)   Lítilla sanda      lítilla sæva :
        lítil eru geþ guma ;
    þvít allir menn      urþut jafnspakir,
     hölf es öld hvár.

54. (53)   Meþalsnotr      skyli manna hverr,
        æva til snotr sé ;
    þeim era fyrþa      fegrst at lifa,
     es vel mart vitu.

55. (54)   Meþalsnotr      skyli manna hverr,
        æva til snotr sé ;
    þvít snotrs manns hjarta      verþr sjaldan glatt,
     ef sá's alsnotr es á.

48. Most blest is he who lives free and bold and nurses never a grief, for the fearful man is dismayed by aught, and the mean one mourns over giving.

49. My garments once I gave in the field to two land-marks made as men; heroes they seemed when once they were clothed; 'tis the naked who suffer shame !

50. The pine tree wastes which is perched on the hill, nor bark nor needles shelter it; such is the man whom none doth love; for what should he longer live?

51. Fiercer than fire among ill friends for five days love will burn; but anon 'tis quenched, when the sixth day comes, and all friendship soon is spoiled.

52. Not great things alone must one give to another, praise oft is earned for nought; with half a loaf and a tilted bowl I have found me many a friend.

53. Little the sand if little the seas, little are minds of men, for ne'er in the world were all equally wise, 'tis shared by the fools and the sage.

54. Wise in measure let each man be; but let him not wax too wise; for never the happiest of men is he who knows much of many things.

55. Wise in measure should each man be; but let him not wax too wise; seldom a heart will sing with joy if the owner be all too wise.

---

49. *Two land-marks, so G. Vigfusson's 'Icelandic-English Dictionary' (Oxford, 1874) explains two tree-men.*

50. *On the hill or in the open. Icelandic 'þorp' has this meaning, beside the more common one of hamlet. The context makes it quite clear that an unsheltered spot is intended, but as the Norwegian pine flourishes on the hill and dies out among houses, we may perhaps infer that the poem did not originate in Norway.*

51. *Five days, the old week before the Christian week of seven days.*

56. (55)　Meþalsnotr　　　skyli manna hverr,
　　　　　　ǽva til snotr sé ;
　　　　　örlög sín　　　viti engi fyrir,
　　　　　þeim's sorgalausastr sefi.

57. (56)　Brandr af brandi　　　brenn unz brunninn es,
　　　　　funi kveykisk af funa ;
　　　　　maþr af manni　　　verþr at máli kuþr,
　　　　　en til dœlskr af dul.

58. (57)　Ár skal rísa　　　sás annars vill
　　　　　fé eþa fjör hafa ;
　　　　　liggjandi ulfr　　　sjaldan lær of getr
　　　　　né sofandi maþr sigr.

59. (58)　Ár skal rísa　　　sás á yrkjendr fá
　　　　　ok ganga síns verka á vit ;
　　　　　mart of dvelr　　　þanns of morgin sefr,
　　　　　halfr es auþr und hvötum.

60. (59)　Þurra skíþa　　　ok þakinna nǽfra,
　　　　　þess kann maþr mjöt,
　　　　　þess viþar　　　es vinnask megi
　　　　　mál ok misseri.

61. (60)　Þveginn ok mettr　　　ríþi maþr þingi at,
　　　　　þót sét vǽdr til vel ;
　　　　　skúa ok bróka　　　skammisk engi maþr,
　　　　　né hests in heldr,
　　　　　þót hann hafit goþan.

62. (61)　Snapir ok gnapir,　　　es til sǽvar kömr,
　　　　　örn á aldinn mar ;
　　　　　svá es maþr　　　es meþr mörgum kömr
　　　　　ok á formǽlendr fá.

63. (62)　Fregna ok segja　　　skal fróþra hverr,
　　　　　sás vill heitinn horskr ;
　　　　　einn vita,　　　né annarr skal,
　　　　　þjóþ veit, ef þrír 'ú.

64. (63)　Ríki sitt　　　skyli ráþsnotra hverr
　　　　　í hófi hafa ;
　　　　　þá þat fiþr　　　es meþ frœknum kömr,
　　　　　at engi's einna hvatastr.

65. (64)　[Gǽtinn ok geyminn　　　skyli gumna hverr
　　　　　ok varr at vintrausti]
　　　　　orþa þeira,　　　es maþr öþrum segir,
　　　　　opt hann gjöld of getr.

56. Wise in measure should each man be, but ne'er let him wax too wise: who looks not forward to learn his fate unburdened heart will bear.

57. Brand kindles from brand until it be burned, spark is kindled from spark, man unfolds him by speech with man, but grows over secret through silence.

58. He must rise betimes who fain of another or life or wealth would win; scarce falls the prey to sleeping wolves, or to slumberers victory in strife.

59. He must rise betimes who hath few to serve him, and see to his work himself; who sleeps at morning is hindered much, to the keen is wealth half-won.

60. Of dry logs saved and roof-bark stored a man can know the measure, of fire-wood too which should last him out quarter and half years to come.

61. Fed and washed should one ride to court though in garments none too new; thou shalt not shame thee for shoes or breeks, nor yet for a sorry steed.

62. Like an eagle swooping over old ocean, snatching after his prey, so comes a man into court who finds there are few to defend his cause.

63. Each man who is wise and would wise be called must ask and answer aright. Let one know thy secret, but never a second, if three a thousand shall know.

64. A wise counselled man will be mild in bearing and use his might in measure, lest when he come his fierce foes among he find others fiercer than he.

65. Each man should be watchful and wary in speech, and slow to put faith in a friend. For the words which one to another speaks he may win reward of ill.

---

62. *The meaning of this strophe is somewhat obscure, but perhaps the idea is that the eagle, wont to seek his food in the quiet mountain pools, is baffled in face of the stormy sea.*

66. (65)    Mikilsti snimma       kvamk í marga staþi,
             en til síþ í suma ;
             öl vas drukkit,         sumt vas ólagat :
             sjaldan hittir leiþr í liþ.

67. (66)    Hér ok hvar        mundi mér heim of boþit,
             ef þyrftak at málungi mat
             eþa tvau lǽr hengi       at ens tryggva vinar,
             þars hafþak eitt etit.

68. (67)    Eldr es baztr        meþ ýta sunum
             auk sólar sýn,
             heilyndi sitt       ef maþr hafa naïr,
             án viþ löst at lifa.

69. (68)    Esat maþr alls vesall,       þót sé illa heill ;
             sumr's af sunum sǽll,
             sumr af frǽndum,       sumr af fé œrnu,
             sumr af verkum vel.

70. (69)    Betra's lifþum       an sé ólifþum,
             ey getr kvikr kú ;
             eld sák upp brinna       auþgum manni fyrir,
             en úti vas dauþr fyr durum.

71. (70)    Haltr ríþr hrossi,       hjörþ rekr handarvanr,
             daufr vegr ok dugir ;
             blindr es betri       an brendr sé,
             nýtr mangi nás.

72. (71)    Sunr es betri,       þót sé síþ of alinn
             ept genginn guma ;
             sjaldan bautarsteinar       standa brautu nǽr,
             nema reisi niþr at niþ.

73. (72)    Tveir'u einherjar,       tunga's höfuþs bani ;
             erumk í heþin hverjan       handar vǽni.
             Nótt verþr feginn       sás nesti truir,
             skammar'u skips rár
             hverf es haustgrima ;
             fjölþ of viþrir       á fimm dögum,
             en meira á mánaþi.

66. At many a feast I was far too late, and much too soon at some; drunk was the ale or yet unserved: never hits he the joint who is hated.

67. Here and there to a home I had haply been asked had I needed no meat at my meals, or were two hams left hanging in the house of that friend where I had partaken of one.

68. Most dear is fire to the sons of men, most sweet the sight of the sun; good is health if one can but keep it, and to live a life without shame.

69. Not reft of all is he who is ill, for some are blest in their bairns, some in their kin and some in their wealth, and some in working well.

70. More blest are the living than the lifeless, 'tis the living who comes by the cow; I saw the hearth-fire burn in the rich man's hall and himself lying dead at the door.

71. The lame can ride horse, the handless drive cattle, the deaf one can fight and prevail, 'tis happier for the blind than for him on the bale-fire, for no man hath care for a corpse.

72. Best have a son though he be late born and before him the father be dead: seldom are stones on the wayside raised save by kinsmen to kinsmen.

73. Two are hosts against one, the tongue is the head's bane, 'neath a rough hide a hand may be hid; he is glad at night fall who knows of his lodging, short is the ship's berth, and changeful the autumn night, much veers the wind ere the fifth day and blows round yet more in a month.

---

66. *Hits the joint; or, as we should say, hits the nail on the head.*

72. *Stones: Icelandic 'bautarsteinar' were monumental stones set upon the high road, many thousands of which are preserved, some with runic inscriptions.*

73. *This agrees with the Icelandic proverb : A man's hand may oft be found beneatti\*a wolf- skin; but others understand : There is chanee of a fist from under a cloak.*

74. (73)  Veita maþr          hinns vætki veit :
          margr verþr af öþrum api ;
          maþr es auþugr,          annarr óauþugr,
          skylit þann vætkis vá.

75. (74)  Deyr fé,          deyja frændr,
          deyr sjalfr et sama,
          en orþstírr          deyr aldrigi
          hveims sér góþan getr.

76. (75)  Deyr fé,          deyja frændr,
          deyr sjalfr et sama ;
          ek veit einn          at aldri deyr :
          dómr of dauþan hvern.

77. (76)  Fullar grindr          sák fyr Fitjungs sunum,
          nú bera vánarvöl ;
          svá es auþr          sem augabragþ,
          hann es valtastr vina.

78. (77)  Ósnotr maþr,          ef eignask getr
          fé eþa fljóþs munugþ,
          metnaþr þroask,          en manvit aldri,
          fram gengr hann drjúgt í dul.

79. (78)  Þat's þá reynt,          es at rúnum spyrr,
          enum reginkunnum :
          þeims görþu ginnregin,
          ok fáþi fimbulþulr,
          þá hefr bazt ef þegir.

80. (79)  At kveldi skal dag leyfa,          konu es brend es,
          mæki es reyndr es,          mey es gefin es,
          ís es yfir kömr,          öl es drukkit es.

81. (80)  Í vindi skal viþ höggva,          veþri á sjó roa,
          myrkri viþ man spjalla,          mörg 'ru dags augu ;
          á skip skal skriþar orka,          en á skjöld til hlífar,
          mæki höggs,          en mey til kossa.

82. (81)  Viþ eld skal öl drekka,          en á ísi skríþa,
          magran mar kaupa,          en mæki saurgan,
          heima hest feita,          en hund á búi.

83. (82)  Meyjar orþum          skyli manngi trua,
          né þvís kveþr kona ;
          þvít á hverfanda hvéli          vöru þeim hjörtu köpuþ
          ok brigþ í brjóst of lagiþ.

84. (83)  Brestanda boga,          brinnanda loga,
          gínanda ulfi,          galandi kráku,
          rýtanda svíni,          rótlausum viþi,
          vaxanda vági,          vellanda katli,

74. He that learns nought will never know how one is the fool of another, for if one be rich another is poor and for that should bear no blame.

75. Cattle die and kinsmen die, thyself too soon must die, but one thing never, I ween, will die, fair fame of one who has earned.

76. Cattle die and kinsmen die, thyself too soon must die, but one thing never, I ween, will die, the doom on each one dead.

77. Full-stocked folds had the Failing's sons, who bear now a beggar's staff: brief is wealth, as the winking of an eye, most faithless ever of friends.

78. If haply a fool should find for himself wealth or a woman's love, pride waxes in him but wisdom never and onward he fares in his folly.

79. All will prove true that thou askest of runes those that are come from the gods, which the high Powers wrought, and which Odin painted then silence is surely best.

## MAXIMS FOR ALL MEN

80. Praise day at even, a wife when dead, a weapon when tried, a maid when married, ice when 'tis crossed, and ale when 'tis drunk.

81. Hew wood in wind, sail the seas in a breeze, woo a maid in the dark, for day's eyes are many, work a ship for its gliding, a shield for its shelter, a sword for its striking, a maid for her kiss.

82. Drink ale by the fire, but slide on the ice; buy a steed when 'tis lanky, a sword when 'tis rusty; feed thy horse neath a roof, and thy hound in the yard.

83. The speech of a maiden should no man trust nor the words which a woman says; for their hearts were shaped on a whirling wheel and falsehood fixed in their breasts.

84. Breaking bow, or flaring flame, ravening wolf, or croaking raven, routing swine, or rootless tree, waxing wave, or seething cauldron,

85. (84)     fljúganda fleini,     fallandi báru,
            ísi einnættum,      ormi hringlegnum,
            brúþar beþmálum     eþa brotnu sverþi,
            bjarnar leiki     eþa barni konungs,

86. (85)     sjúkum kalfii,      sjalfráþa þræli,
            völu vilmæli,       val nýfeldum—
     (86)     bróþurbana sínum,      þót á brautu mœti,
            húsi halfbrunnu,      hesti alskjótum—
            þá's jór ónýtr,       ef einn fótr brotnar :—
            verþit maþr svá tryggr,     at þessu truï öllu.

87. (85)     Akri ársánum       trui engi maþr
               né til snimma syni :
            veþr ræþr akri,      en vit syni,
               hætt es þeira hvárt.

88. (87)     Svá's friþr kvenna      es flátt hyggja,
            sem aki jó óbryddum     á ísi hálum,
            teitum, tvévetrum,     ok sé tamr illa,
            eþa í byr óþum      beiti stjórnlausu,
            eþa skyli haltr henda     hrein í þáfjalli.

89. (88)     Bert ek nú mæli      þvít ek bæþi veit,
               brigþr es karla hugr konum ;
            þá vér fegrst mælum,     es vér flást hyggjum,
               þat tælir horska hugi.

90. (89)     Fagrt skal mæla       ok fé bjóþa
               sás vill fijóþs ást fá,
            líki leyfa       ens ljósa mans :
               sá fær es friar.

91. (90)     Ástar firna        skyli engi maþr
               annan aldrigi ;
            opt fá á horskan,      es á heimskan né fá,
               lostfagrir litir.

92. (91)     Eyvitar firna      es maþr annan skal
               þess's of margan gengr guma ;
            heimska ór horskum     görir hölþa sunu
               sá enn mátki munr.

93. (92)     Hugr einn þat veit,      es býr hjarta nær,
               einn's hann sér of sefa ;
            öng es sótt verri      hveim snotrum manni
               an sér öngu at una.

85. flying arrows, or falling billow, ice of a night time, coiling adder, woman's bed-talk, or broken blade, play of bears or a prince's child,

86. sickly calf or self-willed thrall, witches flattery, new-slain foe, brother's slayer though seen on the highway, half burned house, or horse too swift useless were it with one leg broken be never so trustful as these to trust.

87. Let none put faith in the first sown fruit nor yet in his son too soon; whim rules the child and weather the field, each is open to chance.

88. Like the love of women whose thoughts are lies is the driving un-roughshod o'er slippery ice of a two year old, ill-tamed and gay; or in a wild wind steering a helmless ship, or the lame catching reindeer in the rime-thawed fell.

## LESSONS FOR LOVERS

89. Now plainly I speak, since both I have seen; unfaithful is man to maid; we speak them fairest when thoughts are falsest and wile the wisest of hearts.

90. Let him speak soft words and offer wealth who longs for a woman's love, praise the shape of the shining maid he wins who thus doth woo.

91. Never a whit should one blame another whom love hath brought into bonds: oft a witching form will fetch the wise which holds not the heart of fools.

92. Never a whit should one blame another for a folly which many befalls; the might of love makes sons of men into fools who once were wise.

93. The mind knows alone what is nearest the heart and sees where the soul is turned: no sickness seems to the wise so sore as in nought to know content.

94. (93)    Þat ek þá reynda,      es ek í reyri sat
          ok vættak míns munar ;
       hold ok hjarta      vörumk en horska mær,
       þeygi at heldr hana hefik.

95. (94)    Billings mey      ek fann beþjum á
          sólhvita sofa ;
       jarls ynþi      þóttumk etki vesa,
       nema viþ þat lík at lifa.

96. (95)    ' Auk nær aptni      skaltu, Óþinn ! koma,
          ef þú vill þér mæla man ;
       allt eru ósköp,      nema einir viti
       slíkan löst saman.'

97. (96)    Aptr ek hvarf      ok unna þóttumk,
          vísum vilja frá ;
       hitt ek hugþa,      at ek hafa mynda
       geþ hennar allt ok gaman.

98. (97)    Svá kvam ek næst,      at en nýta vas
          vígdrótt öll of vakin ;
       meþ brinnöndum ljósum      ok bornum viþi—
       svá var mér vílstígr vitaþr.

99. (98)    Auk nær morni,      es ek vas enn of kominn,
          þá vas saldrótt of sofin ;
       grey eitt fannk þá      ennar góþu konu
       bundit beþjum á.

100. (99)    Mörg es góþ mær,      ef görva kannar,
          hugbrigþ viþ hali :
       þá ek þat reynda,      es et ráþspaka
       teygþak á flærþir fijóþ ;
       háþungar hverrar      leitaþi mer et horska man,
       ok hafþak þess vætki vífs.

ODIN'S LOVE QUESTS

94. This once I felt when I sat without in the reeds, and looked for my love; body and soul of me was that sweet maiden yet never I won her as wife.

95. Billing's daughter I found on her bed, fairer than sunlight sleeping, and the sweets of lordship seemed to me nought save I lived with that lovely form.

96. ' Yet nearer evening come thou, Odin, if thou wilt woo a maiden: all were undone save two knew alone such a secret deed of shame.'

97. So away I turned from my wise intent, and deemed my joy assured, for all her liking and all her love I weened that I yet should win. When I came ere long the war troop bold were watching and waking all: with burning brands and torches borne they showed me my sorrowful way.

99. Yet nearer morning I went, once more, the housefolk slept in the hall, but soon I found a barking dog tied fast to that fair maid's couch.

100. Many a sweet maid when one knows her mind is fickle found towards men: I proved it well when that prudent lass I sought to lead astray: shrewd maid, she sought me with every insult and I won therewith no wife.

89. Odin has had many love adventures in disguise.
95. Billing, a dwarf.

101. (100)   Heima glaþr gumi      ok viþ gesti reifr
           sviþr skal of sik vesa ;
           minnugr ok málugr,      ef hann vill margfróþr vesa,
           opt skal góþs geta ;
     (101)   fimbulfambi heitir      sás fátt kann segja,
           þat's ósnotrs aþal.

102. (102)   Enn aldna jötun sóttak,      nu emk aptr of kominn,
           fátt gatk þegjandi þar ;
           mörgum orþum      mæltak í minn frama
           í Suttungs sölum.

103. (104)   Rata munn      létumk rúms of fá
           auk of grjót gnaga,
        yfir ok undir      stóþumk jötna vegir,
           svá hǽttak höfþi til.

104. (103)   Gunnlöþ göfumk      gollnum stóli
           drykk ens dýra mjaþar ;
        ill iþgjöld      létk hana eptir hafa
           síns ens heila hugar,
           síns ens svára sefa.

105.   Vel keypts litar      hefk vel notit,
           fás es fróþum vant ;
        þvít Óþrörir      es nú upp kominn
           á alda vés jaþar.

106.   Ifi 'rumk á,      at værak enn kominn
           jötna görþum ór,
        ef Gunnlaþar né nytak,      ennar góþu konu,
           þeirars lögþumk arm yfir.

107.   Ens hindra dags      gengu hrímþursar
           [Háva ráþs at fregna]
           Háva höllu í ;
        at Bölverki spurþu,      ef væri meþ böndum kominn
           eþa hefþi Suttungr of soit.

108.   Baugeiþ Óþinn      hykk at unnit hafi,
           hvat skal hans trygþum trua ?
        Suttung svikvinn      hann lét sumbli frá
           ok grǿtta Gunnlöþu.

## ODIN'S QUEST AFTER THE SONG MEAD

101. In thy home be joyous and generous to guests discreet shalt thou be in thy bearing, mindful and talkative, wouldst thou gain wisdom, oft making mention of good.

He is ' Simpleton ' named who has nought to say, for such is the fashion of fools.

102. I sought that old Jötun, now safe am I back, little served my silence there; but whispering many soft speeches I won my desire in Suttung's halls.

103. I bored me a road there with Rati's tusk and made room to pass through the rock; while the ways of the Jötuns stretched over and under I dared my life for a draught.

104. 'Twas Gunnlod who gave me on a golden throne a draught of the glorious mead, but with poor reward did I pay her back for her true and troubled heart.

105. In a wily disguise I worked my will; little is lacking to the wise, for the Soul-stirrer now, sweet Mead of Song, is brought to men's earthly abode.

106. I misdoubt me if ever again I had come from the realms of the Jötun race, had I not served me of Gunnlod, sweet woman, her whom I held in mine arms.

107. Came forth, next day, the dread Frost Giants, and entered the High One's hall: they asked was the Baleworker back mid the Powers, or had Suttung slain him below?

108. A ring-oath Odin I trow had taken how shall one trust his troth? 'twas he who stole the mead from Suttung, and Gunnlod caused to weep.

---

*101, Sentence #2. Many scholars agree that this line is an interpolation, as it spoils both sense and metre.*

*102. Suttung, a giant of the underworld,*

*103. Rati or the Gnawer, a tool.*

*105. The Soul-stirrer: One of Odin's characters is that of Songgiver to man;.*

*107. Baleworker, the name which Odin had given himself in disguise.*

109.    Mál's at þylja       þular stóli á :
         Urþar brunni at
   sák ok þagþak,      sák ok hugþak,
      hlýddak á manna mál.

110.    of rúnar heyrþak dœma,      né of ráþum þögþu
      Háva höllu at,
      Háva höllu í ;
      heyrþak segja svá.

111. (110)    Ráþumk þér, Loddfáfnir !      en þú ráþ nemir,
      njóta mundu, ef nemr,
      þér munu góþ, ef getr :
      nótt þú rísat      nema á njósn sér
      eþa leitir þér innan út staþar.

112. (111)    Ráþumk þér, Loddfáfnir !      en þú ráþ nemir,
      njóta mundu, ef nemr,
      þer munu góþ, ef getr :
      fjölkunnigri konu      skalta í faþmi sofa,
      svát hón lyki þík liþum.

113. (111)    Hón svá görir,      at þú gaïr eigi
      þings né þjóþans máls ;
      mat þú villat      né mannskis gaman,
      ferr þú sorgafullr at sofa.

114. (112)    Ráþumk þér, Loddfáfnir !      en þú ráþ nemir,
      njóta mundu, ef nemr,
      þér munu góþ, ef getr :
      annars konu      teyg þér aldrigi
      eyrarúnu at.

## II. LODDFÁFNISMÁL:
## THE COUNSELLING OF THE STRAY-SINGER

109. 'Tis time to speak from the Sage's Seat;
hard by the Well of Weird I saw and was silent,
I saw and pondered,
I listened to the speech of men.

110. Of runes they spoke, and the reading of runes
was little withheld from their lips:
at the High One's hall, in the High One's hall,
I thus heard the High One say:

111. 'I counsel thee, Stray-Singer, accept my counsels,
they will be thy boon if thou obey'st them,
they will work thy weal if thou win'st them:
rise never at night time except thou art spying
or seekest a spot without. '

113. 'I counsel thee, Stray-Singer, accept my counsels,
they will be thy boon if thou obey'st them,
they will work thy weal if thou win'st them :
thou shalt never sleep in the arms of a sorceress,
lest she should lock thy limbs;

114. 'So shall she charm that thou shalt not heed
the council or words of the king,
nor care for thy food or the joys of mankind,
but fall into sorrowful sleep.

---

*109. Well of Weird, the most sacred spot in the world, where the
gods meet in council under the tree Yggdrasil.*

115. (113)Ráþumk þér, Loddfáfnir !     en þú ráþ nemir,
    njóta mundu, ef nemr,
    þér munu góþ, ef getr :
    á fjalli eþa firþi     ef þik fara tíþir,
    fásktu at virþi vel.

116. (114)  Ráþumk þér, Loddfáfnir !     en þú ráþ nemir,
    njóta mundu, ef nemr,
    þér munu góþ, ef getr :
    illan mann     láttu aldrigi
      óhöpp at þér vita,
    þvít af illum manni     fær þú aldrigi
      gjöld ens góþa hugar.

117. (115)  Ofarla bíta     ek sá einum hal
      orþ illrar konu :
    fláráþ tunga     varþ hánum at fjörlagi,
      ok þeygi of sanna sök.

118. (116)  Ráþumk þér, Loddfáfnir !     en þú ráþ nemir,
    njóta mundu, ef nemr,
    þér munu góþ, ef getr :
    veiztu ef vin átt     þanns þú vel truir,
      farþu at finna opt,
    þvít hrísi vex     ok hávu grasi
      vegr es vætki tröþr.

119. (117)  Ráþumk þér, Loddfáfnir !     en þú ráþ nemir,
    njóta mundu, ef nemr,
    þér munu góþ, ef getr :
    góþan mann teyg þér at gamanrúnum
    ok nem líknargaldr meþan lifir.

115. 'I counsel thee, Stray-Singer, accept my counsels,
they will be thy boon if thou obey'st them,
they will work thy weal if thou win'st them :
should thou long to fare over fell and firth
provide thee well with food.

116. 'I counsel thee, Stray-Singer, accept my counsels,
they will be thy boon if thou obey'st them,
they will work thy weal if thou win'st them:
tell not ever an evil man
if misfortunes thee befall,
from such ill friend thou needst never seek
return for thy trustful mind.

117. 'Wounded to death, have I seen a man
by the words of an evil woman;
a lying tongue had bereft him of life,
and all without reason of right.

118. 'I counsel thee, Stray-Singer, accept my counsels,
they will be thy boon if thou obey'st them,
they will work thy weal if thou win'st them:
hast thou a friend whom thou trustest well,
fare thou to find him oft;
for with brushwood grows and with grasses high
the path where no foot doth pass.

119. 'I counsel thee, Stray-Singer, accept my counsels,
they will be thy boon if thou obey'st them,
they will work thy weal if thou win'st them :
in sweet converse call the righteous to thy side,
learn a healing song while thou livest.

120. (118)    Ráþumk þér, Loddfáfnir !      en þú ráþ nemir,
           njóta mundu, ef nemr,
           þér munu góþ, ef getr :
           vin þínum       ves þú aldrigi
             fyrri at flaumslitum ;
           sorg etr hjarta,       ef þú segja né naïr
           einhverjum allan hug.

121. (119)    Ráþumk þér, Loddfáfnir !      en þú ráþ nemir,
           njóta mundu, ef nemr,
           þér munu góþ, ef getr :
           orþum skipta      þú skalt aldrigi
           viþ ósvinna apa ;

122. (119)    þvít af illum manni      mundu aldrigi
           góþs laun of geta,
        en góþr maþr      mun þik görva mega
           líknfastan at lofi.

123. (120)    Sifjum's þá blandat,      hverrs segja ræþr
           einum allan hug :
        allt es betra      an sé brigþum at vesa,
           esat vinr es vilt eitt segir.

124. (121)    Ráþumk þér, Loddfáfnir !      en þú ráþ nemir,
           njóta mundu, ef nemr,
           þér munu góþ, ef getr :
           þrimr orþum senna      skalta þér viþ verra mann ;
           opt enn betri bilar,
        as enn verri vegr.

125. (122)    Ráþumk þér, Loddfáfnir !      en þú ráþ nemir,
           njóta mundu, ef nemr,
           þér munu góþ, ef getr :
           skósmiþr þú vesir      né skeptismiþr,
             nema þér sjölfum sér :
           skór's skapaþr illa      eþa skapt sé rangt,
             þá's þér böls beþit.

120. 'I counsel thee, Stray-Singer, accept my counsels,
they will be thy boon if thou obey'st them,
they will work thy weal if thou win'st them :
be never the first with friend of thine
to break the bond of fellowship;
care shall gnaw thy heart if thou canst not tell
all thy mind to another.

121. 'I counsel thee, Stray-Singer, accept my counsels,
they will be thy boon if thou obey'st them,
they will work thy weal if thou win'st them :
never in speech with a foolish knave
shouldst thou waste a single word.

122. 'From the lips of such thou needst not look
for reward of thine own good will;
but a righteous man by praise will render thee
firm in favour and love.

123. 'There is mingling in friendship when man can utter
all his whole mind to another;
there is nought so vile as a fickle tongue;
no friend is he who but flatters.

124. 'I counsel thee, Stray-Singer, accept my counsels,
they will be thy boon if thou obey'st them,
they will work thy weal if thou win'st them :
strive not in three words with a man worse than thee;
oft the worst lays the best one low.

125. 'I counsel thee, Stray-Singer, accept my counsels,
they will be thy boon if thou obey'st them,
they will work thy weal if thou win'st them :
be not a shoemaker nor yet a shaft maker
save for thyself alone:
let the shoe be misshapen, or crooked the shaft,
and a curse on thy head will be called.

126. (123)Ráþumk þér, Loddfáfnir !     en þú ráþ nemir,
     njóta mundu, ef nemr,
     þér munu góþ, ef getr :
     hvars böl kannt,      kveþu þer bölvi at
     ok gefat fiöndum friþ.

127. (124)      Ráþumk þér, Loddfáfnir !     en þú ráþ nemir,
     njóta mundu, ef nemr,
     þér munu góþ, ef getr :
     illu feginn      ves þú aldrigi,
     en lát þer at góþu getit.

128. (125)      Ráþumk þér, Loddfáfnir !     en þú ráþ nemir,
     njóta mundu, ef nemr,
     þér munu góþ, ef getr :
     upp líta      skalattu í orrostu—
     gjalti glíkir      verþa gumna synir—
     síþr þitt of heilli halir.

129. (126)      Ráþumk þér, Loddfáfnir !     en þú ráþ nemir,
     njóta mundu, ef nemr,
     þér munu góþ, ef getr :
     ef vill þér góþa konu      kveþja at gamanrúnum
     ok fá fögnuþ af,
     fögru skalt heita      ok láta fast vesa ;
     leiþisk manngi gótt, ef getr.

130. (127)      Ráþumk þér, Loddfáfnir !     en þú ráþ nemir,
     njóta mundu, ef nemr,
     þér munu góþ, ef getr :
     varan biþk þik vesa      ok eigi ofvaran ;
     ves viþ öl varastr      ok viþ annars konu
     ok viþ þat et þriþja,      at þik þjófar né leiki.

126. 'I counsel thee, Stray-Singer, accept my counsels,
they will be thy boon if thou obey'st them,
they will work thy weal if thou win'st them :
when in peril thou seest thee, confess thee in peril,
nor ever give peace to thy foes.

127. 'I counsel thee, Stray-Singer, accept my counsels,
they will be thy boon if thou obey'st them,
they will work thy weal if thou win'st them :
rejoice not ever at tidings of ill,
but glad let thy soul be in good.

128. 'I counsel thee, Stray-Singer, accept my counsels,
they will be thy boon if thou obey'st them :
they will work thy weal if thou win'st them :
look not up in battle when men are as beasts,
lest the wights bewitch thee with spells.

129. 'I counsel thee, Stray-Singer, accept my counsels,
they will be thy boon if thou obey'st them,
they will work thy weal if thou win'st them :
wouldst thou win joy of a gentle maiden,
and lure to whispering of love,
thou shalt make fair promise, and let it be fast,
none will scorn their weal who can win it.

130. 'I counsel thee, Stray-Singer, accept my counsels,
they will be thy boon if thou obey'st them,
they will work thy weal if thou win'st them :
I pray thee be wary, yet not too wary,
be wariest of all with ale,
with another's wife, and a third thing eke,
that knaves outwit thee never.

131. (128)　Ráþumk þér, Loddfáfnir !　　en þú ráþ nemir,
　　　　　njóta mundu, ef nemr,
　　　　　þér munu góþ, ef getr :
　　　at háþi né hlátri　　　hafþu aldrigi
　　　　　gest né ganganda ;

132.　opt vitu ógörla　　　þeirs sitja inni fyrir,
　　　　　hvers þeir'u kyns es koma.
　　　Esat maþr svá góþr,　　　at galli né fylgi,
　　　　　né svá illr, at einugi dugi.

133.　Ráþumk þér, Loddfáfnir !　　en þú ráþ nemir,
　　　　　njóta mundu, ef nemr,
　　　　　þér munu góþ, ef getr :
　　　at hárum þul　　　hlæþu aldrigi,
　　　　　opt's gott þats gamlir kveþa ;
　　　opt ór skörpum belg　　　skilin orþ koma
　　　　　þeims hangir meþ hám
　　　　　ok skollir meþ skrám
　　　　　ok váfir meþ vilmögum.

134.　Ráþumk þér, Loddfáfnir !　　en þú ráþ nemir,
　　　　　njóta mundu, ef nemr,
　　　　　þér munu góþ, ef getr :
　　　gest né geyja　　　ne á grind hrökkvir,
　　　　　get þú váluþum vel.

131. 'I counsel thee, Stray-Singer, accept my counsels,
they will be thy boon if thou obey'st them,
they will work thy weal if thou win'st them :
hold not in scorn, nor mock in thy halls
a guest or wandering wight.

132. 'They know but unsurely who sit within
what manner of man is come :
none is found so good but some fault attends him,
or so ill but he serves for somewhat.

133. 'I counsel thee, Stray-Singer, accept my counsels,
they will be thy boon if thou obey'st them,
they will work thy weal if thou win'st them :
hold never in scorn the hoary singer;
oft the counsel of the old is good;
come words of wisdom from the withered lips
of him left to hang among hides,
to rock with the rennets
and swing with the skins.

134. 'I counsel thee, Stray-Singer, accept my counsels,
they will be thy boon if thou obey'st them,
they will work thy weal if thou win'st them :
growl not at guests nor drive them from the gate
but show thyself gentle to the poor.

---

133. *Rennets, in Iceland the maw rennets of a calf were, and are still hung up to dry, and used for curdling milk.*

135.    Ramt's þat tré         es ríþa skal
        öllum at upploki :
        baug þú gef,        eþa þat biþja mun
        þér lǽs hvers á liþu.

136.    Ráþumk þér, Loddfáfnir !        en þú ráþ nemir,
        njóta mundu, ef nemr,
        þér munu góþ, ef getr :
        hvars öl drekkr,        kjóstu þér jarþarmegin—
        [þvít jörþ tekr viþ ölþri,        en aldr viþ sóttum,
        eik viþ abbindi,        ax viþ fjölkyngi,
        viþ haulvi hýrogi,        heiptum skal mána kveþja,
        beiti viþ bitsóttum,        en viþ bölvi rúnar—]
        fold skal viþ flóþi taka.

135. 'Mighty is the bar to be moved away
for the entering in of all.
Shower thy wealth, or men shall wish thee
every ill in thy limbs.

136. 'I counsel thee, Stray-Singer, accept my counsels,
they will be thy boon if thou obey'st them,
they will work thy weal if thou win'st them :
when ale thou quaffest call upon earth's might
'tis earth drinks in the floods.

[Earth prevails o'er drink, but fire o'er sickness,
the oak o'er binding, the earcorn o'er witchcraft,
the rye spur o'er rupture, the moon o'er rages,
herb o'er cattle plagues, runes o'er harm.]

_136. Deals with magic, and belongs to the spell songs rather
than here._

137. (134)  Veitk at hekk      vindga meiþi á
            nætr allar niu,
      geiri undaþr      ok gefinn Óþni,
            sjalfr sjölfum mér,
      á þeim meiþi,      es manngi veit,
            hvers hann af rótum rinn.

138. (135)  Viþ hleifi mik sældu      né viþ hornigi ;
            nýsta ek niþr :
      namk upp rúnar,      œpandi namk ;
            fell ek aptr þaþan.

139. (136)  Fimbulljóþ niu      namk af enum frægja syni
            Bölþorns Bestlu föþur ;
      ok drykk of gatk,      ens dýra mjaþar
            ausenn Óþröri.

140. (137)  Þá namk frævask      ok fróþr vesa
            ok vaxa ok vel hafask :
      orþ mér af orþi      orþs leitaþi,
            verk mér af verki verks.

## III RÚNATAL
## ODIN'S QUEST AFTER THE RUNES

137. I trow I hung on that windy Tree
nine whole days and nights,
stabbed with a spear, offered to Odin,
myself to mine own self given,
high on that Tree of which none hath heard
from what roots it rises to heaven.

138. None refreshed me ever with food or drink,
I peered right down in the deep;
crying aloud I lifted the Runes,
then back I fell from thence.

139. Nine mighty songs I learned from the great
son of Bale-thorn, Bestla's sire;
I drank a measure of the wondrous Mead,
with the Soulstirrer's drops I was showered.

140. Ere long I bare fruit, and throve full well,
I grew and waxed in wisdom;
word following word, I found me words,
deed following deed, I wrought deeds.

---

*137. 'A windy Tree;' this must be Yggdrasil. The same words are used with regard to it under the name of Mimir's tree.*
*138. 'Back I fell:' the attainment of the runes had released him from the tree.*
*139. Mimir, who was a Jötun and Odin's teacher, is presumably the son of the giant Bale-thorn, the grandfather of Odin, although his name is not given here.*

141. (138)    Rúnar munt finna      ok ráþna stafi,
           mjök stóra stafi,
           mjök stinna stafi
           es fáþi fimbulþulr      ok görþu ginnregin,
           es reist Hróptr ragna :

142. (139)    Óþinn meþ ásum,      en fyr ölfum Daïnn,
           Dvalinn dvergum fyrir,
           Alsviþr jötnum fyr      *en fyr ýta sunum*
           reistk sjalfr sumar.

143. (140)    Veiztu hvé rísta skal,      veiztu hvé ráþa skal ?
           veiztu hvé fá skal,      veiztu hvé freista skal ?
           veiztu hvé biþja skal,      veiztu hvé blóta skal ?
           veiztu hvé senda skal,      veiztu hvé soa skal ?

144. (141)    Betra's óbeþit      an sé ofblótit,
           ey sér til gildis gjöf ;
           betra's ósent      an sé ofsoït

           .   .   .   .   .   .   .   .

           Svá Þundr of reist      fyr þjóþa rök,
           þar hann upp of reis,      es hann aptr of kvam.

141. Hidden Runes shalt thou seek and interpreted signs,
many symbols of might and power,
by the great Singer painted, by the high Powers fashioned,
graved by the Utterer of gods.

142. For gods graved Odin, for elves graved Dam,
Dvalin the Dallier for dwarfs,
All-wise for Jötuns, and I, of myself,
graved some for the sons of men.

143. Dost know how to write, dost know how to read,
dost know how to paint, dost know how to prove,
dost know how to ask, dost know how to offer,
dost know how to send, dost know how to spend?

144. Better ask for too little than offer too much,
like the gift should be the boon;
better not to send than to overspend.
· · · · · · · ·
Thus Odin graved ere the world began;
Then he rose from the deep, and came again.

---

142. *All-wise, this giant is unknown, unless identical with*
Fjölsvith, *which mean 'Much-wise'*.
*i44.--Odin, here called by his name Thund, the meaning of*
*which is unknown.*

145. (142) Þau ljóþ kannk   es kannat þjóþans kona
     né mannskis mögr :
     hjölp heitir eitt,   en þat þér hjalpa mun
     viþ sökum ok sorgum ok sútum görvöllum.

146. (143) Þat kannk annat   es þurfu ýta synir
     þeirs vilja læknar lifa

147. (144) Þat kannk et þriþja,   ef mér verþr þörf mikil
     hapts viþ heiptmögu :
     eggjar deyfik   minna andskota,
     bítat þeim vápn né velir.

148. (145) Þat kannk et fjórþa,   ef mér fyrþar bera
     bönd at boglimum :
     svá ek gel,   at ek ganga má,
     sprettr af fötum fjöturr,
     en af höndum hapt.

149. (146) Þat kannk et fimta,   ef sék af fári skotinn
     flein í folki vaþa :
     flýgra svá stint,   at ek stöþvigak,
     ef ek hann sjónum of sék.

150. (147) Þat kannk et sétta,   ef mik særir þegn
     á rótum rás viþar :
     ok þann hal,   es mik heipta kveþr,
     eta mein heldr an mik.

151. (148) Þat kannk et sjaunda,   ef sék hávan loga
     sal of sessmögum :
     brinnrat svá breitt,   at ek bjargigak ;
     þann kannk galdr at gala.

## THE SONG OF SPELLS

145. Those songs I know, which nor sons of men
nor queen in a king's court knows;
the first is Help which will bring thee help
in all woes and in sorrow and strife.

146. A second I know, which the son of men
must sing, who would heal the sick.

147. A third I know : if sore need should come
of a spell to stay my foes;
when I sing that song, which shall blunt their swords,
nor their weapons nor staves can wound.

148. A fourth I know : if men make fast
in chains the joints of my limbs,
when I sing that song which shall set me free,
spring the fetters from hands and feet.

149. A fifth I know : when I see, by foes shot,
speeding a shaft through the host,
flies it never so strongly I still can stay it,
if I get but a glimpse of its flight.

150. A sixth I know : when some thane would harm me
in runes on a moist tree's root,
on his head alone shall light the ills
of the curse that he called upon mine.

151. A seventh I know: if I see a hall
high o'er the bench-mates blaming,
flame it ne'er so fiercely I still can save it,
I know how to sing that song.

152. (149)   Þat kannk et átta,      es öllum es
             nytsamlikt at nema :
          hvars hatr vex       meþ hildings sunum,
            þat mák bœta brátt.

153. (150)   Þat kannk et niunda,      ef mik nauþr of stendr
            at bjarga fari minu á floti :
          vind ek kyrri      vági á,
            ok svæfik allan sæ.

154. (151)   Þat kannk et tiunda,      ef ek sé túnriþur
            leika lopti á :
          ek svá vinnk,     at þær villar fara
            sinna heim hama,
            sinna heim haga.

155. (152)   Þat kannk et ellifta,      ef skalk til orrostu
            leiþa langvini :
          und randir gelk,     en þeir meþ ríki fara
            heilir hildar til,
            heilir hildi frá,
            koma þeir heilir hvaþan.

156. (153)   Þat kannk et tolfta      ef sék á tré uppi
            váfa virgilná :
          svá ek ríst     ok í rúnum fák,
            at sá gengr gumi
            ok mælir viþ mik.

152. An eighth I know: which all can sing
for their weal if they learn it well;
where hate shall wax 'mid the warrior sons,
I can calm it soon with that song.

153. A ninth I know: when need befalls me
to save my vessel afloat,
I hush the wind on the stormy wave,
and soothe all the sea to rest.

154. A tenth I know : when at night the witches
ride and sport in the air,
such spells I weave that they wander home
out of skins and wits bewildered.

155. An eleventh I know : if haply I lead
my old comrades out to war,
I sing 'neath the shields, and they fare forth mightily
safe into battle,
safe out of battle,
and safe return from the strife.

156. A twelfth I know: if I see in a tree
a corpse from a halter hanging,
such spells I write, and paint in runes,
that the being descends and speaks.

---

*154. The witches, or 'hedge-riders' who could change their shapes
or skins (Icel. hama), were thus deprived of their magic powers.*

157. (154) Þat kannk et þrettánda,    ef skalk þegn ungan
verpa vatni á :
munat hann falla,    þót í folk komi,
hnígra sá halr fyr hjörum.

158. (155) Þat kannk et fjogrtánda,    ef skalk fyrþa liþi
telja tíva fyrir :
ása ok alfa    ek kann allra skil,
fár kann ósnotr svá.

159. (156) Þat kannk et fimtánda,    es gól þjóþrœrir
dvergr fyr Dellings durum :
afl gól hann ásum,    en ölfum frama,
hyggju Hróptatý.

160. (157) Þat kannk et sextánda,    ef vilk ens svinna mans
hafa geþ allt ok gaman :
hugi ek hverfi    hvítarmri konu
ok snýk hennar öllum sefa.

161. (158) Þat kannk et sjautjánda,    *ef* . . . . . .

. . . . . . . . . . . .

*svá ek* . . . . . .    at mik seint mun firrask
et manunga man.

162. (158) Ljóþa þessa    mundu, Loddfáfnir !
lengi vanr vesa,
þót þér góþ sé,    ef þú getr,
nýt, ef þú nemr,
þörf, ef þú þiggr.

157. A thirteenth I know: if the new-born son
of a warrior I sprinkle with water,
that youth will not fail when he fares to war,
never slain shall he bow before sword.

158. A fourteenth I know : if I needs must number
the Powers to the people of men,
I know all the nature of gods and of elves
which none can know untaught.

159. A fifteenth I know, which Folk-stirrer sang,
the dwarf, at the gates of Dawn;
he sang strength to the gods, and skill to the elves,
and wisdom to Odin who utters.

160. A sixteenth I know : when all sweetness and love
I would win from some artful wench,
her heart I turn, and the whole mind change
of that fair-armed lady I love.

161. A seventeenth I know : so that e'en the shy maiden
is slow to shun my love.

162. These songs, Stray-Singer, which man's son knows not,
long shalt thou lack in life,
though thy weal if thou win'st them, thy boon if thou obey'st them,
thy good if haply thou gain'st them.

---

*157. Sprinkle with water, a rite of purification.*
*159. Folk-stirrer, this dwarf is not mentioned elsewhere.*

163. (159)    Þat kannk et áttjánda,     es ek æva kennik
         mey né manns konu —
   allt es betra      es einn of kann,
         þat fylgir ljóþa lokum —
   nema þeiri einni,     es mik armi verr
         eþa mín systir sé.

164. (160)    Nú 'ru Háva mál      kveþin höllu í,
         allþörf ýta sunum,
         óþörf jötna sunum ;
   heill sás kvaþ !      heill sás kann !
         njóti sás nam !
         heilir þeirs hlýddu !

163. An eighteenth I know : which I ne'er shall tell
to maiden or wife of man,
save alone to my sister, or haply to her
who folds me fast in her arms;
most safe are secrets known to but one
the songs are sung to an end.

164. Now the sayings of the High One are uttered in the hall
for the weal of men, for the woe of Jötuns,
Hail, thou who hast spoken ! Hail, thou that knowest !
Hail, ye that have hearkened ! Use, thou who hast learned !

# ᚻYᛗIᛋKVIᚦA
## ᚦHE ᛚAY Oᚠ ᚻYᛗIᚱ
### SYNOPSIS

Two, or perhaps three, motifs are combined in Hymiskviða. The poem contains fragments of a number of myths. There is little structure to it, and scenes follow each other in a very rough logical order. Some of the allusions are not known from other sources and it contains unusually many kennings for an Eddic poem.' (Kennings are figures of speech, usually two words, often hyphenated, eg calling a sword a 'wound-hoe'.) Its contents are somewhat confusing but can be summarized as follows:

The Æsir - the principal race of Norse gods - are assembled after their hunting expedition, to consult the oracle, and learn where they shall hold their banquet. According to old Germanic custom the twigs, which have been sprinkled with sacrificial blood and graven with runes, are cast on a cloth. By the manner of their falling it is shown to the gods that they will find plenty to eat and drink in the halls of the wild Sea-giant Ægir.

It is a momentous occasion, for not only have they chosen their banqueting-room for all time, but they must win the alliance of Ægir, god of the ocean and king of the sea creatures. Ægir's fierce wife Ran, who catches drowned men in her net, is well known to skalds and minstrels, as are his nine children, the waves.

The gods pay a visit to the sea-halls. Thor, a strange ambassador for peace, is sent to greet the giant, who is found seated in proud contemplation of his daughters, the merry, sparkling waves tumbling one over the other in their sport, when his peace is shattered by the harsh voice of the Thunderer demanding that he provide a feast for the newcomers.

Small wonder that he takes offence, and bids them fetch a cauldron large enough for him to warm the mead for all of them at once.

That presents a problem, until Týr remembers a particularly large cauldron in the possession of his father, the Frost-giant Hymir (which is odd, as Týr is otherwise said to be the son of Odin).' Tyr is the god of law, justice, the sky, and heroic glory. He was also equated with Mars, the Roman god of war. 'Tuesday' is named after him.

Speedily, Thor harnesses his famous goats Tooth-gnasher and Tooth-grinder, and swiftly he drives with Tyr to the borders of Giant-land (Jötunheim). The rumbling car and goats must be left behind while they cross the river which flows between Asgarth and Jötunheim and fare on foot to Hymir's halls.

Here they feast, and Thor eats so much that Hymir and his guests have no alternative but to go fishing to provide more provisions. In a manner characteristic of the god, whose deeds are all on colossal scale, Thor fares to the wood and slays the biggest ox he can find, called Heaven-hitter, to provide the fishing bait. The Thunderer has designs upon a nobler prey than mere fish or even whales. He compels the reluctant Hymir to row further and further out to sea, where Thor almost catches the great sea-serpent Jörmungandr, also called the World Serpent and Midgard's Worm

Thor has shown off his strength. Moodily Hymir rows them

back to land and they return to his hall.

Here the Frost-giant taunts Thor and says that he can hardly be called strong if he is unable to smash Hymir's chalice of ice. The chalice is a magic one and cannot be broken unless slung against Hymir's head. Thor is eventually informed of this by Hymir's friendly wife, and proceeds to do so.

Hymir is annoyed at the destruction of his treasure, not to mention his headache. As he shows the god the door he tells them that they can take the cauldron with them if they are strong enough to carry it. The brimming kettle has become incredibly heavy. Tyr cannot lift it but Thor, 'the Father of Wrath', heaves it up off the floor and the Æsir depart. leaving the sore-headed Hymir without chalice or cauldron.

Hymir understandably peeved, quickly gathers his comrades and sets out after them. There follows the obligatory slaying of hordes of giants, whereupon the victorious Æsir take the cauldron and booze contentedly at Ægir's place ever after (or at least until Lokasenna).

*Source: Olive Bray and Wikipedia*

*Thor Slays the Ox*

# HYMISKVIPA

1. Ár valtívar     veiþar námu
    ok sumblsamír,     áþr saþir yrþi,
    hristu teina     ok á hlaut söu :
    fundu at Ægis     örkost hverjan.

2. Sat bergbui     barnteitr fyrir
    mjök glíkr megi     Mistorblinda ;
    leit í augu     Yggs barn í þrá :
    ' þú skalt ásum     opt sumbl görva.'

---

*The motive of this illustration is from a pre-Norman monument at Tullie House, Carlisle.*

*Thor's Fishing*

# HYMISKVIÞA

1. Of old when the war-gods their prey had won them,
in mood for feasting, and still unsated,
they shook divining twigs, scanned the blood drops,
and found all dainties in Ægir's halls.

2. As the rock-giant sat in his wave-brood rejoicing,
and seemed in likeness the son of Mist-blind,
came Thor and looked in his eyes with threatening
'Make now a goodly feast for the gods ! '

---

*1. Divining twigs: the oracle.*
*2. Ægir, a sea god, had nine daughters, and 'Ægir's children' was*
*a poetical synonym for the waves.*

3. Önn fekk jötni     orþbæginn halr,
    hugþi at hefndum     hann næst viþ goþ :
    baþ Sifjar ver     sér fœra hver,
    ' þanns öllum yþr     öl of heitak.'

4. Né þat máttu     mærir tívar
    ok ginnregin     of geta hvergi,
    unz af trygþum     Týr Hlórriþa
    ástráþ mikit     einum sagþi :

5. ' Býr fyr austan     Élivága
    hundvíss Hymir     at himins enda :
    á minn faþir     móþugr ketil,
    rúmbrugþinn hver,     rastar djúpan.'

Þórr kvaþ :

6. ' Veiztu ef þiggjum     þann lögvelli ? '

Týr kvaþ :

' Ef, vinr ! velar     vit görvum til.'

7. (6) Fóru drjúgum     dag þann framan
    Ásgarþi frá,     unz til Egils kvámu ;
    hirþi hafra     horngöfgasta ;
    hurfu at höllu     es Hymir átti.

8. (7) Mögr fann ömmu     mjök leiþa sér,
    hafþi höfþa     hundruþ niu ;
    en önnur gekk     algollin fram
    brúnhvit bera     bjórveig syni :

3. But the harsh-voiced hero angered the giant,
who forthwith pondered revenge on the Powers;
He bade the Thunderer bring him a cauldron
' Wherein for all of you ale I may brew.'

4. The glorious gods, the holy Powers
such vessel as this could nowhere find;
till Tyr the trusty whispered in secret
words of friendly counsel to Thor.

Tyr:
5. ' There dwells to the east of Stormy Billow
the all-wise Hymir, at heaven's end,
my fierce-souled father, who owns the kettle,
the broad-roomed cauldron, a full mile deep.'

Thor:
6. 'Dost know can we win that water-seether? '

Tyr.:
'If we use wiles thereto, my friend ! '

7. So forth they drove through the live-long day
till they came from Asgarth to Egil's home.
He stalled the goats of the splendid horns,
while they turned to the hall which Hymir owned.

8. Unsightly seemed to Tyr his granddam
for heads she had nine hundred in all;
but another came all golden forth,
fair-browed, and bearing to her son the ale-cup.

---

*4. Tyr, the god of war, is usually called the son of Odin.*
*Hymir, a frost giant, who binds the wintry sea.*
*7. Egil is probably the giant mentioned in st.*
*39. The goats, called Tooth-gnasber and Tooth-cracker, drew*
*Thor's chariot.*

9. (8)　' Áttniþr jötna !　　ek viljak ykkr
　　　　hugfulla tvá　　und hvera setja :
　　　　es minn fri　　mörgu sinni
　　　　glöggr viþ gesti,　　görr ills hugar.'

10. (9)　En váskapaþr　　varþ síþbuinn
　　　　harþráþr Hymir　　heim af veiþum :
　　　　gekk inn í sal,　　glumþu jöklar,
　　　　vas karls es kvam　　kinnskógr frörinn.

Frilla kvaþ :

11. (10)　' Ves heill, Hymir !　　í hugum góþum :
　　　　nú's sunr kominn　　til sala þinna
　　　　sás vit vættum　　af vegi löngum ;
　　　　fylgir hánum　　Hróþrs andskoti,
　　　　vinr verliþa,　　Veorr heitir sá.

12. (11)　Seþu hvar sitja　　und salar gafli !
　　　　svá forþa sér,　　stendr súl fyrir.'
　　　　Sundr stökk súla　　fyr sjón jötuns,
　　　　en afr í tvau　　áss brotnaþi.

13. (12)　Stukku átta,　　en einn af þeim
　　　　hverr harþsleginn　　heill, af þolli ;
　　　　fram gengu þeir,　　en forn jötunn
　　　　sjónum leiddi　　sinn andskota.

14. (13)　Sagþit hánum　　hugr vel þás sá
　　　　gýgjar grœti　　á golf kominn :
　　　　þar váru þjórar　　þrir of teknir,
　　　　baþ senn jötunn　　sjóþa ganga.

Hymir's wife:

9. ' Kinsman of giants ! fain would I hide you
'neath yon cauldrons, though bold of heart;
for my lord and master ofttimes shows him
mean to strangers, moved soon to wrath.'

10. Long tarried that monster, fierce-mooded Hymir,
ere he came from his hunting home.
He entered the hall, and icicles clashed
all frozen was the bushy beard on his chin.

Wife:

11. ' Hail to thee, Hymir ! Be gracious in mood :
for here in thy halls is come our offspring
whom long we awaited from distant ways;
and with him fares the foe of giants,
the friend of man, whose name is Warder.

12. ' Dost see where they hide, the hall-gable under,
sheltering themselves with a pillar between? '
But the column was shattered at the glance of the giant,
the mighty rafter was reft asunder :

13. Down from the beam eight cauldrons crashed,
one, hard-hammered, alone was whole.
Then forth they stepped, but the ancient Jötun
ever followed the foe with his eyes.

14. For evil whispered his mind when he saw
the bane of giant-wives stand on the hearth;
yet took they soon of the oxen three,
and Hymir bade them cook forthwith.

---

*11. Warder: Thor always appears as the defender of mankind
against the giants.*

15. (14)    Hverjan létu      höfþi skemra
           auk á seyþi       síþan báru :
           át Sifjar verr,      áþr sofa gengi,
           einn meþ öllu      yxn tvá Hymis.

16. (14)    Þotti hárum       Hrungnis spjalla
           verþr Hlórriþa      vel fullmikill :
           ' Munum at apni    öþrum verþa
           viþ veiþimat      vér þrír lifa.'

17.       Veorr kvazk vilja      á vág roa,
           ef ballr jötunn      beitur gǽfi.

Hymir kvaþ :

18. (15)    ' Hverf til hjarþar,    ef hug truir,
           brjótr bergdana !      beitur sǿkja :
           þess vǽntir mik,      at þer myni
           ögn af oxa       auþfeng vesa.'

19. (16)    Sveinn sýsliga      sveif til skógar,
           þars uxi stóþ       alsvartr fyrir :
           braut af þjóri      þurs ráþbani
           hátún ofan       horna tveggja.

Hymir kvaþ :

20. (17)    'Verk þykkja þín     verri miklu
           kjóla valdi,       an kyrr sitir.'

21. (18)    Baþ hlunngota      hafra dróttinn
           áttrunn apa       útar fǿra ;
           en sá jötunn       sína talþi
           litla fýsi        lengra at roa.

15. Each one left they less by a head,
and laid them soon on the seething tire;
then ere he slumbered the Thunderer ate,
himself alone, of the oxen, twain.

16. But Hymir the hoary friend of Hrungnir
deemed too ample the meal of Thor :
'To-morrow at eve shall we three have nought
save our hunting spoil whereon to sup.'

17. Spake Thor, and said he would fish in the sea,
if the fierce-souled giant would find him bait.

Hymir:
18. 'Go, if thou darest, slayer of rock-giants,
seek thy bait from the herd thyself :
for such as thou I ween 'twill seem
that bait from an ox were easy to win.'

19. Forthwith sped Thor, bold youth, to the wood
and soon, all swart, stood an ox before him;
then over its horns the slayer of Jötuns
struck, and sundered the head, high-towering.

Hymir:
20. ' Methinks thou art worse by far afoot
than at table sitting, Steerer of barks !

21. Then the Lord of goats, bade the low-born churl
drive the launched sea-horse further from shore;
but little he wished, that wary giant,
to row any further over the ocean.

---

*16. Hrungnir, a giant of great renown*

22. (19)  Dró mærr Hymir          móþugr hvali
          einn á öngli            upp senn tvá ;
          en aptr í skut          Óþni sifjaþr
          Veorr viþ vélar         vaþ görþi sér.

23. (20)  Egndi á öngul           sás öldum bergr
          orms einbani            oxa höfþi :
          gein viþ agni           sús goþ fia
          umbgjörþ neþan           allra landa.

24. (21)  Dró djarfliga           dáþrakkr Þórr
          orm eitrfán             upp at borþi ;
          hamri kníþi             háfjall skarar
          ofljótt ofan            ulfs hnitbróþur.

25. (22)  Hreingölkn hlumþu,      en hölkn þutu,
          fór en forna           fold öll saman :

          .  .  .  .  .  .        .  .  .  .  .

          sökþisk síþan           sá fiskr í mar.

26. (22)         .  .  .  .  .  .      .  .  .  .  .  .

          óteitr jötunn,          es aptr röru :
          svát at ár Hymir        etki mælti,
          veifþi rœþi             veþrs annars til.

                    Hymir kvaþ :

27. (23)  ' Mundu of vinna        verk halft viþ mik,
          at þu flotbrúsa         festir okkarn,
          eþa heim hvali          haf til bœjar
          ok holtriþa             hver í gögnum.'

22. Alone the famous and fierce-souled Hymir
caught on his hook two whales at once;
but aft in the stern the son of Odin
fashioned with craft his fishing line.

23. Lone Serpent-slayer, and Shield of Men,
he baited his hook with the head of the ox,
and he whom the gods hate gaped thereat,
the Girdle lying all lands beneath.

24. Then Thor drew mightily swift in his doing
the poison-glistening snake to the side.
His hammer he lifted and struck from on high
the fearful head of Fenrir's brother.

25. Moaned the wild monster, the rocks all rumbled,
the ancient earth shrank into itself.
Then sank the serpent down in the deep.

26. So cheerless was the giant as back they rowed
that for a while not a word he spake;
then anew he turned the tiller of thought.

Hymir:
27. ' Now half the work shalt thou share with me
or moor thou fast our floating steed,
or bear the whales to the dwellings home,
all through the hollows of the wooded hills.

---

23. *The Girdle is the World-serpent, called also Midgarth's worm.*
*He is one of Loki's children .*
24. *Fenrir, the famous Wolf.*
26. *Either Hymir has formed a fresh scheme for defeating Thor*
*or he has simply turned the boat towards land.*

28. (24)  Gekk Hlórriþi,          greip á stafni,
          vatt meþ austri        upp lögfáki ;
          einn meþ árum          ok austskotu
          bar til bœjar          brimsvín jötuns.

29. (25)  Ok enn jötunn          of afrendi
          þrágirni vanr          viþ Þór senti :
          kvaþat mann ramman,        þót roa kynni
          kröpturligan,          nema kalk bryti.

30. (26)  En Hlórriþi,           es at höndum kvam,
          brátt lét bresta       brattstein gleri :
          sló sitjandi           súlur í gögnum,
          báro þó heilan         fyr Hymi síþan.

31. (27)  Unz þat en fríþa        frilla kendi
          ástráþ mikit           eitt es vissi :
          ' Drep viþ haus Hymis !      hann's harþari
          kostmóþs jötuns        kalki hverjum.'

32. (28)  Harþr reis á kné        hafra dróttinn,
          fœrþisk allra          í ásmegin :
          heill vas karli        hjalmstofn ofan,
          en vínferill           valr rifnaþi.

                    Hymir kvaþ :

33. (29)  ' Mörg veitk mæti        mér gengin frá,
          es kalki sék           ór knëum hrundit ; '
          karl orþ of kvaþ :       ' knákak segja
          aptr ævagi :           þú ert, ölþr ! of heitt.

34. (30)  Þat's til kostar,        ef koma mættiþ
          út ór óru              ölkjól hofi.'
          Týr leitaþi            tysvar hrœra,
          stóþ at hváru          hverr kyrr fyrir.

28. Then the Thunderer rose, laid hold on the stem,
he landed the boat with the water therein,
and the ocean-swine, with the baler and oars
himself he bore to the giant's home.

29. But still the Jötun, stubborn as ever,
questioned anew the Thunderer's might.
' I deem none strong, row he ne'er so well,
save he who hath power to break my cup.'

30. Then the Storm god, swift, when it came to his hands
dashed into pieces a pillar of stone :
yea, sitting, he hurled the cup through the columns
but whole 'twas borne to Hymir again.

31. At length the fair mistress with friendly words
made known the secret she only knew :
' Strike at Hymir's skull, the food-filled giant's,
'tis harder than ever a wine cup was.'

32. Then rose to his knees the strong Lord of goats,
and girt him with all the might of the gods;
still sound above was the head of Hymir,
shattered below was the shapely wine cup.

Hymir:
33. ' Gone already I trow is my treasure,
when I see the cup now cast by thee kneeling.'
So spake the churl 'I can say never more,
' Ale in my cauldron now art thou brewed.'

34. 'But 'tis yet to prove if ye can bear
the mighty vessel forth from our court.'
Twice in vain sought Tyr to move it;
ever unstirred the cauldron stood.

35. (31)   Faþir Móþa     fekk á þremi
         ok í gögnum sté    golf niþr í sal ;
         hófsk á haufuþ     hver Sifjar verr,
         en á hǽlum       hringar skullu.

36. (32)   Fórut lengi,      áþr lita nam
         aptr Óþins sunr     einu sinni :
         sá ór hreysum      meþ Hymi austan
         folkdrótt fara       fjölhöfþaþa.

37. (33)   Hófsk af herþum     hver standandi,
         veifþi Mjöllni      morþgjörnum fram ;

       .   .   .   .   .   .      .   .   .   .   .   .

         ok hraunhvali     hann alla drap.

38. (34)   Fórut lengi,      áþr liggja nam
         hafr Hlórriþa      halfdauþr fyrir ;
         vas skǽr skökuls    skakkr á beini :
         þvi enn lǽvísi     Loki of olli.

39. (35)   En ér heyrt hafiþ     —hverr kann of þat
         goþmálugra      görr at skilja ?—
         hver af hraunbua     hann laun of fekk,
         es bǽþi galt      börn sin fyrir.

40. (36)   Þróttöflugr kvam      á þing goþa
         ok hafþi hver      þanns Hymir átti ;
         en vear hverjan     vel skulu drekka
         ölþr at Ægis      eitt hörmeitiþ.

35. Then the Father of Wrath laid hold on the rim
and heaved the cauldron high on his head,
against his heels the handles clinked,
as across the hearth he strode down the hall.

36. Far had they fared ere Odin's son
had turned him once, to look behind
and eastward saw from the cairns forthcoming
with Hymir, a war-host hundred headed.

37. From his shoulders raised he the resting cauldron,
swung he Mjollnir, death-craving hammer,
and the monsters all from the mountains slew.

38. But they fared not far ere the Thunderer's goat
had laid him down half dead in the way;
for lame in the leg was the shaft-bound steed,
'twas the work of Loki, crafty in wiles.

39. But ye have heard for who knows it better
of sages learned in the lore of the gods?
what amends made the dweller in wastes,
who paid to the Thunderer both his bairns.

40. Swelling with might to the meeting of gods
came Thor with the cauldron which Hymir had owned,
and the Holy Ones ever shall well drink ale
each harvest of flax in the Sea-god's hall.

---

35. *Wrath or Modi. This son is mentioned in Vafþrúðnismál, stanza 51.*
39. *The dweller in wastes, or mountain giant (presumably Egil), belongs to another story of Thor's adventures tn Jötunheim, the Home of the Giants.*

# ÞRYMSKVIÐA
## THE LAY OF THRYM

### SYNOPSIS

In Thrymskvitha we come to one of the best known and most frequently sung of all the Scandinavian myths. Strong and vigorous like Thor striding into Jötunheim, crisp and clear as a northern snow-scene in the sunlight, this narrative poem is very perfect of its kind, and needs little explanation.

Thor is discovered in helpless plight, his red beard quivering in impotent rage, a Thunder-god searching vainly for his thunder-hammer, 'which the Frost-giants and Mountain-giants well know when they see it uplifted, and small wonder, for many a head has it broken of their forefathers and their kindred.'

But now it is stolen, and Thor must tell no-one the dire secret except Loki, the mischievous fire-god and the swiftest of all messengers, who on this occasion uses his cunning in the service of the gods, and soon discovers the lost treasure. The hammer, like the thunderbolt of superstition, which is silent during the winter months, is deep hidden below the earth in the keeping of the Frost-giant Thrym - nor will he surrender it until he has seen the fair Spring-goddess Freyja coming as bride to his dark realms, like the sunshine which she personifies. He has never yet beheld the bright maiden, though he may have heard her light footfall overhead.

Thor hastens to her court and bids her at once put on her bridal veil, not dreaming that, with Asgarth in danger and the precious hammer stolen, she will refuse to go meekly into Jotunheim.

But she is not so weak-spirited, and flies into a rage as god-like as that of Thor himself when the great sea-serpent refused to be caught upon his fish-hook.

Thor must fetch the hammer himself. Then Heimdal who, though one of the warlike Æsir, is as wise and far-seeing as the Vanir, counsels that Thor should deceive the Frost-giant disguised as Freyja.

In this scene one can almost hear the laugh that goes through Asgarth at the rueful picture of the Thunderer thus decked with jewels and feminine trifles, his sturdy figure draped in woman's weeds.

Thrym seems to accept his strange bride without expressing surprise, perhaps because Frost-giants and Spring-goddesses have seldom a chance of meeting. But Thor can control his appetite as little as his temper, and the giant wonders much at his capacity.

He wonders yet more when he stoops to kiss her, and sees beneath the veil those flaming eyes, half hidden by the bushy brows. The wedding, however, must be completed. The hammer which hallowed the wedding feast of man is brought forth, and Thor seizing it becomes once more the god, and summer is first announced by the crashing thunder peal.

Mjollnir is one of the mythical treasures forged by the dwarfs. A belief in it was not confined to Old Norse mythology, for it appears in many traditions and fairy tales of Germany. Two other famous objects are mentioned in Thrymskvitha - Freyja's feather coat in stanza 3, and her necklace, called Brisingamen, in stanza 12. If the story of the last could be reconstructed, it might prove to be one of the most poetical in mythology. It is undoubtedly old. It was known in England, the earliest reference to it being in Beowulf, and in Denmark, where it is mentioned as the property of Frigg.

In the Sörlaþattr, we have the following story: Once Freyja, mistress of Odin, spied a necklace lying in a cave. It was the work of certain dwarfs, perhaps the Brisings, and when she looked at it she longed to possess it. They promised to give it her if she would stay with them four nights, and this she did.

Odin was angry when he discovered it, and caused Loki to steal the necklace from her chamber, and would only give it back to her on condition that she stirred up war between two kings, whence comes the legend of the 'Everlasting Battle.'

The poet Ulf Uggason tells of the battle between Loki and Heimdal: 'The famous and skilled one of the bridge of the Powers (Bifrost) wrestled with the evil and cunning son of Farbauti (Loki) at Singastone, ere the mighty son of nine mothers gained the shining necklace of sea-stones.'

What is the meaning of this fragmentary tale? The shining necklace must have been a symbol of light, especially the light cast upon the ocean waves.

We can scarcely venture, like some critics, to define it as the moon, the morning and evening star, or the rainbow. It belonged to the Sun goddess, whether called Freyja, Frigg (wife of the heaven god), or Gefjon, for that the three were originally one is suggested by the frequent confusion between them.

But Brisingamen in Old Norse tradition is the property of Freyja, who is also called Mardoll, or Sea-shining, and Menglod, the Necklace-glad.

Freyja loses her necklace, and Heimdal, the god of light, wins it back for her in a conflict with darkness.


*Source: Olive Bray and Wikipedia*

*Loki's Flight*

# ÞRYMSKVIÐA

1.  Vreiþr vas Vingþórr        es vaknaþi
    ok síns hamars        of saknaþi ;
    skegg nam hrista,        skör nam dýja,
    réþ Jarþar burr      umb át þreifask.

2.  Auk þat orþa        ails fyrst of kvaþ :
    ' Heyr nú, Loki !        hvat nú mǽlik,
    es engi veit        jarþar hvergi
    né upphimins :        áss's stolinn hamri ! '

3.  Gengu fagra        Freyju túna,
    ok hann þat orþa        alls fyrst of kvaþ :
    ' Muntu mer, Freyja !        fjaþrhams lea,
    ef minn hamar        mǽttak hitta ? '

*Thrym's Wedding Feast*

# ÞRYMSKVIÐA

1. Wroth was the Thunderer when he awakened
aud missed his hammer, the mighty Mjollnir.
His beard was quivering, his locks were shivering,-
as he groped around him, the Son of Earth.

2. ' List now, Loki, to this I shall tell thee!'
these, first of all his words, he spake
' no wight in high heaven or earth yet weens it:
The god of Thunder is reft of his hammer.'

3. Then sought they the shining halls of Freyja,
and these, first of all his words, spake Thor:
'Wilt than, Freyja, lend me thy feather-coat,
that perchance I may find my hammer? '

---

*i. Mjollnir, the Crusher, Thor's thunder hammer.*

Freyju kvaþ :

4.   ' Munda ek gefa þér        þót væri ór golli,
     ok þó selja          at væri ór silfri.'
     Fló þá Loki,         fjaþrhamr dunþi,
     unz fyr útan kvam         ása garþa
     ok fyr innan kvam         jötna heima.

5. (4)   Þrymr sat á haugi,        þursa dróttinn,
         greyjum sínum        gollbönd snöri
         ok mörum sínum        mön jafnaþi.

Þrymr kvaþ :

6. (5)   ' Hvat's meþ ásum,        hvat's meþ ölfum ?
         hví'st einn kominn        í jötunheima ? '

Loki kvaþ :

     ' Illt's meþ ásum,        illt's meþ ölfum !
     hefr Hlórriþa        hamar of folginn ? '

Þrymer kvaþ :

7. (6)   ' Ek hefi Hlórriþa        hamar of folginn
         átta röstum        fyr jörþ neþan ;
         hann engi maþr        aptr of heimtir,
         nema fœri mér        Freyju at kvæn.'

8. (7)   Fló þá Loki,        fjaþrhamr dunþi,
         unz fyr útan kvam        jötna heima
         ok fyr innan kvam        ása garþa ;
         mœtti Þóri        miþra garþa,
         ok hann þat orþa        alls fyrst of kvaþ :

Freyja:
4. ' I would give it thee though 'twere golden,
still would I grant it though 'twere silver!'
Away flew Loki, the feather-coat rustled,
till he came without the dwellings of Asgarth,
came within the Jötun realms.

5. Thrym sat on a mound, the lord of giants,
for his grayhounds twisting golden circlets,
smoothing over the manes of his steeds.

Thrym:
6. ' How do the gods fare? how do the elves fare?
Why alone art come into Jötunheim? '

Loki:
' Ill do the gods fare, ill do the elves fare.
Speak ! hast thou hidden the Thunderer's hammer? '

Thrym:
7. ' Yea, I have hidden the Thunderer's hammer
eight miles under, deep in the earth:
and never a being back shall win it
till he bring me as bride fair Freyja.'

8. Away flew Loki, the feather-coat rustled,
till he came without the realms of the Jötuns,
came within the garths of the gods.
There 'midst the courts the Thunderer met he,
and these, first of all his words, spake Thor.

---

5. *Thrym's name, like that of other Jötuns, signifies noise .*

9. (8)   ' Hefr eyrindi     sem erfiþi ?
        segþu á lopti     löng tíþindi !
        opt sitjanda     sögur of fallask
        ok liggjandi     lygi of bellir.'


            Loki kvaþ :

10. (9)   ' Hefk erfiþi     ok eyrindi :
        Þrymr hefr hamar,     þursa dróttinn ;
        hann engi maþr     aptr of heimtir,
        nema hánum fǿri     Freyju at kvæn.'


11.   Gengu fagra     Freyju at hitta,
     ok hann þat orþa     alls fyrst of kvaþ :
     ' Bitt þik, Freyja !     brúþar líni,
     vit skulum aka tvau     í jötunheima.'


12.   Vreiþ varþ Freyja     ok fnásaþi,
     allr ása salr     undir bifþisk,
     stökk þat et mikla     men Brísinga :
     'Mik veizt verþa     vergjarnasta,
     ef ekk meþ þér     í jötunheima.'


13.   Senn váru æsir     allir á þingi
     ok ásynjur     allar á máli,
     ok of þat réþu     ríkir tívar,
     hvé Hlórriþa     hamar of sǿtti.


14.   Þá kvaþ Heimdallr,     hvítastr ása—
     vissi vel fram     sem vanir aþrir— :
     Bindum Þór pa     brúþar líni,
     hafi et mikla     men Brísinga !

9. ' Hast thou had issue meet for thy labour?
Tell out aloft and at length thy tidings.
For oft when sitting a tale is broken;
oft when resting a lie is spoken.'

Loki:
10. ' I have had toil and issue also.
Thrym has thy hammer, lord of giants :
never a being back shall win it
till he bring him as bride fair Freyja.'

11. Forthwith went they to find fair Freyja,
and these, first of all his words, spake Thor:
' Bind thee, Freyja, in bridal linen,
we twain must drive into Jötunheim.'

12. Wroth then was Freyja; fiercely she panted;
the halls of Asgarth all trembled under,
burst that mighty necklet of Brisings.
' Know me to be most wanton of women
if I drive with thee into Jötunheim.'

13. Straight were gatherecj all gods at the doomstead;
goddesses all were in speech together;
and the mighty Powers upon this took counsel,
how the Thunderer's hammer they should win again.

14. Spake then Heimdal, of gods the fairest;
even as the Wanes could he see far forward
' Come bind we Thor in bridal linen,
let him wear the mighty Brisinga-men.

12. *Necklet of Brisings. This famous mythological treasure,
called Brisinga- nieu, like many others, was won from the dwarfs.*

15. Látum und hánum     hrynja lukla
    ok kvennváþir     of kné falla,
    en á brjósti     breiþa steina,
    ok hagliga     of höfuþ typpum ! '

16. Þá kvaþ þat Þorr,     þrúþugr áss :
    'Mik munu æsir     argan kalla,
    ef bindask lætk     brúþar líni.'

17. Þá kvaþ þat Loki,     Laufeyjar sunr :
    ' Þegi þú, Þórr !     þeira orþa :
    þegar munu jötnar     Ásgarþ bua,
    nema þinn hamar     þér of heimtir.'

18. Bundu þór þá     bruþar líni
    auk enu miklu     meni Brísinga.

19. (18) Létu und hánum     hrynja lukla
    ok kvennváþir     of kné falla,
    en á brjósti     breiþa steina,
    ok hagliga     of höfuþ typþu.

20. (19) Þá kvaþ þat Loki,     Laufeyjar sunr :
    ' Munk auk meþ þér     ambátt vesa,
    vit skulum aka tvær     í jötunheima.'

21. (20) Senn váru hafrar     heim of vreknir,
    skyndir at sköklum,     skyldu vel rinna :
    björg brotnuþu,     brann jörþ loga,
    ók Ópins sunr     í jötunheima.

15. Let us cause the keys to jingle under him,
weeds of a woman to dangle round him,
and over his breast lay ample jewels,
and daintily let us hood his head.'

16. Spake the Thunderer of gods the sturdiest:
' Womanish then the Powers will call me
if I let me be bound in bridal linen.'

17. Spake then Loki, the son of Laufey:
' Silence, Thor ! with words so witless!
Soon shall the Jötuns dwell in Asgarth
unless thou get thee again thy hammer.'

18. Then bound they Thor in bridal linen,
eke with the mighty Brisinga-men.

19. They caused the keys to jingle under him,
weeds of a woman to dangle round him,
and over his breast laid ample jewels
and daintily they hooded his head.

20. Spake then Loki, the son of Laufey:
' I will fare with thee as thy serving-maiden:
we twain will drive into Jötunheim.'

21. Forthwith the goats were homeward driven,
sped to the traces, well must they run!
Rent were the mountains, earth was aflame;
fared Odin's son into Jötunheim.

---

*17. Loki and Lgufey, or Leaf-isle, Loki's mother; also called Nál, or Pine-needle, by Snorri.*

22. (21) Þa kvaþ þat Þrymr,    þursa dróttinn :
' Standiþ upp, jötnar !    ok straiþ bekki :
nú fœriþ mér    Freyju at kvæn,
Njarþar dóttur    ór Noatúnum.

23. (22) Ganga hér at garþi    gollhyrndar kýr,
öxn alsvartir,    jotni at gamni :
fjölþ ák meiþma,    fjölþ ák menja,
einnar Freyju    ávant þykkjumk.'

24. (23) Vas þar at kveldi    of komit snimma
auk fyr jötna    öl fram borit ;
einn át oxa,    átta laxa,
krásir allar    þærs konur skyldu,
drakk Sifjar verr    sáld þriu mjaþar.

25. (24) Þá kvaþ þat Þrymr,    þursa dróttinn :
` Hvar sátt brúþir    bíta hvassara ?
sákak brúþir    bíta breiþara,
né enn meira mjöþ    mey of drekka.

26. (35) Sat en alsnotra    ambátt fyrir,
es orþ of fann    viþ jötuns máli :
'Át vætr Freyja    átta náttum,
svá vas óþfús    í jötunheima.'

27. (26) Laut und línu,    lysti at kyssa,
en útan stökk    endlangan sal :
' Hví 'ru öndótt    augu Freyju ?
þykkjumk ór augum    *eldr* of brinna.'

22. Spake then Thrym, the lord of giants:
' Stand up, Jötuns! and strew the benches!
Now shall ye bring me as bride fair Freyja,
daughter of Njörð, from Noatun.

23. ' Golden-horned kine are found in my dwellings
and oxen all swarthy, the joy of the giant.
I own many treasures I rule many riches,
and Freyja alone to me seems lacking.'

24. Swiftly drew the day to evening,
borne was the ale cup forth to the Jötuns,
Thor ate an ox and eight whole salmon,
with dainties all as should a damsel,
three full cups of mead he quaffed.

25. Spake then Thrym, the lord of giants,
Didst ever see damsel eat so bravely?
Ne'er have I seen one bite so boldly,
nor a maiden quaff more cups of mead! '

26. All crafty sat by the serving-maiden,
who answer found to the giant's asking :
' Nought has Freyja these eight nights eaten,
so sore her yearning for Jötunheim.'

27. Stooped then Thrym 'neath the veil, to kiss her,
back he leapt the hall's whole length :
' Why are fair Freyja's eyes so fearful?
Meseems from those eyes a fire is flaming.'

---

27. *Eyes so fearful: When Thor was angry he let his bushy brows drop over his eyes 'so that you could scarce get a glimpse of them.' (Snorri).*

28. (27)  Sat en alsnotra        ambátt fyrir,
          es orþ of fann         viþ jötuns máli :
          'Svaf vætr Freyja        átta náttum,
          svá vas óþfús          í jötunheima.'

29. (28)  Inn kvam en arma        jötna systir,
          hins brúþfear        biþja þorþi :
          ' Lát þér af höndum        hringa rauþa,
          ef öþlask vill        ástir mínar
          ástir mínar        alla hylli.'

30. (29)  Þa kvaþ þat Þrymr,        þursa dróttinn :
          ' Beriþ inn hamar        brúþi at vígja,
          leggiþ Mjöllni        í meyjar kné,
          vígiþ okkr saman        Várar hendi ! '

31. (30)  Hló Hlórriþa        hugr í brjósti,
          es harþhugaþr        hamar of þekþi ;
          Þrym drap fyrstan,        þursa dróttin,
          ok ætt jötuns        alla lamþi.

32. (31)  Drap ena öldnu        jötna systur
          hinas brúþfear        of beþit hafþi :
          hón skell of hlaut        fyr skillinga,
          en högg hamars        fyr hringa fjölþ.

   (32)  Sva kvam Óþins sunr        endr at hamri.

28. All crafty sat by the serving-maiden,
who answer found to the giant's asking:
'Not a whit has Freyja these eight nights slumbered,
so sore her yearning for Jötunheim.'

29. In came the wretched sister of Jötuns
and dared to beg for a bridal token :
' Take the red rings from off thy fingers
if thou wilt win thee mine affection,
mine affection, all my favour ! '

30. Spake then Thrym, the lord of giants:
'Bring in the hammer, the bride to hallow.
Mjollnir lay on the knee of the maiden!
Hallow us twain with the hand of the Troth-goddess!'

31. Laughed in his breast the heart of the Thunderer;
strong was his soul when he spied his hammer.
He first smote Thrym, the lord of giants,
and all the Jötun's kindred crushed.

32. Smote he the ancient sister of Jötuns,
her who had begged for a bridal token.
She got but a stroke in the place of shillings;
Mjollnir's mark and never a ring.

And thus Thor won him again his hammer.

---

30. *Thor was called on by the old Norse peasants to bless their marriage feasts with his hammer. Troth- goddess, or Var, was the guardian of oaths and plightings.*

# SKÍRNISMÁL
## THE STORY OF SKÍRNIR

### SYNOPSIS

The prose prologue to the poem opens with the god Frey, the son of Njörð, sitting in Odin's throne, Hliðskjálf and looking over all the worlds. On turning his gaze to Jötunheimr, the land of the giants, Frey sees a beautiful girl and is immediately seized by love. She is Gerðr, the fair earth, daughter of the Jötun Gymir. Fearing that the object of his heart's desire is unattainable, Frey sinks into gloom.

The poem itself starts with the wife of Njörð telling Frey's messenger Skírnir to ask Frey why he is so sad. Skírnir, fearing his master's wrath, nevertheless does as he is bidden.

Frey's response is sullen, yet he pours his heart out. Skírnir agrees to undertake a journey 'through the dim enchanted flickering flame' to woo Gerðr on behalf of his master, and Frey furnishes him with his magical steed and sword.

When Skírnir arrives in Jötunheim at the hall of the giant Gymir, Gerðr bids him enter. Without further ado, Skírnir tries to woo Gerðr on Frey's behalf, offering first gifts then threats (in other versions Skírnir does not use threats but still manages to successfully woo Gerðr).

He threatens her with a curse, which he describes in detail. The curse pictures the hell of Northern belief, which is widely different from the fiery kingdom of other mythologies. It is a far stretching waste, hemmed in by snow-clad mountains, bleak and cold, dark and desolate of all inhabitants save three-headed monsters or eagles rending corpses, and the dim form of Frost-giants stalking to and fro, and binding all things in their chains of ice.

In this lonely land, without speech with human kind, without love, without the good cheer which gladdens winter in the North, Gerðr risks being prey to madness.

Eventually the daughter of Gymir succumbs and agrees to accompany Skírnir to Frey's side.

There are indications that this poem is not exclusively Icelandic or Norwegian. The romance and sentiment are more fully expressed than is usual. One or two familiar forms and objects suggest that the author had a knowledge of international literature, and the best known motives of legend and mythology. There is the watcher who greets Skírnir, the newcomer, and demands the reason of his coming magic, flickering flames are one of the perils of the journey. The sword which he borrowed from Frey must have been one like that in Beowulf, or that of Sigurd or other ancient weapons, forged with magic craft, and graven with stories of old battles and runes of protection and victory.

The golden apples of youth, which were the property of Iðunn, and either borrowed or stolen by Skírnir, are scarcely known to the Edda, though mentioned by Snorri. They were a fruit almost unknown in Norway and Iceland, and the poet, it seems, also has been borrowing, perhaps from the golden apples of the Hesperides.

More peculiar to the North is another object, the ring Draupnir, which was forged by the dwarfs. It belongs to Odin, and the allusion to it having been burned with Odin's son shows that Baldr is already slain at this point in time.

All the magical treasures are symbols of light, growth, fertility, and other beneficent powers. Frey was especially regarded as the patron of harvests, and in this aspect he is known to the Eddas.

Snorri says: 'Frey rules over the rain, and the shining of the sun and the growth of fruits in the ground.' Hence the symbols of fertility and lipht which Skírnir is allowed to carry with him, and hence too the gods' gift of Elf-home to Frey, where the elf-folk work his kindly will in nature (see Grimnismal, stanza 5). In this poem his more original character is apparent. He is the Sun-god who awakens earth out of her winter sleep.

*Source: Olive Bray and Wikipedia*

*The Lovesickness of Frey*

# SKÍRNISMÁL

Freyr sonr Njarþar hafþi einn dag sez í Hliþskjálf ok sá um heima alla ; hann sá í jötunheima ok sá þar mey fagra, þá er hon gekk frá skála föþur síns til skemmu. Þar af fekk hann hugsóttir miklar. Skirnir hét skósveinn Freys ; Njörþr baþ hann kveþa Frey máls. Þá mælti Skaþi :

1.   ' Rís nú, Skirnir !       ok gakk at beiþa
      okkarn mála mög,
    ok þess at fregna,       hveim enn fróþi se
      ofreiþi afi.'

*Skírnir's message to Gerðr*

# ꩜KÍRNI꩜MÁL

Once Frey, son of Njörð, had seated himself on Window-shelf, and was gazing out over all worlds. When he looked into Jötunheim he beheld a fair maiden going from her father's hall to the bower, and at the sight of her he was seized with great sickness of heart.

Now Frey's servant was called Skírnir, and Njörð bade him ask speech of his master; and Skaði, wife of Njörð, said:

I. Rise, bright Skírnir! run thou swiftly,
and beseech our son to speak :
ask the wise youth to answer thee this,
'gainst whom his wrath is aroused.

*Window.shelf: Odin's seat.*
*Skírnir's name means the Light-bringer.*

Skirnir kvaþ :

2.  ' Illra orþa        erumk ón at ykrum syni,
       ef gengk at mæla viþ mög,
    ok þess at fregna,        hveim enn fróþi sé
       ofreiþi afi.'

Skirnir kvaþ :

3.  ' Segþu þat, Freyr,        folkvaldi goþa !
       auk ek vilja vita :
    hví einn sitr        endlanga sali,
       minn dróttinn ! of daga ? '

Freyr kvaþ :

4.  ' Hvi of segjak þér,        seggr enn ungi !
       mikinn móþtrega ?
    þvít alfröþull        lýsir of alla daga,
       ok þeygi at mínum munum.'

Skirnir kvaþ :

5.  ' Muni þína        hykkak svá mikla vesa,
       at mér, seggr ! né segir ;
    þvít ungir saman        várum í árdaga,
       vel mættim tveir truask.'

Freyr kvaþ :

6.  'Í Gymis görþum        ek sá ganga
       mér tíþa mey ;
    armar lýstu,        en af þaþan
       allt lopt ok lögr.

Skírnir spake:

2. If I seek for speech with him, your son,
ill words I shall haply win,
if I ask the wise youth to answer me this,
'gainst whom his wrath is aroused.

Skírnir spake: (to Frey).
3. Tell me truly, Frey, thou ruler of gods,
what I fain would learn from thy lips :
why sitt'st thou lone in the hall, my lord,
lingering the live-long day?

Frey spake:
4. How shall I ever own to thee, youth,
the great heart's burden I bear?
the Elf-light shines each day the same,
but works not yet my will.

Skírnir spake:
5. Scarce are the longings of thy love so great
but I trow thou canst tell them to me;
we were young together in days of yore,
we twain may well trust each other.

Frey spake:
6. In the courts of Gymir, the frost-giant, saw I
that maiden most dear to me;
light shone out from her arms and thence
all the air and sea were ashine.

---

4. *Elf-light, a name for the sun from its power over dwarfs or elves.*

7.    Mær's mér tíþari      an manni hveim
      ungum í árdaga ;
     ása ok alfa       þat vil engi maþr,
     at vit samt sém.

Skirnir kvaþ :

8.    ' Mar gef mér þá,      þanns mik of myrkvan beri
      vísan vafrloga,
     ok þat sverþ,      es sjalft vegisk
     † viþ jötna ætt.'

Freyr kvaþ :

9.    ' Mar þér þann gefk,      es þik of myrkvan berri
      vísan vafrloga,
     ok þat sverþ,      es sjalft mun vegask,
     ef sá's horskr es hefr.'

Skirnir mælti viþ hestinn :

10.    ' Myrkt es úti,      mál kveþk okkr fara
      úrig fjöll yfir,
      þursa þjóþ yfir ;
     báþir vit komumk,      eþa okkr báþa tekr
     enn ámátki jötunn.'

Skirnir reiþ í jötunheima til Gymis garþa. Þar váru hundar ólmir ok bundnir fyr skíþsgarþs hliþi þess er um sal Gerþar var. Hann reiþ at þar er féhirþir sat á haugi ok kvaddi hann :

11.    ' Seg þat, hirþir !      es þu á haugi sitr
      ok varþar alla vega :
     hve at andspilli      komumk ens unga mans
     fyr greyjum Gymis ? '

Hirþir kvaþ :

12.    ' Hvárt est feigr      eþa estu framgenginn,
         . . . . . . . ?
     andspillis vanr      þú skalt æ vesa
     góþrar meyjar Gymis.'

7. She is dearer to me than ever was maiden
to youth in days of yore :
but none among all the gods and elves
hath willed that we twain should wed.

Skírnir spake:
8. Give me steed to bear me safe through the dim
enchanted flickering flame,
and the sword which wages war of itself
'gainst the fearful Jötun folk.

Frey spake:
9. Here is steed to bear thee safe through the dim
enchanted flickering flame,
and the sword which wages war of itself,
if he who bears it be bold.

Skírnir (speaking to the horse).
10. Dark 'tis without ! 'tis time, I ween,
to fare o'er the dewy fells :
'mid the throng of giants we shall both win through,
or the awful Jötun have both.

Then Skírnir rode into Jötunheim to the dwellings of Gymir,
where fierce dogs were chained up before the gate of the enclosure
which surrounded Gerðr's hall. He rode up to a herdsman who was
sitting on a mound, and said:

11. Speak, thou herdsman, who sitt'st on a mound
and watchest every way !
How, for Gymir's hounds, shall I e'er hold speech
with that Jötun's youthful maid?

The Herdsman spake:
12. Either doomed art thou, or one of the dead
going forth to the halls of Hel!
never a word shalt thou win, I ween,
with Gymir's goodly maid.

13.  ' Kostir'u betri       heldr an at klökkva sé
      hveims fúss es fara ;
   einu dœgri      vörumk aldr of skapaþr
   ok allt líf of lagit.'

Gerþr kvaþ :

14.  ' Hvat's þat hlymja      es ek hlymja heyri til
      ossum rönnum í ?
   jörþ bifask,      en allir fyrir
     skjalfa garþar Gymis.'

Ambótt kvaþ :

15.  ' Maþr's hér úti,     stiginn af mars baki,
     jó lætr til jarþar taka.'

Gerþr kvaþ :

16.  ' Inn biþ hann ganga      í okkarn sal
     ok drekka enn mæra mjöþ ;
   þo ek hitt oumk,     at hér úti sé
     minn bróþurbani.'

Gerþr kvaþ :

17.  ' Hvat's þat alfa      né ása suna
     né víssa vana ?
   hvi einn of kvamt     eikinn fúr yfir
     ór salkynni at sea ? '

Skírnir spake:
13. A wiser choice than to whine makes he
who is ready to run his race :
my time was set to a certain day
and my length of life decreed.

Gerðr spake (within the hall):
14. What is the clanking and clashing of sounds
which echoing I hear in our halls?
Trembles the earth and before it all
the courts of Gymir are shook.

A Serving-maid spake:
15. See! A man without ! He is sprung from his steed,
which he now lets graze on the grass.

Gerðr spake:
16. Bid.him come in; let him enter our halls,
let him quaff the glorious mead!
Yet I fear me much lest that man without
the slayer of my brother should be.

Gerðr to Skírnir (who has entered).
17. Who comes, nor of elves' nor of gods' race seeming,
nor yet of the all-wise Wanes?
why hast fared alone through the raging fire
to visit the folk in our hails?

---

*16. Slayer of my brother. Frey slew the giant Belt, who was
perhaps Gerðr's brother; but, according to Snorri, this was after
the loss of his sword, for he used a stag's horn.*

Skirnir kvaþ :

18.  ' Emkak alfa        né ása suna
       né víssa vana :
     þó einn of kvamk        eikinn fúr yfir
       yþur salkynni at sea.


19.  Epli ellifu        hér hefk algollin,
        þau munk þér, Gerþr ! gefa,
     friþ at kaupa,        at þú per Frey kveþir
       óleiþastan lifa.'


Gerþr kvaþ :

20.  ' Epli ellifu        ek þigg aldrigi
       at manzkis munum ;
     né vit Freyr,        meþan okkart fjör lifir,
       byggum bǽþi saman.'


Skirnir kvaþ :

21.  ' Baug þér þá gefk        þanns brendr vas
        meþ ungum Óþins syni ;
     átta 'ru jafnhöfgir        es af drjúpa
       ena niundu hverju nótt.


Gerþr kvaþ :

22.  ' Baug ek þikkak,        þót brendr sé
        meþ ungum Óþins syni ;
     í görþum Gymis        era mér golls vant,
       at deila fé föþur.'

Skírnir spake:

18. I come, nor of elves' nor of gods' race am I,
nor yet of the all-wise Wanes;
yet have I fared through the raging fire
to visit the folk in your halls.

Eleven apples, all golden have I.
these I will give thee, Gerðr
To win thy heart, that from henceforth Frey
Be deemed thy dearest in life.'

Gerðr spake:

20. 'Not e'er will I take those eleven apples
At the will of any wight;
Nor will we twain live, Frey and I,
Together while life shall last.'

Skírnir spake:

21. 'Then do I bring thee the ring that was burned
With Odin's youthful son;
It lets fall ever, eight golden rings
Of a like weight every ninth night.'

Gerðr spake:

22. 'No ring do I want, though once 'twas burned
With Odin's youthful son;
Gold is not lacking in Gymir's courts,
for my father's wealth I share.'

---

*19. Apples: the apple was the symbol of fruitfulness, and also of eternal youth. According to Snorri, the goddess Iðun had charge of the apples which the gods ate whenever they felt themselves growing old.*

Skirnir kvaþ :

23.  ' Sér þú þenna mæki, mær !  mjóvan, málfán,
es hefk í hendi hér ?
haufuþ höggva  munk þér halsi af,
nema mér sætt segir.'

Gerþr kvaþ :

24.  'Ánauþ þola  viljak aldrigi
at manzkis munum ;
þó bins getk,  ef it Gymir finnisk,
[vigs ótrauþir] at ykkr vega tíþi.'

Skirnir kvaþ :

25.  'Sér þú þenna mæki, mær !  mjóvan, málfán,
es hefk í hendi hér ?
fyr þessum eggjum  hnígr sa enn aldni jötunn,
verþr þinn feigr faþir.

26.  Tamsvendi þik drepk,  en ek þik temja mun,
mær ! at mínum munum ;
þar skalt ganga,  es þik gumna synir
síþan æva sea.

27.  Ara þúfu á  skaltu ár sitja,
horfa [heimi ór, snugga] heljar til ;
matr sé þer leiþari  an manna hveim
enn fráni ormr meþ firum.

Skírnir spake:

23. 'Seest thou, maiden, this keen, bright sword
That I hold here in my hand?
Thy head from thy neck shall I straightway hew,
If thou wilt not do my will.'

Gerðr spake:

24. 'For no man's sake will I ever suffer
To be thus moved by might;
But gladly, methinks, will Gymir seek
To fight if he finds thee here.'

Skírnir spake:

25. See'st thou this sword, maiden, slender, rune-graven,
which here I hold in my hand?
Before its keen edge shall fall that old Giant,
thy father is doomed to death.

26. With a taming wand I will touch thee, maid!
and win thee soon to my will.
I will send thee far off where thou shalt be seen
never more by the sons of men.

27. On an eagle's mound shalt thou sit from morn,
gazing out of the world toward Hel:
thy food shall seem loathlier than bright-hued serpent
seemed ever to man among men.

---

*21. Ring: the ring Draupnir ('Dropper') was made by the dwarfs
for Odin, who laid it on Baldr's pyre when the latter's corpse
was burned (Cf. Voluspa and Baldrs' Draumar). Baldr, however,
sent the ring back to Othin from Hel. How Frey obtained it is
nowhere explained Andvari's ring (Andvaranaut) had a similar
power of creating gold.*
*27. An eagle, Corpse-swallower, who sits at the end of heaven.*

28. At undrsjónum verþir,      es þú út kömr,
    á þik Hrimnir hari,
    á þik hotvetna stari ;
    viþkunnari verþir      an vörþr meþ goþum ;
    gapi þú grindum frá.

29. (30)  Tramar gneypa      þik skulu görstan dag
    jötna görþum í ;
    til hrímþursa hallar      þú skalt hverjan dag
    kranga kostalaus,
    kranga kostavön.
    grát at gamni      skaltu í gögn hafa,
    ok leiþa meþ tárum trega.

30. (31)  Meþ þursi þríhöfþuþum      þú skalt æ nara
    eþa verlauss vesa ;
    þitt geþ grípi,      þik morn morni !
    ves sem þistill      sás þrunginn vas
    í önn ofanverþa.

31. (35)  Hrímgrimnir heitir þurs      es þik hafa skal
    fyr nágrindr neþan :
    Þar þér vílmegir      á viþar rótum
    geita hland gefi :
    (36)  œþri drykkju      fá þú aldrigi,
    mær ! af þinum munum,
    mær ! at mínum munum !

32. (29)  Tópi ok ópi,      tjösull ok óþoli
    vaxi þér tár meþ trega ;
    sezktu niþr,      mun ek ségja þér
    sváran súsbreka
    ok tvinnan trega.

28. Sight of wonder when thou walkest,
all beings shall stare on thee,
and the Frost Giant fix thee with his eye!
Known wider than Heimdal the Watchman of gods,
thou shalt gape through the gates of Hel.

29. Trolls shall torment thee from morn till eve
in the realms of the Jötun race,
each day to the dwellings of Frost giants must thou
creep helpless, creep hopeless of love;
thou shalt weeping have in the stead of joy,
and sore burden bear with tears.

30. With a three-headed giant must thou abide
or lack ever husband in life.
Care shall lay hold on thy heart and mind,
thou shalt waste with mourning away,
as a thistle shalt be which hath thrust itself up
in the latter season full late.

31. The Frost-hooded giant shall hold thee fast
beneath the doors of the dead;
at the tree's roots there shall wretched thralls
give thee foul water of goats;
and other draught shalt thou never drink,
at thy wish, maiden, with my will, maid.

32. Sit thee down ! I will further woes two-fold bespeak thee,
a whelming wave of care.
May madness and shrieking, bondage and yearning,
burden thee, with trouble and tears.

---

*31. At the tree's roots: Presumably Yggdrasil's roots stretching over Jötunheim.*

33. Vreiþr's pér Óþinn      vreiþr's þér ása bragr,
    þik skal Freyr fiask,
en firinilla mær !    es þú fengit hefr
    gambanvreiþi goþa.

34. Heyri hrímþursar,    heyri jötnar,
    Suttunga synir,
    sjalfir ásliþar :
hvé fyrbýþk,    hvé fyrbannak
    manna glaum mani,
    manna nyt mani.

35. (32)    Til holts ek gekk    ok til hrás viþar,
    gambantein at geta :

. . . . . . . . . . . . .

    gambantein ek gat.

36. (36)    Þurs rístk þér    ok þria stafi :
    ergi ok œþi ok óþola ;
svá ek þat af rist,    sem ek þat á reist,
    ef görvask þarfar þess.'

Gerþr kvaþ

37.    ' Heill ves heldr, sveinn !    ok tak viþ hrímkalki
    fullum forns mjaþar :
þó hafþak ætlat,    at myndak aldrigi
    unna vaningja vel.'

33. Wroth is Odin ! Wroth is the Thunderer!
Frey too shall hate thee, I trow:
thou evil maiden, well hast thou earned
the awful anger of the gods !

34. Hear now, Jötuns, Frost-giants hear me,
Suttung's sons 'neath the earth,
ye god-folk, too ! how I ban and forbid
man's love to the maiden, man's joy to the maid.

35. I went to the forest to find and fetch
a magic wand of might;
to a green-wood tree, and I got me there
this mighty magic wand.

36. I have cut thee a giant, and carved thee three staves,
lust and raving and rage.
Even as I cut them on so can I cut them off,
if haply I have the will.

(Gerðr offers him a foaming cup.)
37. Be gracious rather, youth ! Take now this rimy cup
filled with famous old mead.
Little I thought that ever in life
I should love a Waneling well.

---

33. *Thunderer. Thor is here called prince of gods. These three Odin, Thor, and Frey are usually ranked together, and appear as the chief gods in temple worship.*
34. *Sutting, a giant of the underworld.*
35. *A green-wood tree, see Havamal, stanza 150.*
36. *Giant : Icelandic burs. The name of some object was given to each runic Utter, and here the symbol b would represent burs.*
37. *Waneling. Frey's father Njörð was a Wane, or Vanir.*

Skirnir kvaþ :

38.  ' Eyrindi mín      viljak öll vita,
      áþr ríþak heim heþan :
   nær þu at þingi      munt enum þroska
      nenna Njarþar syni.'

Gerþr kvaþ :

39.  ' Barri heitir,      es vit bæþi vitum,
      lundr lognfara :
   en ept nætr niu      þar mun Njarþar syni
      Gerþr unna gamans.'

Þá reiþ Skirnir heim. Freyr stóþ úti ok kvaddi hann ok
spurþi tíþinda :

40.  ' Seg mer pat, Skirnir !      áþr verpir söþli af mar
      ok stígir feti framarr :
   hvat þu árnaþir      í jötunheima
      pins eþa míns munar ? '

Skirnir kvaþ :

41.  ' Barri heitir,      es vit báþir vitum,
      lundr lognfara :
   en ept nætr niu      þar mun Njarþar syni
      Gerþr unna gamans.'

Freyr kvaþ :

42.  ' Löng es nótt,      langar'u tvær,
      hvé of þreyjak þriar ?
   opt mér mánuþr      minni þótti
      an sjá hölf hynótt.'

Skírnir spake:

38. All my errand will I know to the end
before I ride homeward hence.
When wilt thou, maiden, meet at the trysting
the stalwart son of Njörð?

Gerðr spake:

39. Pine-needle is the wood of peaceful faring,
we twain know well the way:
there shall Gerðr bestow on the son of Njörð
her heart's love nine nights hence.

Then Skírnir rode home. Frey was standing without, and
he greeted him and asked for tidings.

Frey spake:

40. Speak, Skírnir! Cast not saddle from the steed,
and stir not one step hence :
what hast thou won of thy will and mine
in the realms of the Jötun race?

Skírnir spake:

41. Pine-needle is the wood of peaceful faring,
we twain know well the way:
there shall Gerðr bestow on the son of Njörð
her heart's love nine nights hence.

Frey spake:

42. Long is one night, long are two nights
how shall I live through three !
Shorter a month has seemed to me oft
than waiting this half night here.

# SVIPDAGSMÁL
## A COMBINATION OF THE POEMS
## 'GROUGALDR' (THE SPELL-SONGS OF GRÓA)
## AND
## 'FJOLSVINNSMOL' (THE SAYINGS OF FJÖLSVITH)

## SYNOPSIS

In the original edition of this translation, Svipdagsmál is entitled 'Dayspring and Menglod'.

Svipdagsmál or The Lay of Svipdagr is an Old Norse poem, a part of the Poetic Edda, comprising two poems, The Spell=Songs of Gróa and The Lay of Fjölsviðr. The two works are grouped since they have a common narrator, Svipdagr, or Day-spring. Moreover they would appear to have a common origin since they are closely similar in use of language, structure, style and metre.

Gróugaldr

The cruel stepmother of the youth Day-spring (Svipdag) has compelled him to seek the maiden Menglöð. The maiden dwells far away, 'where none may go'. It will be a long and dangerous journey.

To accomplish this seemingly impossible task, Day-spring-summons the shade of his dead mother, Gróa, a Völva/Vala, (a witch or seeress) to aid him. She casts nine spells (a significant number in Norse mythology).

Fjölsvinnsmál

In the second poem Day-spring, having survived the rigours of the journey, is confronted by the eponymous giant watchman, Much-wise (Fjölsviðr). 'Much-wise' is one of the names of the principal of the gods of Asgard, Odin.

Much-wise tells the youth to go away, while asking him his name; Day-spring wisely conceals this. A game ensues, consisting of question and answer riddles whereby Day-spring learns that Menglöð lives in the castle guarded by Much-wise, and that the castle may not be entered by any man save one . . .

*Groa's Incantation*

# I GRÓUGALDR

Svipdagr kvaþ :

1. ' Vaki þú, Groa !        vaki þú, góþ kona !
   vekk þik dauþra dura :
ef þat mant,        at þinn mög bæþir
   til kumbldysjar koma.'

Gróa kvaþ :

2. ' Hvat's nú ant        mínum einga syni,
   hverju 'st bölvi borinn :
es þú móþur kallar        es til moldar es komin
   ok ór ljóþheimum liþin ? '

*Day-spring and Menglod*

# I GRÓUGALDR
## THE SPELL-SONGS OF GRÓA

(Groa's chant, which her ghost sang to her son.)

Son:
1. Wake thou, Groa, wake, sweet woman,
at the doors of the dead, awake !
Thy child, thou bad'st me, dost thou not mind thee?-
come to the cairn of thy grave.

Groa:
2. What sorrow grieves thee, mine only son,
with what burden art overborne,
that thou callest thy mother who is turned to dust
and gone from the folk-world forth?

Svipdagr kvaþ :

3. ' Ljótu leikborþi     skaut fyr mik en lævísa kona
   sús faþmaþi minn föþur :
   þar baþ mik koma,     es kvæmtki veit,
   móti Menglöþu.'

Gróa kvaþ :

4. ' Löng es för,     langir'u farvegar,
   langir'u manna munir ;
   ef þat verþr,     at þu þinn vilja bíþr,
   ok skeikar þó Skuldar at sköpum.'

Svipdagr kvaþ :

5. ' Galdra mer gal     þás góþir'u,
   bjarg þú, móþir  ! megi :
   á vegum allr     hykk at ek verþa muna,
   þykkjumk til ungr afi.'

Gróa kvaþ :

6. ' Þann gelk þér fyrstan,     þann kveþa fjölnýtan,
   þann gól Rindr Rani :
   at of öxl skjótir     þvís þér atalt þykkir ;
   sjalfr leiþ sjalfan þik  !

7. Þann gelk þér annan,     ef þú árna skalt
   viljalauss á vegum :
   Urþar lokur     haldi þér öllum megum,
   es þu á smán sér  !

Son:

3. A fearful task hath that false woman set me,
who fondly my father hath clasped:
she hath sent me where none may go, to seek
the gay-necklaced maiden Menglod.

Groa:

4. Long is the faring, long are the pathways,
long are the loves of men:
well it may be that thou gain thy will,
but the end must follow fate.

Son:

5. Sing me spell-songs, sweet and strong ones!
Mother, shield me thy child!
Dead on the way I ween I shall be,
for I feel me too young in years.

Groa:

6. I sing thee the first well it serves, they say
which Rindr sang to Ran:
be thy burden too heavy, may it fall from thy back
and may self lead self at will.

7. I sing thee the second : if haply thou strayest
joyless on journeys far,
may the web of Weird be around thy way
and save thee from shameful plight.

---

6. *Rindr, another name for Odin as husband of the giantess
Rind, who is here called Ran. Odin long wooed her in vain, and
won her at last by enchantments.*
7. *Weird or Urd, the goddess of fate.*

8. Þann gelk þer enn þriþja,      ef þér þjóþaar
    falla at fjörlotum :
til heljar heþan      snuisk Horn ok Ruþr,
    en þverri æ fyr þér.

9. Þann gelk per enn fjórþa,      ef þik fiandr standa
    görvir á galgvegi :
hugr þeim hverfi      til handa þér
    ok snuisk til sátta sefi.

10. Þann gelk þer enn fimta,      ef þér fjöturr verþr
    borinn at boglimum :
leysigaldr      lætk þer fyr legg of kveþinn,
    ok stökkr þá láss af limum,
    en af fótum fjöturr.

11. Þann gelk þer enn sétta,      ef á sjó kömr
    meira an menn viti :
lopt ok lögr      gangi þer í lúpr saman
    ok lé per æ friþdrjúgrar farar.

12. Þann gelk per enn sjaunda,      ef þik sœkja kömr
    frost á fjalli há :
hrævakulpi      megit þínu holdi fara,
    ok haldi þér lík at liþum.

13. Þann gelk þer enn átta,      ef þik úti nemr
    nótt á niflvegi :
at því firr megi      þér til meins görva
    kristin dauþ kona.

8. I sing thee the third: if mighty streams
with their waters o'erwhelm thy life,
may those floods of Hel flow back, and dry
be the paths before thy feet.

9. I sing thee the fourth: if foes should lurk
in ambush, armed for thy death,
be their hearts forthwith toward thee turned
and their minds be moved to peace.

10. I sing thee the fifth: if men make fast
a charm on the joints of thy limbs,
that loosening spell which I sing o'er thy legs
shall break fetters from hands and feet.

11. I sing thee the sixth: if thou fare o'er seas
mightier than men do know,
may wind and wave for thee work thy boat,
and make peaceful thy path o'er the deep.

12. I sing thee the seventh: if thou art assailed
by frost on the rimy fell,
may thy flesh not die in the deadly cold;
be thou sound in life and limb.

13. I sing thee the eighth: if night o'ertake thee,
wandering on the misty way,
none the more may ghosts of Christian women
have power to work thy woe.

---

8. *Floods of Hel, here called Horn and Kud, not mentioned in
the list of the rivers which flow from Roaring-kettle.*
13. *Ghosts of Christian women. This line must have been written in heathen days, when Christianity was regarded as a mysterious power of evil.*

14. Þann gelk þer enn niunda,    ef viþ enn naddgöfga
    orþum skiþtir jötun :
    máls ok mannvits    sé þer á *munn ok* hjarta
    gnóga of gefit.

15. Far þú nu æva    þas forap þikkir
    ok standit þer mein fyr munum !
    \*    \*    \*    \*    \*    \*    \*
    á jarþföstum steini    stóþk innan dura,
    meþan þér galdra gólk.

16. Móþur orþ    berþu, mögr ! heþan
    ok lát þer í brjósti bua !
    iþgnóga heill    skalt of aldr hafa,
    meþan mín orþ of mant.'

# II FJOLSVINNSMAL

1. Útan garþa    hann sá upp of koma
    þursa þjóþar sjöt.

        Svipdagr kvaþ :

(2)  ' Hvat's þat flagþa,    es stendr fyr forgörþum
    ok hvarflar umb hǽttan loga ? '

        Fjölsviþr kvaþ :

2. (1)  ' Hvers þú leitar    eþa hvers á leitum est,
    eþa hvat vilt, vinlauss ! vita ?
    úrgar brautir    árnaþu aptr heþan !
    áttat hér, verndarvanr ! veru.'

14. I sing thee the ninth: when thou needs must stand
in speech with that spear-famed giant,
may words and wisdom to lips and heart
in abundance be bestowed.

15. May thou ne'er be led, where danger lurks,
may harm not hinder thy will!
At the doors I stood, on an earth-bound stone,
while I sang these songs to thee.

16. Child, bear with thee a mother's words,
let them abide in thy breast!
Wealth enough in life thou shalt win
if thou keepst my counsel in mind.

# II FJOLSVINNSMAL
## THE SAYINGS OF FJÖLSVITH

1. Stood Day-spring without the walls, and saw
loom high the Jötuns' home.

Day-spring:
What monster is that who guards the threshold,
and prowls round the perilous flames?

Much-wise:
2. Whom dost thou seek? Of whom art in search?
What, friendless wight, wouldst thou learn?
Back wander hence on thy dewy way;
not here is thy haven, lone one!

---

14. *'That spear-famed giant' must be Much- wise, the warder of
Menglod's halls.*

3. ' Hvat's þat flagþa,      es stendr fyr forgarþi
    ok býþrat liþöndum löþ ?
  Sœmþarorþa lauss     hefr þú, seggr ! of lifat,
    ok haltu heim heþan ! '

        Fjölsviþr kvaþ :

4. ' Fjölsviþr ek heiti,     en ek á fróþan sefa,
    þeygi emk mins mildr matar :
  innan garþa     þú kömr aldrigi,
    ok dríf þu nú vargr at vegi ! '

        Svipdagr kvaþ :

5. ' Augna gamans     fýsir aptr at fá,
    hvars getr svást at sea :
  garþar gloa     þykkjumk of gollna sali,
    hér mundak öþli una.'

        Fjölsviþr kvaþ :

6. ' Seg mér, hverjum     estu, sveinn ! of borinn
  eþa hverra'st manna mögr ? '

        Svipdagr kvaþ :

  ' Vindkaldr heitik,     Várkaldr hét minn faþir,
  þess vas Fjölkaldr faþir.

7. Seg mér þat, Fjölsviþr !     es ek þik fregna mun
    auk ek vilja vita :
  hverr hér ræþr     —ok ríki hefr—
    eign ok auþsölum ? '

Day-spring.
3. What monster is that who guards the threshold
and bids not welcome to wanderers?
Lacking all seemly speech wert thou born;
hence, speaker, hie thee home!

Much-wise:
4. Much-wise I am called, for I am wise in mind,
though none too free with my food.
Here in the courts shalt thou never come;
get thee hence like a wolf on thy way!

Day-spring.
5. Longs the lover again for the light of his eyes,
with his sweet-heart back in sight:
glowing are the walls of that golden hall;
I would fain make here my home.

Much-wise:
6. Tell me, bold youth, from whom thou art sprung,
son of what being wert born?

Day-spring.
They call me Wind-cold, the son of Spring-cold,
whose father was Fierce-cold named.

7. Now answer me, Much-wise, this that I ask
and fain would learn from thy lips:
who here doth rule and hold in power
the wealth and wondrous halls?

---

5. *This strophe, like 49, suggests that Day-spring and Menglod
have met before.*

Fjölsviþr kvaþ :

8. ' Menglöþ of heitir,      en hana móþir of gat
viþ Svafnþorins syni :
hón hér ræþr     —ok ríki hefr—
eign ok auþsölum.'

Svipdagr kvaþ :

9 ' Seg mér þat, Fjölsviþr !     es ek þik fregna mun
auk ek vilja vita :
hvat sú grind heitir,     es meþ goþum söut
menn at meira foraþ ? '

Fjölsviþr kvaþ :

10. ' Þrymgjöll hón heitir,     en hana þrír görþu
Sólblinda synir ;
fjöturr fastr     verþr viþ faranda hverjan,
es hana hefr frá hliþi.'

Svipdagr kvaþ :

11. ' Seg mér þat, Fjölsviþr !     es ek þik fregna mun
auk ek vilja vita :
hvat sá garþr heitir,     es meþ goþum söut
menn et meira foraþ ? '

Fjölsviþr kvaþ :

12. ' Gaststropnir heitir,     en ek hann görvan hefk
ór Leirbrimis limum ;
svá hefk studdan,     at hann standa mun
æ meþan öld lifir.'

Much-wise:
8. There is one called Menglod, who of her mother
was born to Sleep-thorn's son:
'tis she doth rule and hold in power
the wealth and wondrous halls.


Day-spring.
9. Now answer me, Much-wise, this that I ask
and fain would learn from thy lips:
what is that gate called? Ne'er among gods
was more fearful barrier found.


Much-wise:
10. Sounding-clanger the gate is called,
wrought by three sons of Solblind.
Fast is the chain to each wanderer who seeks
to lift that door from the latch.


Day-spring.
11. Now answer me, Much-wise, this that I ask
and fain would learn from thy lips :
what is that wall named? Ne'er among gods
was more fearful barrier found.


Much-wise:
12. Guest-crusher 'tis called; from the Clay-giant's limbs
I built that barrier myself :
so fast have I set it that firm 'twill stand,
for ever while life shall last.

---

10. *Solblind or Sun-blinded must be a dwarf name for one who,
like All-wise, fears the light, and whose children are forgers like
Brokk and Sindri.*
12. *The Clay-giant or Leirbrimir. From the giant Ymir or Brimir
was made the whole framework of earth, and the expression is
only a poetical term for the solid ground.*

Svipdagr kvaþ :

13. (19)   ' Seg mér þat, Fjölsviþr !      es ek þik fregna mun

auk ek vilja vita :

hvat þat barr heitir,      es breiþask of

lönd öll limar ? '

Fjölsviþr kvaþ :

14. (20)   ' Mimameiþr hann heitir,      en þat mangi veit,

hvers hann af rótum rinnr ;

viþ þat hann fellr,      es fǽstan varir :

flǽrat hann eldr né jarn.'

Svipdagr kvaþ :

15. (21)   ' Seg mér þat, Fjölsviþr !      es ek þik fregna mun

auk ek vilja vita :

hvat af moþi verþr      þess ens mǽra viþar,

es hann flǽrat eldr né jarn ? '

Fjölsviþr kvaþ :

16. (22)   ' Út af hans aldni      skal á eld bera

fyr killisjúkar konur :

útar hverfa þess      þeirs innar skyldu,

sás hann meþ mönnum mjötuþr.'

Day-spring.
13. Now answer me, Much-wise, this that I ask
and fain would learn from thy lips:
what is that tree, which far and wide,
spreads limbs over every land?

Much-wise:
14. 'Tis the tree of Mimir, but no man knows
by what roots it rises to heaven :
'twill fall at last by what least one weens,
for nor fire nor weapons will wound it.

Day-spring.
15. Now answer me, Much-wise, this that I ask
and fain would learn from thy lips:
what befalls the fruit of that famous tree
which nor fire nor weapons will wound?

Much-wise:
16. The fruit thereof must be laid on the fire
for the weal of travailing women;
they shall then come out who had been within.
To mankind 'tis the giver of life.

---

14. *The tree of Mimir: Yggdrasil. Mimir's well, like that of
Weird, was situated beneath it, and here, in Giant-home, the tree
would be called his.*
16. *Giver of life, or, according to another reading, the Fate-tree.*

17. (23)  ' Seg mér pat, Fjölsviþr !      es ek þik fregna mun
              auk ek vilja vita :
          hvat sá hani heitir,        es sitr í enum háva viþi,
          allr viþ goll gloir ? '

                    Fjölsviþr kvaþ :

18. (24)  ' Viþofnir heitir,        en hann stendr veþrglasi
              á meiþs kvistum Mima :
          einum ekka        þryngr hann örófsaman
          *Surt ok Sinmöru.*'

                    Svipdagr kvaþ :

19. (13)  ' Seg mér þat, Fjölsviþr !      es ek þik fregna mun
              auk ek vilja vita :
          hvat þeir garmar heita,       es gífrir rata
          görþum fyr  . . . . . . .

                    Fjölsviþr kvaþ :

20. (14)  ' Gífr heitir annarr,        en Geri annarr,
              ef þú vill þat vita :
          *verþir' u öflgir,*        er þeir varþa,
          unz rjúfask regin.'

Day-spring.
17. Now answer me, Much-wise, this that I ask
and fain would learn from thy lips:
what cock sits perched in yon lofty tree,
who is glistening all with gold?

Much-wise:
18. Wood-snake he is called, who storm-bright sits
in the boughs of Mimir's Tree:
with one long dread he galls beyond measure
giant and giant-wife.

Day-spring.
19. Now answer me, Much-wise, this that I ask
and fain would learn from thy lips:
what fierce hounds watch in front of the courts
ravening and roaming around?

Much-wise:
20. One is called Greed, the other Glutton,
if haply thou wouldst hear:
mighty warders they are who watch
for aye till the Powers perish.

---

*17. Wood-snake, a poetical name for bird. This cock may be Golden Comb, who wakes the gods at the coming of the giants and is hence the dread of giant and giant-wife, or, more probably Fjalar, who sits 'in the roosting tree,' and sounds the first note of doom. The names of Surt and Sininara, found in the text, are used in a general sense.*
*20. Mighty warders, or, if another reading is taken, eleven warders there are who watch, named perhaps in stanza 34.*

Svipdagr kvaþ :

21. (15)　' Seg mér þat, Fjölsviþr !　　　es ek þik fregna mun
　　　　　　auk ek vilja vita :
　　　　　　hvárt sé manna nekkvat　　　þats megi inn koma,
　　　　　　meþan sókndjarfir sofa ? '

Fjölsviþr kvaþ :

22. (16)　' Missvefni mikit　　　vas þeim mjök of lagit,
　　　　　　síþans þeim vas varzla vituþ :
　　　　　　annarr of nǽtr sefr,　　　en annarr of daga,
　　　　　　ok kömsk þá vǽtr, ef kvam. '

Svipdagr kvaþ :

23. (17)　' Seg mér þat, Fjölsviþr !　　　es ek þik fregna mun
　　　　　　auk ek vilja vita :
　　　　　　hvárt sé matar nekkvat　　　þats menn hafi,
　　　　　　ok hlaupi inn, meþan eta ? '

Fjölsviþr kvaþ :

24. (18)　' Vǽngbráþir tvǽr　　　liggja í Viþofnis liþum,
　　　　　　ef þú vill þat vita :
　　　　　　þat eitt's svá matar,　　　at þeim menn of gefi,
　　　　　　ok hlaupi inn, meþan eta.'

Svipdagr kvaþ :

25.　　　' Seg mér þat, Fjölsviþr !　　　es ek þik fregna mun
　　　　　　auk ek vilja vita :
　　　　　　hvárt sé vápna nekkvat,　　　þats knegi Viþofnir fyrir
　　　　　　hníga á Heljar sjöt ? '

Fjölsviþr kvaþ :

26.　　　' Lǽvateinn heitir,　　　es görþi Loptr rúinn
　　　　　　fyr nágrindr neþan ;
　　　　　　í Sǽgjarns keri　　　liggr hjá Sinmöru,
　　　　　　ok halda njarþlásar niu.'

Day-spring.
21. Now answer me, Much-wise, this that I ask
and fain would learn from thy lips:
is there never a being may pass within
while the fierce hounds are held in sleep?

Much-wise:
22. Division of sleep was ever their lot
since 'twas given them to guard:
sleeps one by night, and the other by day,
and none who comes may win through.

Day-spring.
23. Now answer me, Much-wise, this that I ask
and fain would learn from thy lips:
is there no food which man can find them
and dart through the doors while they feast?

Much-wise:
24. There lie two wings in the Wood-snake's sides,
if haply thou wouldst hear:
this alone is that food which if man can find,
he shall dart through the doors while they feast.

Day-spring.
25. Now answer me, Much-wise, this that I ask
and fain would learn from thy lips:
is there no weapon to strike the Wood-snake
down to the halls of Hel?
Much-wise:

26. Tis the Wounding Wand which Loki plucked
beneath the doors of the dead :
Sinmara keeps it with nine fast locks,
shut in Sea-lover's chest.

---

*26. The Wounding Wand must be the mistletoe with which
Baldr was slain. Snorri tcils us that it grew to the west of Vallhall.*

Svipdagr kvaþ :

27. ' Seg mér þat, Fjölsviþr !      es ek þik fregna mun
     auk ek vilja vita :
     hvárt aptr kömr      sás eptir ferr
     ok vill þann tein taka ? '

Fjölsviþr kvaþ :

28. Aptr mun koma      sás eptir ferr
     ok vill þann tein taka,
     ef þat fœrir,      sem fair eigu,
     eiri aurglasis. '

Svipdagr kvaþ :

29. ' Seg mér þat, Fjölsviþr !      es ek þik fregna mun
     auk ek vilja vita :
     hvárt sé mæta nekkvat,      þats menn hafi,
     ok verþr því en fölva gýgr fegin ? '

Fjölsviþr kvaþ :

30. ' Ljósan lea      skaltu í lúþr bera
     þanns liggr í Viþofnis völum,
     Sinmöru at selja,      áþr hón söm telisk
     vápn til vígs at lea.'

Svipdagr kvaþ ;

31. ' Seg mér þat, Fjölsviþr !      es ek þik fregna mun
     auk ek vilja vita :
     hvat sá salr heitir      es slunginn es
     vísum vafrloga ? '

Day-spring.
27. Now answer me, Much- wise, this that I ask
and fain would learn from thy lips:
comes he ever again, who goes to seek,
and craves to win that wand?

Much-wise:
28. He shall come again who goes to seek
and craves to win that wand;
if he brings the treasure which none doth own,
the gold-bright goddess to please.

Day-spring.
29. Now answer me, Much-wise, this that I ask
and fain would learn from thy lips:
is there no treasure which man can take
to rejoice that pale-hued giantess?

Much-wise:
30. In its quill must thou bear the bright sickled plume,
which was taken from Wood-snake's tail,
and give to Sinmara ere she will grant thee
that weapon of war to use.

Day-spring.
31. Now answer me, Much-wise, this that I ask
and fain would learn from thy lips:
what hall is yonder, all girt around
by enchanted flickering flames?

---

9. *Sinmara: This giantess is only mentioned in st. 18, where she
is coupled with Surt, as though his wife.*
28. *Gold-bright goddess. A poetical term for woman.*
30. *Quill, a suggestion for Ititr, which means case or box; but
whose significance is here doubtful.*

Fjölsviþr kvaþ :

32. ' Hyrr hann heitir,     en hann lengi mun
    á brodds oddi bifask ;
auþranns þess     munu of aldr hafa
    frétt eina firar.'

Svipdagr kvaþ :

33. ' Seg mér þat, Fjölsviþr !     es ek þik fregna mun
    auk ek vilja vita :
hverr þat görþi,     es fyr garþ sák
    innan ásmaga ? '

Fjölsviþr kvaþ :

34. ' Uni ok Iri,     Bari ok Ori,
    Varr ok Vegdrasill,
Dori ok Uri, Dellingr, Atvarþr,
    Líþskjalfr, Loki.'

Sviþdagr kvaþ :

35. ' Seg mér þat, Fjölsviþr !     es ek þik fregna mun
    auk ek vilja vita :
hvat þat bjarg heitir,     es ek sé brúþi á
    þjóþmæra þruma ? '

Fjölsviþr kvaþ :

36. ' Lyfjaberg heitir,     en þat hefr lengi verit
    sjúkum ok sárum gaman :
heil verþr hver,     þót hafi † árs sótt,
    ef þat klífr, kona.'

Much-wise:
32. Ember 'tis called and long must it quiver
as though on the spear's point set;
far tidings only, throughout all time,
man hears of this wondrous hall.

Day-spring.
33. Now answer me, Much-wise, this that I ask
and fain would learn from thy lips:
what beings, born of the gods have built
what I saw inside the court?

Much-wise:
34. Uni and Iri, Bari and Ori,
Var and Vegdrasil,
Dori and Uri, Delling, Atvard,
Lidskjalf and Loki were these.

Day-spring.
35. Now answer me, Much-wise, this that I ask
and fain would learn from thy lips:
what hill is that on whose height I see
yon wondrous Woman resting?

Much-wise:
36. 'Tis the Hill of Healing; long hath it held,
for the sick and sorrowful, joy:
each woman is healed who climbs its height,
even of year-long ills.

---

35. Dori, Ori, and Delling are dwarfs; Loki, the god. The others
are unknown; their names do not seem to indicate their powers
like those of stanza 38.

Svipdagr kvaþ :

37. ' Seg mér þat, Fjölsviþr !    es ek þik fregna mun
auk ek vilja vita :
hvat þǽr meyjar heita,    es fyr Menglaþar knëum
sitja sáttar saman ? '

Fjölsviþr kvaþ :

38. ' Hlíf heitir ein,    önnur Hlífþrasa,
þriþja Þjóþvara,
Björt ok Blíþ,    Blíþr ok Fríþ,
Eir ok Aurboþa.'

Svipdagr kvaþ :

39. ' Seg mér þat, Fjölsviþr !    es ek þik fregna mun
auk ek vilja vita :
hvárt þǽr bjarga    þeims blóta þǽr,
ef görvask þarfar þess ? '

Fjölsviþr kvaþ :

40. ' Bjarga svinnar    hvars menn blóta þǽr
á stallhelgum staþ :
ey svá hátt foraþ    kömr at hölþa sunum,
hverjan ór nauþum nema.'

Svipdagr kvaþ :

41. ' Seg mér þat, Fjölsviþr !    es ek þik fregna mun
auk ek vilja vita :
hvárt sé manna nekkvat,    þats knegi á Menglaþar
svásum armi sofa ? '

Fjölsviþr kvaþ :

42. ' Vǽtr's þat manna,    es knegi á Menglaþar
svásum armi sofa,
nema Svipdagr einn,    hánum vas en sólbjarta
brúþr at kván of gefin.

Day-spring:
37. Now answer me, Much-wise, this that I ask
and fain would learn from thy lips:
who are the maidens, at Menglod's knees
all gathered in peace together?

Much-wise:
38. They are spirits, Sheltering, Shielding giants,
Guarding warriors in war,
Bright and Tender, Blithe and Peaceful,
Gentle, Generous maids.

Day-spring:
39. Now answer me, Much-wise, this that I ask
and fain would learn from thy lips:
will they shelter all who make offering to them,
if need thereof arise?

Much-wise:
40. Those Wise Ones shelter where men make offering
in the sacred altar-stead:
no peril so mighty can man befall
but they save him soon from need.

Day-spring:
41. Now answer me, Much-wise, this that I ask
and fain would learn from thy lips:
is there never being in the world may lie
in Menglod's soft arms sleeping?

Much-wise:
42. There is never being in the world may lie
in Menglod's soft arms sleeping
save Day-spring, to whom of yore was given
that sun-bright maiden as bride.

Svipdagr kvaþ :

43.    ' Hritt á hurþir,      láttu hliþ rúm !
     hér mátt Svipdag sea ;
   þó vita far,      ef vilja muni
     Menglöþ mitt gaman.'

Fjölsviþr kvaþ :

44.    ' Heyrþu, Menglöþ !      hér es maþr kominn,
     gakk á gest sea !
   hundar fagna,      hús hefr upp lokizk :
     hykk at Svipdagr seï.'

Menglöþ kvaþ :

45.    ' Horskir hrafnar      skulu þer á hám galga
     slíta sjónir ór,
   ef þat lýgr,      at hér sé langt kominn
     mögr til minna sala.

46.    Hvaþan þú fórt,      hvaþan þú för görþir,
     hvé þik hétu hiu ?
   at ætt ok nafni      skalk jartegn vita,
     ef ek vas þer at kván of kveþin.'

Svipdagr kvaþ :

47.    ' Svipdagr heitik,      Sólbjartr hét faþir,
     þaþan vrákumk vindar kalda vegu ;
   Urþar orþi      kveþr engi maþr,
     þót sé viþ löst lagit.'

Day-spring:
43. Fling open the door, make wide the gate,
Day-spring is here, behold!
Yet hie thee first, and find if in truth
Menglod longs for my love.

Much-wise to Menglod:
44. Hearken, Menglod, a guest is here!
Come thou this stranger behold!
The hounds are joyous, the hall hath opened.
'Tis Day-spring, well I ween

Menglod:
45. Now may fierce ravens rend thine eyes out,
high on the gallows hanging,
if falsely thou sayest that from far away
comes Day-spring here to my halls !

To Day-spring:
46. Whence hast thou come, whence made thy way,
how do thy home-folk call thee?
Show race and name ere I know that to thee
in truth I have been betrothed.

Day-spring:
47. Day-spring am I, the child of Sun-bright,
by winds on my chill way wafted;
the doom of Weird may no wight withstand
e'en though meted amiss.

---

*47. The doom of Weird, see Spell-songs, stanza 4.*

Menglöþ kvaþ :

48.   ' Vel þú nú kominn !       hefk minn vilja beþit,
      fylgja skal kveþju koss ;
    forkunnar sýn       mun flestan glaþa,
      hverrs hefr viþ annan ást.

49.   Lengi satk       Lyfjabergi á,
      beiþk þin dœgr ok daga :
  nú þat varþ       es ek vætt hefi,
      at aptr kvamt, mögr ! til minna sala.

50.   Þrár hafþar       es ek hef til þíns gamans,
      en þú til míns munar ;
  nú's þat satt,       es vit slíta skulum
      ævi ok aldr saman.'

Menglod:
48. Now welcome art thou ! My will is won;
with greeting comes the kiss.
Never sweeter is sight of heart's desire
than when one brings love to another.

49. Long have I sat on the Hill of Healing,
awaiting thee day by day;
till that I looked for at length is come,
thou art back, youth, here in my halls.

50. Yearnings had I oft for thy heart,
and thou didst long for my love:
now all is made sure, we twain shall share
together the days of time.

# ɦÁRBARÞSLJÓÞ
## GREYBEARD AND ꞇɦOR

### SYNOPSIS

Hárbarþsljóþ is a flyting poem with figures from Norse mythology. Flyting, or fliting, is a contest consisting of the exchange of insults, often conducted in verse, between two parties.

In this poem, the ferryman Hárbarðr (Greybeard) and the god Thor compete in a flyting or verbal contest with one other. Greybeard is rude and obnoxious towards Thor, who is returning, battle-stained and weary, to Asgard from Jötunheim, where he has just been engaged in the never-ending task of fighting the giants.

Greybeard obstructs Thor's way and refuses him passage across a swollen river. Rough in his appearance and harsh in his speech as when he met Allwise the dwarf, straightforward and simple in his thoughts and actions, Thor takes literally the sneer of Greybeard when told that his mother must be dead or she could scarce have thus neglected his appearance. Many of the labours which he proudly boasts and the failures with which he is taunted are well known.

In the course of the poem, Greybeard boasts of his sexual prowess, his magical and tactical abilities, asking Thor about his. Thor responds, telling how he defeated giants. Ultimately, after mocking Thor at length, Greybeard curses him and tells him to walk around.

*Sources: Olive Bray and Wikipedia.*

*Thor Threatens Greybeard*

## HÁRBARÞSLJÓÞ

Þórr fór ór austrvegi ok kom at sundi einu ; öþrum megum sundsins var ferjukarlinn meþ skipit. Þórr kallaþi :

Þórr kvaþ :

1. ' Hverr es sá sveinn sveina,　　es stendr fyr sundit handan ?
'

Ferjukarlinn kvaþ :

2. ' Hverr es sá karl karla,　　es kallar of váginn ? '

*Greybeard mocks Thor*

# HÁRBARÞSLJóÞ

As Thor was journeying from the Eastern Land of the Jötuns he came to a sound. On the other side was a ferryman with his boat.

Thor:
1. What swain of swains art thou who thus
on yonder side of the sound art standing?

Greybeard:
2. Tell me rather what carle of carles
thus calls across the wave.

---

*Prose: The ferryman is presumably Odin in disguise.*

Þórr kvaþ :

3.　' Ferþu mik of sundit !　　　fǿþik þik á morgin :
　　meis hefk á baki　　　verþra matr enn betri.
　　Át ek í hvílþ,　　　áþr ek heiman fór,
　　sildr ok hafra :　　　saþr emk enn þess.'

Ferjukarlinn kvaþ :

4.　' Árligum verkum hrósar þú verþinum ;　veiztattu fyrir görla :
　　döpr eru þín heimkynni,　　　dauþ hykk at þín móþir sé.'

Þórr kvaþ :

5.　' Þat segir þú nú,　　　es hverjum þykkir
　　mest at vita,　　　at mín móþir dauþ sé.'

Ferjukarlinn kvaþ :

6.　' Þeygi es sem þú　　　þrjú bú góþ eigir :
　　berbeinn þú stendr　　　ok hefr brautinga görvi ;
　　þatki at þú hafir brǿkr þínar ! '

Þórr kvaþ :

7.　' Stýrþu hingat eikjunni !　　　ek mun þér stöþna kenna ;
　　eþa hverr á skipit　　　es þú heldr viþ landit ? '

Thor:

3. Row me over! A meal this morn I'll pay thee,
choicer fare thou shalt never find thee.
Here on my back there hangs a basket;
in peace I ate, myself, ere I started,
herrings and goat's flesh, and still am I sated.

Greybeard:

4. As a morning's work thou dost boast thy meal;
but thou art not all forseeing:
filled with care at home are thy kindred,
dead I trow is thy mother.

Thor:

5. Worst of all tidings art thou telling,
when thou sayest me now that dead is my mother.

Greybeard:

6. At least thou lookst not like one who owns
a lot of three fair lands;
bare-legged thou standest, clad like a beggar,
and not even breeks hast thou on.

Thor:

7. Steer the bark hither ! I will show thee a haven.
Who owns yon boat which by the brink thou boldest?

---

3. *Herrings and goat's flesh. For Thor as a fisherman, see Hymiskvipa stanzas 17-25. He usually ate his goats for supper, and restored them to life in the morning. This rendering of 'bafra' seems more probable than the more common alternative oats; for Thor's meal of goat's flesh was famous, and a burlesque like the present poem would be incomplete without some allusion to it.*

Ferjukarlinn kvaþ :

8.  ' Hildolfr sá heitir,      es mik halda bap,
    rekkr enn ráþsvinni,      es býr í Ráþseyjarsundi ;
    baþat hann hlennimenn flytja      eþa hrossa þjófa,
    góþa eina      ok þás ek görva kunna.
    Segþu til nafns þíns,      ef þú vill of sundit fara.

Þórr kvaþ :

9.  ' Segja munk til nafns míns,      þót ek sekr seak,
    ok til alls öþlis :      ek em Óþins sunr,
    Meila bróþir,      en Magna faþir,
    þrúþvaldr goþa ;      viþ þór knáttu hér dœma.
    Hins viljak nú spyrja,      hvat þú heitir.'

Ferjukarlinn kvaþ :

10.  ' Hárbarþr ek heiti.      hylk of nafn sjaldan.'

Þórr kvaþ :

11.  ' Hvat skaltu of nafn hylja, nema þú sakar eigir ? '

Hárbarþr kvaþ :

12.  ' En þót ek sakar eiga,      fyr slíkum sem þú est
     munk forþa þó      fjörvi mínu,
     nema ek feigr sé.'

Greybeard:

8. Battle-wolf bade me wise-counselled hero,
who dwells in Counsel-Isle Sound
to keep it and ferry nor rogues nor robbers
but the worthy and those I know well.
Now shalt thou tell me thy name if thou fain
wouldst hither fare o'er the flood.

Thor:

9. Were I outlawed, yet my name would I tell thee,
eke my race. I am son of Odin,
the brother of Meili, and father of Magni,
gods' Strength-wielder; thou speak'st with Thor.
Fain would I know now thy name and kinship.

Greybeard:

10. They call me Grey-beard; 'tis seldom I care
to hide my own name from any.

Thor:

11. Wherefore shouldst thou not show thy name,
except thou have cause of strife with thy foemen?

Greybeard:

12. Have I cause, 'gainst such as thee will I hold
my life unless I be doomed.

---

8. *Battle-wolf, meaning himself, the patron of war.*
9. *Meili: Nothing is known concerning this son of Odin.*
*Magni or Might.*
10. *Greybeard: Odin's wonted disguise was that of a Grey
-bearded old man.*

Þórr kvaþ :

13. ' Harm ljótan      mér þikkir í þuí at vaþa,
of váginn til þín      ok væta ögur minn ;
skyldak launa kögursveini þínum      kanginyrþi,
ef ek komumk of sundit.'

Hárbarþr kvaþ :

14. ' Hér munk standa      ok þín heþan bíþa ;
fanntattu mann enn harþara      at Hrungni dauþan.'

Þórr kvaþ :

15. ' Hins vildu nú geta,      es vit Hrungnir deildum,
sá enn stórúþgi jötunn,      es ór steini vas höfuþit á ;
þó létk hann falla      ok fyrir hníga.—
Hvat vanntu þá meþan, Hárbarþr ? '

Hárbarþr kvaþ :

16. ' Vask meþ Fjölvari      fimm vetr alla
í eyju þeiri      es Algrœn heitir ;
vega vér þar knáttum      ok val fella,
margs at freista,      mans at kosta.'

Þórr kvaþ :

17. ' Hversu snúnuþu yþr konur yþrar ? '

Hárbarþr kvaþ :

18. ' Sparkar áttum vér konur,      ef oss at spökum yrþi ;
horskar áttum vér konur,      ef oss hollar væri :
þær ór sandi      síma undu
ok ór dali djúpum      grund of grófu
Varþk þeim einn öllum      öfri at ráþum,
hvíldak hjá þeim systrum sjau
ok hafþak geþ þeira allt ok gaman.
Hvat vanntu þá meþan, Þórr ? '

Thor:

13. Sore shame 'twould be to wet my burden
in wading thus thro' the water toward thee.
Those mocking words would I pay thee, mannikin,
could I but reach yon side of the sound now.

Greybeard:

14. Here I stand and await thee !
Ne'er metst thou with sturdier hero since Hrungnir was slain,

Thor.:

15. Dost tell how we once fought, I and Hrungnir,
that hard-hearted giant whose head was rock-hewn?
Yet did he fall and bow before me.
What, the while, wast thou working, Greybeard?

Greybeard:

16. I dwelt with Wary-wise five whole winters
in the island called All-green.
Battles we fought there and felled the doomed,
much daring, and wiling women.

Thor:

17. Got ye weal or woe from those wives of your winning?

Greybeard:

18. Merry wives had we owned had they borne them wisely;
shrewd wives, had they shown them true:
all out of sand they spun them ropes
and dug from the deep dales earth.
Yet slyest was I, who with seven sisters slept,
and won all their liking and love.
What, the while, wast thou working, Thunderer?'

---

14. *Hrungnir. The slaying of this giant was one of Thor's famous deeds.*

16. *Wary-wise, unknown.*

Þórr kvaþ :

19. ' Ek drap Þjaza,       enn þrúþmóþga jötun,
upp ek varp augum      Alvalda sunar
á þann enn heiþa himin ;
þau eru merki mest      minna verka,
þaus allir menn síþan of sé.
Hvat vanntu meþan, Hárbarþr ? '

Hárbarþr kvaþ :

20. ' Miklar manvélar      ek hafþa viþ myrkriþur,
þás ek vélta þær frá verum ;
harþan jötun       hugþak Hlébarþ vesa :
gaf hann mér gambantein,
en ek vélta hann ór viti.'

Þórr kvaþ :

21. ' Illum huga launaþir þú þá góþar gjafar.'

Hárbarþr kvaþ :

22. ' Þat hefr eik       es af annarri skefr :
of sik es hverr í slíku.
Hvat vanntu meþan, Þórr ? '

Þórr kvaþ :

23. ' Ek vas austr       ok jötna barþak
brúþir bölvísar      es til bjargs gengu :
mikil mundi ætt jötna,     ef allir lifþi,
vætr mundi manna      und miþgarþi.
Hvat vanntu meþan, Hárbarþr ? '

Hárbarþr kvaþ :

24. ' Vask á Vallandi      ok vígum fylgþak,
attak jöfrum,      en aldri sættak.
Óþinn á jarla      þás í val falla,
en Þórr á þræla kyn.'

Thor:
19. Slew I Thiazi, son of All-wielder,
strong-souled Jötun, and flung his eyes up
where men shall behold in the shining heavens
the tokens great of my deeds hereafter.
What, the while, wast thou working, Greybeard?

Greybeard:
20. I had dealings in love with the dark witch-riders,
from their husbands I wiled them away:
stout giant seemed Hlebard till his wand he. gave me
and I wiled him out of his wits.

Thor:
21. Then spite for those goodly gifts thou gavest?

Greybeard:
22. Let one oak take what it scrapes off another,
and let each man seek his own.
What, the while, wast thou working, Thunderer?

Thor:
23. Slew I the evil wives of Jötuns,
far in the east, . as they fled to the mountains:
were they all left in the land of the living,
huge would have been now the host of giants,
and never a man would there be in Midgarth.
What, the while, wast thou working, Greybeard?

Greybeard.:
24. In the Land of the Slain I warred and stirred up
princes to strife without peace.
Odin has earls who fall on the battlefield,
Thor has the race of thralls.

Þórr kvaþ :

25. ' Ójafnt skipta      es þú mundir meþ ásum liþi,
ef þú ættir vilgi mikils vald.'

Hárbarþr kvaþ :

26. ' Þórr á afl œrit,      en etki hjarta :
af hrǽzlu ok hugbleyþi      vas þér í hanzka troþit
[ok þóttiska þú þá Þorr vesa ;]
hvárki þú þá þorþir      fyr hrǽzlu þinni
hnjósa ne físa,      svát Fjalarr heyrþi.'

Þórr kvaþ :

27. ' Hárbarþr enn ragi !      ek munda þik í hel drepa,
ef ek mǽtta seilask of sund.'

Hárbarþr kvaþ :

28. ' Hvat skyldir þú of sund seilask,      es sakar'u alls öngvar ?
Hvat vanntu þá, Þórr ? '

Þórr kvaþ :

29. ' Ek vas austr      ok ána varþak,
þás mik sóttu      þeir Svárangs synir ;
grjóti þeir mik börþu,      gagni urþu þeir þó lítt fegnir,
urþu þeir mik fyrri      friþar at biþja.
Hvat vanntu þá meþan, Hárbarþr ? '

Thor:
25. Unfairly wouldst thou divide the slain
among gods if power too great were given thee !

Greybeard:
26. Strength enough has the Thunderer, nought of daring;
from fear and faintness of heart
thou wert thrust, I ween, in a glove-thumb once,
and scarce couldst deem thyself Thor :
lest Fjalar should hear thee, for fright thou durst not
sneeze nor stir a hair.

Thor.
27. Greybeard, thou craven ! Could I but stretch
o'er the sound I would smite thee soon into Hel-home.

Greybeard.
28. Why shouldst thou stretch o'er the sound and smite me?
No reason have we for wrath.
What, the while, wast thou working, Thunderer?

Thor.
29. Eastward held I the flood of Ifing
against the sons of Svarang the Whelmer;
with stones they beset me but small gain got they
and first were found to ask peace of foemen.
What, the while, wast thou working, Greybeard?

---

26. *Fjalar: a giant, otherwise known as Utgard-loki.*
*Glove-thumb: this refers to the time Thor and his comrades took*
*shelter in the thumb of Fjalar's glove.*
29. *Ifing: The name is not mentioned in the text, but it may be*
*assumed that the river is that which flowed between the realms*
*of gods and giants.*

Hárbarþr kvaþ :

30. ' Ek vas austr     ok viþ einhverja dœmþak,
lék ek viþ ena línhvítu     ok launþing háþak,
gladdak ena gollbjörtu,     gamni mær unþi.'

Þórr kvaþ :

31. ' Góþ áttuþ ér mankynni þar þá.'

Hárbarþr kvaþ :

32. ' Liþs þíns værak þá þurfi, þórr !     et ek helda þeiri enni
línhvítu mey.'

Þórr kvaþ :

33. ' Ek munda þér þá þat veita,     ef ek viþr of kvæmumk.'

Hárbarþr kvaþ :

34. ' Ek munda þér þá trua,    nema þú mik í trygþ véltir.'

Þórr kvaþ :

35. ' Emkat ek sá hælbítr     sem húþskór forn á vár.'

Hárbarþr kvaþ :

36. ' Hvat vanntu meþan, þórr ? '

Þórr kvaþ ;

37. ' Brúþir berserkja     barþak í Hléseyju,
þær höfþu verst unnit     vilta þjóþ alla.'

Hárbarþr kvaþ :

38. ' Klæki vanntu þá, þórr !     es þú á konum barþir.'

Greybeard.
30. In the East I dallied with one, my chosen;
I played with that linen-fair lass,
kept secret trysting, and gladdened the gold-bright
maiden, merry in the game.

Thor.
31. Glad meetings of love had ye there with maidens?

Greybeard.
32. Need had I then of help from Thor,
to have kept that linen-fair lass.

Thor.
33. Fain would I give it thee could I but get there.

Greybeard.
34. Fain would I now put trust in thy faith,
wert thou not wont to betray me.

Thor.
35. No heelbiter I, like an old shoe in spring-time!

Greybeard.
36. What, the while, wast thou working, Thunderer?

Thor.
37. Slew I berserk-wives in the Isle of Ægir;
vile things wrought they, all men-folk wiling.

Greybeard.
38. A base deed then wast thou doing, Thunderer
waging war with women!

Þórr kvaþ :

39. ' Vargynjur váru þǽr,      en varla konur ;
skeldu skip mitt      es ek skorþat hafþak ;
œgþu mér ïarnlurki,      en eltu þjalfa.
Hvat vanntu meþan, Hárbarþr ? '

Hárbarþr kvaþ :

40. ' Ek vask í hernum      es hingat görþisk
gnǽfa gunnfana,      geir at rjóþa.'

Þórr kvaþ :

41. ' Þess vildu nú geta, es þú fórt oss óljúfan at bjóþa.'

Hárbarþr kvaþ :

42. ' Bœta skal þér þat þá      munda baugi,
sem jafnendr unnu      þeirs okkr vilja sǽtta.'

Þórr kvaþ :

43. ' Hvar namtu      þessi en hnœfiligu orþ,
es ek heyrþa aldri      in hnœfiligri ? '

Hárbarþr kvaþ :

44. ' Nam ek at mönnum      þeim enum aldrœnum
es bua í heimis haugum.'

Þórr kvaþ :

45. ' Þá gefr þú      gott nafn dysjum,
es þú kallar þǽr heimis hauga.'

Hárbarþr kvaþ :

46. ' Svá dœmi ek of slíkt far.'

Thor:

39. She- wolves were they, and scarcely women.
My ships laid up on the shore they shattered,
with clubs they threatened me, Thialfi chased they.
What, the while, wast thou working, Greybeard?

Greybeard.

40. To raise the war flag and redden the spear,
hither I came in the host.

Thor.

41. Wouldst tell how with hate thou cam'st to harm us?

Greybeard.

42. Let a ring make atonement as the daysmen meted,
who sought to set us at peace.

Thor:

43. Where didst thou learn those scornful speeches?
Never were words more wounding said me.

Greybeard.

44. I learnt them once from ancient beings
who dwell in the hills of home.

Thor.

45. Fair name for cairns to call them home-hills !

Greybeard.

46. 'Tis even as I think concerning such things.

---

44. Hills of home, the ancestral graves.

Þórr kvaþ :

47. ' Orþkringi þín      mun þér illa koma,
ef ek ræþ á vág at vaþa ;
ulfi hæra      hykk þik œpa munu,
ef þú hlýtr af hamri högg.'

Hárbarþr kvaþ :

48. ' Sif á hór heima,      hans mundu fund vilja,
þann mundu þrek drýgja,      þat es þér skyldara.'

Þórr kvaþ :

49. ' Mælir þú at munns ráþi,    svát mér skyldi verst þykkja,
halr enn hugblauþi :      hykk at þú ljúgir.'

Hárbarþr kvaþ :

50. ' Satt hykk mik segja ;      seinn estu at för þinni ;
langt mundir þú nú kominn, Þórr !   ef þú litum fœrir.'

Þórr kvaþ :

51. ' Hárbarþr enn ragi !   heldr hefr þú nú mik dvalþan.'

Hárbarþr kvaþ :

52. ' Ásaþórs      hugþak aldri mundu
glepja farhirþi farar.'

Þórr kvaþ :

53. ' Ráþ munk þér nú ráþa :      ró þú hingat bátinum ;
hættum hœtingi,      hittu föþur Magna ! '

Thor.
47. Sorely thy skill in words should serve thee,
could I but wade to thee through the water.
Louder, I ween, than a wolf wilt thou howl
if haply thou get'st a stroke from my hammer.

Greybeard.
48. Sif has a lover, thy wife at home,
art thou not eager to meet him?
That a deed of daring now must thou do,
a work which well befits thee.

Thor.
49. Faint-heart ! Speak'st thou as worst meseems,
by the cojunsel of thy lips; for I trow thou liest!

Greybeard:
50. Truly I ween that my words are spoken:
too slow art thou in thy travelling.
Far on thy way hadst thou fared now, Thor,
if thou hadst but gone in disguise.

Thor:
51. Greybeard, thou craven ! Too long thou delay'st me.

Greybeard:
52. I had ne'er weened boatman would hinder the way
of Thor, the Thunderer of gods.

Thor:
53. Now will I counsel thee; come in thy boat hither;
fetch Magni's father, and cease we from mocking.

---

*48. Sif's lover, is Loki.*

Hárbarþr kvaþ :

54. ' Farþu firr sundi !      þér skal fars synja.'

Þórr kvaþ :

55. ' Vísa þú mér nú leiþina, alls þú vill mik eigi of váginn
ferja ! '

Hárbarþr kvaþ :

56. ' Lítit es at synja,      langt es at fara :
stund es til stokksins,      önnur til steinsins,
haltu svá til vinstra vegsins,      unz þú hittir Verland.
Þar mun Fjörgyn      hitta þór sun sinn
ok mun hón kenna hánum áttunga brautir      til Óþins
landa.'

Þórr kvaþ :

57. ' Mun ek taka þangat í dag ? '

Hárbarþr kvaþ :

58. ' Taka viþ víl ok erfiþi
at uppvesandi sólu, es ek get þána.'

Þórr kvaþ :

59. ' Skamt mun nú mál okkat,      alls þú mér skœtingu einni
svarar ;
launa munk þér farsynjun,      ef vit finnumsk í sinn annat.'

Hárbarþr kvaþ :

60. ' Farþu nú þars þik haft allan gramir ! '

Greybeard:
54. Hie thee hence away from the sound!
The ferry to thee is refused.

Thor:
55. Show me a path then, since thou wilt not
ferry me over the flood betwixt us.

Greybeard:
56. Tis little to withhold, 'tis far to fare
a while to the stock and the stone:
thus shalt thou hold to the left-hand path,
till thou light on the Land of Men;
there will Earth meet her son and show him the way
of his race to the realms of Odin.

Thor:
57. Shall I to-day reach the dwellings of Odin?

Greybeard:
58. With weariness and toil when the dew is wet
at sunrise, I ween, thou wilt win them.

Thor:
59. Short be our speech now, with but jeering thou answerest.
When we meet next I'll pay thee for denying me passage.

Greybeard:
60. Hie thee hence away where the fiends
may seize thee, body and soul !

---

56. *Earth, or Jord, who is here called Fjbrgyn, is one of Odin's
wives.*
58. *When the dew is wet: about that time,.*

# RIGSÞULA
## THE SONG OF RIG

SYNOPSIS

Once of old the god Heimdal, who was not wont to leave the seat where he kept watch in heaven, came to earth as a kingly being called Ríg. He was walking along the shore and came to a farm-hut owned by Ái (great-grandfather) and Edda (great-grandmother). They offered him shelter and poor, rough food for a meal.

That night Ríg sleeps between the pair in their bed and then departs. Nine months later, Edda gives birth to a son who is svartan (dark). They name him Þræll (Thrall: serf, or slave).

Thrall grows up strong but ugly. He marries a woman named Thír (slave girl or bondswoman), and they have twelve sons and nine daughters with names mostly suggesting ugliness and squatness. They become the race of serfs.

Traveling further, Ríg comes across a pleasant house where a farmer/craftsman, Afi (grandfather) lives with his wife Amma (grandmother). This couple gives him good food and also lets him sleep between them.

Nine months later, a son, Churl (karl, or freeman) is born, who has a ruddy complexion. Churl marries a woman named Snör (daughter-in-law), and they have twelve sons and ten daughters with names mostly suggesting a neat appearance or being of good quality. One of the names is smiðr (smith). These become the ancestors of free farmers, craftsmen and herdsmen.

Traveling further, Ríg arrives at a mansion inhabited by Faðir (Father) and Móðir (Mother). They give him excellent food served splendidly, and nine months later, Móðir gives birth to a beautiful baby named Earl (a nobleman), whose hair is blond and who is bleikr (bright white in color).

When Earl grows up and begins to handle weapons and to use hawks, hounds, and horses, Ríg reappears, claims him as his son, gives him his own name of Ríg, makes him his heir, teaches him runes, and advises him to seek lordship.

Thus Heimdal is the father of the three classes of mankind as conceived by the poet, but kings especially have their right to claim descent from the god.

The first-born son (stanza 6) is Thrall. The Old Norse thralls were serfs, little better than slaves, who could be sold at the will of their masters. In the Viking period they were often prisoners of war. It was sometimes possible for them to obtain freedom, but never any share in the government, or influence in the popular assembly. As their names indicate, their social condition and occupations were very low. Great-grandfather's table is set with coarse brown bread and broth, which are the best that he can lay before his guest.

In the home of Grandfather and Grandmother there is more comfort; their appearance and clothing are neat, and even ornamental; their work and that of their children requires skill; the son who is born to them has a fair and ruddy skin, his bride does not travel on foot, and she is graced by a wedding veil.

Mother and father are found (stanza 21) in a lordlier dwelling; she has no task but to admire and adorn her fair white neck and arms; his work is the honourable pursuit of warfare, and the fashioning of weapons. Their son, Earl, with bright eyes and shining hair, lives the glorious life of a conqueror, distributing spoils and wealth among his dependents. He resembles one of the great lords who are mentioned in Hyndla's Lay, or those who give rise to the epithets used by poets, 'the ring-breaker' and 'gold-giver.'

Through warfare Earl becomes lord of eighteen homesteads with much wealth besides. He also gains the hand of Erna (Brisk), daughter of Hersir (lord). Erna bears eleven sons to Ríg-Earl but no daughters. All the sons are given high-sounding names, mostly meaning 'son.' They are destined to become the ancestors of the warrior nobility, and are required only to inherit the rights and follow the customs which belong to their noble birth.

But Kon, the youngest, is the best of them. He alone learns rune-craft as well as other magic, and is able to understand the speech of birds, to quench fire, and to heal minds. He also has the strength of eight normal men.

Kon becomes a king and is given a higher heritage, not of his father, but from Ríg, who bestows his own name upon him, and endows him with the wisdom of gods. He shares their powers, he learns to understand and use the sacred runes, he interprets nature, and is alone the true son of Heimdal and the father of all kings.

One day, when Kon is riding through the forest hunting and snaring birds, a crow speaks to him and suggests he would win more if he stopped hunting mere birds and rode to battle against foemen; that he should seek the halls of Dan and Danp, who were wealthier than he. At that point the poem abruptly cuts off.

*Sources: Olive Bray and Wikipedia*

*Ríg in Great-grandfather's Cottage*

# RIGSÞULA

Svá segja menn í fornum sögum, at einhverr af ásum, sá
er Heimdallr hét, fór ferþar sinnar ok fram meþ sjóvarströndu
nökkurri, kom at einum húsabœ ok nefndiz Rígr. Eptir þeiri
sögu er kvæþi þetta :

1. Ár kvöþu ganga      grœnar brautir
   öflgan ok aldinn    ás kunnigan,
   ramman ok röskvan      Ríg stíganda,

   . . . . . . . . . . . . . . . . .

2. Gekk meirr at þat      miþrar brautar ;
   kvam hann at húsi,      hurþ vas á gætti ;
   inn nam ganga,      eldr vas á golfi,
   hjón sátu þar      hár at arni.
   Ai ok Edda      aldinfalda.

*The Crow Warns Kon*

# RIGSÞULA

It is told in the sagas of old .time that a certain god called Heimdal was passing on. his way along the sea shore when he came to a farm. He entered, calling himself Ríg according to the story which thus relates :

## I. THE BIRTH OF THRALL

1. Once walked, 'tis said, mighty and ancient,
strong and vigorous, the green ways along,
a god most glorious; striding, Ríg.

2. Ever on he went in the middle of the way,
till he came to a house with door unclosed.
He entered straight; there was fire on the floor
and a hoary couple sitting by the hearth,
Great-grandfather and mother in ancient guise.

---

*Ríg or King. A Celtic word.*

3.   Rígr kunni þeim      ráp at segja,
     meirr settisk hann     miþra fletja,
     en á hlip hvára        hjón salkynna.

4.   Þá tók Edda       ökkvinn hleif,
     þungan ok þykkvan,     þrunginn sápum ;
     bar meirr at þat       miþra skutla,
     soþ vas í bolla,        setti á bjóþ.

5. (4)  Reis upp þaþan,      rézk at sofna ;
 (5)  Rígr kunni þeim      ráp at segja,
      meirr lagþisk hann    miþrar rekkju,
      en á hliþ hvára       hjón salkynna.
      Þar vas at þat        þriar nætr saman,
      gekk meirr at þat      miþrar brautar,
      liþu meirr at þat      mánuþr niu.

6.   Jóþ ól Edda,       jósu vatni,
     hörvi svartan        hétu Þræl.
     Hann nam at vaxa      ok vel dafna,
     vas þar á höndum      hrokkit skinn,
     kropnir knuar,        . . . . . .
     fingr digrir,         fúlligt andlit,
     lútr hryggr,         langir hælar.
 (7)  Nam meirr at þat      megins of kosta,
      bast at binda,        byrþar görva,
      bar heim at þat       hrís görstan dag.

7.   Þar kvam at garþi     gengilbeina,
     örr vas á iljum,      armr sólbrunninn,
     niþrbjúgt es nef,      nefndisk Þír.

3. Well knew Ríg how to give them counsel,
he sat him down in the middle of the floor,
with the home-folk twain upon either side.

4. Great-grandmother fetched a coarse-baked loaf,
all heavy and thick and crammed with husk:
she bore it forth in the middle of the dish,
with broth in a bowl, and laid the board.

5. Thence Ríg uprose, prepared to rest;
well he knew how to give them counsel
he laid him down in the middle of the bed
and the home-folk twain upon either side.
Thus he tarried three nights together,
then on he strode in the middle of the road
while thrice three moons were gliding by.

6. Great-grandmother bore a swarthy boy;
with water they sprinkled him, called him Thrall.
Forthwith he grew and well he throve,
but rough were his hands with wrinkled skin,
with knuckles knotty and fingers thick;
his face was ugly, his back was humpy,
his heels were long. . .
' Straightway 'gan he to prove his strength,
with bast a-binding loads a-making,
he bore home faggots the livelong day.

7. There came to the dwellings a wandering maid,
with wayworn feet, and sunburned arms,
with down-bent nose, the Bond-maid named.

---

*6. Thrall, the lowest class, who were little better than slaves.*
*7. Wandering. The other brides (stanzas 18 and 30) came not on*
*foot, but driving to their husbands.*

8.   Meirr settisk hón      miþra fletja,
       sat hjá henni      sunr húss,
       rœddu ok rýndu,      rekkju görþu
       þræll ok Þír      þrungin dœgr.

9. (8)   Börn álu þau,      bjuggu ok unþu ;
       hykk at héti      Hreimr ok Fjósnir,
       Klúrr ok Kleggi,      Kefsir, Fúlnir,
       Drumbr, Digraldi,      Dröttr ok Hösvir,
       Lútr, Leggjaldi :      lögþu garþa,
       akra töddu,      unnu at svínum,
       geita gættu,      grófu torf.

10. (9)   Dœtr váru þær      Drumba ok Kumba,
       Ökkvinkalfa      ok Arinnefja,
       Ysja ok Ambátt,      Eikintjasna,
       Tötrughypja      ok Trönubeina :
       þaþan eru komnar      þræla ættir.

11. (10)   Gekk Rígr at þat      réttar brautir ;
       kvam hann at höllu,      hurþ vas á skíþi ;
       inn nam ganga,      eldr vas á golfi :
       Afi ok Amma      áttu hús.

12. (10)   Hjón sátu þar,      heldu á sýslu :
       maþr telgþi þar      meiþ til rifjar ;
       vas skegg skapat,      skör vas fýr enni,
       skyrtu þröngva,      skokkr vas á golfi.

13. (11)   Sat þar kona,      sveigþi rokk,
       breiddi faþm,      bjó til váþar ;
   (12)   sveigr vas á höfþi,      smokkr vas á bringu,
       dúkr vas á halsi,      dvergar á öxlum.

8. She sat her down in the middle of the floor;
beside her sat the son of the house:
they chatted and whispered, their bed preparing
Thrall and Bond-maid the long day through.

9. Joyous lived they and reared their children.
Thus they called them: Brawler, Cowherd,
Boor and Horsefly, Lewd and Lustful,
Stout and Stumpy, Sluggard, Swarthy,
Lout and Leggy. They fashioned fences,
they dunged the meadows, swine they herded,
goats they tended and turf they dug.

10. Daughters were there, Loggv and Cloggy,
Lumpy-leggy, and Eagle-nose,
Whiner, Bondwoman, Oaken-peggy,
Tatter-coat and the Crane-shanked maid.
Thence are come the generations of thralls.

## II THE BIRTH OF CHURL

11. Ever on went Ríg the straight roads along
till he came to a dwelling with door unclosed;
he entered straight; there was fire on the floor;
Grandfather and Grandmother owned the house.

12. The home-folk sat there hard aworking;
by them stood on the floor a box;
hewed the husband wood for a warp-beam;
trim his beard and the locks o'er his brow,
but mean and scanty the shirt he wore.

13. The wife sat by him plying her distaff,
swaying her arms to weave the cloth,
with snood on her head and smock on her breast,
studs on her shoulders, and scarf on her neck.

14.    Rígr kunni þeim       ráþ at segja,
       meirr settisk hann       miþra fletja,
       en á hliþ hvára       hjón salkynna.

15.    Þá tók Amma      . . . . . .

       . . . . . .        . . . .
       fram setti hón       fulla skutla,
       vas kalfr soþinn       krása baztr.
       Reis frá borþi,       rézk at sofna,
       Rígr kunni þeim       ráþ at segja,
       meirr lagþisk hann       miþrar rekkju,
       en á hliþ hvára       hjón salkynna.

16.    Þar vas at þat       þriar nǽtr saman,
       gekk meirr at þat       miþrar brautar,
       liþu meirr at þat       mánuþr niu.

17. (15)   Jóþ ól Amma,       jósu vatni,
          kölluþu Karl ;       kona sveip ripti
          rauþan ok rjóþan,       riþuþu augu.
          Hann nam at vaxa       ok vel dafna,
          öxn nam temja,       arþr at görva,
          hús at timbra       ok hlöþur smíþa,
          karta at görva       ok keyra plóg.

18. (16)   Heim óku þá       hanginluklu,
          geitakyrtlu,       giptu Karli ;
          Snör heitir sú,       settisk und ripti,
          bjuggu hjón,       bauga deildu,
          breiddu blǽjur       ok bú görþu.

14. Well knew Ríg how to give them counsel;
he sat him down in the middle of the floor,
and the home-folk twain upon either side.

15. Grandmother set forth plenteous dishes;
cooked was the calf, of dainties best.
Thence Ríg uprose prepared to rest.
Well he knew how to give them counsel
he laid him down in the middle of the bed
and the home-folk twain upon either side.

16. Thus he tarried three nights together,
then on he strode in the middle of the road
while thrice three moons were gliding by.

17. A child had Grandmother, Churl they called him,
and sprinkled with water and swathed in linen,
rosy and ruddy, with sparkling eyes.

He grew and throve, and forthwith 'gan he
to break in oxen, to shape the harrow,
to build him houses and barns to raise him,
to fashion carts and follow the plough.

18. Then home they drove with a key-hung maiden
in goat-skin kirtle, named Daughter-in-Law.
They wed her to Churl in her bridal linen:
the twain made ready, their wealth a-sharing,
kept house together, and joyous lived.

---

*17. Churl or karl, the free-born peasant proprietor.*

19. (16)  Börn ólu þau,      bjuggu ok unþu ;
          hét Halr ok Drengr,      Hölþr, þegn ok Smiþr,
          Breiþr, Bóndi,      Bundinskeggi,
          Bui ok Boddi,      Brattskeggr ok Seggr.

20. (16)  Enn hétu svá      öþrum nöfnum :
          Snót, Brúþr, Svanni,      Svarri, Sprakki,
          Fljóþ, Sprund ok Víf,      Feima, Ristill :
          þaþan eru komnar      karla ǽttir.


21. (17)  Gekk Rígr þaþan      réttar brautir,
          kvam hann at sal,      suþr horfþu dyrr ;
          vas hurp hnigin,      hringr vas í gǽtti,
          gekk inn at þat :      golf vas straït.
          Sátu hjón,      söusk í augu,
          Faþir ok Móþir,      fingrum at leika.
          Sat húsgumi      ok snöri streng,
          alm of bendi,      örvar skepti ;
          en húskona      hugþi at örmum,
          strauk of ripti,      sterti ermar,
          keistr vas faldr,      kinga á bringu,
          síþar slœþur      serk bláfaan,
          brún bjartari,      brjóst ljósara,
          hals hvítari      hreinni mjöllu.

22. (18)  Rígr kunni þeim      ráþ at segja,
          meirr settisk hann      miþra fletja,
          en á hlip hvára      hjón salkynna.

19. Children reared they thus they called them:
Youth and Hero, Thane, Smith, Yeoman,
Broad-limb, Peasant, Sheaf-beard, Neighbour,
Farmer, Speaker and Stubbly-beard.

20. By other names were the daughters called:
Dame, Bride, Lady, Gay, and Gaudy,
Maid, Wife, Woman, Bashful, Slender.
Thence are come the kindreds of churls.

### III THE BIRTH OF EARL

21. Still on went Ríg the straight roads along
till he came to a hall whose gates looked south.
Pushed was the door to, a ring in the post set:
he forthwith entered the rush-strewn room.
Each other eyeing, the home-folk sat there
Father and Mother, twirling their fingers.
There was the husband, string a-twining,
shafting arrows and shaping bows:
and there was the wife o'er her fair arms wondering,
smoothing her linen, stretching her sleeves.
A high-peaked coif and a breast-brooch wore she,
trailing robes and a blue-tinged sark.
Her brow was brighter, her breast was fairer,
her throat was whiter than driven snow.

22. Well knew Ríg how to give them counsel;
he sat him down in the middle of the floor,
and the home-folk twain upon either side.

23. (19)  Þa tók Móþir          merkþan dúk,
          hvítan af hörvi,       hulþi bjóþ ;
          hón tók at þat         hleifa þunna,
          hvíta af hveiti,       ok hulþi dúk.
          Fram setti hón         fulla skutla
          silfri varþa,      *setti* á bjóþ,
          faïn fleski,       fogla steikþa ;
          vín vas í könnu,       varþir kalkar,
          drukku ok dœmþu,       dagr vas á sinnum.

24. (21)  Rígr kunni þeim        ráþ at segja,
          reis hann at þat,      rekkju görþi ;
          meirr lagþisk hann     miþrar rekkju,
          en á hliþ hvára        hjón salkynna.

25. (22)  Þar vas at þat         þriar nætr saman,
          gekk meirr at þat      miþrar brautar,
          liþu meirr at þat      mánuþr niu.

26. (23)  Svein ól Móþir,        silki vafþi,
          jósu vatni,       Jarl létu heita ;
          bleikt vas hár,        bjartir vangar,
          ötul váru augu         sem yrmlingi.

27. (24)  Upp óx þar        Jarl á fletjum,
          lind nam skelfa        leggja strengi,
          alm at beygja,         örvar skepta,
          fleini fleygja,        frökkur dýja,
          hestum ríþa,           hundum verpa,
          sverþum bregþa,        sund at fremja.

23. Then took Mother a figured cloth,
white, of linen, and covered the board;
thereafter took she a fine-baked loaf,
white, of wheat and covered the cloth:
next she brought forth plenteous dishes,
set with silver, and spread the board
with brown-fried bacon and roasted birds.
There was wine in a vessel and rich-wrought goblets;
they drank and revelled while day went by.

24 Well knew Ríg how to give them counsel;
he rose ere long and prepared his couch:
he laid him down in the middle of the bed,
and the home-folk twain upon either side.

25. Thus he tarried three nights together;
then on he strode in the middle of the road
while thrice three moons were gliding by.

26. Then a boy had Mother; she swathed him in silk,
and with water sprinkled him; called him Earl.
Light were his locks, and fair his cheeks,
flashing his eyes like a serpent's shone.

27. Grew Earl forthwith in the halls and 'gan
to swing the shield, to fit the string,
to bend the bow, to shaft the arrow,
to hurl the dart, to shake the spear,
to ride the horse, to loose the hounds,
to draw the sword, and to swim the stream.

28. (25-27)   Kvam þar ór runni      Rígr gangandi,

Rígr gangandi,      rúnar kendi ;

sitt gaf heiti,      sun kvezk eiga,

þann baþ eignask      óþalvöllu,

óþalvöllu,      aldnar bygþir.

29. (28)   Reiþ meirr þaþan      myrkvan viþ,

hélug fjöll,      unz at höllu kvam.

Skapt nam dýja      skelfþi lind,

hesti hleypþi      ok hjörvi brá ;

víg nam vekja,      völl nam rjóþa,

val nam fella,      vá til landa.

(29)   Réþ einn at þat      átján buum,

(30)   auþ nam skipta,      öllum veita :

meiþmar ok mösma,      mara svangrifja ;

hringum hreytti,      hjó sundr baug.

30. (31)   Óku ǽrir      úrgar brautir,

kvámu at höllu      þars Hersir bjó ;

mey átti hann      mjófingraþa,

hvíta ok horska :      hétu Ernu.

31. (32)   Báþu hennar      ok heim óku,

giptu Jarli,      gekk und líni ;

saman bjuggu þau      ok sér unþu,

ǽttir jóku      ok aldrs nutu.

28. Forth from the thicket came Ríg a-striding,
Ríg a-striding, and taught him runes,
his own name gave him, as son he claimed him,
and bade him hold the ancestral fields,
the ancestral fields and the ancient home.

29. Then on rode Earl through the murky wood,
through the rimy fells till he reached a hall.
His shaft he shook, his shield he brandished,
his steed he galloped, his sword he drew;
war he wakened, the field he reddened,
the doomed he slew, and won him lands
till alone he ruled over eighteen halls.
Gold he scattered and gave to all men
treasures and trinkets and slender-ribbed horses;
wealth he strewed and sundered rings.

30. Along dewy roads his messengers drove
till the hall they reached where Ruler dwelt.
A daughter owned he, dainty fingered,
fair and skilful, Erna called.

31. They wooed her and brought her home a-driving;
to Earl they wed her in veil fine- woven :
husband and wife lived happy together,
their children waxed and life enjoyed.

---

*30. Erna. No satisfactory meaning has been suggested for this name.*

32. (33)  Burr vas énn élzti,      en Barn annat,
          Jóþ ok Aþal,       Arfi, Mögr,
          Niþr ok Niþjungr      (námu leika)
          Sunr ok Sveinn      (sund ok tafl) ;
          Kundr hét einn,      Konr vas enn yngsti.

33. (34)  Upp óxu þar      Jarli bornir,
          hesta tömþu      hlífar bendu,
          skeyti skófu,      skelfþu aska.
          En Konr ungr      kunni rúnar,
          æfinrúnar      ok aldrrúnar ;
          meirr kunni hann      mönnum bjarga,
          eggjar deyfa,      ægi lægja.
          Klök nam fogla,      kyrra elda,
          sefa of svefja,      sorgir lægja ;
          afl ok eljun      átta manna.

34. (34)  Hann viþ Ríg Jarl      rúnar deildi,
          brögþum beitti      ok betr kunni ;
          þá öþlaþisk      ok eiga gat
          Rígr at heita,      rúnar kunna.

## IV THE BIRTH OF KING

32. Heir was the eldest, Bairn the second,
Babe, Successor, Inheritor, Boy,
Descendent, Offspring, Son, Youth, Kinsman;
Kon the kingly was youngest born.

33. Forthwith grew up the sons of Earl;
games they learned, and sports and swimming,
taming horses, round shields bending,
war shafts smoothing. ash spears shaking;
but King the youngest alone knew runes,
runes eternal and runes of life.
Yet more he knew, how to shelter men,
to blunt the sword-edge and calm the sea:
he learnt bird language, to quench the fire flame,
heal all sorrows and soothe the heart;
strength and might of eight he owned.

34. Then he strove in runes with Ríg, the Earl,
crafty wiles he used and won,
so gained his heritage, held the right thus
Ríg to be called and runes to know.

---

*32. Kon is the masculine of kona, a woman. It is a word only
found in poetry, applied to men of gentle or royal birth. The
poet plays upon its resemblance to konungr, a king, and suggests
a false derivation from kon and ungr, the young in order to show
that Kon rose to the highest rank and became Ríg, the king;
stanza 34.*

35.   Reiþ Konr ungr        kjörr ok skóga,
      kolfi fleygþi,         kyrþi fogla ;
      þá kvaþ þat kráka,      sat á kvisti ein :
      ' hvat skalt, Konr ungr !      kyrra fogla ?
      Heldr mættiþ ér        hestum ríþa

      .   .   .   .   .           .   .   .   .   .
      .   .   .   .   .           .   .   .   .   .

      [hjörum of bregþa]        ok her fella.

36.   Á Danr ok Danpr         dýrar hallir,
      œþra óþal        an ér hafiþ ;
      þeir kunnu vel        kjól at ríþa,
      egg at kenna,        undir rjúfa.' .   .   .

35. Young King rode once through thicket and wood,
shooting arrows and slaying birds,
till spake a crow, perched lone on a bough:
'Why wilt thou thus kill birds, young King?
'Twould fit thee rather to ride on horses,
to draw the sword and to slay the foe.

36. 'Dan and Damp have dwellings goodlier,
homesteads fairer than ye do hold;
and well they know the keel to ride,
the sword to prove and wounds to strike.

---

*36. Dan and Damp appear as Danish kings in the historical sagas.
The end of this poem is missing, which tells of Kon's descendants,
and probably of his invasion and conquest of Denmark.*

# VOLUSPA EN SKAMMA
## THE VALA'S SHORTER SOOTHSAYING

### SYNOPSIS

In this poem someone is holding converse with a witch, perhaps summoned from the dead. The unknown questioner wants to know the origin and kinship of all mythical beings. He asks first concerning the gods' race, and learns that once, before the death of Baldr, the Æsir were twelve in number. Here a gap in the poem leaves their names unrecorded, but they may be conjectured from descriptions by Snorri and in Lokasenna of the full assembly in Ægir's halls. At these banquets were present Odin, Thor, Heimdal, Tyr, Vidar, Vali, Forseti, Uil, Hcenir, Bragi, and Loki, who, with Baldr, make the twelve.

Another passage is missing which should tell how the Wanes Njord, Frey, and Freyja came among the other gods, and throughout the poem there is such confusion and lack of sequence that it takes some knowledge and skill to explain.

The questioner would next learn whence came other powers beside the ruling gods, those tumultuous forces ever warring with them, the Jötuns; those wise women, the Valas, who could interpret dreams and foretell the future; and whence all wizards and witches and monsters like the great wolf Fenrir, and prodigies such as Odin's eight-footed steed Sleipnir.

The answers to these questions are unfortunately often too dark to understand, or tell us only what is known from other sources. One awful being (stanza 8), the mother of all witches, was born in mysterious fashion from a burning heart, which Loki, as firegod, had devoured. She, it has been suggested, is the same as Golden-draught, who was burned and reburned in Odin's hall, and who caused the first war between gods and Wanes.

In alluding to Loki, who is half god, half giant, the questioner turns once more to higher beings, and the birth of One is related, whose name is not mentioned, but who is easily recognised as Heimdal. The description agrees with what is told of him elsewhere, and belongs to his character as a god of nature.

'Heimdal,' says Snorri, 'is called the White god. He is great and holy. Sometimes he is called Golden-tooth, for his teeth are of gold. His steed is Goldy-lock, and his dwelling place is Heavenhill, by the bridge Bifrost. He is warder of the gods, and sits at the end of heaven guarding the bridge against the Mountain Giants. He needs less sleep than a bird; he can see, by night as well as by day, a hundred miles around him. He hears grass growing on the earth and wool on the backs of sheep, besides all else that makes more sound. He owns the trumpet Gjailar-horn, whose blast is heard throughout the worlds.'

Thus shown as the dazzling god of light, he is unapproachable; far seen, aloof, he sits on his mountain throne, guarding Bifrost where the rainbow reaches heaven. He is no less mysterious in his birth, which Snorri also describes, quoting from some lost 'Song of Heimdal':-

Child am I of mothers nine,
of sisters nine the son.

These maidens, from their names in stanza 12, are ocean waves, and it is again as the god of light that he is born at the world's edge, on the horizon where the sky meets the earth and sea. It is there at sunrise that he drinks of the crimson splendour which is like the blood of sacrifice offered to the gods.

Heimdal stands apart from other deities in the Edda. He is less human, except when, as Rig, he passes through the world of men and becomes the kinsmen of all peoples. His epithet of the 'richest ruler' belongs to him perhaps as owner of the wide and glorious dwelling place of Heaven-hill.

All the revelations so far have been of the past; the Vala now becomes prophetic. She foretells the fearful signs and wonders in nature, the 'long dread winter' which shall herald the fulfilment of Weird with the Doom of the first ruling powers, the gods of war, and the coming of the new Power, some say of Christianity, but whose nature is here kept secret.

*Heimdal and his Nine Mothers*

# VOLUSPA EN SKAMMA

1. (28)    Váru ellifu      æsir talþir,
            Baldr es hné      viþ banaþúfu ;
            þess lézk Váli      verþr at hefna,
            es síns bróþur      sló handbana.

2. (29)    Vas Baldrs faþir      Burs arfþegi
            . . . . .        . . . . . .
            . . . . .        . . . . . .
            . . . . .        . . . . . .

3. (29)    Freyr átti Gerþi,      vas Gymis dóttir,
            jötna ættar      ok Aurboþu :
            þá vas Þjazi      þeira frændi,
            skautgjarn jötunn,      vas Skaþi dóttir.

---

*This poem is generally regarded as an independent work*

*The Vision of the Mighty One*

# VOLUSPA EN SKAMMA

1. Eleven only the war gods numbered
when Baldr sank on the bale fire down;
but Vali showed him strong to avenge it
and slew ere long his brother's slayer.

2. Father of Baldr was Odin, Bur's son.

3. Frey wedded Gerðr; she was Gymir's daughter,
and Aurboda's of Jötun race;
Thiazi also came of their kindred,
the shape-shifting giant, Skaði's sire.

---

*Vala or Witch. From Old Norse valr 'the fallen,' 'the slain,' 'the
dead.' Vali: one of Loki's sons.*
*2. Bur means son, e.g. of Buri, the first-born of the god's race,
and according to Snorri, the grandfather of Odin.*
*3. Gerðr: Aurboda, or Moisture-bringer? Thiazi took the form
of an eagle.*

4. (30)   Mart segjum þér      ok munum fleira ;
        vörumk at viti svá,      vilt enn lengra ?

5. (31)   Heiþr ok Hrossþjófr     Hrimnis kindar.

6. (31)   Eru völur allar      frá Víþolfi,
        vitkar allir     frá Vilmeiþi,
        en seiþberendr     frá Svarthöfþa,
        jötnar allir     frá Ymi komnir.

7. (32)   Mart segjum þér      ok munum fleira ;
        vörumk at viti svá,      vilt enn lengra ?

8. (38)   Ól ulf Loki     viþ Angrboþu,
        en Sleipni gat     viþ Svaþilfera ;
        eitt þótti skars     allra feiknast,
        þat vas bróþur frá     Býleists komit.

9. (39)   Loki *át* hjarta—     lindi brendu
        fann halfsviþinn     hugstein konu— ;
        varþ Loptr kviþugr     af konu illri :
        þaþan's á foldu     flagþ hvert komit.

10. (34)   Mart segjum þér      ok munum fleira ;
        vörumk at viti svá,      vilt enn lengra ?

11. (35)   Varþ einn borinn     í árdaga
        rammaukinn mjök     ragna kindar ;
        niu báru þann,     naddgöfgan mann,
        jötna meyjar     viþ jarþar þröm.

4. Much have I told thee, yet more I remember;
needs must one know it thus, wilt thou yet further?

5. Witch and Horse-thief are sprung from Rime-bringer,

6. All the Valas sprung from Forest-wolf,
all the wizards sprung from Wish-giver,
all the sorcerers sprung from Swart-head;
and all the Jötuns come from Ymir.

7. Much have I told thee, yet more I remember;
needs must one know it thus, wilt thou yet further?

8. Woe-bringer bore the wolf to Loki,
with Swadilfari begat he Sleiphir.
But one was deemed the deadliest of all
the monster brood from Loki born.

9. When the heart of a woman home of love
he ate half-burned with linden wood,
and bore ere long a loathly being
whence witches all in the world are sprung.

10. Much have I told thee, yet more I remember,
needs must one know it thus, wilt thou yet further?

11.One was there born in days of old,
girt with great power, of the kindred of gods.
Nine giant maidens bore that being
armed with glory on the rim of earth.

---

6. *Ymir, see Vm. st. 21.*
8. *Woe-bringer, or Angrboþa: a giantess, who was the mother of Fenrir, the World Serpent and Hel.*
9. *This stanza is perhaps explained by Voluspa stanza. 21, when the gods burn Golden-draught, the witch who is ever born anew.*
11-14. *No name is mentioned in the text, but these stanzas clearly refer to Heimdal or Ríg.*

12. (35)  Hann Gjölp of bar,        hann Greip of bar,
          bar hann Eistla        ok Eyrgjafa,
          hann bar Ulfrún        ok Angeyja,
          Imþr ok Atla        ok Ïarnsaxa.

13. (36)  Sá vas aukinn        jarþar megni,
          svalköldum sæ        ok sonardreyra.

14. (41)  Varþ einn borinn        öllum meiri,
          sá vas aukinn        jarþar megni ;
          þann kveþa stilli        stórúþgastan,
          sif sifjaþan,        sjötum görvöllum.

15. (37)  Mart segjurn þér        ok munum fleira ;
          vörumk at viti svá,        vilt enn lengra ?

16. (40)  Haf gengr hríþum        viþ himin sjalfan,
          líþr lönd yfir,        en lopt bilar ;
          þaþan koma snjóvar        ok snarir vindar,
          þá's í ráþí,        at regin of þrjóti.

17. (44)  Þa kömr annarr        enn mátkari,
          þó þorik eigi        þann at nefna ;
          faïr sea nú        fram of lengra,
          an Óþinn mun        ulfi mœta.

12. Yelper bore him, Griper bore him,
Foamer bore him, Sand-strewer bore him,
She-wolf bore him, Sorrow-whelmer,
Dusk and Fury and Ironsword.

13. He was girt with all the power of Earth,
of the ice-cold sea, and of sacred swine-blood.

14. He was the One born greater than any;
girt with all the power of Earth.
Men call him ever the richest ruler,
Ríg, the kinsman of every race.

15. Much have I told thee, yet more I remember,
needs must one know it thus, wilt thou yet further?

16. The sea shall rise in storms to heaven
it shall sweep o'er the land and the skies shall yield
in showers of snow and biting blasts
at the Doom of the Powers, the gods of war.

17. There shall come hereafter another mightier
whose name I dare not now make known :
few there are who may see beyond
when Odin fares to fight with the Wolf.

# HYNDLULJÓÐ
## THE LAY OF HYNDLA

SYNOPSIS

In the poem, the goddess Freyja meets the Völva Hyndla and they ride together towards Valhalla. Freyja rides on her boar Hildisvíni and Hyndla on a wolf. Their mission is to find out the pedigree of Óttarr so that he can touch his inheritance, and the lay consists mostly of Hyndla reciting a number of names from Óttarr's ancestry. The poem may be a twelfth-century work.

The Lay of Hyndla tells of Óttarr the Simple, a chieftain who is unknown to history, but who seems to have belonged to the famous family of Hordaland. He is here identified with Od, the human lover of Freyja, whose story is thus told by Snorri:

'Freyja was wedded to a mortal called Óttarr, and their daughter Hnoss, the Treasure, is so beautiful that all things fair and costly are named after her. But Óttarr went far away, and Freyja followed him weeping, and her tears were of red gold.'

Óttarr of 'Hyndla' has wagered his inheritance with another personage, Angantyr, that his descent, could he only trace it, is the nobler. Freyja is willing to help her favourite, and she takes him with her disguised as Goldenbristle, the famous boar which belonged to Frey. They seek Hyndla,who, like other Valas or witches, dwells in a cave, and rides forth upon a wolf at night. She is a giantess, and thus knows all the history of mankind. But as such she must be propitiated by a goddess, and Freyja promises to win her the favour of Odin, the War-father, who at times can be so gracious; Thor too, the enemy of giant-wives, shall be appeased by sacrifice such as men offered to the gods.

Hyndla suspects the presence of Óttarr, but Freyja denies it, and in answer to questions of the latter she rehearses the generations of kings while they ride through the night, and Óttarr's heart must beat with pride as she marshals forth the host of his dead forbears. It is shown how he is allied to the most ancient and noble races, and heroes who can trace their line back to the gods.

To us all these great names mean nothing, or merely call up shadowy figures in the land that lies between history and romance. But recited in ancient days by the skalds, before the warriors and women gathered in the hall, the famous race names of Skjoldung, Skilfing, Odling, Yngling were full of deep meaning, and expressed their ideal of glory in heroic deeds.

The Skjoldungs are ancient mythical figures who centre round the birth cradle of the Germanic race. In the various Old English, Icelandic, and Danish sources, which do not always agree in their details, is found the legend of an old culture hero, deemed perhaps a god in human form. He came as a child drifting over the sea in a boat, surrounded by treasures, with a sheaf of corn from which he took his name Skef, though the poem Beowulf has transferred the legend to his son Scyld. The boat approached a land called Skania, where Skef rescued a people in great misery, and taught them to cultivate their territory and defend it against the enemy. He died in old age, leaving Skjold or Scyld to inherit the kingdom, and was sent forth once more over the sea in a boat no less richly endowed than when he came, ' but no man,' it is said, ' knew who received the precious burden.'

From Skjold came the Skjoldungs, or, as we learn from Beowulf, the Danes, whose home was Leira in the island of Seeland. Skef or Sceaf in Old English genealogies is the ancestor of the Angles and Saxons.

With him we must identify Skilvir, also said to be the father of Skjold, the progenitor of the Skilfings, another name for the Swedes.

But who are the Ynglings? Ing or Yng is also a great race-hero, and ancestor of the Swedes and Angles. In the poem Ynglinga-tal, the name Yngling and Skilfing is used interchangeably. Thus Yng must be identical with Skilvir, and Skilvir, as we have seen, is the same as Scef, or, according to Beowulf, Skjold. There is much confusion!

Then Hyndla turns to Óttarr's immediate family, and those with which it is connected. The first great hero mentioned is Halfdan the Old (stanza 18). He was the king of Denmark, and one of the patriarchs of the Germanic race, known to Saxo Grammaticus and to the author of Beowulf. His most famous achievement was the slaying of Sigtrygg, a mythical king. He sacrificed to the gods in order to obtain long life, but he was granted no more than 'a man's life' of three hundred years, and the promise that no ignoble offspring should be born in his line - hence Óttarr would desire to claim kinship with him.

The twelve berserk brothers of stanza 23, sons of Arngrim and Eyfora, belong to Hervarar Saga, and their chieftain Angantyr is the principal figure in one of the finest of the Old Norse heroic poems.

The word berserk had its origin in a superstitious belief that some men were 'hamramr,' or able to change their forms, and become bears or wolves, and were hence called berserks or were-wolves. Later on the name was given to those wild beings who from time to time were seized by fits of madness and rage, when they seemed possessed of more than human strength, and wrought fearful deeds in battle.

The saga in question tells of a magic sword called Tyrfing which came into the hands of Angantyr. It had been forged by dwarfs, and stolen from them; therefore a curse followed it, and though it might serve its bearer well for a lifetime, it would at last bring him to death.

The viking brothers ranged over land and sea, till in consequence of Angantyr's love for Ingibjorg they met in battle, and were defeated by, two warriors, Odd and Hjalmar, in the island of Samsey.

Hervor, Angantyr's warlike daughter, had inherited the berserk spirit, and presently it came upon her. She armed herself like a warrior, and went forth to seek Tyrfing from her father's grave. Fearlessly she passed through the haunted land with its magic flickering flames until she stood on the howe, crying:

'Harvard, Hjorvard, Hrani, Angantyr !
Wake where ye rest the tree-roots under
with helm and byrnie, shield and harness,
sword keen-whetted and reddened spear !
All are they come, the sons of Arngtim,
death-thirsting warriors, to dust of earth;
and not one comes forth of Eyfora's offspring
in Munavagi to speak with me:'

Till at length, while the whole land was aflame with enchanted fires, the grave opened, and she won her heritage from the dead.

Stanza 25 scarcely requires explanation. With the mention of the famous but ill-starred Niflung and Volsung races, a note of warning comes into the poem. This great saga is so widely known and has been so oft repeated that it no longer belongs only to the people of the North, who told it first and best in written form.

Jormunrek married Svanhild, daughter of Sigurd; he caused his wife to be trampled to death by wild horses in consequence of a slander, and her brothers sought to avenge the deed.

Stanza 29 alludes to another famous saga, After this passage follows an old fragmentary poem, placed there, not perhaps by the author of Hyndla's Lay, but by some later copyist who was ignorant of the old genealogies, and knew little of the distinctions between gods and men.

The scene now returns to Freyja and Hyndla, whose ride is ended. Hyndla wants to be left to sleep in peace once more, and bids Freyja hie homewards on her wild night journey, with the darkness lit up only by the flickering of enchanted fires like those which surrounded Hervor, and ever haunt the places of the dead.

Freyja's mocking request to pass the ale-cup to her boar is the acknowledgment of Óttarr's presence. The dialogue between her and Hyndla grows dramatic and breathless, ending with a curse from the witch and a blessing from the goddess upon Óttarr.

*Freyja awakes Hyndla*

# ꜰYNDᴄUᴄᴊÓꝹ

Freyja kvaþ :

1. ' Vaki, mær meyja !      vaki, mín vina !
   Hyndla systir,     es í helli býr !
   nú's rökkr rökkra :    ríþa vit skulum
   til Valhallar,     til vés heilags.

2. Biþjum Herföþr     í hugum sitja ;
   hann geldr ok gefr    goll verþungu :
   gaf Hermóþi     hjalm ok brynju,
   en Sigmundi     sverþ at þiggja.

*The Ancestry of Óttarr*

# ᚻYᚿᛞᛚᚢᛚᛃᚯᛞ

Freyja:
1. Wake, maid of maidens, friend, awaken,
sister Hyndla, in a rock-hole biding!
Comes the gloom of gloaming, we twain together
must ride to Valhöll, the holy dwelling.

2. The War-father bid we be mild in his mood,
who grants and gives to his followers gold;
he gave to Hermod a helm and byrnie
and to Sigmund gave a sword to take.

---

2. *Hermod belongs to some lost tradition. He appears sometimes as a god and sometimes as a hero. In the Prose Edda he is the son of Odin; in the old English poem of Beowolf he is a Danish King. Sigmund, father of Sigurd: Odin arrived at a wedding feast and thrust his sword into a tree from which only Sigmund, the gods' favourite, could draw it.*

3.   Gefr sigr sonum,      en sumum aura,
     mælsku mörgum      ok mannvit firum ;
     byri gefr brögnum     en brag sköldum,
     gefr mannsemi      mörgum rekki.

4.   þór mun blóta,      þess munk biþja,
     at æ viþ þik      einart láti ;

     . . . . . .     . . . . . .

     þó's hánum ótítt     viþ jötuns brúþír.

5.   Nú tak ulf þinn      einn af stalli,
     lát hann rinna      meþ runa mínum.

Hyndla kvaþ :

     seinn es göltr þinn     goþveg troþa,
     vilkak mar minn      mætan hlœþa.'

6.   ' Flá est, Freyja !     es freistar mín,
     vísar augum      á oss þanig,
     es hefr ver þinn     I valsinni,
     óttar unga,      Innsteins bur.'

Freyja kvaþ :

7.   ' Dulin est, Hyndla !    draums ætlak þér,
     es kveþr ver minn     í valsinni,
     þars göltr gloar      gollinbursti,
     Hildisvíni,      as mer hagir görþu
     dvergar tveir      Daïnn ok Nabbi.

3. To some grants he wealth, to his children war-fame,
word-skill to many and wisdom to men:
fair winds to sea-farers, song-craft to skalds,
and might of manhood to many a warrior.

4. To Thor will I offer and this will I ask him,
to bear him truly ever toward thee,
e'en though foe of the wives of Jötuns.

5. Now of thy wolves take one from the stall
and swift let him run by the side of my boar.

Hyndla:
Nay ! loth is thy swine, to tread the gods' way,
nor will I burden my noble beast.

6. False art thou, Freyja ! thou fain wouldst tempt me;
thine eyes betray thee; thou turnest ever
to where on the Dead's way thy lover is with thee,
Óttarr the youthful, Instein's son.

Freyja:
7. Dull art thou, Hyndla! I trow thou art dreaming,
when thou deemst my lover is here on the Dead's road,
where Golden-bristle, the boar, is glowing,
the swine of battle which once they made me,
Dain and Nabbi, the crafty dwarfs.

---

6. *The Dead's way : A road by which the dead warriors went to Valhull. Óttarr: The story of Freyja's human lover Óttarr or Odd is told by Snorri.*

7. *The boar: Frey owned the boar called Golden-bristle, which was forged by the dwarfs. Snorri tells us that Freyja, rode on a cat, though here she rides a wolf. Dam, the Dead one, is mentioned in Voluspa.*

8.   Sennum vit ór söþlum :      sitja skulum
auk of jöfra        ættir dœma ;
gumna þeira      es frá goþum kvámu
. . . . . .     . . . . . .

9. (8)  Þeir hafa veþjat    Vála malmi,
Óttarr ungi       ok Angantýr :
skylt's at veita,    svát skati enn ungi
föþurleifþ hafi     ept frændr sína.

10.  Hörg mér görþi    *of* hlaþinn steinum—
nú es grjót þat     at gleri orþit—,
(10) rauþ í nýju      nauta blóþi ;
æ trúþi Óttarr    á ásynjur.

11.  Nú lát forna     niþja talþa
ok upp bornar    ættir manna :
hvat's Skjöldunga,   hvat's Skilfinga,
*hvat's Öþlinga,*    hvat's Ynglinga,
hvat's hölþborit,   hvat's hersborit,
mest manna val    und miþgarþi ? '

Hyndla kvaþ :

12.  ' Þú est, Óttarr !    borinn Innsteini,
en Innsteinn vas    Alfi gamla,
Alfr vas Ulfi,     Ulfr Sæfara,
en Sæfari      Svan enum rauþa.

13.  Móþur áttir     menjum göfga,
hykk at héti      Hlédís gyþja ;
Fróþi vas faþir,   en † Friaut móþir :
öll þótti ætt sú   meþ yfirmönnum.

8. Let us now strive in our saddles sitting,
and hold converse o'er the long long lines of kings,
heroes all who are come from the gods.

9. Óttarr the youthful, and Angantyr
on this have wagered their wealth of gold;
needs must I help the youthful hero
to hold the heritage after his fathers.

10. He built me an altar with stone o'erlaid;
like glass all riven is that rock with fire,
for he reddened it oft with the fresh blood of oxen;
aye to the goddesses Óttarr was true.

11. Come now let ancient kinsman be numbered,
and let be told the long lines of men:
who is of Skjoldungs, who of Skilfings,
who is of Athlings, who of Ynglings,
who is freeborn, who is gentleborn,
choicest of all the men under Midgarth?

## ÓTTARR'S RACE

Hyndla:
12. Thou art Óttarr, born of Instein;
Instein came from Alf the Old,
Alf was from Wolf, Wolf from Seafarer,
and Seafarer sprang from Swan the Red.

13. Thou hadst a mother shining in jewels,
Hledis, I ween, she was named, the priestess;
her father was Frodi, and Friaut her mother.
All of this race among lords are reckoned.

14. (17)   Vas Hildigunn    hennar móþir,
      Svávu barn    ok Sækonungs ;
      allt's þat ætt þin,    Óttarr heimski !
      varþar at viti svá,    vilt enn lengra ?

15. (19)   Ketill vas vinr peirar,    Klypps arfþegi,
      vas móþurfaþir    móþur þinnar ;
      þar vas Fróþi    fyrr an Kári,
      enn eldri vas    Álfr of getinn.

16.    Nanna vas næst þar    Nökkva dóttir,
     vas mögr hennar    mágr þíns föpur ;
     fyrnd es sú mægþ,    fram telk lengra
     allt's þat ætt þín,    Óttarr heimski !

17.    Ísolfr ok Ásolfr    Ölmóþs synir
     ok Skúrhildar    Skekkils dóttur,
     skalt til telja    skatna margra :
     allt' s þat ætt þín,    Óttarr heimski !

18. (14)   Áli vas ápr    öflgastr manna,
      Halfdanr fyrri    hæstr Skjöldunga ;
      fræg vöru folkvíg    þaus framir görþu,
      hvarfla þóttu hans verk    meþ himins skautum.

19. (15)   Efldisk viþ Eymund,    œztan manna,
      en Sigtrygg slô    meþ svölum eggjum ;
      átti Almveigu,    œzta kvenna,
      ólu ok áttu    átján sunu.

14. Hildigunn was the mother of Friaut;
child was she of Svafa and Sea-king.
All this race is thine Óttarr the Simple!
Needs must one know it thus, wilt thou yet further?

15. Klyp's son Ketil was spouse of Hildigun;
he was the father of thy mother's mother.
Older than Karl yet was Prodi,
but Alf was of all the eldest born.

16. Next came Nanna, the daughter of Nokkvir;
her son was thy father's brother by wedlock.
Old is that kindship, still on will I tell thee,
for all this race is thine, Óttarr the Simple.

17. Isolf and Osolf were sons of Olmod,
and born of Skurhild, daughter of Skekkil.
Thou shalt reckon back to many a chieftain.
All this race is thine Óttarr the Simple!

HALFDAN'S RACE

18. Far back was Ali, mightiest of men:
Halfdan before him highest of Skjoldungs,
whirled were his deeds round the skirts of heaven,
great wars of nations the chieftains waged.

19. He joined him to Eymund, highest of heroes;
Sigtrygg slew with the icy sword-edge,
wedded Almveig, loftiest of ladies;
so he begat him sons eighteen.

---

*18. Halfdan, a mythical King of Denmark.*
*19. Eymund, King of Novgorod and father of Almveig.*

20. (16)  Þaþan Skjöldungar,    þaþan Skilfingar,
           þaþan Öplingar,      þaþan Ynglingar,
           þaþan hölþborit,     þaþan hersborit,
           mest manna val        und miþgarþi ;
           allt's þat ætt pín,      Óttarr heimski !

21. (18)  Dagr átti Þóru         drengja móþur,
           ólusk í ætt þar        œztir kappar :
           Fraþmarr ok Gyrþr    ok Frekar báþir,
           Ámr ok josurmarr,     Álfr enn gamli :
           varþar at viti svá,      vilt enn lengra ?

22. (23)  Þeir í Bolm austr      bornir váru
           Arngríms synir        ok Eyfuru ;
           brökun berserkja,      böls margskonar,
           of lönd ok of lög       sem logi fœri :

23. (25)  Hervarþr, Hjörvarþr,     Hrani, Angautyr,
           Bui ok Brámi,         Barri ok Reifnir,
           Tindr ok Tyrfingr,      tveir Haddingjar :
           allt's þat ætt þin,       Óttarr heimski !

24. (22)  Gunnarr balkr,        Grímr harþskafi,
           jarnskjöldr Þórir,       Ulfr gínandi ;
           kunnak báþa         Brodd ok Hörvi,
           váru þeir í hirþ       Hrolfs ens gamla.

20. Thence are the Skjoldungs, thence the Skilfings,
thence are the Athlings, thence the Ynglings,
thence are freeborn, thence are gentleborn,
all the choicest of men under Midgarth.
All this race is thine, Óttarr the Simple;

21. Dag's wife was Thora, mother of warriors;
reared in that race were the mightiest heroes,
Fradmar and Gyrd, and both the Wolf-cubs,
Josurmar, Am, and Alf the Old.

Needs must one know it thus, wilt thou yet further?

## THE BERSERKS

22. Born in Bolm in the eastern land
were Arngrim's sons and Eyfora's;
woes unnumbered the berserks worked,
like the faring of fire o'er land and sea.

23. Hervard, Hjorvard, Hrani, Angantyr,
Bui and Brami, Barri and Reifnir,
Tind and Tyrfing, and Haddungs twain.
All this race is thine, Óttarr the Simple!

24. Gunnar Battle-wall, Grim Strongminded,
Thorir Iron-shield, Wolf the Gaper;
Brod and Horvi, once I knew them,
both in the train of Hrolf the Old.

---

*21. Dag, son of Halfdan, father of Arngrim.*

25. (27)  Þeir váru gumnar      goþum signaþir,
        allir bornir     Jörmunreki,

   (24)  Sigurþar mági,     —hlýþ sögu minni !—
        folkum grims    es Fáfni vá.

26. (25)  Sá vas vísir     frá Völsungi
        ok Hjördís     frá Hrauþungi,
        en Eylimi     frá Öþlingum :
        allt's þat ætt pín,    Óttarr heimski !

27. (26)  Gunnarr ok Högni   Gjúka arfar
        ok et sama Guþrún,   systir þeira :
        eigi vas Gotþormr   Gjúka ættar,
        þó vas bróþir    beggja þeira :
        allt's þat ætt þín,    Óttarr heimski !

28. (31)  Haki vas Hveþnu   hóti baztr sona,
        en Hveþnu vas    Hjörvarþr faþir

        . . . . .    . . . . .

        . . . . .    . . . . .

## THE VOLSUNG RACE

25. Given to the gods were the warrior sons,
all the children of Jormunrek,
the kinsman of Sigurd list to my saga!
Fear of Nations, who Fafnir slew.

26. That ruler was born of the race of Volsungs,
and Hjordis came, his mother, of Hraudungs,
and Eylimi, her sire, of Athlings.
All this race is thine, Óttarr the Simple!

27. Gunnar and Hogni were sons of Gjuki;
Gudrun their sister, was eke his offspring;
but not of their kin was Guthorm Battle-snake,
though of the twain he was held the brother.
All this race is thine, Óttarr the Simple!

28. Best was Haki of Hvedna's children;
the father of Hvedna was Hjorvard.

---

*22-23. The story of Angantyr and the famous berserks is told in
Hervarar Saga and Orvar Odds Saga .
24. Hrolf: probably Half, a famous King of Gauta-land, and hero
of Half's Saga
25. Jormunrek: the heroicised Ermanric, King of the Goths in
the fourth century. Sigurd: the hero of the Volsunga Saga, and
later Niebelungenlied (The Song of the Nibelungs, The Professor's Bookshelf #1).
27. Gjuki, of Niflung race, a King of the Burgundians. Guthorm,
his stepson, slew Sigurd at the desire of Hrynliild.*

29. (27)  Haraldr hilditönn      borinn Hrœreki  
         slöngvanbauga,      sunr vas hann Auþar,  
         Auþr djúpúþga        Ívars dóttir,  
         en Ráþbarþr vas      Randvés faþir :  
         allt's þat ætt þín,      Óttarr heimski ! '

Freyja kvaþ :

30.   ' Ber minnisöl        mínum gelti,  
      svát öll muni        orþ at tína,  
      þessa rœþu,         á þriþja morni,  
      þás þeir Angantýr    ættir rekja.'

Hyndla kvaþ :

31.   ' Snuþu braut heþan !    sofa lystir mik,  
      fær fátt af mér       fríþra kosta :  
      hleypr, eþlvina !       úti á náttum,  
      sem meþ höfrum     Heiþrún fari.

32.   Rannat at Óþi       ey þreyjandi :  
      skutusk þér fleiri     und fyrirskyrtu ;  
      hleyþr, eþlvina !       úti á, náttum,  
      sem meþ höfrum     Heiþrún fari.'

Freyja kvaþ :

33.   ' Ek slæ eldi         of íviþju,  
      svát eigi kömsk     óbrend heþan.

## RACE OF HARALD WAR-TOOTH

29. Born from Aud was Harald War-tooth,
son of Hrderik, Slinger of Rings.
Aud Deep-thoughted was Ivar's daughter,
and Randver the son of Radbard born.
All this race is thine, Óttarr the Simple !

Freyja:
30. To my boar now bear the ale of memory,
so shall he tell forth all this tale
when the third morn comes, and with Angantyr
he shall trace back the mighty men of their race.

Hyndla:
31. Hie away hence! for I fain would sleep,
and few fair words shalt thou win from me.
Thou gaddest forth, good friend, at nights
like a she-goat straying bold among bucks.

32. Yearning ever thou hast followed Odd;
many a sweetheart has slept in thine arms.
Thou gaddest forth, good friend, at nights
like a she-goat straying bold among bucks.

Freyja:
33. I will strike tire about thee, giantess,
so that unburnt thou hie not hence.

---

29. *Harald War-tooth, a King of Denmark. Hruirik, a King of Sweden, husband of Aud.*
31. *A she-goat : The name of the mythical goat Heidnui is here used in a general sense.*

Hyndla kvaþ :

' Hleypr, eþlvina !     úti á náttum,
sem meþ höfrum     Heiþrun fari.'

34.  ' Hyr sék brinna     en hauþr loga,
verþa flestir     fjörlausn þola :
ber Óttari     bjór at hendi
eitrblandinn mjök,     illu heilli !
Hleypr, eþlvina !     úti á náttum
sem meþ höfrum     Heiþrun fari.'

Freyja kvaþ :

35.  ' Orþheill þín skal     öngu ráþa,
þót, brúþr jötuns !     bölvi heitir ;
hann skal drekka     dýrar veigar,
biþk Óttari     öll goþ duga.'

Hyndla.
Thou gaddest forth, good friend, at nights
like a she-goat straying bold among bucks.

34. Lo ! all around us the earth is flaming !
Many must render their lives as ransom.
Bear now the ale-cup to Óttarr's hand,
all mingled with poison and omens of ill.
Thou gaddest forth, good friend, at nights
like a she-goat straying bold among bucks.

Freyja.
35. The word of thine omen shall work no evil,
albeit thou cursest, vile wife of Jötuns;
sweet shall the draught be that Óttarr drinks,
for I pray all the Powers to shield him well.

# BALDRS DRAUMAR
## BALDR'S DREAMS

SYNOPSIS

This poem relates information on the myth of Baldr's death in a way consistent with Gylfaginning. (Gylfaginning, or the Tricking of Gylfi, is the first part of Snorri Sturluson's Prose Edda after Prologue. It deals with the creation and destruction of the world of the Norse gods, and many other aspects of Norse mythology.)

In Baldrs Draumar, Baldr has been having nightmares. Odin rides to Hel to investigate. He finds the grave of a Völva and resurrects her. Their conversation follows, where the Völva tells Odin about Baldr's fate. In the end Odin asks her a question which reveals his identity and the Völva tells him to ride home.

This poem belongs to a closing chapter in the history of the gods. Baldr's death is the great tragedy which foreshadows their Doom.

No facts are recorded of him in his lifetime; here and there in some passing allusion he enters a poem and flits across its pages like some gleaming ray of light, but only in his death does he become the most human and best loved of all the gods.

Baldr was the son of Odin and Frigg. Unlike Thor, he had no kinship with earth; both of his father and mother, he was born of heaven.

'He was the best among the gods, and praised by all beings. He was so fair to behold and so bright that a glory streamed from him, and no white herb, even though it were the whitest of all herbs, could compare with the whiteness of Baldr's brow. He was the wisest of gods, the fairest spoken and the most pitiful, and yet of such nature that none might overrule his judgments. His home was in the heavens called Broad-beam, where nought unclean might enter.'

Nothing further is told of Baldr's life, nor what part he played in the history of the gods; how he shared in their warring and striving, but not in their sinning; for of him 'there is nought but good to tell.' He must have had a love story which recounted the wooing of Nanna, his fair wife, who must perish with him; but now, in this poem, we hear that Baldr, while still youthful, has had evil dreams and forseen his fate.

All the gods gather in alarm and hold council, but none can tell, though all can guess, the meaning of Baldr's Dreams. Odin journeys down to Hel to seek tidings from a Vala, who, as one of the dead, has power to trace the workings of Weird before and behind. He rides thither by the same road which Herrnod took afterwards and on the same steed, his own eight-footed Sleipnir, and stands calling on the Vala until she obeys the spell of the Master Magician, and comes forth from the grave.

The Vala is heard in speech with Odin. Her words are not the mere fortune-telling of a witch, but like the oracle of old she pronounces the doom of Baldr. The Weird motif now sounds in the poem, and continues like a grim undertone throughout as the Vala interprets one by one the visionary pictures of Baldr's dreams.

He has first seen the interior of a great hall being prepared for the reception of an honoured guest; the benches are strewn, the mead cup is filled and overlaid with the bright shield, and all the place adorned as though for the coming of some king. But Baldr has guessed that this is Hel's abode, and is troubled. Now Odin learns the name of this expected king, and wrothfully asks who would dare thus 'to slay his son, the best loved among all the gods?'

He is answered that no dread Frost-giant or Mountain-giant, but one among themselves will shoot the fatal shaft. Who then shall avenge the deed before ever Baldr is laid on the bale-fire? The father's anger is appeased when he is told that the giantess Rind shall bear him a mighty child, who shall work vengeance on the author of the Woe.

The Vala is next questioned on the second vision which Baldr has seen - a mourning world, maidens weeping and in wild despair casting their veils to the winds. Why does she now break out in fierce indignant reproaches, and know that her tormentor is Odin? None living save a god could thus see into the future, and perhaps as a dweller in the underworld she resents the attempt which will be made to deprive Hel of its victim.

Then Odin, with mocking fury and refusal to believe the prophecy of the Vala, bears the dread tidings home to Asgarth. But she has the last word, reminding him how even the gods must suffer Doom; for all their after efforts, the devices of the fond mother to save her son, are only a hopeless striving against Weird.

Here Snorri takes up the story: 'The gods resolved to ask protection for Baldr against all harm, and Frigg took an oath from fire and water, from iron and all metals, from rocks and earth and trees, from poison and serpents that they would spare Baldr. When this was done and made known, it became the sport of Baldr and the gods to make him stand up at their meetings while some shot at him, some struck him, and some cast stones; but whatever they did he was unharmed, and they deemed it a glorious feat save Loki, son of Leaf-isle, who was ill pleased. He went in the likeness of a woman to Fen Halls, where Frigg dwelt, who asked what all the gods were doing at their assembly.

The goddess made answer that they were shooting at Baldr, but that nought harmed him. Said Frigg 'Nor weapons nor trees will hurt Baldr, for I have taken an oath from them all.' And Loki disguised as a woman asked 'Have all things taken the oath to spare Baldr?

Frigg answered

'There grows indeed, to the west of Valhöll, a tender shoot called the Mistletoe, which seemed too young to ask an oath from.'

Then all in a moment the visiting woman vanished.

But Loki went and plucked the Mistletoe, and joined the gathering of the gods. There was one, Hod, who stood without the circle, for he was blind. Loki asked ' Why art thou not shooting at Baldr?' and he answered, 'Because I cannot see where he stands, and moreover I am without weapon.'

'Thou must do as the others,' said Loki, 'and show honour to Baldr. Shoot now this wand; I will show thee where he stands.' So Hod took the Mistletoe, and aimed as Loki showed him. The shaft flew and pierced Baldr, who fell dead to the earth, and 'tis deemed the direst shot that ever was shot among gods and men. When Baldr had fallen, speech failed the gods and likewise power in their hands to lift him. Each looked at the other, and all were of one mind about him who had wrought the deed, but they could not seek revenge there, for it was a holy place of peace. When the gods sought to speak there was only sound of weeping, and the one could not tell his sorrow to the other. But the greatest sorrow was to Odin, for he best fore-knew what loss and woe had befallen the gods with the death of Baldr.

When at length they had come to themselves again, Frigg asked who among them all desired to win her grace and favour, and would ride the Hel road and seek if haply he might find Baldr, and offer ransom to Hel that she should let him return home to Asgarth. And Hermod, the Eager-hearted son of Odin, was chosen for the journey.

Then gliding Sleipnir, the steed of Odin, was brought forth, and Hermod mounted and rode swiftly away.

But the gods took the body of Baldr to send it floating out to sea. His vessel, called Ring-horn, was the greatest of all ships, and when the gods sought to launch it forth and kindle the bale-fire thereon for Baldr, it could nowise be stirred.

So they sent to Jotunheim after the giantess, fire-shrivelled Hyrrok, who came riding on a wolf, using serpents for the reins. When she had dismounted Odin called four berserks to mind the steed, but they could not hold it until they had felled it to the ground.

Hyrrok went forward to the prow, and in one push she launched the boat with such force that sparks flew from the rollers, and the whole ground was shaken. Then was the Thunderer wroth! He seized his hammer, and would have broken her head it all the other gods had not asked mercy for her.

Then they bore forth the dead form of Baldr and laid it in the vessel, and when his wife Nanna, Nep's daughter, beheld it her heart broke from sorrow, and she died. She too was laid on the bale-tire, and the flame was kindled.

Thor stood by, and hallowed the pile with Mjollnir. At his feet ran a dwarf called Lit, and Thor spurned it with his loot into the fire, and it was burned.

All manner of folk came to the burning of Baldr. First came Odin, and with him Frigg and the valkyries and his ravens Hugin and Munm. Frey came driving in a car drawn by the boar called Golden-bristle or Fierce-tang, and Heimdal riding the steed Golden-lock. Freyja was there with her cats. Thither came, too, a host of Frost-giants and Mountain-giants.

Then Odin laid on the bale-fire that ring called Draupnir, which is of such value that therefrom fall eight like rings every ninth night. And Baldr's steed was led to the bale-fire in all its trappings. Meanwhile Hermod rode nine whole nights through dales so dark and deep that he could see nought till he came to the loud roaring river Gjallar, and rode over the echoing Gjallar-bridge, which is thatched with shining gold.

There the maiden called Modgud keeps watch. She asked Hermod his race and name, and told him how yesterday five phantom troops had ridden over the bridge,

' but under thee the bridge echoes full as loud, nor hast thou the hue of a dead man. Why art thou riding on the Hel-road?'

He answered 'I must needs ride to Hel, and seek Baldr; hast thou seen aught of him on the Hel-road?'

'Baidr,' said she, ' has ridden over the Gjallar-bridge; downward and northward lies the way to Hel.'

So Hermod rode on till he came to the Hel-gates. There he sprang from horseback, tightened his saddlegirths, and mounting again he spurred his steed so fiercely that it leapt high over the gates, and not so much as touched them with its heels.

Then he rode onward to the hall, where he dismounted and entered. He saw there his brother Baldr sitting on the high seat, and he stayed the night. In the morning he besought Hel to let Baldr ride home with him, and told her how great mourning there was among the gods.

Hel said that she would make trial whether Baldr was as much beloved as men said ' If all things, both quick and dead, in all the worlds, shall weep for Baldr, then shall he fare home to the gods, but if aught refuse, let Hel keep what she has.'

Then Hermod arose, and Baldr brought him forth from the hall, and gave him the ring Draupnir to bear to Odin as a token of remembrance, while Nanna sent a veil to Frigg and a golden veil to Fulla. Then Hermod went his way home to Asgarth, and told them all the things which he had seen and heard.

The rest of the story is given with the Fragments.

*Odin Rides to Hel*

# BALDRS DRAUMAR

1.    Senn váru æsir      allir á þingi
     ok ásynjur    allar á máli,
     ok of þat répu      ríkir tívar,
     hví væri Baldri      ballir draumar.

2.    Upp reis Óþinn,      aldinn gautr,
     auk á Sleipni      söþul of lagþi ;
     reiþ nipr þaþan      Niflheljar til,
     mœtti hvelpi      es ór helju kvam.

3. (2)    Sá vas blóþugr      of brjóst framan
     ok galdrs föþur      gó of lengi ;
   (3)    fram reiþ Óþinn      foldvegr dunþi,
     hann kvam at hávu      Heljar ranni.

*The Death of Baldr*

# BALDRS DRAUMAR

1. Straight were gathered all gods at the doomstead,
goddesses all were in speech together;
and the mighty Powers over this took counsel,
why to Baldr came dreams forboding.

2. Up rose Odin the ancient creator;
he laid the saddle on gliding Sleipnir,
and downward rode into Misty Hel.
Met him a hound from a cavern coming;

3. all its breast was blood-besprinkled,
long it bayed at the Father of Spells.
Onward he rode, the Earth's way rumbled,
to the lofty hall of Hel came Odin.

---

*2. Sleipnir: Odin's eight-footed steed. Misty Hel: The dwelling
place of the goddess Hel, daughter of Loki and Angrbofya. A
hound: Garm .*
*3. The father of spells or magic: Odin.*

4.   Þá reiþ Óþinn        fyr austan dyrr,
     þars hann vissi      völvu leiþi,
(4)  nam vittugri         valgaldr kveþa,
     unz nauþug reis      nás orþ of kvaþ :

5. (4)  ' Hvat's manna þat        mér ókunnra
        es höfumk aukit          erfitt sinni ?
        vask snivin snjóvi        ok slegin regni
        ok drifin döggu,         dauþ vask lengi.'

                    Óþinn kvaþ :

6.   ' Vegtamr heitik,       sunr emk Valtams ;
     seg mer ór helju,       ek mun ór heimi :
     hveim eru bekkir        baugum sánir.
     flet fagrliga     flóiþ gulli ? '

                    Völva kvaþ :

7. (6)  ' Hér stendr Baldri       of brugginn mjöþr,
        skírar veigar,          liggr skjöldr yfir ;
        en ásmegir      í ofvæni.
        Nauþug sagþak,       nú munk þegja.'

                    Óþinn kvaþ :

8. (6)  ' Þegjat, völva !        þik vilk fregna,
        unz alkunna,           vilk enn vita :
        hverr mun Báldri       at bana verþa
        ok Óþins sun          aldri ræna ?

4. Round he rode to a door on the eastward
where he knew was a witch's grave.
He sang there spells of the dead to the Vala;
needs she must rise a corpse and answer :

5. 'What man is this to me unknown,
who torment adds to my toilsome way?
I was snowed on with snow, and dashed with rain,
I was drenched with dew, I have long been dead.'

Odin:
6. ' They call me Way wont I am son of Warwont;
tell me tidings of Hel, I will tell of the world.
For whom are the benches strewn with rings,
for whom is the fair dais flooded with gold?'

Vala:
7. ' Here stands for Baldr brewed the mead,
the shining cup, the shield lies over,
but the gods' race all are in despair.
Needs have I spoken, now will I cease.'

Odin:
8. 'Cease not, Vala ! still will I ask thee,
I must see yet onward till all I know:
who will be the slayer of Baldr,
who Odin's son will of life bereave?'

---

*6. Way wont: Odin as wanderer. The Fame- bough or mistletoe which, according to Snorri, Loki puts 'into the hands of blind Hud'*

Völva kvaþ :

9. (7)    'Höþr berr hávan      hróþrbaþm þinig,
       hann mun Baldri       at bana verþa
       ok Óþins sun         aldri ræna.
       Nauþug sagþak,      nú munk þegja.'

Óþinn kvaþ :

10. (7)   ' Þegjat, völva !       þik vilk fregna,
       unz alkunna,         vilk enn vita :
       hverr mun heiptar [Heþi]     hefnt of vinna
       eþa Baldrs bana       á bál vega ? '

Völva kvaþ :

(8)    ' Rindr berr Vála       í vestrsölum,
       sa mun Óþins sunr     einnættr vega ;
       hönd of þværat       né höfuþ kembir,
       áþr á bál of berr      Baldrs andskota.
       Nauþug sagþak,      nú munk þegja.'

Óþinn kvaþ

12. (8)   ' Þegjat, völva !      þik vilk fregna,
       unz alkunna,        vilk enn vita :

(9)    hverjar'u meyjar     es at muni gráta
       ok á himin verpa     halsa skautum ? '

Völva kvaþ :

13. (10)   ' Estat Vegtamr,     sem ek hugþa,
       heldr est Óþinn,     aldinn gautr ! '

Vala:

9. 'Hod shall bear thither the high-grown Fame-bough,
he will be the slayer of Baldr,
yea, Odin's son will of life bereave.
Needs have I spoken, now will I cease.'

Odin:

10. 'Cease not, Vala, still will I ask thee,
I must see yet onward till all I know:
who shall work revenge for the woe on Hod,
and lay on the bale fire Baldr's foe?'

Vala:

11. ' Rind shall bear Vali in the western halls;
he, Odin's son, shall fight one night old.
Nor hand will he wash, nor head will he comb
till he lay on the bale fire Baldr's foe.
Needs have I spoken, now will I cease.'

Odin:

12. 'Cease not, Vala, still will I ask thee,
I must see yet onward till all I know:
who are the maidens who weep at will,
and up toward heaven their neck veils fling?'

Vala:

13. 'Not Waywont art thou as I had weened,
but thou art Odin, the ancient creator!'

---

11. Rind, the giant wife of Odin.

Óþinn kvaþ :

' Estat völva       né vís kona,
heldr est þriggja      þursa móþir ! '

Völva kvaþ :

14. (11)    ' Heim ríþ, Óþinn !       ok ves hróþugr :
svá komir manna     meirr aþtr á vit,
es lauss Loki      líþr ór böndum
ok í ragna rök     rjúfendr koma.'

Odin.

'No Vala art thou nor woman wise,
but of three giants thou art mother!'

Vala:

14. ' Ride homeward, Odin, glorying in thy gain!
for thus shall no being ever meet me more,
ere Loki roves from his fetters free,
and the Destroyers come at the Powers' great Doom.'

# LOKASENNA
## LOKI'S MOCKING

SYNOPSIS

Lokasenna ('Loki's flyting,' 'Loki's wrangling,' 'Loki's quarrelling') presents a trading of insults between the gods and Loki.

'There is one,' writes Snorri, 'who is numbered among the gods, although some call him their reviler, and the shame both of gods and men. His name is Loki, or Lopt, the Rover of Air, son of the Jotun Fierce-beater. His mother is called Leaf-isle or Pine-needle, and his brothers are Byleipt and Hel-dazzler. Loki is beautiful and fair of face, but evil of mind and fickle in his ways. He is more versed in the art of cunning than others, and is crafty in all things. Oft he brings the gods into great plight, and delivers them oft by his wily counsel.'

This bright elusive figure, like a spark of the fire which he personifies, kindles with life and humour every tale into which he enters, appearing and reappearing in different forms, a god in his power, and a devil in his deeds. He well deserves a place among the portraits which art has drawn of the latter personality. No stormy power of evil like the Satan of Paradise Lost, he yet provokes war in heaven, and snares by his tempting the wives of gods. His rebellion is more dangerous to them than a wild assertion of the individual, for he is the undermining instrument of fate. Compared too with Mephistopheles, Loki, rich in human life and mirth and beauty, finds more victims among men than the cold seducer of the spirit.

In the poems he may be traced back to some old Germanic fire god, perhaps called 'Logi,' flame, who lent his name and attributes to Loki, the 'ender' or destroyer of the gods. However this may be, his double nature and the poetical contradictory myths which are told concerning him find explanation in his origin as a fire god.

Fire is mighty, beneficent, life-restoring, swift, and beautiful to the eye; such character has Loki when, as Lodur, he bestows the gift of warmth and goodly hue on man, when he fetches Iðunn out of Jötunheim, and appears a god of wondrous beauty.

But fire may also be cruel, treacherous, fierce, and destructive; and was it not Loki himself who enticed Iðunn out of Asgarth, who betrayed Freyja, mocked the gods at their banquet, worked the death of Baldr, and led the Hel hosts at the Doom?

In all his mythical adventures Loki appears sometimes as the friend of the gods, and especially as the companion of Odin and Hcenir, and sometimes in alliance with the giants. He commits some folly or crime, he bring the gods into danger, and then by his power and cunning he extricates them and is forgiven, until he works the evil which can never be atoned or remedied the death of Baldr. After this he must suffer punishment till Ragnarök.

Snorri relates how Loki had three terrible children by the giantess Sorrow-bringer Fenrir, the World-serpent, and Hel.

'All-father bade the gods bring them to him, and he cast the Serpent into the deep, where it lies encircling all lands, and grown so huge that it bites its own tail.

Hel he cast into Mist-home; and the Wolf was reared at home. Tyr alone had courage to approach the latter with food. And when they beheld how the Wolf waxed mightier each day they remembered the prophecy, how it was foretold that he should work their woe.

And after they had taken counsel together they forged a very strong fetter called Landing, and brought it to the Wolf and bade him try his strength upon it.

Seeing that it was not over mighty, Fenrir let the gods bind him as they willed, and at his first struggle the fetter was broken. Thus he loosed himself from Laeding.

'Then the gods forged another fetter, twice as strong, which they called Drómi, and bade the Wolf try his strength upon this, and told him that he would become famed for his might if a chain of such forging would not hold him. Fenrir knew well how strong was the fetter, but he knew likewise that he had waxed mightier since he broke Laeding. Moreover, it came into his mind that one must needs risk somewhat for the sake of fame, and he allowed himself to be bound.

When the gods said they were ready Fenrir shook himself, and loosened the fetter till it touched the ground; then he strove fiercely against it and spurned it off him, and broke it so that the pieces flew far and wide. Thus Fenrir freed himself from Drómi.

'Then were the gods filled with fear and deemed they would never be able to bind the Wolf, and All-father sent Skirnir, Frey's shining courier, down to the Underworld, where dwelt the Dark Elves or dwarfs, who forged for him the fetter called Gleipnir. Out of six things they wrought it the footfalls of cats, the beards of women, the roots of mountains, the sinews of bears, the breath of fish, and the spittle of birds. It was soft and smooth as a silken band, yet strong and trusty withal.'

The Wolf would consent to be bound only with this fetter on condition that one among the gods would lay a hand in his mouth.

'And each god looked at the other, and weened that here was choice of two ills; but none made offer until Tyr put forth his right hand, and laid it in the Wolf's mouth.'

So they bound Fenrir, and watched him struggle, while the fetter grew tighter and sharper, and they laughed, one and all, save Tyr alone, who lost his hand. But this attempt, as with Baldr, to stay the course of Weird is in vain, and the Wolf will remain bound only till Ragnarok.

'Loki's Mocking' is the best poem of its kind in the whole collection of the Edda. Continually striving after more and more vivid representation, Old Norse art has at last attained its perfection in an inimitable dramatic poem, where the whole interest is centred in living personality. The characters are drawn in masterly fashion with a neat, crisp touch; the dialogue is racy, humorous, forcible, and has a bitterness which flavours the whole. Much skill is shown in the introduction of new speakers, with their ever varying tones, and quick repartees.

The setting is a feast given by the sea god Ægir. In continuity, the prose introduction says: 'Ægir, also named Gymir, had made ale for the Æsir, when he had received the great kettle of which was told' (see Hymiskviða).

Many of the Æsir and the Vanir attend, and elves also. The servants of Ægir, Fimafeng (Nimble-snatcher) and Eldir (Fire-stirrer), do a thorough job of welcoming the guests to the peaceful sea-halls, but Loki is jealous of the praise being heaped upon the servants and slays Fimafeng. The gods are angry with Loki and drive him out of the hall, before returning to their carousing.

On returning Loki encounters Eldir. He threatens him and bids him reveal what the gods were talking about in their cups. Eldir's response is that they were discussing their might at arms, and that Loki is not welcome.

After trading insults and threats with Eldir, Loki enters the hall of Ægir. A hush falls. Loki calls upon the rules of hospitality, demanding a seat and ale. Bragi responds that he is unwelcome. Loki demands fulfillment of an ancient oath sworn with Odin that they should drink together. Odin asks his son Vidar to make a space for Loki.

Vidar rises and pours a drink for Loki. Before Loki drains his draught, he utters a toast to the gods but pointedly excludes Bragi from it.

Bragi offers Loki a horse, a ring and a sword to placate him; Loki, however, is spoiling for a fight, and insults Bragi by questioning his courage. Bragi' replies that it would be contrary to the rules of correct behaviour to fight within his hosts' hall, but were they back in Asgard then things would be different.

Iðunn, Bragi's wife, holds him back. Loki then insults Iðunn, calling her sexually loose. Gefjon is the next to speak and then Loki turns his spite on her. Odin then attempts to chide Loki, as do (in turn), Freyja, Niord, Tyr, Freyr and Byggvir. The exchanges between Odin and Loki are particularly vitriolic.

Eventually Thor turns up at the party, and he is not to be placated, nor withheld. Alternating with Loki's insults to him, he says four times that he will use his hammer to knock Loki's head off if he continues. Loki replies that for Thor alone he will leave the hall, because his threats are the only ones he fears. He then leaves.

Finally there is a short piece of prose summarizing the tale of Loki's binding, which is told in fuller form in the Gylfaginning section of Snorri Sturluson's Prose Edda.

Loki is chased by the gods, and caught after an unsuccessful attempt at disguising himself as a salmon. The entrails of his son Nari are used to bind him to three rocks above which Skaði places a serpent to drip venom on him. Loki's wife Sigyn remains by his side with a bowl to catch the venom; however, whenever she leaves to empty the bowl, venom falls on Loki, causing him to writhe in agony; this writhing was said to be the cause of earthquakes.

The text says that Loki's other son, Narfi, was turned into a wolf, but does not make clear that he tears his brother apart; also in the Gylfaginning version it is a son of Loki named Váli whom the Æsir transform into a wolf and who kills Narfi. Some editors have therefore chosen to read the names Nari and Narvi as a mistake in the manuscript, and transcribe Nari as Váli. Nari and Narfi are otherwise considered to be variations of the same name.

*Loki taunts Bragi*

# LOKASENNA

Ægir, er öþru nafni hét Gymir, hann hafþi búit ásum öl, þá er hann hafþi fengit ketil inn mikla, sem nú er sagt. Til þeirar veizlu kom Óþinn ok Frigg kona hans. þórr kom eigi, þuiat hann var í austrvegi. Síf var þar, kona þórs ; Bragi ok Iþunn kona hans. Týr var þar, hann var einhendr : Fenrisúlfr sleit hönd af hánum, þá er hann var bundinn.

Þar var Njörþr ok kona hans Skaþi, Freyr ok Freyja, Víþarr sonr Óþins. Loki var þar, ok þjónustumenn Freys Byggvir ok Beyla. Mart var þar ása ok álfa.

*Loki Bound*

# LOKASENNA

## AT THE BANQUET OF ÆGIR

Ægir, who is also called Gymir (the Binder), bade the gods to an ale feast after he had got possession of the great cauldron as already told. To this banquet came Odin and Frigg, his wife. Thor came not because he was journeying in the East-country, but his wife Sif was there, and Bragi, with his wife Iðunn; Tyr also, who was one-handed, because the wolf Fenrir had torn off the other hand while the gods were binding him.

There were Njörð and his wife Skaði, Frey and his servants Barley and Beyla, Freyja, Vidar, the son of Odin, with many other gods and elves; there, moreover, was Loki.

---

*As already told: See Hymiskviþa. East-country, or Jötunheim.*

Ægir atti twá þjonustumenn : Fimafengr ok Eldir. Þar var lýsigull haft fyrir elds ljós ; sjálft barsk þar öl ; þar var griþstaþr mikill. Menn löfuþu mjök hversu góþir þjonustumenn Ægis váru. Loki mátti eigi heyra þat, ok draþ hann Fimafeng.

Þa skóku œsir skjöldu sina ok œppu at Loka ok eltu hann braut til skógar, en þeir faru at drekka. Loki hvarf aptr ok hitti úti Eldi ; Loki kvaddi hann :

Loki kvaþ :

1. ' Seg þat, Eldir !      svát þú einugi
     feti gangir framarr :
     hvat hér inni      hafa at ölmálum
     sigtíva synir ? '

Eldir kvaþ :

2. ' Of vápn sin dœma      ok of vígrisni sína
     sigtíva synir :
     ása ok alfa      es hér inni 'rú
     mangi's þér í orþi vinr.'

Loki kvaþ :

3. ' Inn skal ganga      Ægis hallir í
     á þat sumbl at sea ;
     joll ok áfu      fœrik ása sunum
     ok blentk þeim meini mjöp.'

Eldir kvaþ :

4. ' Veiztu, ef inn gengr      Ægis hallir í
     á þat súmbl at sea,
     hrópi ok rógi      ef þú eyss á holl regin,
     á þér munu perra þat.'

Ægir had two servants, Nimble-snatcher and Fire-stirrer. Shining gold was used in the hall for the light of fire, the ale bore itself, and the place was held as a holy peace-stead. Men praised Ægir's servants, and said oft how good they were; but Loki could not brook this, and he slew Nimble-snatcher.

The gods all shook their shields and cried out against Loki, and chased him away to the woods, and then betook themselves again to drink. But Loki turned back, and finding Fire-stirrer standing without, he hailed him:

Loki:
1. Tell me, Fire-stirrer but whence thou standest
move not a single step
what are the sons of the war-gods saying
o'er the ale-cup here within?

Fire-stirrer:
2. Of their weapons are speaking the sons of the war-gods,
they boast of their battle-fame;
but 'mid gods and elves who within are gathered,
not one is thy friend in his words.

Loki:
3. I shall now enter the halls of Ægir
this banquet to behold:
mockery and strife will I bring to the god's sons,
and mingle sorrow with their mead.

Fire-stirrer:
4. Know, if thou enter the halls of Ægir
this banquet to behold,
if reproach and slander on the blest Powers thou pour
they shall wipe out thy words upon thee.

Loki kvaþ :

5.   ' Veizt þat, Eldir !      ef vit einir skulum
     sáryrþum sakask,
    auþugr verþa      munk í andsvörum,
    ef þú mǽlir til mart.'


Síþan gekk Loki inn í höllina, en er þeir sá, er fyrir váru, hverr inn var kominn, þögnuþu þeir allir.

Loki kvaþ :

6.   ' Þyrstr ek köm      þessar hallar til,
    Loptr, of langan veg,
  ásu at biþja,      at mér einn gefi
    mǽran drykk mjaþar.

7. (6)   Hví þegiþ ér svá,      þrungin goþ !
    at ér mǽla né meguþ ?
  sessa ok staþi      veliþ mér sumbli at,
    eþa heitiþ mik heþan.'

Bragi kvaþ :

8. (7)   ' Sessa ok staþi      velja þér sumbli at
    ǽsir aldrigi ;
  þvít ǽsir vitu,      hveim þeir alda skulu
    gambansumbl of geta.'

Loki kvaþ :

9. (8)   ' Mant þat, Óþinn !      es vit í árdaga
    blendum blóþi saman ?
  ölvi bergja      lézt eigi mundu,
    nema okkr væri báþum borit.'

Loki:
5. Know thou, Fire-stirrer, if we twain must fight
together with wounding words,
if thou talk too freely thou soon shalt find me
in answering ready and rich.

Then Loki entered the hall, and when those assembled saw who
was come in they all became silent.

Loki:
6. Thirsty come I, the Rover of Air,
to this feasting hall from afar;
I would ask the gods to give me but one
sweet draught of the mead to drink.

7. Why all silent ye sullen gods?
Can ye speak no single word?
Make me room on the bench, give me place at the banquet,
or bid me hie homeward hence.

Bragi:
8. Nor place at the banquet nor room on the bench
the gods shall give to thee;
well they know for what manner of wight
they should spread so fair a feast.

Loki:
9. Mindest thou, Odin, how we twain of old
like brothers mingled our blood?
Then saidst thou that never was ale-cup sweet
unless 'twere borne to us both.

---

8. *Bragi, the god of poetry.*
9. *The mingling of blood sealed a brotherhood in arms: Loki,*
*Odin, and Hcenir were companions in many strange adventures.*

Óþinn kvaþ :

10. (9)   ' Rís þá, Víþarr !       ok lát ulfs föþur

         sitja sumbli at,

         síþr oss Loki kveþi       lastastöfum

         Ægis höllu í. '

Þá stóþ Víþarr upp ok skenkþi Loka ; en áþr hann drykki, kvaddi hann ásuna :

11. (10)   ' Heilir æsir,       heilar ásynjur

         ok öll ginnheilug goþ !

         nema einn áss       es innar sitr,

         Bragi, bekkjum á.'

Bragi kvaþ :

12. (11)   ' Mar ok mæki       gefk þer míns fear

         ok bœtir svá baugi Bragi,

         síþr þú ásum       öfund of gjaldir ;

         gremjat goþ at þér ! '

Loki kvaþ :

13. (12)   ' Jós ok armbauga       mundu æ vesa

         beggja vanr, Bragi !

         ása ok alfa       es hér inni 'rú

         þú'st viþ víg varastr

         ok skjarrastr viþ skot.'

Bragi kvaþ :

14. (13)   ' Veitk, ef fyr útan værak,       sem fyr innan emk

         Ægis höll of kominn,

         haufuþ þitt       bærak í hendi mér :

         létak þér þat fyr lygi.'

Odin:
10. Rise up, Vidar, and give the Wolf's father
bench-room at the banquet,
lest Loki shame us with scornful speeches
here in Ægir's halls.


Then Vidar arose and poured out ale for Loki, who thus greeted
the gods before he drank:


11. Hail, ye gods, and goddesses, hail!
hail all ye holy Powers!
save only one who sits within,
thou, Bragi, upon the bench !


Bragi:
12. Steed and sword from my store will I give thee
and reward thee well with rings
lest thou pour thy hate on the gracious Powers.
Rouse not their wrath against thee!


Loki:
13. Nor steeds nor rings wilt thou ever own
as long as thou livest, Bragi:
thou art wariest in war, and shyest at shot
of all gods and elves herein.


Bragi:
14. Were I without now even in such mood
as within the halls of ^Egir,
that head of thine would I hold in my hand:
'twere little reward for thy lie !

---

10. *Loki was the father of the wolf Fenrir.*

Loki kvaþ :

15. (14)  ' Snjallr est í sessi,      skalta svá göra,
          Bragi, bekkskrautuþr !
     vega þú gakk,      ef þú vreiþr seïr !
     hyggsk vætr hvatr fyrir.'

Íþunn kvaþ :

16. (15)  ' Biþk þik, Bragi !      barna sifjar duga
          ok allra óskmaga,
     at þú Loka kveþjat      lastastöfum
          Ægis höllu í.'

Loki kvaþ :

17. (16)  ' Þegi þú, Íþunn !      þik kveþk allra kvenna
          vergjarnasta vesa,
     síztu arma þína      lagpir ítrþvegna
          umb þinn bróþurbana.'

Íþunn kvaþ :

18. (17)  ' Loka ek kveþka      lastastöfum
          Ægis höllu i ;
     Braga ek kyrri      bjórreifan :
          vilkak at vreiþir vegisk.'

Gefjun kvaþ :

19. (18)  ' Hvi it æsir tveir      skuluþ inni hér
          sáryrþum sakask ?
     Loka þat veit,      at hann leikinn es
          ok hann fjörg öll fiar.'

Loki:

15. Bold seemst thou sitting, but slack art thou doing,
Bragi, thou pride of the bench!
Come forth and fight if in truth thou art wroth;
a bold warrior bides not to think.

Iðunn:

16. Nay Bragi, I beg for the sake of blood-kindred,
and of all the war-sons of Odin,
upbraid not Loki with bitter speeches
here in Ægir's halls.

Loki.

17. Silence, Iðunn! I swear, of all women
thou the most wanton art;
who couldst fling those fair-washed arms of thine
about thy brother's slayer.

Iðunn:

18. I blame thee not, Loki, with bitter speeches
here in Ægir's halls.
I seek but to sooth the ale-stirred Bragi,
lest in your fierceness ye fight.

Gefjon:

19. Wherefore, ye gods twain with wounding words
strive ye here in the hall?
Who knows not Loki, that he loathes all beings
and mocks in his madness of soul?

---

*16. Iðunn, Bragi's wife. The myth of stanza 17 is unknown.*

Loki kvaþ :

20. (19)   ' Þegi þú, Gefjun !     þess munk nú geta,

hverr þik glapþi at geþi :

sveinn enn hvíti     þér sigli gaf

ok þú lagþir lær yfir.'

Óþinn kvaþ :

21. (20)   ' Œrr est, Loki !     ok örviti,

es þú fær þér Gefjun at gremi :

þvít aldar örlög     hykk at öll of viti

jafngörla sem ek.'

Loki kvaþ :

22. (21)   ' Þegi þú, Óþinn !     þú kunnir aldri

deila víg meþ verum :

opt þú gaft     þeims gefa né skyldir

enum slævurum sigr.'

Óþinn kvaþ :

23. (22)   ' Veizt, ef ek gaf     þeims gefa né skyldak,

enum slævurum sigr :

átta vetr     vastu fyr jörþ neþan

kýr molkandi ok kona

ok hefr þar börn of borit,

ok hugþak þat args aþal.'

Loki:

20. Silence, Gefjon! I will tell that tale
of him who once stole thy heart,
that fair swain who gave thee a shining necklace,
him thou didst hold in thine arms.

Odin:

21. Wild art thou, Loki, and witless now,
thus rousing Gefjon to wrath!
I ween she knows all the fate of the world
even as surely as I.

Loki:

22. Silence, Odin! When couldst thou ever
rule battles of men aright?
Oft hast thou given to them who had earned not,
to the slothful victory in strife.

Odin:

23. Know, if ever I gave to them who had earned not,
to the slothful victory in strife,
eight winters wert thou below in the earth
like a maiden, milking kine,
and there thou gavest birth to bairns,
which I weened was a woman's lot.

---

*20. Gefjon is only mentioned here in the Poetical Edda. The myth
is usually told by Freyja.*
*23. This stanza alludes to a story otherwise unattested; that Loki
once spent eight winters beneath the earth as a woman milking
cows, and during this time bore children.*

Loki kvaþ :

24. (23)   ' En þik sípa      kváþu Sámseyju í,
ok drapt á vétt sem völur :
vitka líki      fórtu verþjóþ yfir,
ok hugþak at args aþal.'

Frigg kvaþ :

25. (24)   ' Örlögum ykkrum      skyliþ aldrigi
segja seggjum frá :
hvat it æsir tveir      drýgþuþ í árdaga,
firrisk æ forn rök firar.'

Loki kvaþ :

26. (25)   ' Þegi þú, Frigg !      þú'st Fjörgyns mær
ok hefr æ vergjörn verit,
es þá Vé ok Vilja      léztu þér, Viþris kvæn !
báþa í baþm of tekit.'

Frigg kvaþ :

27. (26)   ' Veizt, ef inni ættak      Ægis höllum í
Baldri glíkan bur,
út né kvæmir      frá ása sunum,
ok væri at þér vreiþum vegit.'

Loki:

24. But thou in Samsey wast weaving magic
and making spells like a witch:
thou didst pass as wizard through the world of men,
which I weened was a woman's way.


Frigg:

25. Tell ye to no man the shameful tale
of the deeds ye did of old,
how ye two gods wrought in ancient time;
what is gone is best forgot.


Loki:

26. Silence, Frigg! who hast Earth's spouse for a husband,
and hast ever yearned after men!
Vé the holy, and Vili the lustful
both lay in thine arms, wife of Odin.


Frigg:

27. Know, if I had but in Ægir's halls,
a son like my Baldr, the slain,
thou wouldst ne'er come whole through the host of the gods
but fiercely thou shouldst be assailed.

---

*24. Samsey, modern Samsu, north of Funen.*
*26. Line 1: This line has often been misunderstood, by Snorri and later critics. The literal thou art Fjörgynn's maid has been rendered thou art Fjörgynn's daughter. But Fjörgynn is only another name for Odin in his character as the husband of Fjörgynn or Jord, the Earth, and mother of Thor. Vé and Vili, the brothers of Odin, may also be taken as different aspects of the same god. The name used in the text for Odin is Vidrir, the Stormer.*

Loki kvaþ :

28. (27)   ' Enn vill þú, Frigg !     at ek fleiri telja
mína meinstafi :
ek því ræþ,     es þú ríþa sérat
síþan Baldr at sölum.'

Freyja kvaþ :

28. (28)   ' Œrr est, Loki !     es þú yþra telr
ljóta leiþstafi :
örlög Frigg     hykk at öll viti,
þót hón sjölfgi segi.'

Loki kvaþ :

30. (29)   ' Þegi þú, Freyja !     þik kannk fullgörva,
esa þér vamma vant :
ása ok alfa     es hér inni 'rú
hverr hefr hórr þinn verit.'

Freyja kvaþ :

31. (30)   ' Flá's þér tunga,     hykk at þér fremr
myni ógott of gala ;
vreiþir'u þér æsir     ok ásynjur,
hryggr munt heim fara.'

Loki kvaþ :

32. (31)   ' Þegi þú, Freyja !     þú'st fordæþa
ok meini blandin mjök :
síz þík at brœþr þínum     stóþu blíþ regin,
ok mundir þá, Freyja ! frata.'

Loki:

28. Wouldst have me, Frigg, tell a few more yet
of these shameful stories of mine?
'Twas I wrought the Woe, that henceforth thou wilt not
see Baldr ride back to the halls.

Freyja:

29. Mad art thou, Loki, to tell thus the shame
and grim deeds wrought by you gods!
Frigg knows, I ween, all the fate of the world;
though she whispers thereof to none.

Loki:

30. Silence, Freyja ! Full well I know thee
and faultless art thou not found;
of the gods and elves who here are gathered
each one hast thou made thy mate.

Freyja:

31. False thy tongue is ! Too soon 'twill sing
its own song of woe, as I ween.
Wroth are the gods, and the goddesses wroth,
rueful thou soon shalt run home.

Loki:

32. Silence, Freyja ! Thou art a sorceress
all with evil blent:
once at thy brother's the blithe gods caught thee,
and then wast thou frightened, Freyja !

---

28. *The only allusion in the Poetical Edda to Loki's share in the death of Baldr. Possibly it only refers to Loki's refusal to weep.*
32. *No such myth of Frey or Freyja is mentioned elsewhere.*

Njörþr kvaþ :

33. (32)   ' Þat's vá litil,      þót sér vers faï
           varþir, hóss eþa hvárs ;
           undr's at áss ragr      es hér inn of kominn
           ok hefr sá börn of borit.'

Loki kvaþ :

34 (33)   Þegi þú, Njörþr !      þú vast austr heþan
           gísl of sendr at goþum ;
           Hymis meyjar      höfþu þik at hlandtrogi
           ok þér í munn migu.'

Njörþr kvaþ :

35. (34)   ' Sú erumk líkn,      es vask langt heþan
           gísl of sendr at goþum :
           þa ek mög gat      þanns manngi fiar,
           ok þykkir sá ása jaþarr.'

Loki kvaþ :

36. (35)   ' Hætt nú, Njörþr !      haf á hófi þik !
           munkak því leyna lengr :
           viþ systur þinni      gaztu slíkan mög
           ok esa þó ónu verr.'

Týrr kvaþ :

37. (36)   ' Freyr es baztr      allra baldriþa
           ása görþum í ;
           mey né grœtir      né manns konu,
           ok leysir ór höptum hvern.'

Njörð:

33. Small harm it seems if haply a woman
both lover and husband have;
but behold the horror now in the halls,
the vile god who bairns hath borne!

Loki:

34. Silence, Njörð! Thou wast eastward sent
as hostage from hence by the gods;
there into thy mouth flowed the maids of Hymir
and used thee as trough for their floods.

Njörð:

35. Yet was I gladdened when sent afar,
as hostage from hence by the gods;
there a son I got me, the foe of none,
and highest held among gods.

Loki:

36. Silence now, Njörð! Set bounds to thy lying;
I will no longer let this be hid
with thine own sister that son thou gottest,
though he is not worse than one weened.

Tyr:

37. Nay! Frey is the best of all bold riders
who enter the garths of the gods;
nor wife nor maiden he makes to weep,
but he breaks the prisoner's bonds.

---

*34. Njörð figures here in his character of sea god.*
*36. A son, presumably got with the giantess Skaiii, but in*
*Ynglinga S. it is stated that Njörð was married to his sister, and*
*had a son and daughter, Frey and Freyja, before even he was sent*
*as hostage by the Vanir to the Æsir.*

Loki kvaþ :

38. (37)   ' Þegi þú, Týr !       þú kunnir aldri
           bera tilt meþ tveim :
      handar hœgri       munk hinnar geta
           es þér sleit Fenrir frá.'

Týrr kvaþ

39. (38)   ' Handar emk vanr,      en þú Hróþvitnis,
           böl es beggja þrá :
      ulfgi hefr ok vel       es í böndum skal
           bíþa ragna rökkrs.'

Loki kvaþ :

40. (39)   ' Þegi þú, Tyr !       þat varþ þinni konu,
           at hón átti mög viþ mér ;
      öln né penning       hafþir þú þess aldrigi
           vanréttis, vesall ! '

Freyr kvaþ :

41. (40)   ' Ulf sék liggja       árósi fyrir,
           unz of rjúfask regin ;
      því munt næst,       nema nú þegir,
           bundinn, bölvasmiþr ! '

Loki.

38. Silence, Tyr! Who in truth couldst never
bring good will betwixt twain;
the tale will I tell of that right hand
which Fenrir reft from thee once.


Tyr:

39. If I want for a hand for thy Wolf-son, thou;
we both bear burden of want:
and 'tis ill with the Wolf who must bide in bonds
till the twilight come of the Powers.


Loki:

40. Be silent, Tyr, while I tell of the son
whom thy wife got once by me:
not even a penny or ell of cloth
didst thou get for thy wrong, poor wretch!


Frey:

41. I see Fenrir lying at the mouth of the flood;
he shall bide till the Powers perish;
and thou, mischief-maker, shalt meet with like fate
if thou hold not herewith thy peace.

---

*39. Twilight of the Powers or Ragna rokr: This is the only use of
rokr in the poems, which has given rise to the phtase 'twilight of
the gods.' The more usual form was rok or fate.*
*40. A lost myth.*
*41. The flood, called Vamm or Van by Snorri, is a river of Hel
proceeding from the moisture which flowed out of Fenrir 's jaws
while the great Wolf lay bound in torture.*

Loki kvaþ :

42. (41)  ' Golli keypta          léztu Gymis dóttur
          ok seldir þitt svá sverþ ;
          en es Múspells synir          ríþa Myrkviþ yfir,
          veizta þá, vesall ! hvé vegr.'

Byggvir kvaþ :

43. (42)  ' Veizt, ef öþli ættak          sem Ingunar-Freyr,
          ok svá sællikt setr,
          mergi smæra mölþak          þá meinkráku
          ok lemþa alla í liþu.'

Loki kvaþ :

44. (43)  ' Hvat's þat et litla,          es ek þat löggra sék,
          ok snapvíst snapir ?
          at eyrum Freys          mundu æ vesa
          auk und kvernum klaka.'

Byggvir kvaþ :

45. (44)  ' Byggvir heitik,          en mik bráþan kveþa
          goþ öll ok gumar ;
          því emk hér hróþugr,          at drekka Hrópts megir
          allir öl saman.'

Loki kvaþ :

46. (45)  ' Þegi þú, Byggvir !          þú kunnir aldri
          deila meþ mönnum mat ;
          þik í flets straï          finna né máttu,
          þá es vágu verar.'

Loki:
42. Wealth gav'st thou, Frey, for Gymir's maid,
thou didst sell thy sword for Gerðr;
but how shalt thou fight when the sons of fire
through the Murk-wood ride, poor wretch?

Barley:
43. Were I of Ing's race even as Frey
 owned I a land blest as Elfhome
I would crush like marrow yon croaker of ill,
and break all his bones into bits.

Loki:
44. What is that wee thing whining and fawning,
snuffling and snapping, I see?
Ever at Frey's ear, flattering and chattering,
or murmuring under the mill!

45. Barley, I am named, Barley. too bold and brisk
I am called by gods and men!
Here am I glorying that Odin's sons
all are drinking ale together!

Loki:
46. Silence, Barley-corn! Never couldst thou
even serve meat among men:
and when they fought thou couldst scarce be found,
safe 'neath the bed-straw hiding.

---

*42. Frey is slain by Surt, the Fire-giant, at the Doom of the gods.
43. Ing was the half divine ancestor of the Germanic race who
gave his name to the Ynglings or Swedes and to the Ingvines
mentioned by Tacitus. In Sweden he became associated with Frey,
who was there the chief god. Elf-home, see Grimismal, stanza 5.*

Heimdallr kvaþ :

47. (46)    ' Ölr est, Loki !       svát þú'st örviti,
      hví né lezkat, Loki ?
      þvít ofdrykkja       veldr alda hveim,
      es sína mǽlgi né manat.'

Loki kvaþ :

48. (47)    ' Þegi þú, Heimdallr !       þér vas í árdaga
      et ljóta líf of lagit :
      örþgu baki       þú munt ǽ vesa
      ok vaka vörþr goþa.'

Skaþi kvaþ :

49. (48)    ' Létt's þér, Loki !       munattu lengi svá
      leika lausum hala ;
      þvít þik á hjörvi skulu       ens hrímkalda magar
      görnum binda goþ.'

Loki kvaþ :

50. (49)    ' Veizt, ef mik á hjörvi skulu   ens hrímkalda magar
      görnum binda goþ :
      fyrstr ok öfstr       vask at fjörlagi,
      þars ver á Þjaza þrifum.

Skaþi kvaþ :

51. (50)    ' Veizt, ef fyrstr ok öfstr       vast at fjörlagi,
      þás er á þjaza þrifuþ :
      frá vëum mínum       ok vöngum skulu
      þér ǽ köld ráþ koma.'

Heimdal:
47. So drunk art thou, Loki, thou hast lost thy wits;
why wilt thou not cease from thy scoffing?
Ale beyond measure so masters man
that he keeps no watch on his words.

Loki:
48. Silence, Heimdal! That hard life of thine
 was settled for thee long since:
with weary back must thou ever bide,
and keep watch, thou warder of gods !

Skaði:
49. Blithe are thou, Loki, but brief while shalt thou
with free tail frolic thus:
ere long the gods shall bind thee with guts
of thy rime-cold son to a sword.

Loki:
50. If in truth the gods shall bind me with guts
of my rime-cold son to a rock,
know that first and last was I found at the death
when we set upon Thiaxi, thy sire.

Skaði.
51. If first and last thou wert found at the death
when ye set upon Thiazi, my sire,
know that in house or home of mine
shall be shown thee little love!

---

*49. Skaði: Norse goddess of bowhunting, skiing, winter, and mountains. A sword: we are told by Snorri that Loki is bound not to a sword but to three sharp stones.*
*50. Thiazi was slain by Thor.*

Loki kvaþ :

52. (51)   ' Léttari í málum      vastu viþ Laufeyjar sun,
          þás þú lézt mer á beþ þinn boþit :
          getit verþr oss sliks,      ef vér görva skulum
          telja vömm enn vár. '

Þá gekk Sif fram ok byrlaþi Loka, í hrímkalki mjöþ ok mælti :

53. (52)   ' Heill ves nú, Loki !      ok tak viþ hrímkalki
          fullum forns mjaþar,
          heldr hana eina      látir meþ ása sunum
          vammalausa vesa.'

Hann tók viþ horni ok drakk af :

54. (53)   ' Ein þú værir,      ef þú svá værir
          vör ok gröm at veri :
          einn ek veit,      svát ek vita þykkjumk
          hór ok of Hlórriþa
          ok vas þat sa enn lævísi Loki.

Beyla kvaþ :

55. (54)   ' Fjöll öll skjalfa,      hykk á för vesa
          heiman Hlórriþa ;
          hann ræþr ró      þeims rœgir hér
          goþ öll ok guma.'

Loki kvaþ :

56. (55)   ' Þegi þú, Beyla !      þú'st Byggvis kvæn
          ok meini blandin mjök ;
          ókynjan meira      kvama meþ ása sunum,
          öll est, deigja ! dritin.'

Loki:
52. Milder were thy words to Loki once
when thou badst him come to thy bed;
for such tales, I ween, will be told of us twain,
if we own all our acts of shame.

Then Sif came forth, and poured out mead for Loki in the
foaming cup.

Sif:
53. Hail now, Loki! quaff this rimy cup
filled with the old mead full.
At least grant that I, of the kindred of gods
alone am free from all fault.

Loki took the horn and quaffed:

54. Thou alone wert blameless hadst thou in bearing
been sly and shrewish with men;
but Thor's wife had one lover at least, as I know,
even Loki the wily-wise.

Beyla:
55. All the fells are quaking, fast is the Thunderer
faring, I trow, from home !
He will soon bring to silence him who thus slanders
all beings here in the hall.

Loki.
56. Silence, Beyla, wife of Barley-corn
all with foulness filled!
Ne'er 'mid the gods came one so uncouth,
thou bond-maid stained and soiled.

---

52. *Another lost myth.*
53. *Sif: Thor's wife*

Þá kom þórr at ok kvaþ :

57. (56)  ' Þegi þú, rög vættr !    þér skal minn þrúþhamarr
           Mjöllnir mál fyrnema ;
   (57)  herþaklett    drepk þér halsi af,
           ok verþr þá þínu fjörvi of farit.'

Loki kvaþ :

58.  ' Jarþar *burr*    es hér nú inn kominn :
         hví þrasir þú svá, þórr ?
     en þá þorir þú etki    es skalt viþ ulf vega,
         ok svelgr hann allan Sigföþur.'

Þórr kvaþ :

59.  ' þegi þú, rög vættr !    þér skal minn þrúþhamarr
         Mjöllnir mál fyrnema ;
     upp þér verpk    ok á austrvega,
         síþan þik manngi sér.'

Loki kvaþ :

60.  ' Austrförum þínum    skaltu aldrigi
         segja seggjum frá :
     síz í hanzka þumlungi    hnúkþir þú, einheri !
         ok þóttiska Þórr vesa.'

Þórr kvaþ :

61.  ' Þegi þú, rög vættr !    þér skal minn þrúþhamarr
         Mjöllnir mál fyrnema ;
     hendi hœgri    drepk þik Hrungnis bana,
         svát þer brotnar beina hvat.'

Loki kvaþ :

62.  ' Lifa ætlak mér    langan aldr,
         þóttu hœtir hamri mér ;
     skarpar álar    þóttu þer Skrýmis vesa
         ok máttira nesti naa
         ok svalztu hungri heill.'

Then came the Thunderer in, and spake:

57. Silence, vile being! My hammer of might,
Mjollnir, shall spoil thee of speech.
I will strike that rock-head from off thy shoulders,
and soon will thy life-days be spent.

Loki:
58. 'Tis the Son of Earth who enters the hall !
Why dost thou threaten so, Thor?
Ne'er wilt thou venture to fight with the Wolf;
he shall swallow the War-father whole.

Thor:
59. Silence, vile being ! My hammer of might,
Mjollnir, shall spoil thee of speech.
I will drive thee forth to the eastern land
and no man shall see thee more.

Loki:
60. Of thy eastern journeys never shouldst thou
tell unto men the tale;
how once in a glove-thumb thou, warrior, didst crouch,
and scarce couldst think thyself Thor.

Thor.
61. Silence, vile being ! My hammer of might,
Mjollnir, shall spoil thee of speech;
this right hand shall smite thee with Hrungnir's slayer,
till each bone of thee shall be broke.

Loki:
62. Though haply thou threat'nest with'thy hammer of might,
long will my life be, I ween;
sharp were Skrymir's thongs, mindst thou, when starving
thou couldst not get at the food?

63.  ' Þegi pú, rög væittr !    þér   skal minn þrúþhamarr
     Mjöllnir mál fyrnema ;
     Hrungnis bani        mun þer í hel koma
     fyr nágrindr neþan.'

                    Loki kvap

64.  ' Kvapk fyr ásum,        kvaþk fyr ása sunum
     þats mik hvatti hugr ;
     en fyr þér einum        munk út ganga,
     þvít ek veit at vegr.

65.  Öl görþir, Ægir !        en þú aldri munt
     síþan sumbl of göra :
     eiga þin öll,        es hér inni es,
        leiki yfir logi
        ok brinni þér á baki ! '

En eptir þetta falz Loki í Fránangrs forsi í lax líki, þar
tóku æsir hann. Hann var bundinn meþ þörmum sonar *síns*
Narfa, en Váli sonr hans varþ at vargi. Skapi tók eitrorm ok
festi upp yfir annlit Loka ; draup þar ór eitr. Sigyn kona
Loka sat þar ok helt munnlaug undir eitrit, en er munnlaugin
var full, bar hon út eitrit ; en meþan draup eitrit á Loka. Þá
kiptiz hann svá hart viþ, at þaþan af skalf jörþ öll : þat eru
nú kallaþir landskjálftar.

Thor:
63. Silence, vile being! My hammer of might,
Mjollnir, shall spoil thee of speech.
With Hrungnir's slayer I will smite thee to Hel,
down 'neath the gates of the dead.

Loki:
64. Before sons and daughters of gods have I spoken,
even as I was moved by my mind :
now at length I go, and for thee alone,
for well, I ween, thou wilt fight.

65. Thou hast brewed thine ale, but such banquet, Ægir,
never more shalt thou make.
May flames play high o'er thy wealth
in the hall and scorch the skin of thy back!

Then Loki went forth and hid himself in Franang's stream in the form of a salmon, where the gods caught him and bound him with the guts of his son Narfi. But his other son Vali was turned into a wolf.

Skaði took a poisonous snake and fastened it up over Loki, so that poison dripped from it upon his face. Sigyn, his wife, sat by, and held a basin under the drops. And when the basin was full she cast the poison away, but meanwhile the drops fell upon Loki, and he struggled so fiercely against it that the whole earth shook with his strivings, which are now called earthquakes.

# FRAGMENTS FROM THE SNORRA EDDA

## SYNOPSIS

Iðun, the wife of Bragi, appears but this once in the poems. Snorri says 'She keeps in her casket those apples whereof the gods eat when they wax old, and which make them young again; thus they have given a great treasure into the keeping of Iðun, which once was well nigh lost.' These words recall one of the most famous incidents in the history of the gods, which involved the slaying of Thiazi and Njord's periods of exile.

Loki, when journeying with Odin and Hcenir, had once been made prisoner by the giant Thiazi, and was released only on promise of betraying Iðun to the giants. Iðun, like Freyja, was coveted by them as a summer goddess. Loki enticed her out of Asgarth by saying he had found apples as wondrous as her own.

Then there was walling among the gods at the loss of Iðun, and ere long they waxed grey-haired and old. They gathered in council, and each asked the other what he knew last concerning Iðun, and it was found that she was last seen going forth from Asgarth with Loki.

The latter, to save his life, donned Freyja's falcon plumes and flew into Jötunheim, and fetched back Iðun in the form of a nut. Thiazi pursued him as an eagle, and, just missing him, flew into a fire which the gods had kindled outside the walls of Asgarth. His wings were burnt, and there he was slain.

Skaði, his daughter, demanded vengeance, and would make peace only on two conditions one, that the gods should make her laugh, which only Loki could do by acting the part of a buffoon; secondly, that she should choose a husband among them, and she chose Njord.

*Source: Olive Bray and Wikipedia*

*Skaði s Longing for the Mountains*

# FRAGMENTS FROM THE SNORRA EDDA.

En Skaþi, dóttir jötuns, tók hjálm ok brynja ok öll hervápn ok ferr til Asgarþs at hefna föþur síns ; en æsir buþu henni sætt ok yfirbœtr, ok et fyrsta, at hón skal kjósa sér mann af ásum ok kjósa at fótum, ok sjá ekki af fleira.

Þá sá hón eins manns fœtr forkunnarfagra ok mælti: þenna kýs ek, fátt mun Gótt á Baldri ! en þat var Njörþr ór Nóatúnum. (*Bragarœþur LVI.*) Njörþr á þá konu er Skaþi heitir, dóttir Þjaza jötuns.

Skaþi vill hafa bústaþ þann er hafþi faþir hennar, þat er á fjöllum nökkurum þar sem heitir Þrymheimr : en Njörþr vill vera nær sjó. Þau sætuz á þat, at þau skyldu vera niú nætr í Þrymheimi en þá þrjár at Nóatúnum.

*Njörd's desire of the Sea*

# FRAGMENTS FROM
# THE SNORRA EDDA.

### I. HOW NJÖRÐ WAS MADE SKAÐI'S SPOUSE

Then Skaði, daughter of the giant Thiazi, when she heard how the gods had slain her father, donned helm and byrnie and all her weapons of war, and went to revenge him in Asgarth. For the sake of peace they offered her as weregild the choice of a spouse among the gods, but in her choosing she should behold no more than their feet.

And when she saw that the feet of one were exceeding fair and shapely, she cried: 'Him will I choose, for scant is the blemish in Baldr;' but lo! it was Njörð out of Noatun. Thus he took to wife Skaði, daughter of the Jötun Thiazi.

She would fain keep the dwellings of her father among the mountains in the land called Sound-home, but Njörð desired to be near the sea, so they made agreement thus: nine nights they should dwell in Sound-home, and afterwards three in Noatun.

En er Njörþr kom aptr til Nóatúna af fjallinu, þá kvaþ harm
þetta :

    (1)   ' Leiþ erumk fjöll,       vaska þar lengi á,
          nætr einar niu ;
    ulfa þytr       þóttumk illr vesa
    hjá söngvi svana.'

Þá kvaþ Skaþi þetta :

    (2)   ' Sofa né mákat      sævar beþjum á
         fogls jarmi fyrir :
       sá mik vekr,      es af víþi kömr,
         morgin hverjan már.'—*Gylfaginning xxiii.*


## II.

Hana (*Gná*) sendir Frigg í ymsa heima at eyrindum sínum.
Hon á þann hest er rennr lopt ok lög, ok heitir Hófvarpnir.
Þat var eitt sinn er hon reiþ, at vanir nökkurir sá reiþ hennar
í loptinu, þa mælti einn :

    (1)   ' Hvat þar flýgr,     hvat þar ferr
         eþa at lopti líþr ? '

Hon svaraþi :

    (2)   ' Né ek flýg,      þó ek fer
         auk at lopti líþ :
       á Hófvarpni     þeims Hamskerpir,
         gat viþ Garþrofu.'—*Gylfaginning xxxv.*

But when Njörð came back to Noatun from the mountains,
he said:

'Hateful the hills! though not long I lingered,
 nights only nine I dwelt there;
the howling of wolves was ill meseemed,
beside the song of the swans.'

And Skaði spake thus:

'Sleep I could not on ocean's couch
for the wailing cry of the gull:
from the wide sea faring, that bird awoke me
when he came each day at dawn.'

## II. CONCERNING THE GODDESS GNA

Frigg sends Gna, the Floater, on errands into many worlds. She
rides a horse called Hoof-flinger which fares through the sky and
over the sea. Once as she was passing, certain of the Wanes saw her
riding in the air, and one said:

What flies there, what fares there,
what flits there aloft?

And she made answer:

I fly not, yet am faring,
and I flit here aloft,
high on the Hoof-flinger, who was of Hedge-breaker
born, and the Fine-flanked steed.'

## III

Því næst sendu æsir um allan heim eyrindreka at biþja, at Baldr væri grátinn ór helju, en allir görþu þat : menninir ok kykvendin ok jörþin ok steinarnir ok tré ok allr malmr : svá sem þú munt sét hafa, at þessir hlutir gráta þá er þeir koma ór frosti ok í hita. Þá er sendimenn fóru heim ok höfþu vel rekit sín eyrindi, finna þeir í helli nökkurum hvar gýgr sat, hon nefndiz Þökk ; þeir biþja hana gráta Baldr ór helju. Hon svarar :

'  Þökk mun gráta　　þurrum tárum
　　　Baldrs bálfarar ;
　　kviks né dauþs　　nautka karls sonar,
　　　haldi hel þvís hefir. '

En þess geta menn, at þar hafi verit Loki Laufeyjar sonr er flest hefir illt gört meþ ásum.

## IV.

Þá fór Þórr til ár þeirar er Vimur heitir, allra á mest. Þá spenti hann sik megingjörþum ok studdi forstreymis Gríþarvöl, en Loki helt undir megingjarþar ; ok þá er Þórr kom á miþja ána, þá óx svá mjök áin, at uppi braut á öxl honum. Þá kvaþ Þórr þetta :

'  Vaxat nú, Vimur !　　alls mik þik vaþa tíþir
　　　jötna garþa í :
　　veiztu ef vex,　　at þá vex mér ásmegin
　　　jafnhátt upp sem himinn.'

## III. HOW THE WORLD WEPT FOR BALDR

The gods sent messengers throughout all the world to plead that Baldr might be wept out of Hel. And all beings wept; men and living creatures, the earth and rocks and trees and metals even as such things weep when after being fast bound with frost they become warm.

When the messengers had well done their errand they returned and found a certain giantess called Thokk sitting in a cave. They bade her weep Baldr out of Hel, but she answered:

'Thokk shall weep with dry tears alone
that Baldr is laid on the bale-fire :
Never joy have I had from man living or dead :
let Hel hold fast what she hath.'

Thus they knew that Loki, son of Laufey, had been there, who was ever wont to work most evil among the gods.

## IV. HOW THOR SLEW THE DAUGHTERS OF Geirröth

When Thor was faring once into Jötunheim he came to the river Vimur, of all rivers the greatest. There he girt him with his belt of strength, and leant on Gridar's staff as he went down-stream. Loki held on under the belt. When Thor had come into the midst of the flood it had risen so high that it flowed over his shoulders. Then he spake:

Wax not, Vimur, I needs must wade thee
to reach the Jötun-realms;
know ! if thou wax forthwith shall wax
my god's might high as heaven.'

En er Þórr kom til Geirröþar, þá var þeim félögum vísat fyrst í gestahús til herbergis, ok var þar einn stóll til sætis, ok sat þar Þórr. Þá varþ hann þess varr, at stóllinn fór undir hánum upp at ræfri ; hann stakk Gríþarveli upp í raptana ok lét sígaz fast á stólinn ; varþ þá brestr mikill ok fylgþi skrækr ; þar höfþu verit undir stólinum dœtr Geirröþar Gjölp ok Greip, ok hafþi hann brotit hrygginn í báþum. Þá kvaþ Þórr :

'  Einu sinni        neyttak alls megins
   jötna görþum í :
þás Gjölp ok Greip       Geirröþar dœtr,
   vildu hefja mik til himins.'


V.

Í Ásgarþi fyrir durum Valhallar stendr lundr sá er Glasir er kallaþr, en lauf hans allt er gull rautt, svá sem hér er kveþit, at

'  Glasir stendr       meþ gullnu laufi
   firir Sigtýs sölum.'

And when Thor had reached Geirröth's court, he and Loki were taken to lodge in the guest-house. There was but one stool there, and Thor sat down upon it. But presently he became aware that it was rising up to the roof under him. He thrust Gridar's staff against the rafters and pushed the stool down, and then came a great crash, and a shriek was heard for the daughters of Geirröth; Yelper and Gripper had been under the stool, and both their backs were broken.

Then spake Thor

Once only I used my god's might all
in the realms of the Jötun race;
When Yelper and Gripper, Geirröth's maids,
would have raised me high to heaven.

## V. GLISTENER

In Asgarth, before the gates of Valhöll, there stands a grove called Glistener (Glasir), whose leaves are all of red gold, as here is written :

Glistener stands with golden leaves
in front of Odin's halls.

---

*Sigty is another name for Odin.*

# VöLUSPÁ
## THE SOOTHSAYING OF THE VALA

SYNOPSIS

Völuspá (Prophecy of the Völva) is the best known poem of the Poetic Edda. It unites the other Eddic poems in one history, from beginning to end. Of it, Olive Bray says, 'Some poet, who has seen truth in the beauty of these old-world tales, has endeavoured to give them a unity...'

Bray adds that Völuspá 'needs to be read both first and last first, because it sums up and interprets the other poems; and last, because without a previous knowledge of its myths the Vala's words can scarcely be understood.'

The story of the creation of the world and its approaching doom is related by a Völva, or Vala (seeress) addressing Odin. The poem is one of the most important primary sources for the study of Norse mythology.

---

*The Icelandic 'Völva' is here anglicised to 'Vala'.*

A Vala was a wandering prophetess, who, clad in her fur cap
and her dark robes, went from house to house, foretelling and
divining hidden things. The power of second sight which she
claimed was common, not only to such as she, but to many a good
housewife in Icelandic sagas. But while those so gifted knew only of
trivial matters, interpreted dreams and omens, advised and warned,
this Vala, addressing all kindreds of the earth, reveals the fate and
history of the world.

Völuspá commences with the Vala requesting silence from 'the
sons of Heimdall' (human beings) and asking Odin whether he
wants her to recite ancient lore. She says she remembers giants born
in antiquity who reared her.

She tells first of the creation. In the beginning was chaos, when
as yet there was no heaven or earth only, in the north, a region of
snow and ice; and, in the south, one of fire and heat, with a yawning
gap between, from which life arose in the form of Ymir, the stirring,
rustling, sounding Jotun, followed by others of his kind, born out
of the elements, and as yet hardly to be distinguished from them.

Then the gods were born, who forthwith made war upon these
giant powers, and, half subduing them, they ordered the universe
with its worlds of gods and elves, of dwarfs and giants, of men the
living in Midgarth (Middle-earth), the dead in Hel, all held in the
sheltering embrace of a great World Tree; but from whence sprang
this Tree, or when and how it grew, not even the giants could tell.

The Æsir established order in the cosmos by setting the Sun,
Moon and Stars in heaven, thereby starting the cycle of day and
night. And when Sun turned her face towards Earth, and shone
upon its 'threshold' stones, the Earth brought forth fruit, and its
bare surface was overspread with green.

Now the gods bestowed, each after his own nature, gifts upon
two barren trees, and human life was awakened. Odin, as the Wind
god, gave them breath, which has ever been held as the emblem of
the spirit, or even as spirit itself. Hoenir, of whom little is known,
except that he was wise, gave an understanding mind. Loki (here
called Lodur), the fire-god, gave warm blood and the bright hue
of life,

A golden age ensued, when the Æsir had plenty of gold and constructed fair buildings and made tools. They were rejoicing in their work, in their play, and doubtless, too, in their love. It must have been then that Bragi wooed Idun, that Baldr wedded Nanna, that Thor's heart was given to Sif the golden-haired, the most guileless among all the goddesses.

But soon this peaceful age was broken. The first shadow of Doom fell as three mighty maidens arrived from Jotunheim, and sat them down beneath the tree Yggdrasil. These fair Norns wrote the past and present on their tablets and laid down the future fatesof men.

The Æsir then created the dwarves, of whom Mótsognir and Durinn were the mightiest.

At this point ten of the poem's stanzas conclude and six stanzas ensue which contain names of dwarves. This section, sometimes called 'Dvergatal' ('Catalogue of Dwarves'), is usually considered an interpolation and sometimes omitted by editors and translators.

After the 'Dvergatal', the creation of the first man and woman is recounted and Yggdrasil, the world-tree, is described. The Vala tells of the events that led to the first war among kindred races of the gods, the Æsir and the Vanir, and what occurred in the struggle between the Æsir and Vanir.

From the Wanes there came a witch called Golden-draught. Two things she taught a warlike tribe: the lust for gold, and the use of magic. The last was deemed an unpardonable sin among Germanic nations, and was punished by burning. In like manner the Æsir sought to destroy Golden-draught by burning her in Odin's hall; but in vain, for as many times as they burned her she was born anew.

War broke out and the Wanes demanded were-gild, and a council of peace was held; but the War-father arose, and hurling his spear gave the signal for strife to rage anew. It ended in the storming and destruction of Asgarth by the Wanes.

The seeress goes on to describe the beheading of Mimir, the attempted winning of Freya, the slaying of Baldr, best and fairest of the gods, as well as the enmity of Loki, and of others. The Vala proves her power to foretell the future by showing that her knowledge penetrates to the holiest secrets of the gods. She knows of their pledges; Heimdal's hearing, Odin's eye, and Baldr's life and fate, which are bound up with the mistletoe.

Heimdal can hear grass growing in the earth, and wool on the back of sheep. Is it his ear which he has hidden in the sacred well beneath Yggdrasil to obtain this wonderful power which he needs in his watch against the Mountain-giants. The seeress reveals to Odin that she is aware of what he sacrificed of himself in exchange for knowledge, and she knows where his eye is hidden. In several refrains she asks him whether he understands, or if he would like to hear more.

The Vala's description is now growing more and more visualised, and she herself can scarce interpret the floating pictures which represent now some future, now some present scene. She is looking into all the different worlds: Earth, where the Valkyries are speeding to the battlefields of men; Asgarth, where beside Valholl the fateful mistletoe is already high upgrown; the cave where she foresees the torment of Loki; Hel, where evil men are suffering the penalty of their misdeeds; Jotunheim, with, its feasting-hall of giants; dark dwarf-land, where no sun nor moon can penetrate, lit only by the glowing forge fires of .these active beings; and again eastward into Jotunheim, where Skoll was fostered, the dark wolf-son of Fenrir, who follows the fleeing Sun goddess across the heavens until he clutches her in the west, and stains all the sky at sunset with crimson like the blood of men.

She prophesies the destruction of the gods; fire and flood will overwhelm heaven and earth as the gods fight their final battles with their enemies. This is the 'twilight of the gods' - Ragnarök. She describes the summons to battle, the deaths of many of the gods and how Odin, himself, will be slain.

In the earth, among men, she hears wars and rumours of wars, crashing of shields and swords; from below comes the groaning of the imprisoned dwarfs; and throughout, at intervals, waxing louder and wilder, the deep baying of the Hel-hound, Garm. Amid this tumult she catches another sound, more fearful still, the shivering and rustling of the great Ash, the Tree of Fate, as it quivers, but does not fall and yet one other sound, a voice in the storm, the murmur of words : Odin is holding speech with Mimir. Now light falls; once more the Vala can see; the foes are gathering from all quarters on the great battlefield, which measures a hundred miles each way. From the east come Frost and Mountain giants; from the south come Fire-giants; from the north the Helhosts, and Loki; from the west must come the gods, led by Odin, with all his Chosen warriors.

In single combats the last battle is depicted. Thus the war-gods perish, and fire consumes the world.

Finally, augurs the Vala, a beautiful reborn world will rise from the ashes of death and destruction. Baldr will live again and the earth will sprout abundance without seed being sown. A final stanza describes the sudden appearance of Nidhogg the dragon, bearing corpses in his wings, before the seeress emerges from her trance.

*Sources: Olive Bray and Wikipedia.*

*Ragnarök*

# VöLUSPÁ

1. Hljóþs biþk allar     helgar kindir,
   meiri ok minni     mögu Heimdallar :
   viltu at ek, Valföþr,     vel fyr telja
   forn spjöll fira     þaus fremst of mank.

2. Ek man jötna     ár of borna
   þás forþum mik     fœdda höfþu,
   niú mank heima,     niú í viþi,
   mjötviþ mæran     fyr mold neþan.

3. Ár vas alda     þars Ymir bygþi,
   vasa sandr né sær     né svalar unnir ;
   jörþ fannsk æva     né upphiminn,
   gap vas ginnunga,     en gras hvergi.

4. Áþr Burs synir     bjöþum of ypþu
   þeir es miþgarþ     mæran skópu ;
   sól skein sunnan     á salar steina,
   þa vas grund groïn     grœnum lauki.

5. Sól varp sunnan,     sinni mána,
   hendi hœgri     umb himinjöþur ;
   sól né vissi,     hvar sali átti,
   stjörnur né vissu,     hvar staþi áttu,
   máni né vissi,     hvat megins átti.

*The Restoration*

# VöLUSPÁ

1. Hearing I ask all holy kindreds,
high and low-born, sons of Heimdal!
Thou too, Odin, who bidst me utter
the oldest tidings of men that I mind !

## THE WORLD'S BEGINNING

2. I remember of yore were born the Jötuns,
they who aforetime fostered me:
nine worlds I remember, nine in the Tree,
the glorious Fate Tree that springs 'neath the Earth.

3. 'Twas the earliest of times when Ymir lived;
then was sand nor sea nor cooling wave,
nor was Earth found ever, nor Heaven on high,
there was Yawning of Deeps and nowhere grass:

4. ere the sons of the god had uplifted the world-plain,
and fashioned Midgarth, the glorious Earth.
Sun shone from the south, on the world's bare stones
then was Earth o'ergrown with herb of green.

5. Sun, Moon's companion, out of the south
her right hand flung round the rim of heaven.
Sun knew not yet where she had her hall;
nor knew the stars where they had their place;
nor ever the Moon what might he owned.

---

*3. Fate Tree, Yggdrasil*

6. Þá gengu regin öll      á rökstóla,
   ginnheilug goþ,        ok of þat gættusk :
   nátt ok niþjum         nöfn of gáfu,
   morgin hétu            ok miþjan dag,
   undorn ok aptan,       árum at telja.


7. Hittusk æsir          á Iþavelli
   þeirs hörg ok hof      hátimbruþu ;
   afla lögþu,            auþ smíþuþu,
   tangir skópu           ok tól görþu.

8. Tefldu í túni,         teitir váru—
   vas þeim vættergís     vant ór golli—
   unz þriar kvámu        þursa meyjar,
   ámátkar mjök,          or jötunheimum.


9. Þá gengu regin öll     á rökstóla,
   ginnheilug goþ,        ok of þat gættusk :
   hvern skyldi dverga     drótt of skepja
   ór Brimis blóþi        ok ór blám leggjum.

10. Þar vas Mótsognir      mæztr of orþinn
    dverga allra,         en Durinn annarr ;
    þeir mannlíkun        mörg of görþu
    dvergar í jörþu,      sem Durinn sagþi.

## ORDERING OF TIMES AND SEASONS

6. Then went all the Powers to their thrones of doom
the most holy gods and o'er this took counsel :
to Night and the New-Moons they named the Morning,
names they gave: and named the Mid-day,
Afternoon, Evening, to count the years.

## THE GOLDEN AGE TILL THE COMING OF FATE

7. Gathered the gods on the Fields of Labour;
they set on high their courts and temples;
they founded forges, tongs they hammered
wrought rich treasures, and fashioned tools.

8. They played at tables in court, were joyous,
little they wanted for wealth of gold.
Till there came forth three of the giant race,
all fearful maidens, from Jötunheim.

## CREATION OF THE DWARFS

9. Then went all the Powers to their thrones of doom,
the most holy gods, and o'er this took counsel :
whom should they make the lord of dwarfs
out of Ymir's blood, and his swarthy limbs.

10. Mead-drinker then was made the highest,
but Durin second of all the dwarfs;
and out of the earth these twain-shaped beings
in form like man, as Durin bade.

---

*6. Thrones of doom, beneath Yggdrasi*
*8. All-fearful maidens: the Norns,.*

11.  Nyi ok Niþi,            Norþri ok Suþri,
     Austri ok Vestri,       Alþjófr, Dvalinn,
     Nár ok Naïnn,           Nípingr, Daïnn,
     Bífurr, Báfurr,         Bömburr, Nóri,
     Ánn ok Ónarr,           Aï, Mjöþvitnir.

12.  Viggr ok Gandalfr,         Vindalfr, Þraïnn,
     Þekkr ok Þórinn,           Þror, Vitr ok Litr,
     Nýr ok Nýráþr,             nú hefk dverga-
     Reginn ok Ráþsviþr—           rétt of talþa.

13.  Fíli, Kíli,      Fundinn, Náli,
     Heptifíli,       Hannarr, Sviurr,
     Frár, Hornbori,      Frægr ok Lóni,
     Aurvangr, Jari,      Eikinskjaldi.

14.  Mál es dverga        í Dvalins líþi
     ljóna kindum         til Lofars telja ;
     þeir es sóttu        frá salar steini
     Aurvanga sjöt        til Jöruvalla.

15.  Þar vas Draupnir         ok Dolgþrasir,
     Hár, Haugspori,          Hlévangr, Gloïnn,
     Dóri, Óri,         Dúfr, Andvari,
     Skirfir, Virfir,         Skáfiþr, Aï.

16.  Alfr ok Yngvi,          Eikinskjaldi,
     Fjalarr ok Frosti,        Fiþr ok Ginnarr ;
     þat mun æ uppi,          meþan öld lifir,
     langniþja tal      *til* Lofars hafat.

11. New Moon, Waning-moon, All-thief, Dallier,
North and South and East and West.
Corpse-like, Death-like, Niping, Damn,
Bifur, Bafur, Bombur, Nori,
Ann and Onar, AI, Mead-wolf.

12. Vigg and Wand-elf, Thekk and Thorin,
Wind-elf, Thrainn, Thror, Vit, and Lit,
Nyr and Regin, New-counsel, Wise-counsel,
now have I numbered the dwarfs aright.

13. Fili, Kili, Fundin, Nali,
Heptifili, Hannar, Sviur,
Frar, Hornbori, Fraeg and Loni,
Aurvang, Jari, Oaken-shield.

14. 'Tis time to number in Dallier's song-mead
all the dwarf-kind of Lofar's race,
who from earth's threshold, the Plains of Moisture,
sought below the Sandy-realms.

15. There were Draupnir Har and Haugspori,
and Dolgthrasir, Hlevang, Gloin,
Dori, Ori, Duf, Andvari,
Skirfir, Virfir, Skafid, Ai.

16. Elf and Yngvi, Fjalar and Frost,
Oaken-shield, Fin and Ginar.
Thus shall be told throughout all time
the line who were born of Lofar's race.

---

*11-16. A translation of these obscure names has only been given where it seems to suggest the character of the dwarfs.*
*14. Dallier's song-mead is thus taken by scholars. as a synonym for poetry .Dallier is a dwarf well known in the Edda, and is chosen to represent his race who brewed the mead. This dwarf migration from the earth's surface is also suggested by other scholars.*

17.    Unz þrír kvámn      ór því liþi
       öflgir ok ástkir     æsir at húsi ;
       fundu á landi       lítt megandi
       Ask ok Emblu      örlöglausa.

18.    Önd né áttu,       óþ né höfþu,
       lá né læti     né litu góþa ;
       önd gaf Óþinn,     óþ gaf Hœnir,
       lá gaf Lóþurr     ok litu góþa.


19.    Ask veitk standa,     heitir Yggdrasil,
       hár baþmr ausinn     hvíta auri ;
       þaþan koma döggvar    es í dali falla,
       stendr æ of grœnn     Urþar brunni.

20.    Þaþan koma meyjar     margs vitandi
       þriar ór þeim sal     es und þolli stendr ;
       Urþ hétu eina,       aþra Verþandi,
       skáru á skíþi,       Skuld ena þriþju ;
       þær lög lögþu,      þær líf kuru
       alda börnum,       örlög seggja.

## CREATION OF MEN

17. Then came three gods of the Æsir kindred,
mighty and blessed, towards their home.
They found on the seashore, wanting power,
with fate unwoven, an Ash and Elm.

18. Spirit they had not, and mind they owned not,
blood, nor voice nor fair appearance.
Spirit gave Odin, and mind gave Honir,
blood gave Lodur, and aspect fair.

## THE TREE OF LIFE AND FATE

19. An ash I know standing, 'tis called Yggdrasil,
a high tree sprinkled with shining drops;
come dews therefrom which fall in the dales;
it stands ever green o'er the well of Weird.

20. There are the Maidens, all things knowing,
three in the hall which stands 'neath the Tree.
One is named 'Weird,' the second 'Being' -
- who grave on tablets but 'Shall 'the third.
They lay down laws, they choose out life,
they speak the doom of the sons of men.

---

*17. Elm: the meaning of Icelandic embla is doubtful.*
*18. Hönir a god of wisdom. Lodur probably stands for Loki, for these three were always companions.*

21. Þat man folkvig      fyrst í heimi,
     es Gollveigu       geirum studdu
     ok í höllo Hárs      hána brendu,
     þrysvar brendu      þrysvar borna,
     opt ósjaldan—:       þó enn lifir.

22. Heiþi hétu      hvars húsa kvam
     völu velspaa,     vitti ganda ;
     seiþ hvars kunni,     seiþ hugleikin,
     æ vas angan     illrar brúþar.

23. Þá gengu regin öll     á rökstóla,
     ginnheilug goþ,     ok of þat gættusk :
     hvárt skyldu æsir     afráþ gjalda
     eþa skyldu goþ öll     gildi eiga.

24. Fleygþi Óþinn     ok í folk of skaut :
     þat vas enn folkvíg     fyrst í heimi ;
     brotinn vas borþveggr     borgar ása,
     knáttu vanir vígská     völlu sporna.

## THE WAR OF THE GODS

21. I remember the first great war in the world,
when Golden-draught they pierced with spears,
and burned in the hall of Odin the High One;
thrice they burned her, the three times born,
oft, not seldom yet still she lives.

22. Men called her 'Witch,' when she came to their dwellings,
flattering seeress; wands she enchanted,
spells many wove she, light-hearted wove them,
and of evil women was ever the joy.

23. Then went all the Powers to their thrones of doom,
the most holy gods, and o'er this took counsel :
whether the Æsir should pay a were-gild
and all Powers together make peaceful offering.

24. But Odin hurled and shot 'mid the host;
and still raged the first great war in the world.
Broken then were the bulwarks of Asgard,
the Wanes, war wary, trampled the field.

---

21. *The story of this war between the Æsir and Vanir is never
fully told, but is the subject of constant allusions.*
22. *Witch, Seeress or Vala.*

25. Þá gengu regin öll       á rökstóla,
    ginnheilug goþ,          ok of þat gættusk :
    hverr loþt hefþi         lævi blandit
    eþa ætt jötuns           Óþs mey gefna.

26. Þórr einn þar vá         þrunginn móþi—
    hann sjaldan sitr        es slíkt of fregn— :
    á gengusk eiþar,         orþ ok sœri,
    mál öll meginlig         es á meþal fóru.


27. Veit Heimdallar         hljóþ of folgit
    und heiþvönum           helgum baþmi ;
    á sé ausask       aurgum forsi
    af veþi Valföþrs :       vituþ enn eþa hvat ?

28. Ein sat úti,        es enn aldni kvam
    Yggjungr ása         ok í augu leit.
    · · · · · ·        · · · · · ·
    Hvers fregniþ mik,      hví freistiþ mín ?

29. Allt veit, Óþinn !       hvar auga falt,
    í enom mæra         Mímis brunni ;
    drekkr mjöþ Mímir         morgin hverjan
    af veþi Valföþrs :       vituþ enn eþa hvat ?

30. Valþi Herföþr         hringa ok men
    fyr spjöll spaklig         ok spá ganda.
    · · · · · ·        · · · · · ·
    sá vitt ok vítt        of veröld hverja.

## WAR WITH THE JÖTUNS

25. Then went all the Powers to their thrones of doom,
the most holy gods, and o'er this took counsel :
who all the air had mingled with poison
and Freyja had yielded to the race of Jötuns.

26. Alone fought the Thunderer with raging heart
seldom he rests when he hears such tidings.
Oaths were broken, words and swearing,
all solemn treaties made betwixt them.

## THE SECRET PLEDGES OF THE GODS

27. I know where Heimdal's hearing is hidden
under the heaven-wont which I see ever showered
holy tree, with falling streams from All-father's pledge.
Would ye know further, and what?

28. I sat lone enchanting when came the Dread One,
the ancient god, and gazed in my eyes:
What dost thou ask of me? why dost thou prove me?

29. All know I, Odin, yea, where thou hast hidden
thine eye in the wondrous well of Mimir,
who each morn from the pledge of All-father
drinks the mead. Would ye know further, and what?

30. Then Odin bestowed on me rings and trinkets
for magic spells and the wisdom of wands.
I saw far and wide into every world.

---

25. *Freyja is here called the bride of Ud or Ottar.*
27. *Heirndal's hearing was celebrated.*
29. *Mimir, a water giant. He is the wise teacher and counsellor of the gods, although a Jötun.*

31. Sá valkyrjur  vítt of komnar,
  görvar at ríþa  til Gotþjóþar :
  Skuld hélt skildi,  en Skögul önnur,
  Guþr, Hildr, Göndul  ok Geirskögul.
  Nú 'ru talþar  nönnur Herjans,
  görvar at ríþa  grund valkyrjur.

32. Ek sá Baldri  blóþgum tívur,
  Óþins barni  örlög folgin :
  stóþ of vaxinn  völlum hæri
  mær ok mjök fagr  † mistilteinn.

33. Varþ af meiþi  es mær sýndisk
  harmflaug hættlig :  Höþr nam skjóta ;
  Baldrs bróþir vas  of borinn snimma,
  sa nam Óþins sunr  einnættr vega.

34. Þó hendr æva  né höfoþ kembþi,
  áþr á bál of bar  Baldrs andskota ;
  en Frigg of grét  í Fensölum
  vá Valhallar :  vituþ enn eþa hvat ?

35. Hapt sá liggja  und hvera lundi
  lægjarns líki  Loka áþekkjan ;
  þar sitr Sigyn  þeygi of sínum
  ver vel glýjuþ :  vituþ enn eþa hvat ?

31. From far I saw the Valkyries coming
ready to ride to the hero host.
Fate held a shield, and Lofty followed
War and Battle, Bond and Spearpoint.
Numbered now are the Warfather's maidens,
Valkyries, ready to ride o'er Earth.

32. I saw for Baldr, the bleeding god,
the child of Odin, his doom concealed.
High o'er the fields, there stood upgrown,
most slender and fair, the mistletoe.

33. And there came from that plant,
though slender it seemed,
 the fell woe-shaft which Hod did shoot.
But Baldr's brother was born ere long;
that son of Odin fought one night old;

34. for never hand he bathed, nor head,
ere he laid on the bale-fire Baldr's foe.
But Frigg long wept o'er the woe of Valhöll
in Fen's moist halls - Would ye know further, and what?

VISION INTO HEL AND JÖTUNHEIM

35. I saw lying bound in Cauldron-grove
one like the form of guile-loving Loki.
And there sat Sigyn, yet o'er her husband
rejoicing little. Would ye know further, and what?

---

*34. Fen's moist halls : the home of Frigg,*

36. Á fellr austan      of eitrdali
     söxum ok sverþum :     Slíþr heitir sú.

    .   .   .   .   .     .   .   .   .   .
    .   .   .   .   .     .   .   .   .   .

37. Stóþ fyr norþan      á Niþavöllum
     salr ór golli      Sindra ættar,
     en annarr stóþ      á Ókólni
     bjórsalr jötuns,      sá Brimir heitir.

38. Sal sá standa      sólu fjarri
     Náströndu á,      norþr horfa dyrr ;
     fellu eitrdropar      inn of ljóra,
     sá 's undinn salr      orma hryggjum.

39. Sá þar vaþa      þunga strauma
     menn meinsvara      ok morþvarga
     ok þanns annars glepr      eyrarúnu ;
     þar só Níþhöggr      naï framgengna,
     sleit vargr vera :      vituþ enn eþa hvat ?

40. Austr sat en aldna      í Jarnviþi
     ok fœddi þar      Fenris kindir ;
     verþr of öllum      einna nekkverr
     tungls tjúgari      í trolls hami.

41. Fyllisk fjörvi      feigra manna,
     rýþr ragna sjöt      rauþum dreyra ;
     svört verþa sólskin      of sumur eptir,
     veþr öll válynd :      vituþ enn eþa hvat ?

36. From the eastward a flood, the Stream of Fear,
bore swords and daggers through Poison-dales.

37. To the northward stood on the Moonless Plains,
the golden hall of the Sparkler's race;
and a second stood in the Uncooled realm,

38. a feast-hall of Jötuns, Fire,' 'tis called
and far from the sun I saw a third
on the Strand of Corpses, with doors set northward :
down through the roof dripped poison-drops,
for that hall was woven with serpents' backs.

39. I saw there wading the whelming streams
wolf-like murderers, men forworn,
and those who another's love-whisperer had wiled.
The dragon, Fierce-stinger, fed on corpses,
a wolf tore men. Would ye know further, and what?

40. Far east in Iron-wood sat an old giantess,
Fenrir's offspring she fostered there.
From among them all doth one come forth,
in guise of a troll, to snatch the sun.

41. He is gorged, as on lives of dying men;
he reddens the place of the Powers like blood.
Swart grows the sunshine of summer after,
all baleful the storms. Would ye know further, and what?

---

37. *The Sparkler: a dwarf and forger of the gods' treasures.*
39. *Fierce-stinger, see Grminismal, stanza 35.*
40. *Ironwood: a famous mythical forest in Jötunheim. Fenrir's offspring: Skoll, who pursued the sun, and Hati, who followed the moon.*

42.  Sat þar á haugi        ok sló hörpu
     gýgjar hirþir,          † glaþr Eggþér ;
     gól of hánum            í gaglviþi
     fagrrauþr hani          sás Fjalarr heitir.

43.  Gól of ásum            Gollinkambi,
     sá vekr hölþa           at Herjaföþrs ;
     en annarr gelr          fyr jörþ neþan
     sótraupr hani           at sölum Heljar.

44.  Geyr nú Garmr mjök         fyr Gnipahelli,
     festr mun slitna,         en freki rinna !
     fjölþ veitk frœþa,         fram sék lengra
     umb ragna rök,            römm sigtíva.

45.  Brœþr munu berjask         ok at bönum verþask,
     munu systrungar           sifjum spilla ;
     hart's í heimi,           hórdómr mikill ;
     skeggjöld, skalmöld,      skildir 'u klofnir,
     vindöld, vargöld,         áþr veröld steypisk ;
     mun engi maþr             öþrum þyrma.

## SIGNS OF DOOM

42. Sits on a mound and strikes his harp
 the gleeful Swordsman, warder of giant-wives;
o'er him crows in the roosting tree
the fair red cock who Fjalar is called.


43. Crows o'er the gods the Golden-combed;
he wakes the heroes in War-father's dwellings;
and crows yet another beneath the earth,


44. a dark red cock Loud bays Garm
 in the halls of Hel. before Gaping- Hel
 the bond shall be broken the Wolf run free.
Hidden things I know still onward I; see
the great Doom of the Powers, the gods of war.


45. Brothers shall fight and be as murderers;
sisters' children shall stain their kinship.
'Tis ill with the world; comes fearful whoredom,
a Sword age, Axe age - Shields are cloven,
a Wind age, Wolf age, ere the world sinks.
Never shall man then spare another.

---

*42. The gleeful Swordsman is the warder of Jötunheim, and cor-
responds with Heimdal, the watchman of the gods.*
*43. The Golden-combed, see Fjolsvinnsmal. stanza 17.*
*44. Garm, the Hel hound; see Baldrs Draumar stanza 2. He and
Tyr fight and slay one another. Gaping-hel, Icelandic 'Gnipa-
hel', is descriptive of the craggy rock entrance which forms the
mouth of Hel. Mimir : his sons must be the waters of the well,
or the streams that flow from it. The story of Mimir's head is
told in Ynglinga Saga, but here an earlier form of the myth is
implied, in which the head is a well-spring of wisdom. 'The Fate
Tree' has suggested various renderings: 'the judge appears'; 'fate
approaches'.*

46.  Leika Míms synir,    en mjötviþr kyndisk
     at enu gamla    Gjallarhorni ;
     hátt blæss Heimdallr,    horn's á lopti,
     mælir Óþinn    viþ Míms höfuþ.

47.  Ymr aldit tré,    en jötunn losnar,
     skelfr Yggdrasíls    askr standandi,

48.  Hvat's meþ ásum ?    hvat's meþ ölfum ?
     gnýr allr jötunheimr,    æsir'u á þingi ;
     stynja dvergar    fyr steindurum,
     veggbergs vísir :    vituþ enn eþa hvat ?

49.  Geyr nú Garmr mjök    fyr Gnipahelli,
     festr mun slitna,    en freki rinna !
     fjölþ veitk frœþa,    fram sék lengra
     umb ragna rök,    römm sigtíva.

50.  Hrymr ekr austan,    hefsk lind fyrir ;
     snýsk jörmungandr    í jötunmóþi ;
     ormr knýr unnir,    en ari hlakkar,
     slítr naï niþfölr ;    Naglfar losnar.

51.  Kjóll ferr norþan ;    koma munu Heljar
     of lög lýþir,    en Loki stýrir ;
     fara fífimegir    meþ freka allir,
     þeim es bróþir    Býleists í för.

46. Mim's sons arise; the Fate Tree kindles
at the roaring sound of Gjalla-horn.
Loud blows Heimdal, the horn is aloft,
and Odin speaks with Mimir's head.

47. Groans the Ancient Tree, Fenrir is freed,
shivers, yet standing, Yggdrasil's ash.

48. How do the gods fare, how do the elves fare?
All Jötunheim rumbles, the gods are in council;
before the stone doors the dwarfs are groaning,
a rock-wall finding - Would ye know further, and what?

49. Loud bays Garm before Gaping-hel:
the bond shall be broken, the Wolf run free.
Hidden things I know still onward I see;
the great Doom of the Powers, the gods of war.

## GATHERING OF THE DESTROYERS

50. Drives Hrym from the East holding shield on high;
the World-serpent writhes in Jötun-rage;
he lashes the waves; screams a pale-beaked eagle,
rending corpses, the Death boat is launched.

51. Sails the bark from the North; the hosts of Hel
o'er the sea are coming, and Loki steering,
brother of Byleist, he fares on the way
with Fenrir and all the monster kinsmen.

---

47. *Fenrir, not Loki. must be intended by Jötun of the text, for Loki was always reckoned among the gods.*
50. *Hrym, the leader of the Frost-giants. A pale-beaked eagle, Corpse-swallower; see Vm. 37. Death-boat or Naglfar, the Nail-ferry, said by Snorri to be made of the nails of dead men.*
51. *Byleist is unknown except as Loki's brother.*

52.   Surtr ferr sunnan       með sviga lævi,
         skínn af sverþi        sól valtíva ;
         grjótbjörg gnata,       en gífr hrata,
         troþa halir helveg,      en himinn klofnar.

53.   þá kömr Hlínar       harmr annarr fram,
         es Óþinn ferr         við ulf vega,
         en bani Belja         bjartr at Surti :
         þá mun Friggjar       falla angan.

54.   Kömr enn mikli       mögr Sigföþur,
         Víþarr, vega      at valdýri ;
         lætr megi hveþrungs        mund of standa
         hjör til hjarta :       þá's hefnt föþur.

55.   Kömr enn mæri       mögr Hlóþynjar ;
         . . . . . .       . . . . . .
         . . . . . .       . . . . . .
         gengr Óþins sunr       ormi mœta.

56.   Drepr af móþi       miþgarþs vëur ;
         munu halir allir       heimstöþ ryþja ;
         gengr fet niu       Fjörgynjar burr
         neppr frá naþri       níþs ókvíþnum.

57.   Sól tér sortna,       sígr fold í mar,
         hverfa af himni       heiþar stjörnur ;
         geisar eimi      ok aldrnari,
         leikr hár hiti      við himin sjalfan.

58.   Geyr nú Garmr mjök       fyr Gnipahelli,
         festr mun slitna,       en freki rinna !
         fjölþ veitk frœþa,       fram sék lengra
         umb ragna rök,       römm sigtíva.

52. Rides Surt from the South - fire, bane of branches,
sun of the war gods, gleams from his sword.
The rock-hills crash, the troll-wives totter,
men flock Helward, and heaven is cleft.

## THE LAST BATTLES OF THE GODS

53. Soon comes to pass Frigg's second woe,
when Odin fares to fight with the wolf;
then must he fall, her lord beloved,
and Beli's bright slayer must bow before Surt.

54. Comes forth the stalwart son of the War-father,
Vidar, to strive with the deadly beast;
lets he the sword from his right hand leap
into Fenrir's heart, and avenged is the father.

55. Comes forth the glorious offspring of Earth,
Thor, to strive with the glistening Serpent.

56. Strikes in his wrath the Warder of Midgard,
while mortals all their homes forsake;
nine feet recoils he, the son of Odin,
bowed, from the dragon who fears not shame.

## THE END OF THE WORLD

57. The sun is darkened, Earth sinks in the sea,
from heaven turn the bright stars away.
Rages smoke with fire, the life-feeder,
high flame plays against heaven itself.

58. Loud bays Garm before Gaping-hel,
the bond shall be broken, the Wolf run free;
hidden things I know still onward I see;
the great Doom of the Powers, the gods of war.

---

*53. Beli's bright slayer, or Frey. Beli, Snorri tells us, was a giant whom Frey slew with a stag's horn for lack of the sword which he had given for Gerðr.*

59. Sék upp koma      öþru sinni
    jörþ ór ægi     iþjagrœna ;
    falla forsar,     flýgr örn yfir,
    sás á fjalli     fiska veiþir.

60. Finnask æsir     á Iþavelli
    ok of moldþinur     mátkan dœma,
    ok minnask þar     á megindóma
    ok á Fimbultýs     fornar rúnar.

61. Þar munu eptir     undrsamligar
    gollnar töflur     í grasi finnask
    þærs í árdaga     áttar höfþu.

   . . . . . .      . . . . . .

62. Munu ósánir     akrar vaxa,
    böls mun batna,     mun Baldr koma,
    bua Höþr ok Baldr     Hropts sigtoptir,
    vel valtívar :     vituþ enn eþa hvat ?

63. þá kná Hœnir     hlautviþ kjósa

   . . . . . .      . . . . . .

    ok burir byggva     brœþra Tveggja
    vindheim víþan :     vituþ enn eþa hvat ?

64. Sal sék standa     sólu fegra,
    golli þakþan     á Gimlé :
    þar skulu dyggvar     dróttir byggva
    ok of aldrdaga     ynþis njóta.

## THE NEW WORLD

59. I see uprising a second time
earth from the ocean, green anew;
the waters fall, on high the eagle
flies o'er the fell and catches fish.

60. The gods are gathered on the Fields of Labour;
they speak concerning the great World Serpent,
and remember there things of former fame
and the Mightiest God's old mysteries.

61. Then shall be found the wondrous-seeming
golden tables hid in the grass,
those they had used in days of yore.

62. And there unsown shall the fields bring forth;
all harm shall be healed, Baldr will come -
Hod and Baldr shall dwell in Valhöll,
at peace the war gods. - Would ye know further, and what?

63. Then Honir shall cast the twigs of divining,
and the sons shall dwell of Odin's brothers
in Wind-home wide. Would ye know further, and what?

64. I see yet a hall more fair than the sun,
roofed with gold in the Fire-sheltered realm;
ever shall dwell there all holy beings,
blest with joy through the days of time.

---

62. *Valhöll, called here the victory halls of Hropt (Odin).*
64. *Fire-sheltered realm, Icelandic (Gimlé from gim, fire, and hlé, shelter), which has often been translated jewelled; but the above meaning shows this hall in contrast to the others of stanzas 37 and 38.*

65. Kömr enn ríki       at regindómi
    öflugr ofan         sás öllu ræþr.
    . . . . .           . . . . .
    . . . . .           . . . . .

66. Kömr enn dimmi       dreki fljúgandi,
    naþr fránn neþan      frá Niþafjöllum ;
    bersk í fjöþrum      —flýgr völl yfir—
    Níþhöggr naï ;       nú mun sökkvask.

## COMING OF THE NEW POWER, PASSING OF THE OLD

65. Comes from on high to the great Assembly
the Mighty Ruler who orders all.

66. Fares from beneath a dim dragon flying,
a glistening snake from the Moonless Fells.
Fierce-stinger bears the dead on his pinions
 away o'er the plains. I sink now and cease.

# GLOSSARY

## GLOSSARY.

Ægir, a sea giant

Æsir, the race of gods, distinguished from Wanes

Agnar, brother of Geirröd

_____ son of Geirröd.

Ai, name of two dwarfs.

Alf, kinsman of Ottar.

Alf the Old, son of Dag and Thora.

_____ grandfather of Ottar.

Ali, kinsman of Ottar.

All-father, Odin.

All-fleet, a horse.

All-green, an island.

All-thief, a dwarf.

All-wielder, a giant, father of Thiazi.

All-wise (Alvíss) a dwarf.

_____ (Alsviþr) a jötun.

Almveig, wife of Halfdan.

Anm, son of Dag and Thora.

Andvari, a dwarf.

Angantyr, Ottar's rival.

_____ a berserk.

Ann, a dwarf.

Arngrim, father of twelve berserks.

Asgarth, dwelling of the Æsir or gods.

Ash, the first man.

Athlings, a mythical race.

Atvard, one of the builders of Menglöd's hall.

Aud, mother of Harald Wartooth.

Aurboda, mother of Gerd.

Aurvang, a dwarf.

Babe, son of Earl.

Bafur, a dwarf.

Bairn, son of Earl.

Baldr, the god, son of Odin.

Bale-thorn, a giant, grandfather of Odin.

Bale-worker, Odin.

Bari, a builder of Menglöd's hall.

Barley, Frey's servant.

Barri, a berserk.

Bashful, daughter of Churl.

Bathtubs, two rivers.

Battle, (Hildr) a valkyrie.

Battle-wolf, a ferryman.

Being, one of the Norns.

Beli, a giant slain by Frey.

Bergelm, forefather of all Jötuns.

Bestla, a giantess, mother of Odin.

Cauldron-grove, Loki's prison.

Chosen Warriors, heroes of the battle field bidden to Valhöll by Odin.

Churl, son of Rig and Grandmother, father of all freeborn peasants.

Clay-giant, Ymir.

Cloggy, daughter of Thrall.

Cooler, shelterer from the sun.

Corpse-like, a dwarf.

Corpse-swallower, a giant eagle, maker of the wind.

Counsel-fierce, a Valkyrie.

Counsel-isle-sound, home of Battle-wolf.

Counsellor, Odin.

Cow-herd, son of Thrall.

Crane-shanked maid, daughter of Thrall.

Dag, a chieftain of Halfdan's race.

Daïn, a hart.

———— an elf or dwarf.

Dallier, a dwarf.

———— a hart.

Dame, daughter of Churl.

Damp, a chieftain.

Dan, a chieftain.

Daughter-in-law, wife of Churl.

Dawning, Dawn, father of Day.

Day, personification of Day.

Day-spring, Menglöd's lover.

Dazzler of Hel, Odin.

Dead's Way, road to Valhöll.

Death-barrier, the gate of Valhöll.

Death-father, Odin.

Death-like, a dwarf.

Delling, a builder of Menglöd's hall, probably the same being as Dawning.

Descendent, son of Earl.

Dolgthrasir, a dwarf.

Doom of the gods or Ragnarök.

Dori.

Draupnir, a dwarf.

Dread One, Odin.

Duf, a dwarf.

Duneyr, a hart.

Durin, a dwarf.

Dusk, one of Heimdal's mothers.

Dvalin, Dallier, a hart.

Dwarfs.

Dyrathror, a hart.

Eager in War, Odin.

Eagle-nose, dau. of Thrall.

Earl, son of Rig and Mother.

Early-woke, a horse.

Earna, wife of Earl.

Earth, a goddess, wife of Odin and mother of Thor.

East, a dwarf.

Eastern land, the East, Jötunheim, giant-land.

Egil, a giant, father of Thjalfi.

Elf, a dwarf.

Elf-beam, Elf-light, the sun.

Elf-home, Frey's dwelling.

Elm, the first woman.

Elves.

Ember, Menglöd's hall.

Equal-ranked, Odin.

Eyfora, wife of Arngrim.

Eylimi, a hero of the Athling race.

Eymund, a chieftain, Halfdan's ally.

Fafnir, a dragon slain by Sigurd.

Falling-brook, home of Odin and Saga.

Fame-bough, the mistletoe shot by Höd.

Farmer, son of Churl.

Fate, a Valkyrie.

Fate-tree, Yggdrasil.

Father, a nobleman.

Father of Beings, Odin.

Father of Hosts, Odin.

Father of Men, Odin.

Father of Spells, Odin.

Father of Wrath, Thor.

Fear, a river.

Fenrir, the great Wolf; son of Loki.

Fen's Moist halls, Frigg's home.

Fickle, Odin.

Fields of Labour, first home of the gods.

Fierce-cold, grandfather of Day-spring.

Fierce-stinger, the dragon who gnaws the roots of Yggdrasil.

Fili, a dwarf.

Fin, a dwarf.

Fine-flanked-steed, grandsire of Gna's horse, Hoof-flinger.

Fire, feasting hall of the Jötuns.

Fire-sheltered-realm, habitation of the good after Ragnarök.

Fire-stirrer, Ægir's serving-man.

Fjalar, a giant who hoodwinked Thor, called by Snorri Utgard-loki.

Fjalar, a cock.

_____ a dwarf.

Flaming-eyed, Odin.

Flashing-eyed, Odin.

Foamer, one of Heimdal's mothers.

Folk-field, home of Freyja.

Folk-stirrer, a dwarf.

Forest-wolf, forefather of all Valas.

Forseti, a god.

Fradmar, son of Dag.

Franang's-stream, where Loki hid in the form of a salmon.

Fræg, a dwarf.

Frar, a dwarf.

Freight-wafter, Odin.

Frey, a god, son of Njörd. (See Njörd, son of).

Freyja, a goddess, daughter of Njörd.

Friaut, Ottar's grandmother.

Frigg, a goddess, wife of Odin.

Frodi, a hero of Ottar's line.

_____ Ottar's grandfather.

Frost, a dwarf.

Frost-giants.

Fulla, Frigg's handmaiden.

Fundin, a dwarf.

Fury, one of Heimdal's mothers.

Gaping-hel, the rock-entrance of Hel.

Garm, the watch-dog of Hel.

Gaudy, daughter of Churl.

Gay, daughter of Churl.

Gefjon, a goddess.

Geirröd, a Jötun.

_____ King of the Goths.

Generous, one of Menglöd's handmaidens.

Gentle, one of Menglöd's hand-maidens.

Gerd, a giant maiden, daughter of Gymir, wooed by Frey.

Ginar, a dwarf.

Girdle (the), the World-serpent.

Gjallahorn, Heimdal's horn.

Gjuki, King of the Goths.

Glad-home, Odin's dwelling.

Glad-one, a horse.

Gleatner, a horse.

Glistmer (Glasir), a grove in front of Valhöll.

———— (Glitnir), Forseti's mansion.

Gloin, a dwarf.

Glutton, a watch-dog of Menglöd's hall.

Gna, a goddess.

Goïn, a serpent.

Golden-bristle, Freyja's boar.

Golden-comb, a cock.

Golden-draught, a Vala.

Gold-lock, a horse.

Goldy, a horse.

Grand-father, a free-born peasant.

Grand-mother, mother of Churl.

Grave-haunting worm, a serpent.

Grave-monster, a serpent.

Great-grand-father, a thrall.

Great-grand-mother, mother of Thrall.

Greed, á watch-dog of Menglöd's hall.

———— one of Odin's wolves.

Grey-back, a serpent.

Grey-beard, Odin.

Gridar, a giantess.

Grimnir, Odin.

Grim Strongminded, a berserk.

Griper, one of Heimdal's mothers.

Gripper, one of Geirröd's daughters.

Groa, the dead mother of Day-spring.

Guarding-warriors, one of Menglöd's handmaidens.

Gudrun, daughter of Gjuki and wife of Sigurd the Völsung.

Guest-crusher, the rocky barrier in front of Menglöd's hall.

Gunnar Battle-wall, a berserk.

Gunnar, son of Gjuki, brother of Gudrun.

Gunnlöd, a giantess, guardian of the Mead.

Gymir, Ægir.

———— a frost-giant, father of Gerd.

Gyrd, son of Dag.

Guthorm Battle-snake, step-son of Gjuki.

Habrok, a hawk.

Haddings, two berserks.

Haki, son of Hvedna.

Halfdan, a king, of the Skjöldung race.

Hannar, a dwarf.

Har, a dwarf.

Harald War-tooth, King of Denmark.

Haugspori, a dwarf.

Heaven-hill, Heimdall's home.

Hedge-breaker, a horse.

Heimdall, watchman of the gods.

Heir, son of Earl.

Hel, a goddess.

———— home of the dead.

Helm-bearer, Odin.

Heptifili, a dwarf.

Hermod, a warrior, given sword and armour by Odin.

Hero, son of Churl.

Hervard, a berserk.

High One (the), Odin.

Hildigun, Ottar's great-grand-mother.

Hill of Healing, the mountain on which Menglöd sat.

Hjördis, a lady of the Hraudung race.

Hjörvard, a berserk.

Hlebard, a giant.

Hledis, a priestess, mother of Ottar.

Hlevang, a dwarf.

Höd, a god, slayer of Baldr.

Hœnir, a god.

Högni, son of Gjuki, brother of Gudrun.

Home of Strength, Thor's dwelling.

Hoodwinker, Odin.

Hoof-flinger, Gna's horse.

Hornbori, a dwarf.

Horse-thief, a giant, son of Rimebringer.

Hörvi, a warrior in the train of Hrolf the Old.

Hrani, a berserk.

Hraudung, a king, father of Agnar and Geirröd.

Hraudungs, a race.

Hrist, a Valkyrie.

Hroerik, a king, father of Harald War-tooth.

Hrolf the Old, a chieftain.

Hrungnir, a giant slain by Thor.

Hrym, one of the giant destroyers at Ragnarök.

Hugin, a raven.

Hvedna, daughter of Hjövard.

Hymir, a frost-giant.

Hyndla, a giantess.

Idun, a goddess, wife of Bragi.

Ifing, the river between the realms of giants and gods.

Ing, a mythical race founder.

Inheritor, son of Earl.

Innstein, father of Ottar.

Iri, a builder of Menglöd's hall.

Ironsword, one of Heimdal's mothers.

Iron-wood, a forest in Jötúnheim.

Isolf, a hero of Ottar's line.

Jalk, Odin.

Jörmunrek, King of the Goths.

Josurmar, son of Dag.

Jötuns.

Kari, a warrior of Ottar's line.

Keeler, Odin.

Ketil, great grandfather of Ottar.

King, the most famous of Earl's sons.

Kinsman, son of Earl.

Klyp, great grandfather of Ottar.

Kon, King.

Kormt, a river.

Lady, daughter of Churl.

Land of Men.

Land of the Slain, the battlefield.

Laufey, Loki's mother.

Leggy, son of Thrall.

Lewd, son of Thrall.

Lidskjalf, a builder of Menglöd's hall.

Life, Life-craver, the new beings born after Ragnarök.

Light-foot, a horse.

Lightning-abode, Thor's hall.

Lit, a dwarf.

Lodur, a god.

Lofar, a dwarf.

Lofty, a Valkyrie.

Loggy, daughter of Thrall.

Loki, a god, father of Fenrir, Hel and the World-serpent.

Long-beard, Odin.

Loni, a dwarf.

Lord of the Host, Odin.

Lord of goats, Lord of the goat's wain, Thor.

Lout, son of Thrall.

Lumpy-leggy, daughter of Thrall.

Lustful, son of Thrall.

Magni, a god, son of Thor.

Maker, Odin.

Maid, daughter of Churl.

Masked One, Odin.

Mead (the)=Soul-stirrer, the song-mead.

Mead-drinker, a dwarf.

Mead-wolf, a dwarf.

Meili, a god, Thor's brother.

Memory, a raven.

Menglöd, a giantess or goddess wooed by Day-spring.

Midgarth, man's dwelling, the Earth.

Might, a Valkyrie.

Mightiest god, Odin.

Mighty Weaver, a giant who contends with Odin.

Mimir, a giant, guardian of the well of wisdom.

Mimir's Tree, Yggdrasil.

Mist, a Valkyrie.

Mist-blind, a Jötun.

Mist-hel, home of the dead.

Mjöllnir, Thor's hammer.

Modi, Wroth, son of Thor.

Mögthrasir, Son-craver, a Jötun.

Moin, a serpent.

Moon.

Moon-hater, a wolf.

Moonless Plains, Fells, regions of the underworld.

Mother, mother of Earl.

Mover of the Handle, father of Moon.

Much-wise, a giant.

———— Odin.

Munin, a raven=Memory.

Murk-wood, through which the Sons of Fire ride to Ragnarök.

Nabbi, a dwarf.

Nali, a dwarf.

Nanna, a kinswoman of Ottar.

Narfi, son of Loki.

Neighbour, son of Churl.

New-counsel, a dwarf.

New-moon, a dwarf.

Night, personification of night.

Nimble-snatcher, one of Ægir's serving men.

Niping, a dwarf.

Njörd, a god, a hostage from the Wanes.

_____ (son of)=Frey.

Noatun, Njörd's home.

Nökkvir, father of Nanna.

Nöri, a dwarf.

Nörr, father of Night.

North, a dwarf.

Nyr, a dwarf.

Oaken-peggy, daughter of Thrall.

Oaken-shield, a dwarf.

Oak-thorn, a hart.

Odin, the god.

*See also* All-father, Bale-worker, Counseller, Dazzler of Hel, Death-father, Dread One, Eager in War, Equal-ranked, Father of Beings, Father of Hosts, Father of Men, Father of Spells, Fickle, Flaming-eyed, Flashing-eyed, Grey-beard, Grimnir, Helm-bearer, High One, Hood-winker, Jalk, Keeler, Long-beard, Maker, Masked One, Mightiest god, Much-wise, On-driver, On-rider, On-thruster, Riddle-reader, Rindr, Sage, Shaker, Shape-shifter, Sigrani, Singer (the great), Slender, Soother, Sooth-sayer, Stormer, Third-highest, Thror, Thund, Tree-rocker, True, Utterer of gods, Veiled One, Wafter, Wan-derer, War-father, War-wont, Watcher, Wave, Way-wont, Weaver, Well-comer, Wile-wise, Wind-roar, Wise, Wish-giver, Wizard.

Odin's brother's, Vili and Ve.

Odin's son=Baldr.

Odin's son=Thor.

Odin's sons, the chosen warriors,.

Odin's son, Vali.

Ölmod, a kinsman of Ottar.

Onar, a dwarf.

On-driver, On-rider, On-thruster, Odin.

Ori, a dwarf, builder of Menglöd's hall.

Ormt, a river.

Osmund, a giant? .

Osolf, a hero of Ottar's line.

Ottar, Freyja's lover.

Pale-hoof, a horse.

Peaceful, one of Menglöd's handmaidens.

Peasant, son of Churl.

Pine-needle, a grove.

Plains of Moisture, the surface of the earth?

Powers, High Powers, the gods.

Race-giant, a horse.

Radbard, a hero of Harald War-tooth's line.

Ran, one of Odin's wives?

Randver, a hero of Harald War-tooth's line.

Ratatosk, the squirrel gnawing Yggdrasil.

Rati, an awl.

Ravener, a wolf.

Regin, a dwarf.

Reifnir, a berserk.

Riddle-reader, Odin.

Rig=Heimdal.

Rime-bringer, a Frost-giant? father of Witch and Horse-thief.

Rimy-mane, a horse of Night.

Rind, a giantess.

Rindr, Odin as husband of Rind.

Roaring-kettle, a spring, whence flow the rivers of Hel.

Rover of Air, Loki.

Ruler, father of Erna.

Runes (the).

Saga, a goddess, wife of Odin.

Sage, Odin.

Samsey, an island.

Sand-strewer, one of Heimdal's mothers.

Sandy-realms, home of dwarfs.

Sea-farer, one of Ottar's fore-fathers.

Sea-god, Ægir.

Sea-king, one of Ottar's fore-fathers.

Sea-lover, a giant.

Serpent (the), the World-serpent, son of Loki.

Serpent-slayer, Thor.

Shaker, Odin.

Shall, one of the Norns.

Shape-shifter, Odin,.

Sheaf-beard, son of Churl.

Shelterer (the), Yggdrasil.

Sheltering Spirit, one of Men-glöd's maidens.

Sheltering-grove, a wood, the refuge of Sun.

She-wolf, one of Heimdal's mothers.

Shield-fierce, a Valkyrie.

Shield of Men, Thor.

Shielding-giants, one of Men-glöd s maidens.

Shiner, a horse.

Shining-mane, the horse of Day.

Shrieker, a Valkyrie.

Sif, wife of Thor.

Sigrani, Odin.

Sigmund, son of Völsung.

Sigtrygg, a warrior slain by Halfdan.

Sigurd, son of Sigmund, slayer of Fafnir.

Sigyn, wife of Loki.

Silvery-lock, a horse.

Sinewy, a horse.

Singer (the great), Odin.

Sinmara, a giantess.

Skadi, daughter of the giant Thiazi, wife of Njörd.

Skafid, a dwarf.

Skekkil, a kinsman of Ottar.

Skidbladnir, a ship.

Skirfir, a dwarf.

Skilfings, a mythical race.

Skirnir, Frey's servant.

Skjöldungs, a mythical race born of Skjöld..

Sköll, a wolf.

Skrymir, a giant (=Fjalar).

Skurhild, daughter of Skekkil.

Skybright, a goat.

Slayer of Jötuns, Slayer of Rock-giants, Thor.

Sleep-thorn, grandfather of Menglöd.

Sleipnir, Odin's horse.

Slender, daughter of Churl.

———— Odin, 21.

Sluggard, son of Thrall.

Smith, son of Churl.

Solblind, a dwarf?

Son, son of Earl.

Son of Earth, Thor.

Soother, Odin.

———— a serpent.

Soothsayer, Odin.

Sooty-black, a boar.

Sooty-face, a cook.

Sooty-flame, a cauldron.

Sorrow-seed, a Jötun, grandfather of Winter.

Sorrow-whelmer, one of Heimdal's mothers.

Sold-stirrer, the song-mead.

Sound-home, Thiazi's dwelling.

Sounding-clanger, the barrier in front of Menglöd's hall.

South, a dwarf.

Sparkler, a dwarf, forger of treasures.

Speaker, son of Churl.

Spear-fierce, a Valkyrie.

Spear-point, a Valkyrie.

Spring-cold, father of Wind-cold (Day-spring).

Steerer of barks, Thor.

Storm-god, (Thor).

Storm-pale, a hawk.

Stormer, Odin.

Stormy-billow, the river from which Ymir was formed.

Strand of corpses, a region in Hel.

Stray-singer, a poet.

Strength-maiden, a Valkyrie.

Strength-wielder, Thor

Stout, son of Thrall.

Stubbly-beard, son of Churl.

Stumpy, son of Thrall.

Successor, son of Earl.

Summer, personification of summer.

Sun, a goddess.

Sun-bright, father of Day-spring.

Surt, a fire-giant.

Suttung, a giant, owner of the song-mead.

Svafa, mother of Hildigunn, of Ottar's line.

Svarang, a water-giant.

Sviur, a dwarf.

Swadilfari, a mare, mother of Sleipnir.

Swan the Red, ancestor of Ottar.

Swart-head, father of all sorcerers.

Sweet-south, father of Summer.

Swordsman, watchman of the giants.

Tatter-coat, daughter of Churl.

Tender, one of Menglöd's maidens.

Thane, son of Churl.

Thekk, a dwarf.

Thialfi, Thor's servant.

Waning-moon, a dwarf.

War, a Valkyrie.

War-father, Odin.

_____ (son of) =Vidar.

War-fetter, a Valkyrie,.

War-path, the battle-field at Ragnarök.

War-wont, Odin.

Warder, Thor.

Wary-wise, a warrior.

Watcher, Odin.

Watchman of gods, Heimdal.

Wave, Odin.

Way-wont, Odin.

Weaver, Odin.

_____ a serpent.

Weird, one of the Norns.

Well-comer, Odin.

West, a dwarf.

Whiner, daughter of Thrall.

Wielder, a dwarf.

Wife, daughter of Churl,.

Wile-wise, Odin.

Wind-cold, Dayspring.

Wind-cool, father of Winter.

Wind-elf, a dwarf.

Wind-home, home of the sons of Vili and Ve, in the New World.

Window-shelf, Odin's seat.

Wind-roar, Odin.

Winged-thunder, Thor.

Winter, personification of winter.

Wise, Odin.

Wise-counsel, a dwarf.

Wise Ones, Menglöd's maidens.

Wish-giver, Odin.

Witch, a giantess,? daughter of Rime-bringer.

_____ Golden-draught.

Wizard, Odin.

Woe-bringer, a giantess, mother of Fenrir.

Wolf (the), Fenrir.

Wolf, great-grandfather of Ottar.

Wolf-cubs, sons of Dag.

Wolf the Gaper, a berserk.

Woman, a daughter of Churl.

Wood-home, Vidar's home.

Wood-snake, a cock.

World-serpent, the encircler of the world, son of Loki. _See also_ Girdle.

Wounding-wand, the mistletoe.


Yari, a dwarf.

Yelper, one of Heimdal's mothers.

_____ a giantess, daughter of Geirröd.

Yeoman, son of Churl.

Yewdale, home of Ull.

Yggdrasil, the World-tree. _See also_ Fate-tree.

Ymir, the first-born of Jötuns. _See also_ Clay-giant.

Ynglings, a race descended from Yng.

Yngvi, a dwarf.

Youth, son of Churl.

_____ son of Earl.

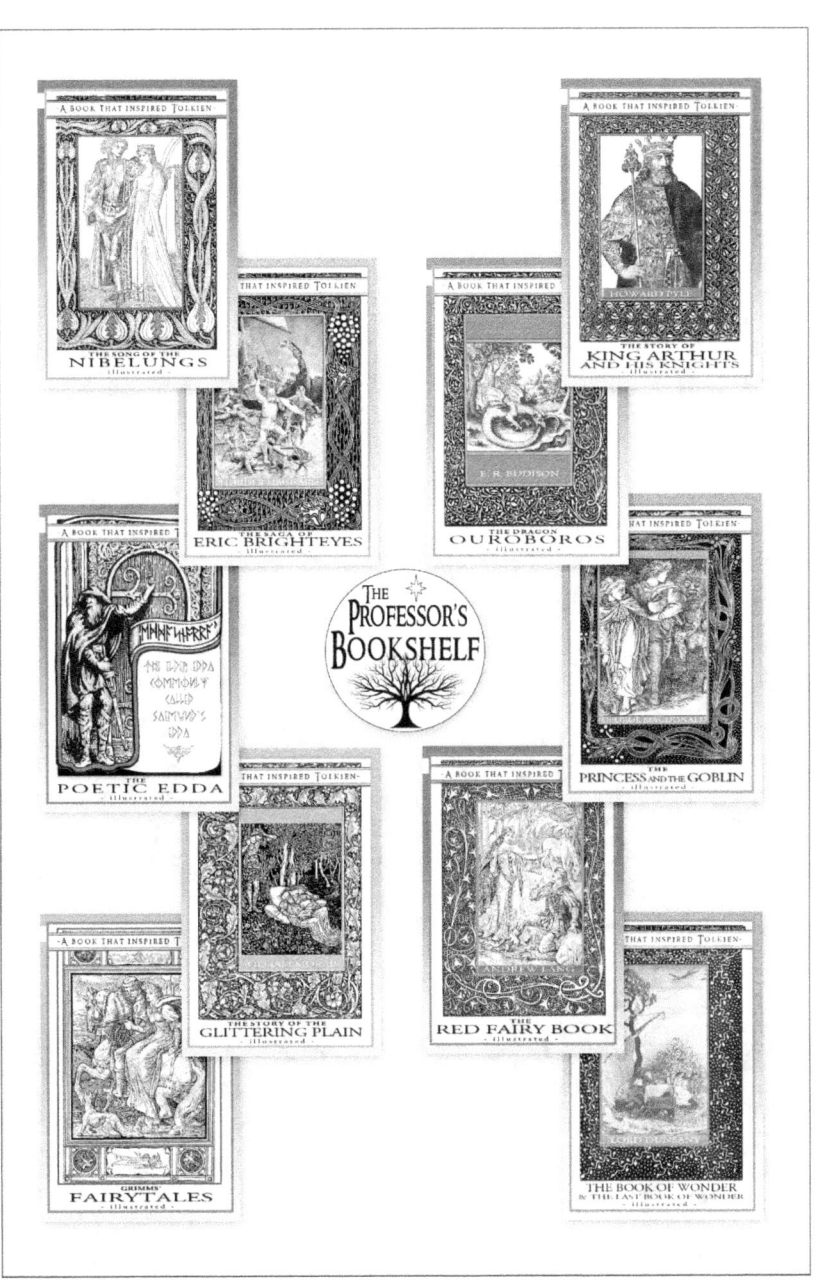

*Some titles in The Professor's Bookshelf series*

THE BITTERBYNDE – BOOK 1

# THE
# ILL-MADE
# MUTE

## CECILIA
## DART-THORNTON

Cecilia Dart-Thornton

THE ILL-MADE MUTE
*Book I of The Bitterbynde Trilogy*

The Stormriders land their splendid winged stallions on the airy battlements of Isse Tower. Far below, the superstitious servants who dwell in the fortress' lower depths tell frightening tales of wicked creatures inhabiting the world outside, a world they have only glimpsed. Yet it is the least of the lowly, a mute, scarred, and utterly despised foundling, who dares to scale the Tower, stow away aboard a Windship, and then dive from the sky.

The fugitive is rescued by a kind-hearted adventurer, who bestows a name, the gift of communicating by handspeak, and an amazing truth never before guessed. Now the foundling begins a journey to distant Caermelor, to seek a wise woman whose skills may prove life-changing.

Along the way, this shunned outsider with an angel's soul and a gargoyle's face must survive in a wilderness of extraordinary danger. And as the challenges grow more deadly Imrhien learns something more terrifying than all the evil eldritch wights combined . . .

In a thrilling debut combining storytelling mastery with a treasure trove of folklore, Cecilia Dart-Thornton creates an exceptional epic adventure.

'Not since Tolkien's *The Fellowship of the Ring*... have I been so impressed by a beautifully spun fantasy.'
ANDRE NORTON, GRAND MASTER OF SCIENCE FICTION.

# ⲦⲎⲈ ⲢⲢⲞⲪⲈⲊⲊⲞⲢ'Ⲋ ⲂⲞⲞⲔⲊⲎⲈⲖⲪ

Stories that inspired Professor Tolkien,
author of 'The Lord of the Rings'

www.professorsbookshelf.com